CLOUD PARLIAMENT

OLIVIA A. COLE

All rights reserved. Published in the United States by Fletchero Publishing

ISBN 978-0-9916155-6-8

Jacket design by Anna Green. Some images used in the creation of cover are attributable to Shutterstock.

CHAPTER 1

TY

Every window on the second floor of the Mahogany was open, and the sounds of the first parade drifted up from the street and into the chamber Ty Redson had just finished cleaning. In two weeks, a man would die down the hall, even if she hadn't yet figured out just how she would kill him.

She stood in the head-to-toe black uniform, making sure each of her tools had been returned to its place in the cleanwork kit at her waist. As Ty had worked her way from the bed frame to the toilet seat, she had drawn each tool one by one: Microbion for invisible bacteria, Bacnobior for odors. Her kit was as shiny as the Mahogany, one of the most prestigious properties in Louisville filled with the most prestigious guests. The guests – one in particular – were why she had come.

Ty moved to the window, frowning at a few bits of dust that floated out into the open air to join the parade's confetti. She was tempted to Vacusac the air itself. She stared down at the passing revelers, the gargantuan floats that bobbed just above the trees lining the street. A white Pegasus. A mint leaf with cartoon eyes. A Thoroughbred, of course. The dense trees blocked out most of the people watching, but Ty could hear them, the way their cheers rose with the biodegradable paper bits they tossed in the air. She could hear, too, the clink of glasses, the occasional shatter. She watched with a combination of disgust and envy – this was the second Kentucky Derby since her mother had been killed, and it all made the bitterness sharper in her mouth.

"Oh, good, you're finished!"

Madame Richmond swept into the chamber, gazing around with satisfaction. When she'd first hired Ty, she'd done the obnoxious white-glove-across-the-dressers bullshit that so many employers thought was intimidating before they realized maids could make or break an establishment. (After the Dirt Riot in Chicago – maids sabotaging high-end hotels with stained sheets and full toilets for wealthy guests checking in; relentless until they received a fair wage – the rest of the industry fell in line quickly before their own cleanwork crews got any ideas.) A pandemic or three was enough to demonstrate the value of cleanwork, so by now Madame Richmond knew that the eight women who made up her staff at the Mahogany were something like gods, and she'd learned not to test them. Still, she was a nervous woman, and her nerves came out in questions.

"You've squared the corners? And vacuumed under the carpet? Here, a quick photo."

Ty didn't bother to answer or pose – standing as she was looking out the window, kit at her waist, was enough. Part of her wanted the photo for herself: the light was perfect and she'd just bleached her shaved head the night before. She used to be what people would call photogenic – the bump in the bridge of her nose looked regal in pictures, her round cheeks peaked with impressive cheekbones. She used to like her eyes: they had once been big and shiny, a step away from anime. Now she always caught herself squinting. Either way, she knew that if she saw the photo all she would see was the deadness in those eyes. She'd rather not.

"We have a very special guest in this suite tonight," Madame was saying, studying the photo on her device. "There cannot be a speck of dirt."

"Honestly, mother," said a voice. "When has Ty ever left a speck of anything anywhere? She came from the Infinity, for god's sake."

Madame's head snapped up.

"Camille," she said sharply. "Where *are* you?"

"Here," said the voice. It came from under the bed. A girl a little younger than Ty rolled out, her blonde curly hair flattened on one side from lying on it. She clutched a device, its screen still glowing.

"What in god's name are you doing under the bed?" her mother sighed.

"Reading."

"Why? Why are you *under* the bed? In *here*?"

"This bedframe is made of cedar and it's a very pleasant smell. Also, Ty sings while she works sometimes and it's very relaxing."

Ty froze at the window, then turned her head to glare at Camille Richmond, a white girl like Ty herself, but pale. Ty had become used to Madame's youngest daughter hanging around the Mahogany – unlike Camille's two socialite older sisters, Camille had few friends and little desire to leave the hotel. She was usually reading one of the hundreds of books stocked on her device, curled up in an antique chair someplace. But Ty didn't know she was a spy, and her mind raced, wondering what Camille might have heard, seen. Every hotel had its thief among the staff, and it wasn't Ty, but she had other plans, plans that were not for Camille or anyone else to know.

"Off she goes," Camille said with a small smile. "She's a daydreamer. An artist in another life. Mother, did you know Ty used to perform at concerts? She really does have a beautiful voice."

Ty shot her another cloudy look. The fact that Ty used to

sing wasn't exactly a secret, but the fact that Camille knew at all meant she had searched her online. *Idle hands*, she thought poisonously.

"She can sing and daydream all she likes as long as this room is perfect," Madame said, satisfied with the photo she had taken. She had probably already posted it. Good. Make Ty seem normal. Legit. She'd worked at the Infinity for this same reason – a life lived as alibi. Madame crossed to the windows and peered out beside Ty, the sounds from the parade audience rising as the clang and thump of a brass band made its way closer, down Magnolia. "There are six inns on this block and Rosario Vicario is only staying at one."

"Did you say Rosario Vicario?" Ty said, before she could catch herself.

Ty caught Camille casting her a curious glance but she didn't care. She needed to know if it was true. The room she'd been cleaning seemed suddenly to swirl with the dust she had dislodged, all making its way into her throat. She'd watched the guestbook meticulously, scanning the names as if seeking treasure, always returning to her target like a line in a palm to be read. But Vicario was a surprise – that name hadn't been in the ledgers.

"Yes," Madame Richmond said. "And if you're going to be starstruck about it I will remove you from this wing in a metalbred's hoofbeat. Do you hear me? I won't have you or any of the others tripping over their dustbins for autographs and ruining her stay. We're lucky she's staying with us – one of the most famous jockeys alive."

"And one of the youngest," Camille added, still looking at Ty, a smile on her lips.

"Which is why she's one of the most famous," her mother sniffed. She directed her gaze back at Ty. "Do I need to reassign you?"

"No," Ty said quickly. "Did she book her room last minute?"

"Why?" Madame said, squinting at her.

Ty couldn't tell her that she'd been scanning the guest logs, of course, so she merely shrugged.

"No," Madame said after a moment. "No, she's been on the books for a year. I didn't know it myself until this morning. Her agent made the reservation, under her own name. I suppose you must take such measures when you're as famous as she is."

Madame swished out of the room. On to the next wing where Hilda was working, and where Madame would find plenty to complain about. Hilda's kit could use some newer tech.

"Were you a fan of Rosario Vicario before or after she won the Derby?" Camille said. She perched on the very edge of the bed Ty had already made up with percale linens. If it were anyone else Ty might snap at her not to ruin the square corners she'd so painstakingly folded. But not only was it not a good idea to snap at the boss's daughter, it was unnecessary. Camille was tall but weighed little more than dust herself. She barely left a dent in the down comforter the color of good china. Ty moved to the mantel, not looking at her.

"Before," she said.

"Before," Camille repeated, sounding delighted. She crossed her legs. "A real Derby girl, then?"

"I grew up with horses," Ty said, then snapped her mouth shut. Like the rooms she carefully set to order, she had created such an order for her life since her mother left it. The past was the past, and now was now. They overlapped in only one very specific way, and it wasn't the sort of thing she would talk to Camille about.

"But you're a Rosario fan?" Camille went on. "Most fans of *real* horses aren't big fans of the new jockeys. People call them glorified video gamers."

Ty stared down, inspecting her kit. The solid, slightly sharp smell of grass filled her nose as it always did whenever she thought of her childhood. The pungent, familiar scent of horse dung. She fought the memories down like vomit.

"I didn't say I was a fan of horses," Ty said, not looking at her. "Just that I grew up with them. Near them."

"Thoroughbreds? Real ones?"

"A few. Mostly Quarter horses and Tennessee Walkers."

Camille looked impressed – she'd probably lived in the city, in this hotel, her entire life, Ty thought. Horseracing with real horses was banned when Ty was just a child, and since then the Thoroughbreds that were once as inextricable from the image of Kentucky as the bluegrass itself became harder and harder to find. Not to mention that tens of thousands of people were put out of work – including Ty's father. For awhile. Until Limestone. But at one point, Ty had known horses and known them well. So had her mother. She fought that thought down too.

"So you could tell a metalbred from a Thoroughbred easily," Camille said.

Ty merely scoffed in answer.

Metalbreds, the creations that had saved Kentucky, the horse lands, from collapse. In 2041 there was a small entertainment robotics company that forged a complex 3D printing process to create animals and creatures for movie sets and faux-hunting resorts. Then someone on the board had the genius idea to create the metalbred, a completely lifelike robot horse that raised horseracing from the grave and turned Cavehill Downs into a fatter cash cow than it had ever been before public outcry over drugs and abuse sank organic horseracing. The small gaming company partnered with one of the oldest horse families in Kentucky and became Limestone Corp. Headquartered in Louisville, they sold thousands of metalbreds a year to the world's wealthiest equinaries.

But in the house where Ty grew up – a yellow farmhouse just outside Louisville's limits – Ty's bedroom window had overlooked the pasture of her neighbors. The girl who lived there was named Joelle, and Joelle's pasture held six horses, two of which were Thoroughbreds; despite Ty's parents' warnings about AC and heating bills, Ty always slept with her window cracked so the smell of manure and sun-baked hay could drift into her room, filling her dreams with the sound of thundering hooves, the glint of moonlight on shining rumps. *Those* had been horses. And when Ty moved into the city when she was twelve – her father in search of work after the racing ban – it was like leaving behind something sacred: the way Joelle had sensed the horse hunger in her shy, boyish neighbor and invited Ty beyond the fence had been a unique kindness, and Ty associated that feeling of warm welcome with horses themselves. Horses. Not equinibots.

"Is that a yes?" Camille prodded, even though Ty had turned her back to her, tidying up to leave. "You can tell them apart?"

"Yes," Ty answered. "But I will say Rosario Vicario's Window Seat looked more like a real horse than any bot I've ever seen before. Jockeys are talented, I know. It takes a lot of work to program metalbreds. But they're machines, and that's not interesting to me. That said, Rosario Vicario loves horses. You can just...tell. It makes her different."

"Ahh," Camille said, and Ty could hear the grin in her voice. "A purist."

"I don't even know what that means," Ty frowned. Outside, the brass band had reached the street just below the Mahogany and she couldn't help but feel the infection of excitement. The Kentucky Derby. Two weeks away from the day that nineteen metalbreds would capture the nation's attention, when the whole city would be flooded with rose petals and mint juleps, costume parties and galas. She would be invited to none of them. She wouldn't attend a single parade (there used to be one: now there were dozens). She wouldn't don an evening dress or a horse mask or sip bourbon. She had other plans, and none of them would happen in daylight. But Derby had a way of casting a spell on the city.

The band passed under the windows and the merry crash began to fade to watercolor. Ty reined herself in.

"Have you ever been?" Camille asked. She had moved to the overstuffed armchair in the corner at some point without Ty ever hearing her move.

"To the Derby?" Ty said. "No. I'd rather make my money off the people that do go."

"Let's hope Rosario Vicario is a good tipper," Camille said. She was standing now, and by the door. Her silent steps were almost creepy.

"She will be," Ty said confidently.

"The people's champion," Camille smiled. "That makes sense. The first non-millionaire to win the New Derby."

"She's rich now," Ty shrugged. "But still. She gets it." She moved to the windows and closed them one by one. The silencing effect was immediate – Madame Richmond had the Mahogany renovated twice to compensate for both climate change and the surging attendance of the new Derbies. The statewide slump had risen from the dead like a seersucker zombie when Limestone and the Claybelle family had partnered to introduce the metalbreds. Slowly at first, the masses curious about this new thing that could justify fashionable drunkenness, and then faster and faster until Cavehill Downs had been forced to build vertically, adding two new levels of seats for the people who flocked in to see the horses that weren't horses, the equinibots that felt no pain, the jockeys, whipless, walking the red carpet in designer gowns and suits and never setting foot on the track or astride a horse.

Then three years ago Rosario Vicario had entered the Derby with an equinibot she built in her parents' basement – Window Seat: a glorious chestnut creature with a white blaze and two white socks – and walked the red carpet in a dress her sister Aracelis had sewn, also in her parents' basement. Window Seat had defeated every Limestone metalbred on the track, and the photos of Rosario and Window Seat smothered in red roses had reached every corner of the world. 17-YEAR-OLD WINS KENTUCKY DERBY WITH HOMEMADE HORSE. Unsurprisingly, the Claybelle family worked quickly to establish a rule that every Derby entrant be a Limestone-base metalbred – "for safety reasons." Monopoly complete. But it kept Kentucky running.

"Are you going to ask for her autograph?" Camille said, teasing. Ty wasn't sure how she felt about buddying up with the boss's daughter. She was still concerned about what Camille might have eavesdropped.

"No," Ty lied. She had planned to go straight home after work and get some rest before coming back to the hotel at four tomorrow morning. But now she planned to lurk in the hallways to get a glimpse of the legendary Rosario Vicario, and perhaps to take her mind off the nagging feeling that her arrival had placed in the back of Ty's head. If one name could appear without prior knowledge, perhaps another could as well, or disappear – and all of Ty's plans relied on one particular guest arriving alone, as the guest log had promised for the past year.

Camille vanished down the hall, feet as light as air, and Ty hoped when it came down to Derby night, her own steps would be that soft.

CHAPTER 2

LUZ

I f she tilted her head a little to the left, Luz Cabo Trejo would be able to see the triple spires of Cavehill Downs jutting up into the dark as if to pierce the moon. She kept still. From here she could see the track and only the track, the dark arc of it bending into shadow, the first lightning bugs like fickle stars, hot then cold. It was only April, and after all her years in Kentucky, born and raised, Luz thought they appeared a little earlier every spring. The earth was warm and strange, confused. So were the bugs.

So was Luz, if she were honest. When she walked out of her parents' house on a Friday night carrying her backpack filled with clothes, her mother had whispered a short phrase in Kaqchikel, and, assuming her daughter had forgotten the little she'd been taught, added in English: "*After all our sacrifice....*" The gap of her silence at the end didn't need to be filled. Luz understood. They had caught Luz in a lie – a long lie – and the pain was enough for her mother to point at the door. Although perhaps she had not expected Luz to actually go.

And that's why Luz was confused. Because she had never ventured from the path her parents envisioned for her. She always stretched to live up to their dreams, and that meant staying away from the Downs, learning coding at the Skyhorse program, and looking at colleges for engineering. Her hair was long and black, even though she'd stood in her bathroom with scissors poised at her nape at least a dozen times, always returning the shears to her mother's sewing box before a single strand felt its teeth. Her round face was like an angel's. She was the perfect daughter.

Until she wasn't.

She moved into the not-moonlight. The moon had dimmed, dawn still hours away. The workers on the backside of Cavehill got up before the sun, so if she wanted to be here and not be seen, she had to come even earlier. She'd ridden her bike all the way from the huge house where she'd been welcomed as a roommate by a girl she barely knew, and now she leaned the rusty ten-speed against the fence. Quiet. Good. Even if her own parents didn't see her, someone else might, would recognize the eyes of Otto, the cheekbones of Sherry. Luz had been away from the track for a few years – obeying her parents – but the people of the backside would still know her. Soon the coffee truck and the doughnut truck and the tamale truck would be pulling in, the warm, familiar smells drawing the workers from their lodging, or maybe from the barn, where they might have fallen asleep whispering to the horses.

She called them horses because her parents called them horses, the creatures that her mother and father had spent most of their lives caring for, first flesh and then metal. The work had changed but the love had not, and Luz wanted nothing more than to be within the circle of warmth that radiated from that love. But her parents had other plans for her, big dreams. It wasn't the size of the dreams that scared Luz; it was the cold of them, the way they felt far from the things that felt close to her heart: the herbs her abuela worked back in Chimaltenango, the photo of her when she was a girl, leading a lanky horse down the road, her hair in two braids.

Luz only glanced at the three spires as she turned away from the track. From here she couldn't quite see the horticultural center, where she had been going every day for the last year instead of Skyhorse. It had been her sweet, green secret, and she hadn't planned on keeping it forever, but she *had* hoped to keep it a little longer. Her father had heard from other backside workers that Skyhorse was doing a pre-Derby exhibition, and he stopped by to see. He'd learned quickly from Dr. Aldana, the program director, that Luz hadn't shown up in too, too long. Her parents had suspected a boy at first, or maybe a girl. She hadn't told them that she hadn't been interested in either in a long time, that she was 21 and hadn't kissed anyone in five years, because somehow the fact that trees and plants eclipsed romance seemed just as bad. And besides, she wasn't a child. She could opt out of the Skyhorse classes if she wanted. Couldn't she? She'd worked away the guilt, hours spent working in the greenhouse, the kind of work her parents imagined her above. They imagined a daughter whose hands had never been dirty, but she only felt like herself when the half-moons of her fingernails were clogged with soil.

She moved now toward the nearest shedrow. The horses didn't hold the same appeal for her as they did for tourists, or even for her parents, but as she stepped under the lip of the roof, she still smiled as one by one their heads popped out to see who was coming. They were machines, she knew, and the doorways where no head emerged were stalls of models that the jockeys powered down. But some of the jockeys liked having the metalbreds already "awake" when they arrived to run morning diagnostics, and scheduled them that way. And here the horses were, greeting her in a way that made her trip here this morning feel justified.

"Early risers," she whispered as she approached. "Or maybe you never sleep. Like me."

She extended her hand to the chestnut model that craned its neck toward her fingers, and she obliged, stroking the velvet nose, dodging its fluttering lips that were curious about the rings she wore. It was easy to forget they weren't real. She knew these were all programmed responses, designed to mimic real horses by experts who believed that the essence of a horse could be distilled into a single chip. There was always the lack of manure though, she thought, the single thing a real horse could create besides applause. She stood under the shedrow smelling the hay and the soil and the dew and the coming of summer, but she didn't smell manure and it felt like a deep loss, somehow. The smell of manure couldn't be more different than her mother's delicious pepián, but they were both deeply familiar, and she couldn't remember the last time she had smelled either of them. It made her wonder if she actually ever had, or if she had inherited the knowledge of it, a download on a chip of her own.

She was petting the horse idly, staring across the backside fence at the geraniums that had already been pulled from the greenhouse and planted. She had helped grow them, had helped study the soil that made them sprout bright and strong. The audience that would crush into the Downs in a few weeks for Derby would see the flowers, but not the people who had planted them. And this is why her mother wanted her out of this world, ascending to a height that would allow the sun to be her own personal spotlight. Luz was looking for another way.

Her ears caught footsteps over by the big barn, where the jockeys like Rosario Vicario, jocks with the big money, kept their horses. Her eyes flew to the sky, where the moon was still shining, but the horizon getting brighter with the coming of sunrise. She darted away from the horse, startling it, and tucked herself around the corner of the shedrow. If her mother found her here, it would be a whole thing. *Two weeks after leaving my house and you're already here, showing off how little you care for your mother's wishes!* Luz wasn't ready, she didn't have the words she wanted to say, the plan taking root in her mind hadn't yet grown the leaves that would enable her to talk about it.

But it wasn't her mother who emerged from the barn. It was

a white man, which surprised her. Usually it was the workers, the men and women from Guatemala and Mexico and El Salvador, the occasional Black horsemen, who were here before the sun, smoothing out the wrinkles that night brings, laying everything straight. A white man – her first thought was ICE. Sometimes they came in the night, skull patches on their sleeves. Luz had practiced hacking the ICE registry at Skyhorse once when Dr. Aldana was out of the room – ICE no longer had to wear badges, and Luz had just wanted to know their names. Conrad Miller was the chief of ICE in Louisville, and Luz had stared at his features on that screen for a long time, memorizing his face the way one might memorize the shape and color of a poisonous leaf or berry. When out in the wild, avoid at all costs.

But this white man wasn't ICE – instead of the black vest, he wore shiny suit pants, and he moved like a rat, quick and furtive, close to the wall. He was too far and it was too dark for Luz to see his face, but she watched him look over his shoulder, then scan the empty backside, his gaze a scalpel. Luz felt herself shrinking deeper into shadow. He didn't see her. She watched him spray something on his hands, cleaning under his nails. He took a few steps to a hand sanitizer station, washed. Then he took one more look around and was gone.

She waited awhile before breathing – something in his step, in the way his footsteps were dark and sharp, made her lungs need to be still. But after he had been gone for many minutes, everything else remained still as well, the only sounds she heard coming from the shedrow beside her, the muted thud and stomp of the horses in their stalls. She gradually moved back into moonlight, and gazed toward the barn. What had he been doing there? An owner, perhaps, she thought, come to check on his model. This thought left a film of doubt over her tongue, but the dirt of the track was calling her, the greenhouse on the other side of the track. A plan was emerging, tiny sprouts pushing through soil. On her finger was the ring scan she used to accesss the greenhouse every morning, given to her by Mr. Benjamin, who had seen her green thumbs and welcomed her under his tutelage. Mr. Benjamin wouldn't be in until after the sun rose, and her ring and the dark promised privacy, at least for awhile. She stared down at her knuckles, a smile forming at one corner of her mouth.

CHAPTER 3

EZZ

The party from the night before had spilled into the kitchen at some point, and Ezzardine Clayton padded through the maze of rubbish and horse-shaped balloons, dragging a trash bag the size of a parachute. Her slides made a smacking sound against the marble floors, echoing up against the granite, the white cabinets she kept spotless. Out of the entire mansion her parents left her, the kitchen was still the only room that felt like home. They had lived here together for only a few months before her parents died, all the rooms full of boxes except the kitchen, where they had meals together, laying out plans for the rest of the house, the gardens. Now, two years after the funerals, Ezz spent most of her days here. She stopped short of sleeping in it, and luckily no partygoers had made that decision last night either. She didn't mind cleaning up – she didn't enjoy kicking people out.

When she'd cleared out enough trash to lend the room some peace, she poured herself a massive bowl of cereal and sat by the window overlooking the garden, eyeing the updated Derby odds on her device. She would bet in the smaller races, of course, and win. But she was interested in how Rosario was ranking now that she had been signed with a traditional owner. Ezz shook her head at the idea of Rosario jockeying for anyone but herself, but since the Limestone law of exclusivity, she didn't have much choice. Ezz put down the device. She'd bet on Rosario no matter the odds. Ezz's inheritance may have made her a millionaire, but betting on Rosario was one way she'd stayed rich.

"You need a line-up," someone said, and Ezz jumped, thinking party guests had stayed over after all, but it was just Luz, letting herself in from outside with her hair in a messy bun, circles under her eyes.

"You look great too," Ezz smirked, then palm-checked her hair. "I'm going to see Shavon at Bay's before the dinner tonight."

"That's why I was reminding you," Luz said, pouring herself a more reasonable bowl of Froot Loops. "You've been so busy. Just making sure it's on your schedule. You should probably text Shav now if you want to get in. Derby season and all."

"Such a mom," Ezz teased, and Luz blushed. Everyone seemed to be uncomfortable about Ezz making parent jokes except Ezz. She pointed at the area under her eye, then at Luz. "Did you not sleep well? The party keep you up? You know you can always work in the lair if you need to."

"No, no." Luz shook her head. "I had my earpods in anyway. I was just working on something and couldn't seem to put it down. Feels better than sleeping sometimes."

"You've already been out," Ezz said, nodding down at her shoes, wet with dew and flecked with grass. "Where'd you go so early?"

"Just had to run an errand," Luz said. "Picking up something at the backside."

Ezz raised an eyebrow. Luz guarded her privacy carefully, and Ezz was more than willing to let her have it. But she couldn't resist prying just a little.

"When's the last time you talked to your parents?" she asked.

Luz seemed suddenly interested in something in the garden, eyes focused on a nonexistent sparrow.

"Been a few days."

"Do they know you're here?"

"Told them I'm staying with a friend."

"Would they care if they knew you'd only known 'the friend' a few weeks?"

Luz shrugged.

"They would care only if I told them you bet at Cavehill. They just want me to stay away from horse people."

"I mean, I'm *not* a horse person," Ezz said, and at this Luz's eyes darted back in the kitchen, catching Ezz's long enough for them both to know her meaning: *Liar.* But so far Luz had allowed Ezz these small denials. These moments of pretending that who she had been before the funerals had died as well. Her love of horses and barns, she told herself, had burned alongside her parents.

"They don't need to know where I am," Luz said after a moment. "As long as it's not the track, they don't care."

"Your call," Ezz said, shrugging.

"Text Shavon," Luz said.

Ezz did. Shavvy had been cutting Ezz's hair for years, well before she opened Bay's. After Ezz's parents died, she couldn't bear to set foot in the mansion for two weeks, and had alternated nights on Rosario and Shavon's couches. On the nights when the mansion had felt like a cell, Shavon came and watched old movies, rubbing Ezz's legs through a blanket. So when Shavon wanted to open Bay's, Ezz had fronted her the money. Then WNBA superstar Danielle Trice had wandered in and put the shop on the map. Ezz got her money back fast, and still quietly paid $25 while tourists lined up to lay down $45 for a mere shape-up.

"What do you want me to work on today?" Luz's voice raised Ezz's eyes from her device.

"What do you mean?"

"Yard stuff," Luz said, the blush back on her cheeks and Ezz wasn't sure why. "Flowers. Ivy? Something."

18

"You don't have to work on something," Ezz said, shaking her head. "Just chill. Relax."

"No," Luz said firmly. "You're letting me stay here. I need to make sure you're getting something in return."

"Girl, do you see this big-ass house?" Ezz cried, throwing her arms out. "This shit is empty and lonely as shit. You being here is all the gift I need, okay?"

"Have you ever thought about selling it?" Luz said, then immediately bit her lip. "Sorry. That was not…that was not…I don't know. Not cool."

Ezz waved her off.

"It's fine. Yeah, I thought about it. But it's paid for. And there are like three cleaning ladies who make their living here. Plus all the artists and shit…"

"Your wards," Luz laughed.

"Stop." Ezz rolled her eyes.

"Seriously, though. I need something to do," Luz insisted. "And you have all this land for me to play with and…" She paused. "I really, really love growing things."

Ezz turned her eyes to the gardens, the square greenness of it. Her mother always had plans to turn it into vegetables, bring in horses, to hell with all the shrubs. *Shrubs and an empty lawn are vestiges of colonialism*, she would always say. Since the fire, Ezz had only paid people to cut the grass to keep the mosquitos at bay. Contemplating doing anything more felt like dipping her head under water for too long.

"I mean, what all can you do?" Ezz said, still studying the landscape. "You can do whatever you like doing."

Luz frowned, and Ezz watched her eyes wander out to the garden beyond the huge arching windows. She stayed silent for awhile, studying the thick bushes and trees that lined the sloping acres of land the mansion was nestled in. Then her face lit up.

"What do you think about…a topiary garden?"

Ezz scrunched her eyebrows.

"Wait, that's like, making the trees into shapes and stuff, right?"

"Yes."

"You can do that?"

"I'm a horticultural genius, remember?" Luz said, rolling her eyes. "What did you think I meant by that?"

"I don't know!" Ezz laughed. "You stay working on computers and shit too. I thought you were a hacker."

"Only because my parents made me," Luz said. "When they were trying to divert me from horses to computers. How annoyed do you think they were when the metalbreds became a thing? But plants were my first love. Before they banned me from the Downs, I used to work in Cavehill's greenhouse."

"That's amazing," Ezz said, watching her. Sometimes talking to Luz was like speaking into the mouth of a cave – dark and silent, but a dragon certainly breathing within. Other times the cave was aglow, words and truths tumbling out like crystals. Ezz had learned to wait for these moments, and not snatch at the gems. Gather them slowly, and look forward to next time. Now, she threw a casual hand out at the garden. "If you're in the mood to topiary, then topiary on, okay? Mi jardín es tu jardín."

"Are elephants okay with you?"

"Elephants...?"

"I'm going to turn the trees into elephants," Luz said flatly.

Ezz stared at her, mouth open.

"See you later," Luz said, clearing her cereal bowl. She washed it in silence and made her way to the door before pausing to look back. "I really appreciate you letting me stay here. I love my parents, and I know they love me. But it's like...they think they don't deserve my love? And sometimes loving someone like that gets...exhausting."

"I get it."

"You really don't mind if I use the lair?"

"Not at all."

"It feels so weird saying 'lair'," Luz said, laughing.

"You get used to it," Ezz grinned.

"It also feels so weird to…work on what I want to work on? Without someone telling me what I should be doing instead. Do you ever get used to that?"

This was a question Ezz could answer comfortably.

"Yes."

Luz brushed a hand across her eyes, nodded once. She had something in her pocket, Ezz noted. A large vial, or a bottle. What she must have picked up from the backside, she assumed. Then Ezz's device buzzed against the counter, and she looked down expecting Shavon, but it was a video call from Rosario. She saw her own face reflected back at her for a moment – her father's wide graceful nose, her mother's doe-like eyes. She resented those sometimes – too girly. Lashes that wouldn't let her live, always tangling and needing froufrou shit like eyelash combs. Her mother had so many little things like that, a table full of delicate tools that she'd touch with her delicate hands. Ezz had those hands too. She swiped her own face aside on the screen and was rewarded with the sight of Rosario.

"Rio-io!" Ezz crowed, grinning at her. "Are you back?"

"Yes, I'm in a car on my way to a meeting with the owner!" Rosario smiled, all teeth and cheekbones. "I'm glad to finally lay eyes on you, and home. Traveling sucks. And I can't even go *home* home until after Derby."

"What do you mean? You're not going to your parents' after this?"

"No, I didn't tell you? They're putting jockeys up in hotels this year. Something about a car route for when they pick us up and drop us off for events and all that nonsense. So I'm staying at the Mahogany – that's where the dinner is tonight."

"Booo," Ezz said. "I know your mom is pissed. You've been gone for weeks!"

"You have no idea!" Rosario laughed. But at the corner of her smile there was a crease, a scroll not fully unfurled.

"Everything cool?" Ezz said.

"Yes," Rosario said, and her eyes lifted, presumably to the driver, and then back down at Ezz. "Everything's fine. Should I pick you up later? Do you still refuse to own a car?"

"I do," Ezz grinned.

"All that damn money and you take the Trolley…"

"I care about the environment, okay?"

"Want a horse?" Rosario laughed.

Ezz didn't reply, and Rosario, looking out the window, snapped her eyes back to the screen.

"I'm sorry," she said. "I shouldn't have said that."

"It's cool." Ezz shook her head. "What's the dress code for tonight?"

"Fancy-ish," Rosario said. "I'm wearing a dress."

"Well, I'm not doing *that*," Ezz chuckled.

"Yes, I know, Your Butchness!" Rosario's laugh was as it always was now, the crease ironed out, and Ezz felt herself relax. "Wear whatever you want. But, uh, are you going to get a haircut?"

"Damn! Everybody is roasting me today!" Ezz cried. "Yes, I'm going to Bay's in a minute, damn! I've been busy!"

"Not too busy to throw a party!" Luz called from the background, just before she stepped out into the garden.

"Who was that?" Rosario said, raising an eyebrow. "Do you have a new girlfriend? I haven't been gone *that* long!"

Ezz shook her head.

"A new friend," she said. "Staying with me for awhile. Luz."

"Where'd you meet her?"

"The track. Her parents have worked on the backside for a couple decades."

"Jealous. Do you ever wonder what I would be like if I had grown up on the backside?"

"Do you?"

"Sometimes. Does Luz work there?"

"No," Ezz said. "They won't let her. Want her to do something other than racetracking."

"Can't say I disagree," Rosario sighed. "It has a way of taking over your life."

"But if you love it, you love it…," Ezz began, but the conversation suddenly felt like a lasso around her chest, squeezing the subject against her lungs. She pivoted. "You hear Limestone instituted a scholarship? Free ride for a Latinx senior to go to groom-tech school? Guaranteed spot on the backside doing the groom work."

Rosario snorted, her eyes lighting up with the spark that had lit the way for every interview where the reporter's questions about fairness in the industry cut too close to the nerve.

"They love making themselves look so good sending Latinx kids to groom school. What about jockeying? How many of these kids actually end up in the jockey booth? How many *own* a metalbred? Just as traditional horseracing started getting Brown, the ban came down. Now they reinvent it whiter than ever…"

"You should really meet Luz," Ezz said, smiling. "Y'all would really hit it off."

"Can't wait."

"She's not as loud with her opinions as you are," Ezz teased, "but I think she's just as fed up with the industry."

At the corner of Rosario's eyes, the crease was back, and she looked like there was something she wanted to say. Her eyes rose once more, quick as hummingbirds, then flitted back. "I'm almost to my meeting, but I'll see you tonight, okay? Six?"

"Sure," Ezz nodded.

They said goodbye, Ezz reluctant to watch her best friend's

face blink away into black. At least she would see her later. Being a world-famous jockey kept Rosario busy, but after Derby things would slow down again – at least for awhile.

Ezz got up and moved through the kitchen back to the ballroom. They'd laughed about it when they'd bought it, a soaring, gilded space with a dome that the realtor said had only ever collected dust. Her father had chatted idly about hosting community concerts in it, chuckling about how the long-dead white people who had built the place would have died sooner if they had imagined a Black family throwing parties with Black guests and Black music under that stupid dome. Since then, Ezz had the outside of the mansion painted candy pink, and hosted parties every weekend. Her neighbors pretended she didn't exist. But she did.

The ballroom was now coated in confetti instead of dust. The stage she had erected in the center still had all the instruments of the band she'd hired to play last night – they'd be back later. She climbed up and let her legs dangle over the edge, a guitar on her lap. When she ran her fingers across the strings, the music sounded small and blue.

CHAPTER 4

LUZ

She watched Ezz leave for the barbershop, strolling down the long curving driveway that never felt the weight of cars. Luz knew the flock of vehicles Ezz had inherited were still sitting in the garage like candy-painted boulders, and she also knew that if Luz asked to drive one, Ezz would say yes in a rush of keys and encouragement. Ezz was full of so many yeses. It made Luz wary, even if she believed the kindness of Ezz's eyes.

She stood there, paused next to the tree she was transforming into an elephant, waiting for Ezz to disappear through the front gate and down the street toward Bay's. Luz felt weightless, detached – she'd felt this way since she'd walked out of her parents' house. That night, she'd gone straight to the backside, watching the hot walkers lead metalbreds to and from the track. She'd considered calling her abuela, telling her what happened. She had a feeling she'd be on Luz's side. But then Cristobal, a groom, paused at her elbow, concerned but warning – *Do your parents know you're here?* – and the guilt had nearly closed her windpipe. She'd walked away in tears, and her tears had led her to Ezz. Ezz, full of yes. Ezz, who offered distraction from her guilt. So here she was, transforming a bush into an elephant, ignoring texts from her eldest cousin, Mariela.

When are you coming back?

Tia Sherry just wants what's best for you!
You can't ignore me forever, Luz Cabo Trejo!

Luz almost wrote back "Yes I can" but knew this is what Mariela was counting on. She slid her device back into her back pocket, and when she looked up, Ezz was gone. The feeling of weightlessness dissolved now, roots shooting down. This is what happened when it was time to work.

"Okay," she whispered to the half-elephant. She gave a few of the leaves a soft caress. "I'll be back."

She set off across the garden then, making her way toward the labyrinth, her hand on her pocket, resting on the vial she'd taken from the greenhouse. The yard was one of the reasons Luz felt she had been brought here for a reason when Ezz gave her a tour on the second day. Two acres full of greenery, with full license to grow and do with it what she wanted. In the year that she'd been secretly working in the greenhouse she had worked with Mr. Benjamin on growth serums, hybrid flowers, soil analysis. When she'd arrived at the Pink, and Ezz had shown her the gardens, and then the lair, Luz had picked up right where she'd left off.

Luz stepped inside the labyrinth, a winding green maze of leaves and roots and ivy that the original owners had probably created from some fascination fixed in Europe-worship. Luz had done some research into the people who owned the mansion before Ezz's family. The Vanders, snub-nosed white people with money that enjoyed its great age, that sought to drag its favorite bits of history – and only those bits – along into the future in a stale, gold parade. It made Luz both bored and nauseated. She liked the changes Ezz had made. The pink paint, even parties, which Luz usually just watched from a quiet distance.

But the labyrinth. Things like this, and like her abuela's work with herbs, had drawn Luz into botanical study to begin with. The way plants could be both friend and enemy, and how those roles might switch depending on how much or how little the hand knew of the seeds. This labyrinth had been planned well, she confirmed as she wandered through, the path to the hidden door like a tattoo in her fingertips. The branches grew slowly but in the right direction. The ivy knew its role. Luz twisted and turned, the feeling of rootedness deepening with every step. By the time she reached the unremarkable place between one curve and another, she felt the sort of calm that came from meditation, legs crossed and palms up.

Reaching through the ivy, she found the door Ezz had shown her. Now she paused, feeling guilt sharpen into a thorn. After everything her parents did for her – funding her comic book obsessions as a kid, paying for Skyhorse's advanced workshops, her father taking a second job to pay for her braces – she had left their house and not gone back. It felt like swimming in shame. But her plan had begun to take hold, even if it wasn't fully formed, and Luz pushed through the leaves.

She stepped through into the dark, paused until the ivy had swung closed at her back. She knew no one would follow – she and Ezz were likely the only two living people who knew this door, this staircase, this underground floor existed. This door. Another door. She walked along the path, and couldn't help but sink into a grief not her own. Ezz had told her that this lair was the one thing her parents had been able to create before the barn fire that claimed their lives: a safe place. An underground secret. It was like a bomb shelter but it felt warmer than that. A burrow.

There were three rooms, one empty, and Luz had been allowed to make the other two her own. The second was full of computers and devices, many of which she had built. She had actually enjoyed Skyhorse: building things, making them tick, was a way to let off steam. It was a side hobby that she happened to be very good at, and she'd carried that activity here as well. It helped to stanch the guilt, as if the occasional fiddling with machines was proxy for her mother's permission to work with the plants, her parents' sacrifice made worthwhile.

And then there was the other door. Luz opened it now and stepped inside, breathed the sweet smell of soil and seed deeply into her lungs. The light was made green by the crush of leaves. She didn't sit down at the rough table right away – instead she extracted the greenhouse bottle from her pocket, stood looking at the unlabeled glass. She'd developed the serum in January, and Mr. Benjamin had been so stunned by what it could do that he'd taken off his glasses, rubbing the bridge of his nose. But Luz knew it could do more.

Luz sank down onto the workbench now, turning the bottle of serum over and over in her hands, the garden in her mind growing. She'd need to tweak it, if the plan flowering in her mind was going to work. What would her parents think? She almost called Dr. Gina, the woman who taught Luz to hack, the woman who had been an MIT professor and brought her skills back to Kentucky to teach girls who looked like her, girls like Luz Cabo Trejo, girls whose parents walked all the way from Guatemala to build something good and gold for their future children. Gina had envisioned Luz at MIT too. Everyone had their ideas about what Luz should be, but she had her eye on something else.

Luz closed her eyes, exhaling a long breath, getting rooted. This was her ritual: finding somewhere peaceful in her mind, where the work would spring from. She always ended up one of two places: beside her abuelita in Chimaltenango, watching the wrinkled old woman whom she'd only ever met twice boil Tagetes lucida. The other place she'd end up was the backside, every sound and sight unfurling in her head. This time she felt herself at the latter: the nearby plod of metalbred feet, the far-off gallop as the jockeys and technicians studied the product of their code. The rise and fall of Spanish being called from stall to stall, echoing from the shedrow in song and complaint and curse. Laughter. The younger kids hanging around, waiting to be asked to help, drawn into the dusty magic that horses – even metalbreds – exuded. People like her mother and father, from Guatemala, from Mexico, from El Salvador, moving on their expert paths, crooning to the animals that, while just machines, still behaved better under these gentle brown hands. The white tourists and owners picking their way through the constant motion, the buzz and snap of reins and flies; seeing only the stars – the equinibots – and not the galaxy that framed their glow.

Now in this moment, Luz again remembered Cristobal asking: *Do your parents know you're here?* The question had become, in her mind, *Does anyone know we're here?*

Luz opened her eyes, rooted. She was ready. She needed to be up to her wrists in dirt, eyes like lasers glaring through the magnifier she had set up to examine the insides of seeds. The seeds were from a plant called kudzu, and she'd never heard of it before she'd been driven to the outskirts of Louisville once on a field trip. Whole fields roiled with it, swallowing cars and garages and caving in the roofs of houses left unattended too long. It seemed straight out of the DC comic books she stacked like tilted cities – an invention of Poison Ivy, her hero. The kudzu had caught her eye like all green things, and she asked the bus driver what it was.

"That!" the driver said. "The plant that swallowed the south! Kudzu. Brought it from Japan a couple hundred years ago to help out with soil erosion, and then it took over! They call it an invasive species now. People been trying to beat it back ever since!"

This had stayed with Luz as she moved through her life in Kentucky, watching her parents work all day as invisible gears in a machine that wouldn't run without them. *Invasive*, the driver had said, and as Luz tinkered with the seeds and the soil, acid, water, electricity, she couldn't help but wonder what the south would look like if after kudzu took a bite, it truly, actually swallowed.

CHAPTER 5

EZZ

Night had fallen, but there was a cardinal in the garden. Ezz had been waiting at the end of the drive waiting for Rosario when the flash of red feathers had drawn her inside the herd of elephants Luz had begun to carve into the green. Now Ezz stood at the base of one, watching the bird flutter around the outer edge of the elephants, as if it too couldn't believe that the statue was made of leaves. Watching it, Ezz's heart felt that fast and red, memories of her first days at the Pink layering onto her skin the way the dew had already begun to creep across the grass. Sometimes living here still felt as strange and lonely as it had those first few weeks after her parents' deaths, grief like a housecat around her ankles. She felt like she could sooner escape the moon, which followed her as she moved back toward the drive.

She paused at the sound of a car slowing on the street. It was long and dark – Rosario. Rosario climbed out of the backseat, her marigold dress swimming into the night air like a koi fish through inky black water. She took a few steps onto Ezz's drive, peering up toward the Pink, and Ezz merely watched for a moment, drinking her in. It had been weeks since she'd seen her friend in person, and seeing her now felt like cool water on a burn she was only just aware of. Shavon had chided Ezz when she'd mentioned it – *you need more friends. I know Rosario is your bestie, but she's too busy traveling the country to be the only egg in your basket.* Shavon was an old woman at heart – she was full of these sayings. Still, maybe she was right.

But as Ezz watched Rosario, the impatience of her hands – raising first her device to check the time and then her wrist – was as familiar as the curve of Ezz's own knuckles. How could there be other friends when Rosario was the only person – besides Shavon – who had known, really known, Ezz before the fire? Ezz may have transformed since the loss of her parents, but as long as Rosario was there to remember who Ezz had once been, maybe she could find her way back to that version of herself.

"We won't be late," Ezz said, emerging from the shadows, and laughed when Rosario squealed, leaping backward.

"Ezzardine! ¡No seas gacho! You know I hate being scared!" She clutched her chest, laughing, but it sounded a little strained and Ezz looked closer.

"Sorry, Rio," she said. "You good?"

"I'm fine," Rosario said, tossing her hair out of her face as she stepped forward for a tight hug. She smelled the way she always smelled – like rose oil and something not quite identifiable: a clean, warm outside smell. "Just shocked you're ready on time. I may not ever recover from this sudden punctuality."

"I mean, can you blame me? I haven't seen my best friend in three weeks – she's been off traveling through the big cities and…"

And there it was again, the strain; although this time it wasn't in Rosario's voice, but across her face, a twitch of a muscle.

"Hey, what's wrong?" Ezz said. "Are you not happy to be back or something? I mean, damn, I'm not saying I expect little ole Louisville to compete with all the fancy shit they have you at, but I thought our Derby was at least in your top five…"

Rosario shook her head, and the black hair she just shoved out of her face cascaded back down. She turned back to her car, where the driver leaned, waiting.

"Of course I'm happy to be back," she said. "I just…"

She paused, and Ezz watched her back, a subtle tan line beyond the straps of the dress from the t-shirts she always wore. Some jockeys worked inside – dark basements or chilly offices. Not Rosario. She liked to be where the horses were, even if the "horses" were made of metal.

"You just what?" Ezz called. Whatever uncertainty was resting there between Rosario's shoulder blades seemed to travel through the air and burrow into her own. *This is why you can't have just one egg*, she could hear Shavon saying. *Because what happens if it breaks?*

"I just…wanted to talk to you about something," Rosario said. She waved the driver back into the car.

"Maybe something about how you didn't bring me any popcorn from Chicago?" Ezz said, trying to tease, trying to get that muscle in Rosario's jaw to lay flat. "That little-ass purse you're carrying is too tiny for it to be in there so…"

Rosario laughed, but her eyes were on the driver, and when he ducked back into the car and the door closed behind him, she returned her gaze to Ezz.

"What if I told you…" she started, and Ezz felt her smile fade, soaked up by the quiet that opened between them when Rosario didn't continue.

"What?" said Ezz. And for some reason she felt the way she did the first time she saw her parents' barn after the fire – the blackened frame, the collapsed walls. Everything sighing the same two words: *too late*. Whatever was in Rosario's eyes had moved past the point of no return. It was too late for something, Ezz just didn't know what.

"What if you told me what?" Ezz repeated, but as she said it, she saw the cardinal of possibility fade out of Rosario's face. She had already put it away, whatever it was.

"What if I told you that the place we're going for dinner is

run by a woman who once appeared on The Great British Baking Show? And she's not even British."

Rosario's grin was a lullaby as she opened the dark car, beckoning her inside.

"That good?" Ezz said, allowing herself to be lulled.

"Better," Rosario smiled.

CHAPTER 6

TY

Madame Richmond could cook. It was half of what made the Mahogany so popular for the elites it served – the appeal of a semi-private chef and the allure of sharing a dinner table with people who could afford to rub their elbow. Every night at 8 o'clock, a bell installed in each suite would ring a soft, welcoming chime informing guests that dinner was ready, and every night the various socialites and minor celebrities would descend from their chambers and alight around the table that seated twenty-four and no more. Madame would be waiting, the cookwork staff poised to carry dishes and take drink orders. Cookwork was afforded more access to the guests, as cleanwork staff were expected to clean and straighten suites while guests were not in them. Ty had never envied the proximity until tonight.

She knew Rosario Vicario's laugh from her unending media circuits. Even when it wasn't Derby season, there were horseraces around the country for metalbreds and the jockeys hired to program them. Rosario's face showed up regularly, her youth part of the national appeal, but also, of course, her beauty. Ty didn't have a crush on her, exactly, but she was fascinated by her. It was one thing to be that smart, and eventually that rich. But Rosario was brave as hell. Ty's mother had been brave: standing outside Cavehill with signs, yelling in the faces of horse owners. But what

Rosario had done was something else – Brown girl, white industry, no fucks. This industry wasn't a friendly one to outsiders, and certainly not to ones that made them look foolish.

But Rosario was friendly to everyone. Rosario emerged for dinner downstairs and her laugh clanged down the hallway like a herd of frying pans – Ty heard her all the way from the staff lockers at the back of the kitchen. Ty poked her head out just in time for one of the cookwork staff, Jessica, to catch her.

"What are you still doing here?" Jessica said, balancing a tray loaded with appetizers, little cups of macaroni and cheese and shot glasses of white bean chili.

"That's Rosario Vicario!" a voice squawked from the dining area, another of the Mahogany's guests who didn't know whose company they'd be dining in this evening.

"For that," said Ty, gesturing to the voice.

"A fan," Jessica said, looking her up and down. "I didn't see that coming."

"You didn't think I'd be a fan of Rosario Vicario? *Everyone's* a fan of Rosario Vicario."

"No," Jessica said before pushing through the doors into the dining room, "I didn't see you as a fan of anything."

She was gone before Ty could reply, and through the slow swing of the service door, Ty got her first in-person glimpse of the girl whose hand-built horse crushed the wealthiest racers in the industry. Her smile was like a slash of electricity in the dim room, all the candles the cookwork staff lit an hour ago like dying stars in the universe her laugh created. The door swung closed, leaving Ty to observe with only her ears. She hovered in the back hall of the kitchen, eavesdropping.

"Coming home to the water here is my favorite part." Rosario's voice carried through, a silver bell. "Louisville's tap water is the best in the country, I swear. I was at a race in New York and the water tastes like someone cleans their tools in it."

"We're not *just* known for our horses," said Madame Richmond. Ty couldn't see her but she knew what she would be doing. Sitting at the head of the table like a grand hawk wearing a scattering of diamonds, the candles positioned to catch them just right. Ty wondered if she knew Rosario was from Louisville too, or if she assumed as so many did that she arrived at the racetrack straight from Mexico. Some white people – Ty included, at one point – would see her skin and stop there, not hearing the accent: *Luh-vul*. A Louisville girl.

"No, but horses are what *we* know Louisville for," said a man's voice, already thick with alcohol. "That's how Limestone got its name, isn't it? Something in Kentucky?"

"I think Ezz here is the one to tell that story," Rosario said.

A lower voice said something Ty couldn't catch, which made Rosario laugh, and then this unknown person's laugh spread through the dining hall like a honeyed mist. It wafted under the service door and into the kitchen where Ty eavesdropped, a laugh she'd never heard the likes of. A brassy sound like a saxophone in a crowd of violins. And Rosario's violin was pleasant. But Ty needed to see the mouth that saxophone was coming out of, and she glowered at the door, wishing she could trade her black cleanwork uniform for a white one of the cookwork, just this once. She tried going to the crack to peer but the cookworks started grumbling every time she was underfoot. She could only hear the tinkle of Rosario's friendly conversation amid the hum of the other guests, and occasionally the melody of that faceless saxophone. Ty sighed the next time she heard it and from somewhere above her came another voice.

"You can see everything from up here, you know," said a soft voice, and Ty jumped a little before gazing around, seeing no one, wondering which cookwork was fucking with her. "Here, Ty. No, *here*. Yes."

The voice said "yes" in confirmation but Ty was only staring up at the blank faces of the many white cabinets, and continued doing so, seeing nothing. A dry chuckle came from the cabinets before one large door at the very top of the airy kitchen swung slowly open with a groan. Camille stuck her head out, gazing down like a squirrel from a tree.

"What the hell are you doing up there?" Ty demanded, shocked. Camille was wearing a black tank top clouded with dust and, from the looks of it, flour. "Is that the baking cabinet? Why are you *inside* it?"

"No, Madame moved the baking things a long time ago," she whispered. "Too high to reach. This is empty now. Back when people still had servants, they must have used this to spy on the household, because there is a nice pair of eyeholes up here that look directly over the dining table."

"What? You're serious?" Ty raised an eyebrow. She found herself liking that the house had secrets. Cleanwork was treated with more respect now, but that wasn't always the case, and imagining maids and cooks taking more from their employers than the pennies they offered put a jagged little line of satisfaction through her heart.

"Rosario brought a guest," Camille said in that rapsy voice of hers, arching her own eyebrow back. "Must be someone significant or Madame wouldn't have allowed her at dinner. She's so strict about it usually. But I don't recognize them."

Ty stared up at her, her mind clicking. Perhaps Rosario had brought Aracelis, the sister who had famously sewn Rosario's rose carpet gown. No, Ty thought, a saxophone laugh like that couldn't come out of a girl that small. Besides, she thought Camille would at least recognize her from the footage.

"Do you want to come see?" Camille whispered, looking sly.

"You're trying to get me fired," Ty said dismissively. She had come to the Mahogany with one goal, and Derby brought it closer and closer to her grasp. Getting fired would make it impossible.

"Never," Camille said. "No one else on the cleanwork staff sings. Who would I listen to?"

"I don't sing anymore," Ty grumbled.

"Besides," Camille said, ignoring her, "you're Madame's favorite. She'd never get rid of you."

"Wait, do you really call your mother *Madame*?"

"Only during Derby season."

Ty frowned.

"Come up," Camille said, shifting sideways to make room. "You'll fit."

Fit isn't the issue, Ty thought. But then there was that saxophone laugh again, a warm swell of sound that found its way through the kitchen to Ty's ears and settled there, both the start and the finale of a symphony. She had to see the mouth it came from; she couldn't go home until she did. So after one more glance around the now empty kitchen, she hauled herself up onto the counter and used the shelves indicated by Camille to climb into the cabinet.

Camille swung the door closed after them almost immediately, plunging the small space into near-darkness. Two round streams of yellow light cut in from the back wall, illuminating a bit of the little flour-dusted cave. Roomier than Ty had anticipated. She sat comfortably cross-legged six inches from Camille, who smelled vaguely of peppermint.

"Be my guest," the girl whispered, gesturing to the two holes. "They just served dinner."

As predicted, Madame Richmond was seated at the head of the table and dripping in sparkly stones. She wore delicate gloves up to her elbows, which Ty knew she would not remove to dine. The other guests were more modern in their fashions – the pair of gentlemen to her right (metalbred owners, Ty knew with one glance) wore the kind of suits that were acceptable for dinner but might be sewn with the spinworm silk that could allow for a more dramatic color-change for whatever clubs they ended up in after this engagement. Most of the women wore dresses, Rosario included. Ty could see her full-on now, wearing a dress the color of marigolds that lit up the sunshine in her skin, a string of jewels along her collar bone, her earing aid decorated with glimmering stones to match. She may have been a poor girl at one point, Ty thought, but she wasn't anymore.

But then there was that laugh.

Ty's eyes flew from the gems at Rosario's neck to the person sitting next to her, and finally took them in, mid-laugh.

A young Black woman, the only woman not in a gown. She wore a suit somewhere between royal blue and robin's egg, tailored to her body as if she'd been born in it. The collar of the white shirt under the jacket was tall, nearly brushing her jaw, which when Ty's eyes found it, would not let go. She followed that jaw down to a pointed chin, up to a broad elegant nose, up to the brown eyes that were lit with candlelight. The close-cropped coils of her hair were dyed a deep fuchsia, purple in places, short on the sides and a little longer on top, a crisp edge along her forehead. Under the curve of her unglossed lips was a bowtie. The lips were moving and Ty eventually got a hold of herself enough to listen.

"…the new Secretariat models are massive. The horse himself was 16.2 hands but the Limestone model is 16.5. Biggest animals Cavehill Downs will have ever seen. Personally I don't see the point in naming it Secretariat if the Limestone animals' statistics are going to be different."

A horse person, Ty thought. Of course. It's Derby and they were all seated at the Mahogany. You came either because you knew horses or because you wanted to.

"You call them animals," a white woman at the other end of the table said. She was elderly and platinum blonde. "Surely you mean robots? Equinibots."

"Sure," the blue-suited diner said, sipping water. "Whatever you want to call them."

"It's hard to keep up," the white woman's date said. "We're old! We remember when real horses ran the tracks. We've been coming to the Derby for sixty years. Those years after the ban were sad ones."

"Limestone's creatures took some getting used to," the woman said. "But really you can't much tell the difference. Only there's no jockeys."

"There are jockeys," Rosario said brightly, rotating her wrists and displaying her palms, as if unveiling herself as a surprise. "We just don't sit on the metalbreds' backs."

"Tell us what your job is like," Madame Richmond said, jumping in. Ty could see she was pleased at the angle of this conversation – an excuse to show off her prized guest. "We've never had a real jockey at our table before."

"I'm just a fancy nerd," Rosario said with a smile, the same charming lilt in her voice that made her so appealing in the interviews. "Now that I'm hired by metalbred owners and not running my own creation – " she paused, her smile tightening ever so slightly " – I work from the Limestone model that the owner has purchased. Those are standard, of course. How many do they make now, Ezz?" She shot her eyes to her blue-suited neighbor and Ty eagerly drank her in.

"Limestone makes around a few thousand models a year. This year is the Secretariat model, designed to resemble the original horse in as many ways as possible. Last year was Man O' War. They choose an historical Derby winner to replicate every year. Then it's up to the geniuses like Rosario – " she nodded affectionately, and Ty wondered if they were in love " – to do their programming magic and make them faster, stronger. Find all the little secret Easter Eggs that the Limestone engineers left for the jockeys to find and exploit."

"Are you a jockey too?" the old man asked, impressed, and at this Rosario and her guest exchanged a swift look.

"Not for a long, long time," she said, but Ty didn't think she could be more than twenty-one or two.

"Ezzardine is a bettor, not a jockey," Rosario said. "But she comes from horse people."

It was subtle, but Ty saw Ezzardine flinch.

Madame Richmond didn't notice – she sat forward in her chair, scattering the light from her earrings over the table.

"A bettor! Ah! I knew I recognized your face!" she said, her hands clasped, elbows on the table. "Ezzardine Clayton. Your parents were…owners? Yes? Winifred and…?"

"James," Ezzardine said, a little more quietly than before. Ty couldn't take her eyes from the young woman's face, the storm spreading across her features. She knew that storm. She walked in that rain.

"Jesus Christ…," Camille whispered, and Ty almost jumped at the sound of her voice, her breath on her shoulder. She'd almost forgotten Camille was there. She glanced sidelong at the boss's daughter, who rolled her eyes. "Read the room, mom."

"Winifred and James Clayton," Madame Richmond went on, nodding. "Yes. I heard about the fire. I'm sorry for your loss. It's been a few years now?"

"Two."

"Doing what they loved. I heard they could only save a few of the horses."

Ty watched Ezzardine Clayton swallow.

"Three," she said. "Horses…real horses…are afraid of fire. You take 'em out of their stall and a lot of the time they go right back in."

Rosario cleared her throat, loudly. There was a long pause, and then another man seated at the table piped up, his voice carrying the pitch that said he intended to pivot toward sunshine.

"Ezzardine Clayton, I know that name too," he said,

eyebrows raised. He snapped his fingers, as if the thought in his mind could be called like a dog. "Ezzardine Clayton...the gambler...didn't you...?"

"She bet on me when no one else would," Rosario said, reaching out to squeeze her guest's hand. Ty watched Ezz's brow unfurrow. "And it turned out that was a smart thing to do."

"I've seen Rosario start a car with a fork and a cinnamon stick, okay?" Ezzardine chuckled. Ty could practically smell the relief for the change in subject. "If Cavehill Downs hadn't banned all equinibots except Limestone models she would have gone on winning with her homemade builds. And all the other racetracks followed suit, of course."

"But you've bet on lots of metalbreds since Rosario's big win with Window Seat," Madame pressed.

"And always with an earpod in your ear!" one of the guests laughed.

"Mhmm."

"Ezz has a nose for money," Rosario said.

"Something like that," Ezz grinned.

They went on talking and Ty went on staring, her forehead pressed against the inside of the cabinet, sometimes forgetting she wasn't at the table with them. She had merely wanted to get a glimpse of Rosario Vicario, but Ezzardine Clayton was an unexpected feature of the evening and Ty couldn't tear her eyes away.

"Smitten?" Camille said softly, and when Ty glanced at her she was grinning.

"I've just never seen her before. Lived in Louisville all my life."

"I've heard of her but never seen her. Surprised the cameras don't follow her around the track."

"Seems like she keeps a low profile," Ty said.

"Yeah, the fuchsia hair is really low profile."

Ty smirked.

"Okay, not like that. But I don't see her parading around the Downs dropping money. If she's rich like they said she probably sends someone to make her bets."

"How would you know?"

"I clean rich people's rooms for a living," Ty shrugged. "You hear stuff."

"Hmm."

"Wait, wait," said one of the guests downstairs, "we never finished the story. How Limestone got its name. Ezzardine, er, Miss Clayton, do you work for Limestone?"

The saxophone laugh.

"No," she said definitively. "I'm just old, old Kentucky blood. One of my ancestors was one of horseracing's very first Black jockeys. He was from New York originally, back when Kentucky and New York competed for betting on horseracing. But he won a couple races and stayed for awhile. Back then New York and other northern states started banning gambling of any kind. But not Kentucky. So the millionaires came running. Bringing horses, building mansions. It was just what Louisville needed. They built Cavehill Downs and then had the first Derby in 1875, and after that…they were off!" She chuckled.

"But where did *Limestone* come from?"

She pointed downward.

"It's in the ground. In our caves. Mammoth Cave? It's all filled with limestone. It releases calcium into the soil, then into the grass, the water. The horses eat – ate – the grass. Drank the water. Everyone believes that's what made the Kentucky Thoroughbreds such great racers. Strong bones." She tapped her legs beneath the table. "Anyway, that's what the horse folks said back then to get everyone's noses turned to Kentucky. And it worked."

She spread her arms wide, as if in reference to the whole

room, the whole house, the whole state.

"Weird that a company that never worked with real horses would call themselves Limestone," Camille said quietly, up in the cupboard. She was gazing through the other set of eyeholes, her attention less rapt than Ty's but still interested.

"It's all about the image," said Ty without looking at her. "When horseracing was banned a lot of people were out of work. Limestone acquired a ton of the old farms' workers. They want everyone to know they're *friends of horse people*."

Camille looked at her in surprise.

"What would farmers know about robotics?"

Ty shrugged.

"Nothing. Just ask my dad. He was one of the trainers they acquired. Can barely work the toaster."

Downstairs, Madame Richmond was prodding Ezzardine with more questions.

"Surely it was more than calcium that made Kentucky Thoroughbreds the best," she said. She had that syrupy nostalgia in her voice.

"It was," Ezz nodded. "Kentucky horses didn't do what they were supposed to do. They had a heart and a mind that you couldn't just train into them. They were smart. Fierce. They gave it all they had even when they shouldn't have. Nothing could bind them."

"Wait, wait," one of the guests said, waving his drink, sloshing it a little. "This sounds like what Limestone has done with the metalbreds! Right? The Artis...the Aristi..."

"The Aristidean component," Rosario finished for him with a smile. "Now you're talking my territory. The Aristidean component is what Limestone installs in all their models, yes. It's a part of the metalbreds' brain that jockeys aren't able to alter. It's what compels the equinibot to run, essentially. It's what responds to all the input we jockeys do to the rest of the build. We can change many things about the model, but the Aristidean component is what keeps the machine safe and ensures it responds to our programming orders."

"Named after Aristides," Ezzardine continued. "The very first Derby winner. Ridden by a Black jockey, you know. Oliver Lewis. They weren't supposed to win – they were supposed to be the rabbit, the horse that the horse the owners *wanted* to win would fixate on and chase. But Artistides was a Kentucky horse. He didn't do what he was supposed to do. He broke away and fought off every horse that tried to catch up. Won by a length. That was a horse that wanted to win."

"You know so much," Madame said with a sugary smile. Ty half-believed she was flirting. "You're sure you won't be a jockey?"

"I have other talents," Ezzardine shrugged. She was attempting to look flippant, but Ty saw the tightness in her jaw. "Riding horses isn't one of them."

"Technically I don't ride horses either..." Rosario said, grinning. "I just program them. I do lots of animal builds though – the metalbreds are just the most profitable!"

"What other animals?" Madame Richmond pried.

"Birds, turtles, dogs..."

"Her dog builds are wild good," Ezzardine said. "I hate dogs – hers are *too* real."

"Even a dog bot is man's best friend," Rosario protested. "They keep all your secrets!"

They all laughed and kept drinking, except Ezz, who Ty watched drink glass after glass of water. Rosario gave the impression of drinking a lot, but she took only small sips of her wine every time she raised it. The rest of the dinner party, however, emptied and filled, emptied and filled. They grew louder and louder, and Ezz spoke less and less, watching them all with a small smile and narrowed eyes.

"I'm going to bed," Camille said. "They'll be winding down

soon. You can stay up here if you want."

"I'm just going to hang out a little longer and then I'll leave too," Ty said. Camille made a sound of acknowledgment, but Ty caught the shadow of a smile on her lips as she cracked the cabinet door open and dropped out of sight into the empty kitchen like a cat. The cookwork staff was all loitering in the dining room, getting all the viewing of Rosario Vicario that they could get away with. And of Ezzardine, Ty thought, with an irrationally green pang.

Ty was just trying to convince herself to climb down and catch the Trolley when the melodious sound of the doorbell traveled in through the crack of the cabinet. Through the eyeholes, Ty observed Madame motion for Jessica to answer the door; she disappeared through the grand entranceway that separated the dining room from the front of the house. Jessica was gone only a moment before she returned with a young white man Ty's age, skin deeply tanned and with a tinge of outdoors-all-day red. He looked a little stunned to have entered a room with so many well-dressed people and took a moment to whisper his business to Jessica. Upon hearing it, Jessica turned to Rosario, equally stunned and pleased to have cause to address the famous guest.

"Ma'am. Miss Vicario," she said. "He's a messenger. He's arrived with a note for you."

"Oh," said Rosario, looking up from her wine. "From who?"

The boy's skin reddened further, heated now by an internal sun.

"Um, it's private, ma'am. If I could just..."

He moved toward the table, then paused, and when no one admonished him, started forward again. He went around to Rosario's side of the table and reached in his pocket. Ty didn't know what she was expecting him to withdraw, but it wasn't a paper envelope.

"Must be *really* private," Ty whispered to herself. No one sent a hard-copy message anymore unless they had serious worries about security.

Rosario took the envelope from the boy's fingers, casting a puzzled smile sidelong at Ezz before opening it. She opened its edge neatly and drew out a square of white paper. Ty watched her black arching eyebrows lower first in focus and then in concern. The puzzled smile faded, then died. All the glitter of her expression turned to ash. Ty couldn't help it – something in her stomach dropped watching Rosario's face transform.

"Ezzardine," Rosario said, standing so quickly her chair groaned against the floor. "We have to go. Right now."

Rosario was nearly out the door before she thought to pause.

"Madame Richmond," she said, recovering her manners. But Ty thought her voice shook. "Thank you for an excellent meal. The Hot Brown was fantastic. Thank you for the wonderful company," she said to everyone else, then nodded quickly, and disappeared. Ezz followed, not stopping to issue a goodbye.

"I wonder what that was all about?" one of the guests said when the messenger had gone and the front door was shut again.

"Derby business perhaps."

"Metalbreds don't sleep, do they?"

"No. I mean, well, she probably puts it to sleep."

"There's a button for everything!"

"That Ezzardine Clayton certainly know how to dress."

The conversation revolved away from any seriousness, and eventually Ty climbed down from the secret cabinet, dusting the flour off her cleanwork uniform. Now it would need to be micropressed tonight, keeping her up later. Even less sleep. But as the Trolley rocked her on the way back to the tiny house she shared with her father, she didn't feel tired. She felt like the Trolley itself: moving, but slightly unbalanced. A tipping back and forth in her head. The sudden storm that had appeared in the eyes of Rosario Vicario left her feeling as if she floated on choppy waters.

Or maybe it was the blue suit and the pink curls of Ezzardine Clayton.

CHAPTER 7

LUZ

Luz walked through the Kentucky Derby Museum imagining she was Poison Ivy. Her shirt bore her face, and so did the tattoo on her arm: green skin and red hair, fingers splayed before her lips as if to blow a kiss but sending vines out instead. On the tip of one vine perched Guatemala's quetzal, bowing its resplendent head. Luz wandered among the glass cases, gazing at hundred-year-old bridles and paintings of jockeys from the first races at the Downs, electronic exhibits where she could sit astride a mechanical horse and virtually run any race from history she selected from a screen. She didn't. Instead she imagined ivy creeping over the walls, choking it all in green leaves like fists. Filling the marble halls with snaking branches that reached into the walls and brought the whole building down. In her pocket, a device that looked like an old-fashioned audio recorder was tapping into Cavehill Downs's walkie system, recording conversations from the security frequency. By the end of the day, she would have hours of protocol. Luz wasn't Poison Ivy, but her mind was full of vines.

She walked slowly along the perimeter of the rooms housing the exhibits, the earpods for the audio tour provided by the admission desk stuffed in her ears. They were silent. Under their guise she listened to the squeak of every shoe, watched the track of the security guards turn at corners and doorways, noticed how they overlapped and where. In her head grew an algorithm, a winding maze like the labyrinth in Ezzardine Clayton's vast backyard. Eventually it felt like a cup whose contents wavered at the brim.

She moved to the center of the brightly lit hallway, staring at the high-definition banners of the last flesh-and-blood horse to win the Triple Crown before horseracing with real horses was banned – Heart of a Tulip. A filly, the first ever to win, who died right in the winner's circle. That was enough to finally seal the bans. Luz vaguely remembered the worry that swept through her house with the news of the ban – her parents had been working with horses since they were both children. They'd been relieved when Limestone stepped in, that horse knowledge still had a place among the metalbreds. Latinx jockeys had been on the rise before the ban, even some trainers. Luz remembered her mother standing at the sink rinsing beans, saying "Still no owners. For now. Go into the world and make some money, mija, and maybe you'll be one."

Luz passed her hand over the neck of one of the mechanical horses on display, thinking of that kitchen prayer and how it had never grown wings. And anyway, where to squeeze in? Limestone had brought in white Silicon Valley bros to be the first to learn the metalbred platforms, leaving girls like Rosario Vicario, with parents born in Tlalpan in Mexico, near the old dead volcano, to learn on their own.

But girls like Rosario – and even like Luz – couldn't be kept away, though Luz couldn't help but weep at her earliest memories of the racetrack, the way kids had arrived in her first-grade classroom saying ICE had come and swept the barns at dawn, taking children's parents away. Luz hadn't known until that afternoon that her own parents were safe, and she had been afraid to even think about the backside for months. It happened every so often, ICE sweeping in like armed roaches, and even with Luz's love, the backside still felt sometimes like a target – so many Guatemalans, Mexicans, El Salvadorians in one place, it felt like a trap, a magnet, a lure. Her mother had said *If you allow them to separate you from what you love, they're winning*, but then her own parents had done something of the same – no flowers, no trees: focus on the wires, the metal – all with the goal of putting their daughter in a boat that would rise with the same tide that kept them half-underwater.

Luz didn't notice the tears running down her face until a soft voice entered her ear.

"Are you okay?"

She'd almost forgotten she was in the museum. She glanced sideways and found a young Brown woman wearing a navy-blue blazer peering at her, eyebrows low in concern. Looking at the young woman's face, something cracked through Luz at the sight of her lips, so full her closed mouth was almost a circle, her nose round and perfect above. For a moment, Luz was cutting her a flower from the greenhouse, slipping it in the young woman's hand. And then she caught up with whatever part of herself had run away, and she swallowed.

"Um…" Luz stared and the woman stared back until Luz's eyes darted down to her blazer –a golden nametag that said *Cavehill Downs & Derby Museum: Irma*. An employee. Luz stood there in broad daylight feeling like a nocturnal animal that had wandered out of its den too soon. She hadn't really looked at a girl or a boy since she was a teenager, since her early days at Skyhorse, when the anxiety about being beautiful enough, interesting enough, had set in. The added complication of liking both boys and girls only widened the field of rejection. For Luz, Irma's face was like déjà vu, a forgotten room in an empty house. And then came the next wave of anxiety: Irma was a museum employee…did she know Luz's parents? Would she recognize her?

Or had Luz's parents' efforts to keep Luz from the racetrack paid off in this current pursuit of anonymity?

"Are you...are you okay?" Irma repeated.

"I'm fine," Luz said softly.

"Okay," Irma said, but looked hesitant. "Are you lost? Can I help?"

"I'm not lost." Luz hurriedly brushed away her tears. There were more of them than she thought. Embarrassed, she searched her purse for a tissue. Irma produced one and held it out, the tissue like an offering of something more than paper. Luz accepted it, muttering her thanks.

"You look like you know your way around," Irma said. Her accent was comfortable in Luz's ear, and she wondered if she should answer in Spanish. She glanced at the white tourists milling nearby. Luz's cousin in Tennessee had been accosted by a white woman at the grocery store for speaking Spanish while waiting in line, the woman as enraged by a rolling *r* as she would have been by flying spit. Luz kept her language tucked in the pocket of her throat. She merely shrugged in reply.

"Is this your first time to the museum?" Irma said this time, trying another tack.

"Yes." Not quite true, but it was her first time coming alone.

"Are you enjoying your experience?" Irma said, and through the remnants of her tears Luz gave her a sour look that actually made them both laugh a little. "Yeah, I see. I'm supposed to ask if you'd fill out a survey next, but something tells me that would be a bad idea."

"For both of us," Luz said, smiling. Was she flirting, an atrophied muscle finding movement?

"They're going to be updating it soon," said Irma, gazing around. "It's all outdated now with the introduction of metalbreds. Everything in this place is about real horses."

"Everything in here is about white people," Luz said before

she could stop herself. Irma just nodded.

"Mostly, yes," she agreed. "There's a section about the contributions of African-American jockeys, but it's too small and doesn't really do them justice. And they talk about some immigrants, about Mexicans and Guatemalans, but it always kind of feels like an afterthought. Like they did the whole 'seat at the table' thing, but it's just a rickety chair when they really needed a whole new table. Or maybe there shouldn't be a table at all. How big can one table be?"

"I have a friend," said Luz, thinking of Ezz. "She knows so much about the Black jockeys. They carried Derby for so long. The same way Latinx people carry it now. In a different way."

"The invisible foundation," Irma said eagerly. She glanced around in a different way now. Luz knew that look – keeping an eye out for bosses. "Have you been to the backside? Everyone is from Guatemala, Honduras, Mexico. Puerto Rico. From the hot walkers to the stable hands. Me, working here in the museum. This whole place would fall apart without us."

Luz merely nodded, wondering what Irma would think if she knew why Luz was really here.

"And the track just eats us alive and swallows the profit," she said bitterly.

"To be fair," Irma said, "and I'm not saying this just because I work here, but the Downs tried really hard to offer protections to undocumented workers. Literacy programs, help with citizenship tests, English classes, all that stuff. But then Limestone came in. Bought everything up. Changed things around. The Board is all billionaires. The president of Limestone? Annie Claybelle and her brother? She was here last week for a ribbon cutting and said she would've advocated for banning real-horse racing a long time ago if she had known she could get all her West Coast friends to move to Kentucky. She doesn't care about the horses – Thoroughbreds or metalbreds. It's all money to them."

Luz frowned, staring at the animated mural of Heart of a Tulip. A real horse, the shining muscles bunching and stretching, much like a machine itself, all speed and power. In her purse, another tiny machine was ticking away, recording all the things she would need to know to set her private plan in motion.

"You saw the way the industry eventually treated the horses," Irma went on softly. "The whips and the drugs. And the *horses* were the stars, the athletes! I don't know why I'm always surprised when they treat *people* just as bad. Have you noticed that ICE always comes in shortly after there's any talk of equity at the backside? Almost like they're Limestone's private army."

All her life Luz had wanted to find her way into the industry. It suddenly felt like fighting her way into a burning room.

"How long have you worked in this world?" Luz said, keeping her eyes on the horses.

"Since I was twelve," Irma said. "Started in the stables at Keeneland. Then I came to Louisville for school and started at the museum."

"Does it bother you?" Luz said. "To work in an industry that doesn't care if you live or die?"

Irma made a scoffing sound, but her eyes were sad.

"If that was the condition," she said, "I'd never hold a job. Not in this country."

Luz nodded wordlessly.

"What are you doing here?" Irma said quietly, and her tone made Luz look, not because it was tender but because it knew something. She found Irma looking right at her, and Luz couldn't help it – she shivered.

"What do you mean?"

"You seem like you're looking for something," Irma said. "I've been watching you. You've barely looked at the exhibits. You've been staying at the edges. I've seen you watching the security guards."

In Luz's chest a stallion reared, nervous and quick-footed. She looked away.

"I'm just here for the tour," she said.

"I know the path of the tour," Irma said, pointing at the earpods in Luz's ears. "That's my voice narrating. It guides you on a specific track, but you've been all over the place."

They were looking at each other again, Luz's eyes squinted in suspicion, Irma's gaze wide and open as a window in summer. Luz said nothing.

"Look, it's okay," Irma shrugged. "I'm just letting you know I'm not the only one with eyes. So if you're casing the joint," she paused and laughed. "Just know you're not being as subtle as you might think."

"I'm not here to steal anything," Luz scowled. Irma was stepping away, back to work, and Luz had the sudden, irrational urge to tell her the plan, anything to keep her close.

"What's there to steal?" Irma laughed. "Some 100-year-old riding leathers? Like I said, I don't know why you're here. But be careful. That's all I'm saying."

"Why do you care?" Luz said as Irma turned to walk away, just to feel her eyes one more time. "Isn't this your job?"

"Yes," Irma said. Her smile was a butterfly, there and then gone. "So make sure you do the survey before you leave."

CHAPTER 8

TY

Like every morning, Ty woke up forgetting that her mother was dead. The reminder was the sound of her father in the kitchen – he never shut cabinets, but rather applied enough force so that they closed themselves. Ty didn't see the point in making noise that could be avoided, and this seemed to be one of his most cherished activities; so unlike her mother, a large woman who moved with the grace and delicacy of a cat. Ty still remembered the way she looked that night, moving out of the dark and into the splash of the streetlight, elegantly, as if the dust tinted with midnight had been a stage. In bed, Ty opened her eyes to fill her mind with something else, if only the water-stained ceiling of her bedroom.

"Go," she said, her voice grating in her own ears. "Get. The fuck. Up."

She got up, and when she had applied her makeup, like war paint for the battle of the day, she entered the kitchen, aimed for the door.

"Where are you going?" her father said, his voice like a harpoon. She would not be a whale – she steered on.

"Work."

"Busy, busy," he said.

"Well, it's Derby season."

"Who are you telling?" he huffed. "Did you forget I make the metalbreds? No Derby without me, toots."

"Is that what you do there?" she asked, pausing, hating it.

"I'm an equine imitation specialist. What do you *think* I do?"

"I have no idea."

"What *do* you know?" he said, and she moved more deliberately toward the door. "Hold on, hold on," he said. "Okay, I'm just kidding. Hold on. I want to give you something."

She paused again, raising her eyebrows in a wordless *What?*

He finished unbuttoning his pale blue shirt – he'd only just returned home: late shift – and draped it over the back of a chair, nodding at the table.

"Check it out."

She peered without moving closer.

"A piece of paper."

"A piece of paper with your name on it," he grinned. She wanted to smash his teeth.

She looked, if only to distract from the fantasy of his teeth like a church window meeting a baseball, and made out the circular logo of Limestone, the horse's face that peered out through the letters. Not a piece of letterhead, but thick bamboo paper, the typography raised and luxurious. Something from his job, then. She read it out loud.

"You're Invited," she read, frowning. "To an Evening Hosted by Limestone Corp. A Private Tour of the Heart of Derby."

She raised her eyes to his.

"What is this?"

His finger, the nail meticulously clean and filed, landed on the finer print under the fancy type.

Tyler Redson and Guest are Formally Invited to a Private Tour of Limestone Headquarters and Printing Facilities, Including an Exclusive Q&A Session with

Top Limestone Engineers.

Keynote Speaker: Dr. Raymond Salt
Special Appearance by Chairwoman Annie Claybelle
Champagne and Red Carpet. Black Tie.

"Celebrities come," he said, and when she raised her eyes to his face she saw how excited he was, a smile that showed teeth. "The mayor. They only invite a chosen few members of the staff. Could mean I'm getting promoted if I play my cards right – I've been trying to get on good terms with Dr. Salt for months. Annie Claybelle is the top dog – you know her from TV. She's got all the clout. And with you as my date, how could they not love us?"

"I wouldn't be your date," she said.

"You know what I mean. My guest."

"If I go."

"If? You don't want to go?"

She stayed silent, and this was enough to make his eyes narrow. Even in the metal suit of her rage, a piece of her cowered, knowing.

"You used to love horses," he said.

"These aren't horses," she said, and realized too late that his words had been a test. Something behind the eyes went steely.

"Just like her, are you?" he said, and the smile that grew on his mouth gave her a chill. "Just like her."

"What are you even talking about?"

"Your mother could never enjoy anything. Did you know that? She was always looking for problems. We'd go to the movies – oh, the script was sexist. We'd go to dinner – oh, they banned tipping. She always loved horses, so we could talk about that, but then she had to protest the industry. *Oh, they drug the horses.* So what! If it helps them run? She never saw the big picture, always her little gripes. Making her signs, going down to Cavehill. Always making me look bad. She changed her tactics toward the end. Met some workers and got involved with workers' rights. So was it ever about the horses? See what I mean? Never satisfied. Always looking for a problem. Her and that –"

"Stop," she snapped, before he could get a slur out. "I don't want to hear that shit."

She'd heard all this before – his monologuing rants, his complaints. Still, her ear caught on "toward the end." He said it like he meant a career, but he was talking about a life.

"You going to start going to protests like her too?" he sneered. "Carrying signs out front of Cavehill Downs? Join a little robot rights group? Where did *that* lead her? A fucking suicide pact with her little salsa-dancing boyfriend."

This was always the hardest part. The lies he swallowed like medicine. She moved toward the door.

"I don't give a shit about horses," she said. "Fake or real."

"You're lying, but that's fine," he snapped. "Focus on being a maid. Stack those little pennies and buy yourself a nice dress for this event I'm being kind enough to invite you to."

"Don't forget that my so-called pennies are almost much as you make at your robot factory," she said over her shoulder.

"You think it's about money?" he laughed. "It's about what it is. You clean up after celebrities. You could've been a singer with that voice – at least that's one good thing you got from your mother – and even that isn't a career, but it's better than being a goddamn maid."

"You still think there's shame in this work," she shrugged as she reached for the doorknob. Her apathy always unnerved him. He was always looking for the trigger that would turn her into the grenade her mother could occasionally become – he didn't know that mechanism had all but frozen over the night she saw her mother die. "I'm not ashamed."

"But can you afford your own house?" he snarled. "Can you support yourself? No. You're stuck here, baby."

"I can't afford it yet," she said, looking back at him, right in the eye. "*Yet.*"

She was moving through the door when she caught his last words, tossed after her in that laughing tone, in that *I'm just kidding, you're too sensitive* tone, the one he would use to gaslight her mother after he'd goaded her into screaming at him.

"Just think about it," he called. Butterfly with stinger. "Think about coming to the event!"

She let the door close after her, and even though she was in no real danger of missing the Trolley, she ran the whole way there, feeling every jolt of her kit in the bag across her chest. By the time she'd climbed the stairs to the station and the sleek snake of the Trolley came humming down the tracks, she'd left her father's voice and her mother's absence in the house down the street, as she did every day. The Trolley was adorned with Derby decals for the entire month of May – when the doors slid open she was walking under the legs of a leaping Thoroughbreds crowned with roses. He thought he needed to convince her to go to the Limestone event – he didn't know that the invitation was like cubes of sugar before a horse's mouth. If a horse had fangs.

Ty pulled open the Staff Only doors to the Mahogany just as Rosario Vicario was walking out. They did the awkward shuffle dance for a moment before Rosario, laughing, put a hand on Ty's shoulder and steered her to the left, stepping outside after her. Ty looked past her inside the doors for a half a heartbeat before she realized she was looking for Ezzardine Clayton. Her cheeks heated and Rosario noticed, misinterpreting her embarrassment.

"It's okay," she said. "I'm so awkward. I'm always doing this. I don't even think I'm supposed to be using this door."

"You're not, really," Ty laughed. "It's technically only for staff."

Rosario laughed again, but this time it seemed to Ty that the sound was a little heavier, a little blue at the edges.

"I had a feeling," Rosario sighed when her laugh had faded. "But sometimes a back door is so comforting, you know?"

"It's probably hard," Ty said. "Being you. Everyone always wanting to talk to you and take a selfie or whatever else."

"Yes," said Rosario. She was gazing over Ty's head at the garden Madame Richmond kept as clean and stocked as her kitchen. Her earing aid was plain white now; the only jewel on her person sparkled from her nose. "But even when no one says anything at all you get the feeling that someone is watching. Sometimes I'd rather they just came and said what they needed to say. Do what they needed to do."

"Hmm," said Ty, because she wasn't sure what else to say, but the little crease that had appeared between Rosario's eyes and at the edge of her smile made Ty frown too. "Well, if you want to take the back door while you're staying here, that's fine with me. I know no one would mind."

At that, Rosario's eyes left the garden and the smile rose back into them.

"No? What about Madame Richmond?"

"Please." Ty rolled her eyes. "She's just happy you're here. You could ask to sleep in her bed and she'd jump out."

"Is her bed comfortable?" Rosario said with mock seriousness. "Because…"

They both laughed and Ty felt an uncomfortable flush of pleasure. She had allowed the concept of friendship to lapse. There was Shavon, who cut her hair at the barbershop: they'd become friendly after two years of bi-weekly cuts. But Shavon was still just her barber – Ty had never seen her without a black cape velcroed around Ty's neck, buzzing clippers in her ear. Rosario was too famous for Ty to envision an actual pathway to friendship, but this conversation felt like a phantom flutter in a limb that had been amputated. She didn't altogether enjoy the sensation.

At the back of the garden, where the tall brick wall covered in flowered ivy ran against the alley, the distant sound of a car horn came. One sharp beep, an announcement.

"My ride," Rosario said. "Okay if I cut through the garden?"

"Of course," said Ty. "Let me get the gate for you."

She escorted Rosario the few additional steps to the gate, scanning the fob that she wore as a ring around her pinky. The gate slid open and Rosario slipped through.

"Thanks," she said with a smile, not the smile that Ty had seen on so many news stations, full of fire and confetti. A real smile, sweet. Normal.

Ty waved and watched as Rosario Vicario weaved her way around the many hedges and explosions of bloom that Madame Richmond spent her weekends cultivating.

"Fraternizing with the guests," Camille said, appearing behind Ty on the narrow walkway. This time Ty didn't jump – she was beginning to get used to Madame's ferret of a daughter.

"Just helping her find her way." Ty turned from the garden and made her way back down to the staff door of the Mahogany, scanning her ring fob once more. She let herself into the hallway where the electronic lockers were lined, the lights on all of them red, indicating she was the first to clock in for the day. She used the far-right locker, trying to ignore Camille, who settled on a stool nearby, watching.

"You always use the same locker," Camille said.

"So?"

"So the lockers are unassigned."

"And?"

"I read a book yesterday," Camille said. "About which habits and methodologies people maintain when they don't have to. Some people would use a different locker every day and enjoy the freedom to do so. But you use the same one every day – always arriving early enough so that there's no chance of someone else getting it – and that, according to this book, indicates that you crave order and sameness, or that you are seeking control where you feel you have none."

"What's the book?" Ty said, not looking at her. "*Pseudoscience for the Heiress's Soul?*"

Camille just smiled.

"You like order," she went on. "There's nothing wrong with that."

"Maybe I just get to work early so I don't have to deal with anyone," Ty said, shooting her a meaningful look, and this time Camille laughed.

"Would you rather I leave you alone?" Camille said. "I really will if you want me to."

"I don't really care," Ty said. She closed the locker gently, keying in the temporary code that made it hers. Camille was half right, she thought. She did enjoy the consistency of having the same locker every day. But knowing that the code was temporary was the real appeal, even if the feeling was like pressing on a bruise. Temporary. Nothing lasts. She hoped Camille hadn't also read a book on how to be a psychic.

"Have you even met any of the other cleanwork staff?" Camille said, following her from the kitchen.

"A couple," Ty said. "Do you bother them too?"

"No," Camille said. "I've watched them all, of course. But they're not as interesting as you are."

"I assure you I'm not interesting either," Ty said, frowning as she made her way to the service elevator. There was something about Camille that was soothing – her attention gave one the feeling of a flower being haunted by a butterfly. But if Ty was going to do what she had come to the Mahogany to do, then having Camille watching all the time was a problem.

"You are though," Camille went on. "You take your work so seriously. And so do they, enough to keep their jobs at least. But you…you see it as an art. Don't you?"

"I think there's honor in cleaning," Ty said, surprising herself with the answer. She pressed the button for the elevator to keep from saying more.

"I believe that," Camille said. "It used to be so belittled. 'Women's work', you know? And especially women of color. It was automatically denigrated. But then it kind of went mainstream."

"Another book?" Ty said, raising an eyebrow, but still not looking at her.

"A few," Camille nodded. "Especially after the 2020 pandemic – clean became a commodity. Read some books about this building too."

She paused, looking up at the darkly arching handrails, the stained-glass windows here and there that Ty was always silently grateful didn't fall within her scope of work. The elevator dinged open, and Ty stepped in. Camille stepped in quickly after her and Ty almost told her she shouldn't be in the service lift, but who swatted a butterfly?

"What made you pick up cleanwork?" Camille said. In the days when vacuums were clumsy machines the size of an oxygen tank, the elevator would've been crowded. Now it was just the two of them in the gentle shudder as they were borne up to the third floor where Ty's schedule had her beginning her shift. It was strange to have company. Usually she'd nestle the skittles of her earpods into her ears and crank Ella Fitzgerald until her brain swayed. The near-silence now was almost dizzying.

"You already said it," Ty told her as the elevator rumbled to a stop. She slid the grate open and it provided a nice, distracting clatter. "Because I seek control. Right?"

"And what makes you feel out of control?"

"Why does it have to be something?"

"There's usually a catalyst. A trauma."

"Are you asking me what my trauma is?"

"Yes."

"Someone killed my mother."

As soon as the words were out of her mouth and in the air, she turned away from them and strode down the plushly carpeted hall toward the linen closet.

"Someone?" Camille said, gently, after a polite pause.

"Someone."

Camille stayed mercifully silent for once, and Ty measured each of her movements carefully, knowing the keen ferret eye was upon her. She mustn't give anything away. She'd already said too much. If Camille got even a glimpse of the truth, it would be like offering a single drop of blood to a hound. Keeping her shoulders down and back, Ty walked from the linen closet to the suite across the hall. A senator was staying there, a senator and her wife. Not the person Ty was here at the Mahogany for. No, he hadn't checked in yet.

"Do you...know who? Was there justice?" Camille said, and as hard as she tried, Ty still faltered in her step, for Camille had now whispered something from her own nightmares, the elephant that sat darkly on the corner of her bed at night, wondering out loud. The knowledge that no, the person who had turned one side of her mother's skull into shattered glass would never, never face justice – unless Ty delivered it.

Ty went to the windows, opening first one and then another. The trick to a fresh room was always starting with fresh air. Down the street she heard the streetcleaners starting their slow humming path toward downtown, sweeping up confetti and bottles and lost hats.

"Ten days 'til Derby," she said, and with the windows open she turned back to Camille and tried a smile that felt as clouded as the panes of glass. "Who do you have your bets on winning?"

"The one that runs the fastest," Camille said. She took the cue admirably, respecting the red light, and Ty's mind categorized her as friend, even as she struggled against it. Camille was sitting on the floor by the bed, prepared to roll under. "Are you going to sing today?"

"I don't sing anymore," Ty said, rolling her eyes, but she was already lifting the buds to her ears, already felt the swimming in her throat. She'd done too much talking about things that made the room feel cluttered and dusty. A song would push the cobwebs back. She reached for the kit at her waist, for the bottle of what the professionals called rubber. She sprayed it along her palms and the back of her hands, feeling the subtle tightening as the solution encased her germs and her loose skin cells in a glove that would be rinsed off with vinegar later when she was finished. She took hold of the bed linens, Camille already out of sight, pulling them onto the floor and exposing the invisible bacteria beneath to the sunlight pouring through the window. Below, the streetcleaners hummed by and the same tune grew in Ty's chest, stronger and stronger until it rose to her mouth and floated toward the ceiling as she shook the linens skyward.

She used to sing like this. Had made good money singing like this. But not like *this*: an audience of percale and curtains. She remembered what it meant to have an audience and had loved it, once upon a time. Now that her imperative was to move in shadow, in silence, the idea of all those eyes on her as she floated toward her mission made her feel untethered. It was important to stay rooted, and she closed her mouth around the song, choking it out as she made the room transform.

The hours went on. The sun began to amber with afternoon, and Ty got lost in her work. Camille left her alone after the second room. Though the girl's presence was quiet, her absence was quieter, somehow, and Ty enjoyed returning to the solitude of square corners. Inch by inch the rooms turned over beneath her hands, the human, lived-in smell of outdoors and breath scrubbed away and replaced with lemon, orange, cedar – smells specified in the guest profiles provided by Madame Richmond, Ty carefully applying each vial of essential oil in her kit. There was power in this, she thought, and privilege. Clean.

She carried the vacuum-sealed parcels of dirty linens out into the hall – Suite 11, she thought, her nose wrinkled. They'd checked in four days ago and each day needed new sheets. Today she didn't even bother to check them, sweeping them off the bed and sealing them away. She piled the neat blocks together beside the elevator – when she finished Suite 12 she would carry the tidy parcels down to the basement and hand them off to the deepclean staff. The scrubbers, the bleachers, the ones whose kits came built into the stones of the Mahogany. They'd process linens overnight and then return them, shrink-wrapped with cedar chips and encased lemon peel, to the dry wooden shelves by the cleanwork elevators.

Ty glanced down at the various softly blinking lights that filled her kit. She'd been allowing the Nanospeck to charge at her waist while she switched the linens for Suite 11, wanting everything to be prepped and ready for Suite 12, which she usually did first. But Rosario Vicario wasn't usually staying in it. It felt sacred now somehow, for reasons she couldn't quite place. It wasn't that she was a jockey, Ty told herself as she checked the levels in her diffuser. It was that in early interviews, when the press first started to notice the pretty Brown girl with the single braid and the glimmering ruby nose ring, Rosario had that same hungry look that Ty knew from the mirror. Sly and shrewd, a lion pacing. Ty didn't know Rosario any better than the other jockeys who walked the red carpet at the Downs, but she felt that they somehow paced the same cage, had the same hungry dreams.

Ty approached the door with her hand raised, the fob ring on her pinky catching a little of the soft light in the wood-walled hallway. She knocked once as she always did, and called "Service," as she always did. She didn't expect an answer – only occasionally did she encounter the strange guest who liked to watch her clean, under the guise of preventing theft – but still she felt the math of her heartbeat in her wrist, fluttering, compounding. She opened the door, unsurprised by the black of the room beyond, and reached down to her waist for her shadowglass, slipping the slim black arms over each ear, the frames over her eyes. She tapped lightly near her right eyebrow and the room sprang alight in pale shades of gray. The bed and its linens thrown back like a shorn lamb. The sofa, its cushions out of place. The armoire, its drawers open and uneven like teeth in a battered mouth. The floor scattered with clothes.

She stepped around the mess, surprised but unjudgmental. Even those who appeared most put together were trash heaps in private, she had learned – she'd seen it over and over. She'd seen discarded, holey clothes, underwear left in sinks to soak. She moved toward the window to pull back the shades. Evening had fallen by Room 10, and had deepened as it followed her here, violet seeping in at the edges. She was passing the ottoman, turned over on its side like a wounded bison, when she looked down at the floor and saw Rosario Vicario staring soundlessly up at her, mouth opening and closing slowly, wetly.

In the gray tones of the shadowglass, her lips dripped black.

Ty stumbled backward, knocking into the ottoman. She would've fallen if her hand had not found one of the tall bedposts in the dark, the one piece of furniture that seemed to have kept its feet. It was as if the entire room had been picked up and shaken, Rosario's twitching form a doll who had fallen and only just come to rest. Ty stared, speechless, into the dark eyes gazing up and couldn't make herself move or scream or speak until from the black-dripping lips croaked a wretched "Help."

Ty moved then. She stumbled to the windows, tripping on more objects and possessions strewn across the room. She thrust the curtains open, the rings grating against the rod, and then spun back to face the scene as she ripped the shadowglass from her eyes, as if the dim remnants of daylight would illuminate the room with the truth.

The truth was worse in light, and Ty felt her heart plunge back to her mother, the dust, the mist of red exploding by her temple. Deeper. This room had been torn apart – pillows sliced, fluffy innards strewn across the sofa. The mattress was turned and torn. Rosario's luggage was open and broken, on its side like the last of a train wreck. "Help," Rosario croaked again. In light, her mouth was wet with pinkish blood.

Ty ran to her side, not tripping this time. She fell to her knees beside Rosario, frantically scanning her body for wounds. She found none, and could only stare into Rosario's eyes, which were blinking over and over like an android whose system has failed.

"What happened?" Ty said, and her hand reached for the other girl's mouth, to wipe it, to help it speak, but she stopped herself.

"Ellos…v-vinieron. They…they…came," the girl wheezed, her eyes squeezing shut now. Her hands shook, clasping and unclasping near her waist. Ty's eyes moved to the inch of stomach exposed there, Rosario's hands clumsily tugging at her shirt. "There," she rasped.

A faint circle imprinted on the flesh, fading before Ty's eyes. A circle with a single point in the center. It was gone a blink later.

"In…injection," Rosario grated.

"I'm calling for help," Ty said, her voice almost a sob, and her hand sprang to the ring fob, ready to press the button hidden on its side for emergencies. Rosario's hand flashed out like a snake, the grip so hard Ty yelped.

"Es-espere," Rosario muttered, gasping. Her body convulsed, but her hand didn't loosen its grip on Ty until it decided its path. Between shakes, Rosario's hand made its way up to her own face, fingers bent and gnarled, unsteady in the journey across her cheek. She stopped at her nose, then convulsed again, this time crying out; her eyes squeezed shut again as if in concentration, willing her fingers to be still. Her thumb and forefinger, shaking, positioned alongside her nose, and then slowly, shakily withdrew the shining stud from her nostril.

The tiny object slipped from Rosario's grasp before she could deliver it to Ty's palm, and Rosario's chest seized with a shrill gasp until Ty scrambled to find it there on the carpet, holding it up for Rosario to see.

"Take...take it to Ezz...Ezzardine Clayton. Take it to her. Tell her they were looking."

A fresh surge of pale blood came from somewhere in the delicate mechanics of her body. The last of the light was fading from the window, leaving Rosario's face in shadow.

"This?" Ty cried, gripping the red jewel of the nose stud.

"Hide it," she said.

When Rosario's body convulsed again, Ty grabbed her hand. She felt stiff.

"Hide it," Rosario repeated slowly. "Th-then take it to...Ezz."

Ty stuffed the stud into one of the vials of her cleanwork kit, sealing it, and somewhere in the agony of Rosario's face, a muscle relaxed. She sighed a ragged sigh.

"N-now you can call," she said, her voice tighter still, forcing its way past whatever was filling her throat.

Ty hit the button. But by the time the blue-and-green lights of the medical emergency police spilled into the black room, Rosario Vicario was gone.

CHAPTER 9

TY

The Mahogany had never seen ants like the Special Police. They infested the corners of the hotel, black uniforms as shiny as beetles, cameras and crime kits that put Ty's belt to shame. A line of them stood on the sidewalk to keep the press back – the news had leaked out quickly, and the streets of Old Louisville were packed with the reflections of recording devices and other various screens, some people even perched in the proud old trees that lined the sidewalks. The deli on the corner had closed its shutters and locked its doors, the owner and her husband come out to join the scene. These were the times when Ty resented Louisville the most. Or maybe this was every town – murder like a bang of light drawing moths from the shadows.

Ty was watching Jessica and Frida touch up their make-up before they picked up trays of cookies when Camille appeared in the kitchen. She had a slightly rumpled look and Ty hadn't seen her come in – she wondered if the ferret daughter had been sleeping in her secret flour-dusted cavern.

"What are you doing?" Camille said, eyebrow raised at the cookworks.

"Getting cute," Jessica said, turning her chin left and right in the mirror. Ty sat on a stool hugging her knees. "The whole country is about to watch us taking these cookies out there."

"Maybe the whole world," Frida said.

"Whole world is about to watch you feed the pigs," Josie said, sniffing from the back door. Her kit was put away, her hair loose around her face now that she was leaving the Mahogany, her antifuzz hairnet tucked away.

"Why are you taking them cookies?" Camille asked, still looking at Jessica and Frida.

"Boss's orders," said Frida, hefting her tray. "Your mom's smart to capitalize on the PR."

"Someone is dead," Camille said, flat.

"Yeah, one of the most famous jockeys in the world," Jessica answered.

"Cookwork!" Madame Richmond's voice came echoing from the front hall. "Let's have our moment!"

Camille shot a look at Ty, who didn't mean to catch it but did, and when the two cookworks pushed through the service doors toward the front door, Ty and Camille waited a beat and then followed. They emerged into the broad entryway just as Madame Richmond swept onto the front porch in a floor-length navy dress, makeup and jewelry all in place and sparkling. She made a gesture to the press, a sort of sorrowful wave.

"Snake," Camille muttered. But Ty didn't answer – she was turning toward the tap on her shoulder, delivered by the director of the Special Police, a shockingly pretty woman named Alexa Spoke. Director Spoke had been called to the scene at 10:30pm – two hours after the medical officers arrived to find the body of Rosario Vicario lying still and silent on the carpet of her suite. Ty hadn't cried yet, answering questions and providing fingerprints, but almost everyone else had. She had trembled outside the open door of Suite 12 while officers came and went, until she had drifted down to the kitchen and sat in the corner, waiting to be told she could leave. It was 11pm now and they had yet to remove the body.

"We're still examining the scene," Director Spoke said to Ty, extracting a bottle of water from a pocket on the side of her wheelchair. Ty looked sideways just in time to see Camille slip back inside. "We're waiting for an eye."

"An eye. You're still hiring private detectives then," Ty said. Her tongue felt like a sodden sponge.

"A bit like the old, old days," Spoke said, shrugging as she took a sip. "The boys in blue kept fucking it up, so they call in the Special Police on certain occasions. We overlap with forensics sometimes, like today. It changes every year, depends on who's on the board. But for a death, protocol always calls in an independent specialist for the actual investigation. He may see something we don't."

Ty merely nodded. They'd called in an eye when her mother's body had been found. Lot of good that did. Now Ty just stood looking at the line of Special Police, their shining beetle backs, and the press beyond turned stark in the pool of flood lights. Ty had to blink several times to stop seeing pale blood bubbling slowly from each of their mouths.

"A mess," the director said, running her fingers through her vibrant red hair. "And ten days before Derby. I don't know what her employer is going to do. Plenty of jockeys who want the job, of course. But only *one* Rosario Vicario. The equinibot might need to be wiped before the next jockey comes in. Who can build out a metalbred in less than 10 days?"

Director Spoke licked her lips, her tongue a nervous pink creature testing the light, her eyes searching the crowd and suddenly finding something. She returned the water to her chair.

"Ah," she said, aiming a stiff nod out at the street. "Here he is."

Ty turned to see the line of officers breaking to admit a white man dressed simply in khaki pants and a somewhat wrinkled white polo, returning his identification to his pocket as he climbed the stairs to the Mahogany. He was young – thirty-five at most – and like the officers he didn't carry a gun. His hair was short and neat, the stubble near his sideburns low and raw as if he had just stepped from the barber's chair. Ty's stomach dropped. She knew him.

"Detective Segrest," Ty said, and when he turned his green-blue eyes on her she knew she was right. The last time she had seen him he was sitting on the sunken couch in her living room at home, asking when the last time was she'd seen her mother, if she'd been acting strange. Had she gotten any messages, a call? Had she noticed anything unusual? Did she have a boyfriend? She had told him only one piece of truth: that she had last seen her mother at Cavehill Downs, talking to Luis Funes, a groom on the backside. Her friend. She didn't tell Segrest that Ty had followed her there, that she had spied on her own mother. That she went looking for proof of an affair but instead found murder. She didn't tell the detective that she'd seen who had held the gun, had watched her mother and Luis freeze when the weapon emerged shining like oil. The gun roared far from Luis and close to her mother, and when Ty closed her eyes all she could see was the way they had fallen, loose-limbed and chaotic, nothing like the movies. She knew how the police had handled such things for decades, and so she had opened her eyes and lied to Detective Segrest.

And now she was going to lie to him again.

"Miss…," he said, his eyes fishing. "Redson. Right? Your mother…"

"Died," she said flatly.

"Yes," he said, meeting her gaze. "I'm sorry. What are you doing here?"

She resisted the urge to snarl at him. Sorry for what? Sorry that she was dead, or sorry that the eyes which made him an eye were useless, that they didn't see anything at all? But then Director Spoke interrupted:

"She found the body," the director said with a pointed look, a look that said to proceed, but with caution.

"She wasn't a body when I found her," Ty said stiffly. She moved her eyes to the street and kept them there.

"She was alive?" Segrest said, eyebrows raised.

"Yes."

"Did you see anyone enter or leave the room?"

"No."

"No one?"

"No."

"What did you see when you entered the room? How did you enter the room?"

"With my scanner," she said, lifting her hand. She swallowed. The scene swam back to her, the ink of the dark sinking into the memory of her eye. "It was…very dark. All the shades closed. I used my shadowglass to see. Everything was a mess. A big mess. I went toward the windows and that's…that's when I found her."

"Where?"

"On the floor."

"Breathing?"

"Yes."

"Talking?"

Ty paused, remembering and unremembering and remembering again.

"Yes," she said.

"What did she say?"

He was staring at her hard, and she couldn't remember if this was the way he stared at her when he sat in her living room asking about blood. Ty had told him things, but not the things that mattered: that her mother had received phone calls, always from the same number, always whispering threats. That her friend Luis got those calls too, that whoever did the calling saw Luis and Ty's mother as a two-pronged problem. Ty shook her head. Detective

Segrest was there at the beginning, when her mother's death had placed the plan in Ty's head. Now here he was again, so close to the plan's fruition. Which is why she had to be careful, she thought, returning his gaze. She had seen the man who killed her mother and Luis – she saw his face often, a pale rock at the bottom of the cold river of her dreams. She knew that man, and he checked into the Mahogany in seven days. She didn't need Detective Segrest poking around.

"She asked me to call for help," Ty said. "So I did."

The eyebrows didn't move. Beside them, Director Spoke shifted, impatient. The press was taking photos, and while Ty stood with her back to them, Spoke was in every shot.

"Let's take this inside," the director said. "They probably brought some lip-readers out."

"I need to see the scene," said Detective Segrest, his eyes still on Ty. "And the body."

Spoke moved for the door and the detective crooked his finger at Ty.

"You too," he said, and she nodded wordlessly. Inside, she led them to the service elevator, scanned, and held the metal gate to the side for them both to enter.

"Did you clean the room?" Detective Segrest said as they hummed upward. "Before you realized something had happened?"

"No. I had cleaned it the day before, before she checked in. That's all."

"Nothing today? Not a Squish or a Nanospeck?"

She glanced at him, surprised he knew the specifics of her trade. He didn't look back.

"No," she said. "I couldn't see anything. I was going to open the shades before I started."

"And you never got to the windows."

"No. Well, yeah. After I found them I opened them."

"I see."

He didn't take notes. She imagined his mind whirring like the engine of a metalbred, recording effortlessly. He'd done the same thing when asking about her mother. The elevator eased to a halt, and the doors slid open to reveal the hallway, crowded with people. Forensic investigators and photographers. Ty saw the white-coated woman with silver hair who had pronounced the time of death. She'd been accurate to the minute.

"You're young to be in cleanwork," Detective Segrest said as they stepped into the hall.

"I'm twenty-one," she said. "Old enough."

The door to 12 was propped open, glaring light pooling just inside. They would have to step into that too-bright light in a moment, and the knowledge made Ty's steps falter. The detective looked at her.

"Is something the matter?"

"I just...would rather not see her again."

"Were you a fan?" he said, and the question caught her sharply with its implication. A fan? Did he suspect her? A stalker who wrote one too many unanswered letters to the beautiful young jockey?

"Sort of," she said, and shook her head. "But that's not...that's not why..."

"Then what?"

"She's *dead*," Ty snapped. "I don't want to stand looking at a dead girl, okay? A dead girl who I saw alive just this morning. It's...wrong."

Detective Segrest studied her for a long moment before directing his gaze at someone over her shoulder.

"Is the body covered?" he said.

"Yes, sir," someone said.

"Good." The eyes were back on Ty, the eyebrows in their same frozen position. "After you."

She had no choice. Did he suspect her? If not of this, of…something?

Compared to the dim hallway, the room felt like diving into the sun. Ty blinked many times to clear the spots, but the investigators seemed to have placed a flood light in every corner, every inch bathed in a too-white glow. Every piece of furniture, every pillow, was still trapped in the frozen chaos, a whole scene caught in a tractor beam. Everything cast shadows – the ottoman, the mattress torn and sideways. Everything except for the white sheet at the end of the bed, the shape beneath it almost impossibly small, as if Rosario's body had been shrinking hour by hour, swallowed by the carpet.

"That's where you found her?" Detective Segrest said, and she almost jumped. She nodded instead. "Anything different?"

"No. I mean, the lights. The sheet. Obviously. But nothing else."

It looked more horrible in the light, even with Rosario's body concealed. He gestured for her to follow, his steps leading them on a winding path through the wreckage. She could hear Director Spoke's voice from out in the hallway, giving orders and murmuring to subordinates. Projected along the back wall were holograms of faces in uniform, shuffling slowly like identity cards.

"What is that?" Ty said, pointing.

The detective glanced up, then back down.

"Crime scene access portfolio. These officers and investigators who have checked into the site and are allowed to be on premises, now and in the future."

As if to demonstrate, his own face appeared on the wall for a long moment before being replaced by another face in uniform.

"A real mess," Detective Segrest said. He stared at Ty. "An overdose, do you think?"

Ty didn't respond until she finally noticed him looking at her.

"Are you asking *me*?"

"Sure."

"What?"

"Does this look like an overdose to you?"

"I have…I have no idea."

"The rapid blood report says it was ketamine," he said, as if talking to himself. "Would have to have been laced with something else for her to wreck her own room. But who knows what jockeys are into these days, right?"

He stopped every now and then, sometimes stooping to study this shred of fabric or that loose shoe.

"Why do you do cleanwork?" he said while peering at a bright red scarf laid out across the white carpet like an entrail.

"Are you talking to me?" Ty said.

"Yes. Cleanwork. Why do you do it?"

"It makes me feel peaceful," she said. This was the story she invented for herself – an organized girl, taking a job where she could organize the world. It led her to peace. It was a paycheck, not a doorway.

"Powerful?"

"I said peaceful."

"Something powerful about that." He poked at the edge of the scarf with a pen he'd pulled from nowhere.

"Maybe so."

"How many bags did Miss Vicario check in with?" he said.

"I'm not sure. I can check the log. At least two."

"I'm interested in this answer," he said. "We have no way of knowing what she checked in with specifically. What was *in* those bags, I mean. But I would very much like to know what, if anything, is missing from this room."

"Missing?"

They were at the far end of the room now. He'd taken them on an indirect route away from Rosario Vicario's body, and now they were by the windows. The shades were closed again, to keep out the eyes of the press, which had doubtlessly bribed their way into neighboring windows by now, cameras aimed like rifles.

"Or maybe she was looking for something," Detective Segrest said quietly, as if to himself. "See the pulled-out drawers? The mattress split? Someone was looking for something. Don't see her making all this mess herself unless she was high."

He pointed idly, the tip of the pen leading her eyes around the room.

"Looking for what?" she said.

He shrugged, almost bored. Had he been like this interviewing possible witnesses about her mother? She felt a surge of rage. This is why she hadn't told. Apathy would never lead to justice, and no one cared more than her.

"Maybe," he said.

He had reached the edge of the white sheet and stood looking down thoughtfully, the pen poised in his fingers like a magic wand. She half expected him to flourish it and send the sheet rippling back off Rosario's face. Instead he squatted down – she heard a faint crack in one knee. He slipped the pen back into his pocket and in the same motion reached down, took the edge of the sheet between thumb and forefinger, and flipped it off.

Ty's breath jumped, gagging her for a short moment. Rosario Vicario's eyes stared somewhere between the chandelier and the bedpost. The brown of her irises had changed, Ty thought, some of the honey gone. Her lips were parted, the space between them red with blood, a trail of it down her cheek, pooling on the carpet by her shoulder. Ty let her eyes go fuzzy, staring just beyond Rosario to forget the sound her last breath made. Ty's eyes ended up on the carpet by the wardrobe. A minuscule white bleach spot. She sharpened her eyes again, focusing in on it. Bleach?

"She told you to call for help?" Detective Segrest said, not looking at Ty, studying Rosario's face.

"Yes," said Ty. Ty jerked her eyes from the spot, staring now at the empty place on Rosario's nostril, the tiny dimple where the nose ring had been before it had been plucked out and placed in Ty's palm, then stowed away in a vial at her waist. She wondered if the detective would notice, if in his quest for what was missing from the room, his eye would fall upon the tiny crater, if he would compare photos of the dead versus the living Rosario Vicario and note the red sparkle, now absent. Ty's kit felt suddenly effervescent.

"Did she say what she saw?" the detective said. "Names? Anything that may not have made sense?"

Ty squeezed her eyes shut, blocking out the chalky face and the empty spot on the nose, the white sheet concealing Rosario neck-down, leaving her strangely dissected.

"No," she said, not elaborating. Adding too many details to a lie made it heavy, unmanageable.

Segrest had slid the sheet farther off Rosario's body and was now holding her hand, examining the gold-polished nails. Ty had the sudden urge to slap him, grab him by the wrist and shake his tanned hand until Rosario was free. Instead she closed her eyes again.

"Can I go?" she said. The nose ring in her kit felt like a cannonball, heavy and explosive. "I feel like I've told you everything I saw."

"There may be something you saw that you didn't know you saw," Segrest said, eyes still on Rosario's fingernails. "Something that may be significant that won't occur to you until later."

Her eyes went back to the bleach stain. It hadn't been there when she cleaned the room yesterday. She didn't have bleach in her kit – no good cleanwork did. How did it get there? He looked up at her, drawing her eyes back.

"Do you have somewhere to be?"

"Bed," she said honestly. "I've been here since 7am."

"Cleaning," he said.

"Yes."

"When did you see Rosario Vicario return?"

"I didn't. I saw her leave."

"Oh? When?"

"Early," she said, numb. "When I got to work."

"Where?"

"The staff door. She went through the garden."

He laid the limp hand down but didn't cover it again.

"The garden?"

"Yeah. Her car was waiting for her in the alley."

Detective Segrest still hadn't taken any notes. His eyes carried no sparkle but had a shrewdness to them, the look of a barn owl.

"That's all I need from you," he finally said. It took her brain a moment to catch up, to tune in. "I know where to find you if I have more questions. I very well may."

"I can go?"

"You can go."

The garden felt clammy. Rain later, perhaps. It didn't stop the revelers – she could see the glow over the trees of a party on the next block, the rise and fall of voices mingling with a blur of music she couldn't make out. She took deep breaths, stepping slowly along the stones. Ty raised her eyes to the back wall, where a dark car had waited in the hours sandwiching dawn. It was gone now, and so was Rosario, and though Ty hadn't known her, had only spoken to her those few brief moments, she felt a dark hollow inside her, lit only by the strangely glowing pinpoint of the nose ring hidden away in her kit. She turned to look back at the Mahogany, its roof glittering with solar panels. All the windows, closed with shades, were filled with moonlight. All except one. A west-facing window on the third floor – Rosario Vicario's room. From the garden she could make out the form of Detective Segrest, watching her. She turned away, forcing her hand to avoid the vial where Rosario's red jewel rested.

Ty had no idea how to get in touch with Ezzardine Clayton. But she knew someone who might.

CHAPTER 10

EZZ

Ezz sat on the couch where she'd been sitting when she'd been told her parents were dead. The small house smelled the same. Vague ancho and strong epazote, then the floral perfume that Rosario's mother wore. Except now there was the trailing scent of smoke – candles lit for their daughter. Rosario was dead, and Ezz sat in the Vicarios' living room, the spaces between them crowded with grief. Ezz was still out of breath. She didn't know if she'd ever catch it. She'd seen the news in all the headlines and ran straight to her best friend's childhood home. 4.3 miles from the Pink. Rosario's mother was just opening the door when Ezz arrived, sweating and crying, as if she had felt her coming like a meteor of sorrow. They'd hugged for a long, long time. Now they sat and stared at each other emptily.

"Where's Aracelis?" Ezz ventured.

"In her room," Rosario's father said. "She doesn't want to come out."

"Rosario should have stayed here," Mrs. Vicario said. "At home where she belonged."

Ezz could tell by the hollowness in her voice that she had said those same words many times already, and Ezz didn't know whether her mother meant this time, for this Derby, or that Rosario never should have left home at all.

"Who called you?" Ezz said. "To tell you. The hotel?"

"The medical officers," said Mrs. Vicario, staring at the floor. "Early this morning. She died last night. My daughter lying cold without her family for 10 hours before they finally thought to reach us. We should be with her."

"I'm so sorry," Ezz said, crushing her fists against her eyes. "I'm so, so sorry."

"My daughter is not on drugs," Mr. Vicario said abruptly, straightening his neck, staring fire at Ezz.

"Is that what they said?" Ezz said, her spine going rigid. "That she overdosed?"

"My daughter is not on drugs," he said again, the mustache his daughter would tease him about trembling. This time it sounded like a question that he demanded that Ezz refute.

"She was not on drugs!" Ezz cried. "Why would they say that?"

"Ketamine, they say," Rosario's father thundered. "What they used to use on horses. They say the jockeys sometimes use it recreationally. Rosario would never do such a thing!"

"There's absolutely no way…," said Ezz. She trailed off, feeling choked. She and Rosario had drifted apart since her first big win – not because of anything so stupid as a fight or jealousy, but because Rosario was…famous. She traveled a lot. When she was in Louisville she had meetings and events. Like a pale ghost, doubt leaked into a corner of Ezz's mind. Surrounded by all those jockeys…high rollers, known for their addictions, as common in the headlines as cheating scandals. But she had never seen Rosario's name mentioned, never a whisper. Maybe she had chosen not to go looking…

"It's impossible," Ezz said out loud, making sure her words sounded like concrete even if they felt like sand in her mouth. Rosario's parents needed concrete.

Mrs. Vicario's face filled with silent tears, her father's neck bending. What was worse? That their daughter might be an addict, and that they had no idea? Or that someone, not something, had killed her? Ezz didn't know.

"When was the last time you saw her?" Ezz said.

"Monday we went to the market," Mrs. Vicario said, looking up through her tears. "Tuesday she went with me to see her abuela in Prospect. Wednesday she –"

"Wait," Ezz interrupted. "But she didn't get back in town until yesterday. Yesterday was Thursday."

For a moment, Mrs. Vicario's confusion overshadowed her grief.

"Ezzardine, what? No. Rosario has been home for nine days. She left Los Angeles for Phoenix and then came here. I suppose we should be grateful for having these days with her before…before…this…"

A sob tore out of her throat, and Ezz pulled her lips in to keep from arguing again. When she'd seen the headlines about Rosario's death, she had come here wanting to be wrong, but also wanting to *know*. But what Rosario's mother had said about being grateful for these days didn't apply to Ezz…because Rosario had lied to her. Not just on their video call but to Ezz's face, as they had sat side-by-side at the Mahogany for dinner, making small talk about Derby as if nothing had changed. But something had. In a bigger way than Ezz ever sensed.

"When did you see her last?" her father said. "She told us she had dinner scheduled with you…"

"Yes," Ezz nodded. They wouldn't notice that her tears were different now, that they sprang from another source. "We had dinner. But it was…"

She stopped, running back through the evening, the abrupt way it ended. Rosario had received a note at the table, had rushed out of the Mahogany. She had the car drop Ezz back at the Pink, saying she had a last-minute meeting with the owner of the metalbred she was jockeying for Derby. When Ezz had pried, Rosario waved her questions away, and that creased smile of hers returned, the one Ezz didn't recognize. It had left part of Ezz's heart feeling shadowed, and it was as if Rosario's father could sense it. He frowned.

"It was what?" he said. "What?"

"Nothing," Ezz said. They didn't need this. Her doubts. Her fears. This house was full enough of grief – any space there was to breathe didn't need to be clouded with the products of her wandering imagination. She chose to be half honest: "It was…too short. I wish…I wish I had told her to blow off her meeting and hang out with me. We shouldn't even have gone to that dinner. We should've just…talked."

"You were her oldest, truest friend," Mrs. Vicario said. Even now, in the midst of this, she was trying to mother Ezz. She always had. "She was very busy since she'd been home. She and her friend Martha seemed to have a lot to do, but nothing could replace you, Ezzardine."

Ezz just stared at her. If her mouth said the words that echoed in her mind, if she actually heard them out loud, it would be admitting the horrible truth: that maybe Rosario had left Ezz behind, as alone as she always feared she would be.

Who's Martha? She couldn't say it. She wouldn't.

"I should go," she said instead, and stood so abruptly Mrs. Vicario's eyes widened.

"Ezz…"

"To let you…be alone," Ezz said. "Together. You should have…time. With each other."

"Ezzardine, you are part of this family," Mr. Vicario said, his mustache curving down. His serious face. Ezz could picture Rosario mocking it when they were ten, hands on hips. Her heart seized.

"Thank you," she whispered. "I just…thank you."

She left without hugging them. She knew if she felt the warmth of Mrs. Vicario's arms like a cradle around her, she might never climb out of this feeling. Maybe she wouldn't anyway. But right now grief was an ocean around her, and anger felt like a sand bar under her feet. It would probably shift, but it felt good to stand on something and keep her chin above water. Rosario. Gone. She wondered if Martha knew, whoever she was.

Ezz didn't run home. She walked, one foot in front of the other, trying not to sink. Derby was nine days away and the street was starting to come alive with tourists and a small parade. The noise was like a balm, drowning out the hum of pain. She needed more. More noise. More brass. She knew just the thing to do to keep her head above the tide.

CHAPTER 11

LUZ

Luz stood at the very back of the crowd, the flames of dozens of candles blurring into a yellow blaze when she let her eyes go unfocused. She wasn't a crier, not really. But watching the tears on everyone's cheeks made her wish she was. She knew so many of these faces, people who had gathered at the waterfront to share their grief over the loss of Rosario Vicario, and Luz wanted to be with them in every way. She wanted to wail with them, to clasp hands. Her cousin Mariela, always the life of the party, always the first person to the dance floor, never understood Luz's anxiety, the way crowds made her feel like an insect squirming on a taxonomist's needle. Even crowds of people she loved. So she stood at the back while Eric Sanchez from the backside read a poem through the megaphone up front.

Luz couldn't focus on the words. She vaguely heard Rosario compared to a butterfly, to a flower, to a ray of sunshine, but never to a horse, which, in Luz's head, was the only possible metaphor. And she was stuck on this. How a girl could gallop through brick walls built specifically to keep her out, and then disappear into death without so much as a crack of lightning, with only faces like hers showing up to mourn her. Luz focused on the statue where people had come to place flowers and stuffed ponies. The statue itself was a bronze metalbred, paid for by Limestone after the first

New Derby. No plaque, no branding, just a horse with gears carved into the shoulders and springs at the knees. The vaguely fishy smell blowing in off the river was unpleasant, but in a familiar way. The Great Lawn was filled with white boys playing frisbee, families walking dogs. They ignored Luz and the others, gathered at dusk to pay their respects to Rosario Vicario. And would Rosario have wanted it any other way? Her memory was enshrined with pure love and the light of candles, not cameras. As it should be.

The prayers went on, fresh tears pouring. Perhaps if Luz had been crying like everyone else, immersed in the scene of grief, she wouldn't have noticed the other thing that hung around the group of mourners like an odor. She'd felt hints of it when someone's abuela got up to lead a prayer, when heads were bowed to pray but eyes cracked open, prying at the dark that had begun to crush against the river. Finally Luz saw it baldly when she gazed across the gathering and caught sight of her cousin Mariela, scanning the crowd and the shadows beyond it.

Fear.

A girl whose face Luz knew from Skyhorse climbed up on the bronze metalbred's base, refusing the megaphone. She barely raised her voice when it was her time to speak, and Luz strained to hear her.

"We gather to grieve Rosario Vicario," she said, her eyes bright with angry tears. "But also the others. Those who won't get a headline, or even 60 seconds on the local news. Those whose lives are snuffed out for no reason, who they put in the dirt without a blink. We honor Rosario, who was one of us even if she didn't grow up on the backside, and we honor the rest of us too. We won't stop looking for answers. They tried to bury us. They didn't know we were seeds."

There were murmurs, raised hands. Luz had heard this quote before – she didn't know who originally said it. The girl climbed down, crying, and hugs were offered, slow circles rubbed on her back. But the fear stayed in the air. Everyone was scared, and it wasn't because Rosario Vicario had been found in a hotel room, supposedly overdosed on ketamine. There was something else, and Luz could smell it; by the time the prayers had finished and the crowd had started to disperse, she couldn't keep the words from spilling out of her mouth when she approached her cousin Mariela.

"What the hell is going on?"

"A girl died," Mariela said immediately, but her eyes were over Luz's shoulder, still sweeping.

"I know, but there's something else happening. Everyone is acting strange…"

"Not Rosario," Mariela whispered. "Someone else. A backside girl. Two nights ago."

Luz felt her eyes become falcons then too, swooping, sweeping, searching.

"A backside girl?" she repeated. "Who?"

"I don't know yet," Mariela said. "It happened in one of the barns and people are freaked out. Some people are saying it's just a rumor…but I saw the medical officers come. They left with a stretcher."

"Puchica," Luz whispered.

"Your mom tried to call you," Mariela said.

"She did?"

"Your device was off."

"Is she here?" Luz's head swiveled anew, taking in the crowd that grew smaller and smaller.

"No," Mariela said. "But she knew you would be, and she told me to pass you a message."

"What?"

Mariela took her cousin firmly by the shoulders, looking her deeply in the eyes.

"Stay. The hell. Away. From the racetrack."

CHAPTER 12

TY

Ty could see the lights of Shavon's shop as soon as she stepped off the Trolley at 1ˢᵗ and Oak – all glass, the many TV screens flickering out into the streets like the aurora borealis. Ty usually avoided the barbershop during Derby season and let her hair go messy: tourists flooded the shop where visiting celebrities were known to get fades and shape-ups – basketball players, jockeys, the occasional Hollywood face.

Tonight, however, the plush waiting chairs were mostly empty aside from faces Ty recognized as regulars. The tourists were all at parties and bars, crowding into Limestone-sponsored events to get a glimpse of last year's Derby winners. Limestone generally recycled the metalbreds for the next year's races, but the winners and other notable builds remained programmed and alert, constantly on parade like beauty pageant winners making appearances at town halls.

"What are you doing here?" Shavon was finishing up a young guy's cut, using a tiny froom to suck up loose fuzz from the back of his neck. She didn't look at Ty but Ty knew she was talking to her by the way her voice rose, a friendly balloon, across to the door.

"Why else?"

At this Shavon shot her a quick evaluative glance, eyes taking in her hairline.

"I just saw you last week. Special occasion coming up?"

"Kinda."

"Be with you in a second."

Ty sat in one of the open chairs, letting her eyes wander over the shop. It had definitely seen some improvements since Shavon reached celebrity stylist status – Ty remembered when all the chairs were folding chairs Shavon borrowed from her church. She would fit them all in her truck and carry them back and forth on Sundays and Wednesdays when they were needed for youth choir practice. Everyone knew back then that if you came for a cut on Sundays and Wednesdays then you would be standing while you waited. Now, Ty thought, sinking into the velvety throne under her butt, things were different.

But some things were the same. Tons of TVs, most of them playing sporting events, throwback music videos, or local news. The walls that weren't mirrors or screens were filled with artwork – many of them colorful, imaginative paintings featuring the first two Black presidents, as well as historic Kentucky celebrities like Muhammad Ali and Lionel Hampton. A random white woman Ty learned was Anne Braden. And then there were the jockeys.

This was another part of Bay's – and Shavon's – fame: its museum. The entire wall alongside the mirrors was covered in old framed photos, some of them so old you had to stand close to separate face from shadow. The photos were arranged in chronological order, one would find, starting with Oliver Lewis, the jockey who won the very first Kentucky Derby in 1875. Like most of the earliest jockeys, Oliver Lewis was Black, a fact that Shavon was currently imparting to the young man in her chair.

"Oliver Lewis was the first to win, but he wasn't the first Black man to ride a horse. Hell no. Not even talking about the Black cowboys – white people think they own Westerns – but jockeys in general. Back then, enslaved people were the ones caring for the horses. They had the knowledge, the connection. White people just had the money and the property. So they had folks like Oliver Lewis race. And he was good as hell."

Ty's mind jumped back to the dinner party at the Mahogany that Ezzardine Clayton had attended alongside Rosario Vicario. History and knowledge – the odds were good that Ezzardine came here for her haircuts. This is why Ty had come to Shavon today, and the purpose of her visit transformed her palms into swamps.

"I never even heard of him," the young man in her chair said, awed.

"I know you haven't," Shavon said, indignant. "Not many people have. I bet you ain't heard of Erskine Henderson, either."

She waited, and the guy stared at her blankly.

"Didn't think so. He was a Black jockey too, and first to win three Derbies in one year – the Kentucky Derby, the Tennessee Derby, and the Coney Island Derby, all in 1885. Riding Joe Cotton."

"Joe Cotton," the guy said. "Wasn't that a Limestone model a couple years ago?"

"Yup. They credit the horse but not the rider." She snorted as she edged one last spot on the back of his neck. "You wouldn't even know that there are Black horse folks all over this country right now. Right now! Los Angeles, Alabama, Mississippi, North Dakota. And don't even get me started on Native folks. There are still people who believe Native folks never saw horses until white folks came. What horseshit."

"Wild," the guy said, eyeing the wall of framed faces, on and on. "I barely knew about some of this. I kinda recognize him though…"

He pointed, his finger wavering in the direction of an ancient-looking portrait of a young Black man wearing an old-fashioned jockey's cap. Ty knew them all by now. She'd heard Shavon's speech many times, and had been on the receiving end of it once, early in their relationship. It was Shavon who had led

Ty down the path of seeing Derby – and the world – outside a narrow white lens.

"Isaac Murphy," Shavon said, triumphant.

"Yeah! I've heard of him."

"Well, thank God for that," Shavon said. "He was arguably the greatest jockey to have ever lived. My cousin owns a little bit of horse land and named it after him. He was one of the best to ever do it. Richest, too. For awhile."

There was a brief, heavy silence. Ty felt it in her chest. She knew what had become of Isaac Murphy. Of Soup Perkins. Albert Isom. Tom Britton.

"You really love the Derby," the guy said seriously.

"Man, I don't give a fuck about the Derby," Shavon laughed. She removed his cape with a flourish. "I just care about Black folks."

He stood, slipping her two twenties.

"Thanks. For the cut and the history lesson." He passed Ty for the door. She stiffened as she so often did when men of any age passed by her. If it wasn't an outright moment of harassment, it was often a veiled one: *You'd be a lot prettier with long hair*, or *You must like the girls, huh*? Even now, in this day and age, they never knew quite what to say when she said "yes."

But the guy ignored her except for a polite nod, and Shavon waved Ty over to the chair, frooming its surface.

"What about them?" Ty said, indicating the few people waiting.

"They're waiting for Lisa."

"I thought you were on vacation?" Ty called to Lisa over the electric snap of Lisa's clippers.

"She came back for Derby," Shavon said, loudly. "She's not from here, remember? Didn't realize how much money she was missing out on. She can take a whole 'nother vacation after the races are through."

"You could've *told* me," Lisa called from the only other chair in the shop. "Taking advantage of my non-localness!"

"I like to let people make their own mistakes," Shavon grinned. "C'mon, Ty."

Ty plopped down, her stomach becoming a knot of cord. Usually this was easy. After so many haircuts at Bay's, she and Shavon began to make friendly conversation. Casual stuff. Work. The city. Occasionally metalbreds or other sports. After eight months of haircuts, they ventured into more personal conversations. Family. Lovers. Fears. But while the conversations occasionally delved deep, they always stayed in the chair, neither of them asking anything of the other. If Ty made an appointment, she contacted Shavon's device, but never saved her number. They never communicated other than to set the time. It was all straightforward. Now Ty felt like she was entering Bay's through a side door, hands hidden. She was going to ask Shavon a favor, to step outside their relationship of careful boundaries. She was going to treat her like a friend.

Why was that so hard?

"So what's the special occasion?" Shavon said, changing out the blades in her clippers. Wireless, sharpened by laser. Like Ty's cleanwork kit, Shavon had her own set of tools.

"I actually needed to talk to you," Ty said quickly before she could stop herself.

The clippers, which had moved to hum beside her right ear, wavered. Ty's heart flinched as she felt the hesitation sputter between them.

"Okay," Shavon said, slowly. The clippers connected with Ty's neck. "About what?"

"Look," Lisa called, and the buzz of her clippers snapped off. Ty and Shavon both looked her way. Lisa and her client were both staring at the largest screen in the shop. Lisa tapped a button built into her mirror shelves and the volume soared.

"Investigators continue to examine the hotel where the body

of Rosario Vicario was found," a woman onscreen was saying, holding her mic solemnly before her. Ty couldn't remember if she had seen this face out in the sea of faces that crowded the street, held back by the shining line of Special Police. "Cause of death has yet to be determined, but early indications point to a drug overdose."

The camera cut to the Mahogany, replaying footage of four figures carrying a long black stretcher down the steep stone stairs under the wash of floodlights. The black bag they bore could be luggage, guns, soil. Not a body. Ty stared until her eyes were dry.

"It's so fucking sad," Lisa said, turning the screen back down. Her eyes shone with tears. She shook her head so hard the ends of her braids swung against her cheeks. "I don't even know what to say. She's my little sister's age. God knows what her family is feeling…"

She and her client continued the conversation, Ty and Shavon staring at the screen where the body bag had been replaced by still photos of Rosario Vicario in a gown on the red carpet of Cavehill Downs last year. Another one of her standing next to Window Seat, the homemade metalbred that had set the industry on fire. Ty had seen the famous equinibot a thousand times – black as the best soil, a white blaze down its perfectly convincing forehead, stopping just between the two flared nostrils.

"This," Ty said softly, wondering if Shavon would hear. She did.

"Huh?"

"This," Ty said. She nodded ever so slightly at the screen. "This is what I needed to talk to you about."

Shavon looked uncomprehending for a moment, the clippers buzzing idly. Then realization sparked in her eyes.

"Oh shit," she said. "The fucking Mahogany. You do cleanwork. Oh my God." A pause, as it sank in further. "Oh my *God*."

Ty didn't respond until the clippers were back against her skull, the sound of her hair being shredded by the razor throwing up a curtain of noise. But then Lisa interrupted.

"You see this?" she said, pointing. A new story had taken over the screen, shots of Cavehill. "Somebody stole a metalbred from the Downs."

"...authorities say a Palomino with face markings worth three million in upgrades disappeared from its stall..." the anchor said.

"What, are they going to sell it for parts?" a waiting customer called, to laughter.

Ty angled her eyes back at Shavon.

"I found her," she murmured.

Shavon almost paused, and Ty caught the frown on her lips.

"What did you say?" she said, her voice lowering now too.

"I found her. Rosario Vicario. In her suite."

The hum and scratch of the clippers filled her left ear and then her right.

"Are you being serious," Shavon said, almost a whisper. She had grasped Ty's desire to be low-key and studied Ty's hairline with a laser focus.

"Yes. I...talked to her. Right before."

"Holy shit, Ty." Ty saw her throat shift out of the corner of her eye, a nervous swallow. "Holy shit. Does anyone know?"

"The investigators. My boss. The staff. This detective interrogated me hardcore. Like he thought I did it or something." She blinked hard, clearing the memory of Segrest watching her from the window. "But there's something I didn't tell him, Shavon."

The clippers inched away from her neck. Shavon was staring at her now, the effort to be low-key replaced by concern.

"What," she said, flat.

"Rosario gave me something," Ty whispered.

"She gave you *what?*"

"Something," Ty said. For the first time, she felt tears prickle in her eyes, remembering the light sinking from Rosario's, the panic when the nose ring had fallen to the carpet. The blood like bubbling soap. "And she asked me to do something for her."

"Something like what? Do what?"

"That's why I came to you," Ty said, and she was embarrassed by the pleading she heard slip into her voice. "I need your help. I figured you of all people might know how…might know how I can…"

She floundered, flustered. Shavon squinted, clicking off the clippers.

"What?"

"I need to find Ezzardine Clayton," Ty said, a whisper. "I need to talk to her."

"Ezzardine Clayton?" Shavon raised an eyebrow.

"Yes."

The clippers clicked back on with a snap that made Ty flinch.

"Girl, that's all you had to say," Shavon said. Ty thought she sounded relieved. She didn't want to imagine what Shavon thought Ty was asking for: aiding and abetting, perhaps, or a safe house. Not something as simple as a chaperone. "What are you doing tonight?"

CHAPTER 13

TY

The pink house owned by Ezzardine Clayton was massive and twinkling, but when Ty approached the front gate, Shavon by her side, the only thing she could see were the elephants.

In the near-dark of Friday night, the lights from the mansion behind the herd of three giants obscured them in shadow. Ty gaped at their ears, their powerful shoulders, their trunks mid-swing.

"Topiaries," Shavon said, laughing lightly. "Amazing, right?"

They passed through the gates, the bars illuminated from within by some softly glowing substance at their core, and once Ty stepped into the perimeter of the pink house's kingdom, she could make out the dense leaves that the elephants were carved from. Thick bushes, the tallest nearly fifteen feet high.

"They're perfect," she breathed.

"Ezz is sponsoring this girl who does botanical art," Shavon said. "She's dope. Ezz says she has some kind of serum that makes the plants grow fast, then she trims them like this."

The gate and path allowed for foot travel only, Ty had been told, and she gazed around, taking it all in as they walked. No cars at the Pink. Ty could already hear the music, traveling through the ground like breath. A Derby party, Shavon had told her, but

Ty hadn't expected topiary, the house glowing like rose quartz.

"Sponsoring?" Ty said. She gazed around at the other animals inhabiting the front yard. She'd never seen anything like this in Louisville. Maybe a small bush cut to look like a horse at the Downs, but nothing like these, the grand jade leaves that built the elephants' backs, and, as she moved deeper into the yard, the hippos, and the lions.

"Yeah, like pays for her supplies and studies and stuff. Ezz usually has three or four people she sponsors at one time, but right now it's just the one. Most of them live here at the Pink for awhile while they work on whatever project she's sponsoring them for. Like a residency. Zora West was my favorite – you heard of her? Fashion designer. Ellen Samudzi was cool – a philosopher. Wrote a book from Ezz's guest suite. The new girl is Luz Cabo Trejo, I think her name is. Botany and, like, nerdy computer stuff I think."

"Where does she find them? Zora West and everybody."

"Sometimes they find her. But with Luz, I think they were both at the track and Luz was in a bind, so Ezz asked what she could do. She found out she did botany, and boom. Now Luz is staying here for awhile."

"Ezzardine just…pays them?" Ty let her fingers trail along the slender leg of a leafy giraffe. A pair of them stood close to where the footpath opened up into the wider pavement that led up to the house, their feet planted on either side of the path, their necks arching overhead and meeting in a kiss.

"Yup. She's wild rich, clearly. Inherited a ton of it but also she's just a mad talented gambler. Like truly talented. Always plays cards with an earpod in – I don't know what music she listens to. Golden fingers, silver eye. Massive bets. She bet on Rosario when no one else would have bothered – Rosario was her best friend. Even closer than me. I'm more like a cousin. Anyway, Ezz's parents died a few years ago, and she inherited this house. She turned it into the Pink after that."

Ty nodded, taking it all in. Rosario's best friend – that's why Ezzardine had been at the Mahogany dinner. She wondered what kind of person could throw a party the day after their best friend was found dead.

Ty and Shavon stepped into the glow emanating from the house, bathing them both in soft pink light that came from…somewhere. Strategically placed lights, Ty thought, but in the moment it felt more as if she were entering a new atmosphere, a new planet where the foliage breathed and moved, where the moon was made of jewels.

Shavon led the way, comfortable in this kingdom of strange beauty, and Ty was surprised by the envy she felt snapping in her veins. Ty had only seen Ezzardine Clayton once, and only from a kitchen peephole, but even that glimpse showed her something magnetic. She turned Ty to metal. Even so, Ty's steps slowed. When Shavon had offered to take her to a Derby party to meet Ezzardine, Ty had imagined the kind of parties she grew up with before her mother disappeared – backyards and grills, a screen or two broadcasting the race while her mother and her mother's friends talked shit about Limestone. Fireworks set off in the street, every year another kid with burns on shins and knuckles. This wasn't a party, Ty thought as Shavon raised her hand to the doorknob. This was an *event*.

"Don't worry," Shavon grinned over her shoulder as the door swung open. "You look great."

The party at the Pink swallowed them in a single bite of jazz and glitter. Ty gaped up at the cathedral ceiling, aware of her mouth hanging open but not quite able to close it. A tightrope sliced high across the room and a person wearing a full rhinestone-studded bodysuit placed one foot in front of the other, the rose light transforming them into a sparkling, celestial idol. The music came from a band on a circular stage at the center of what Ty could only describe as a ballroom – skirted in shimmering gold drapery, the stage held an eight-woman band playing a rendition of "A-Tisket, A-Tasket."

"She got The Belles in here," Shavon said, bobbing her head. The women on stage were all Black and Brown and all wore ballgowns, an assortment of locs and curls swinging as they sent music in brassy waves over the crowd. "*And* they're playing Ella Fitzgerald. Ezz knows how to set a mood."

Ty felt everything inside her lurch back in time. At one point she might have been performing on a stage like this, her voice swelling up into the domed ceiling. It was like looking out a car window and seeing the scenery suddenly reverse. This could have been her life – or something like it. If her mother were alive. If her mother had never left her house at midnight, bound for Cavehill Downs. Maybe even if Ty hadn't followed, and had been allowed to believe the lies in the headlines, rather than seeing the truth herself.

Shavon tugged her forward and Ty shook herself back into the room. Around the stage were a half-dozen different dance cyphers. A girl wearing head-to-toe pink with fuchsia feathers down her back duck-walked to cheers, popped up, then dropped down in a full split. Ty felt her own legs twitch, as if she were already among the dancers, as if she had been there all along.

"Where *is* Ezz?" Shavon said, still looking. "Everybody and their mama here but I don't see..."

"She's right there." Ty pointed at the stage, where the figure of Ezzardine Clayton was scaling a small gold ladder and joining The Belles, bobbing her head of close-cropped fuchsia curls. The band smashed out the final notes, the music clanging and harmonious, and when they drew it to a close, all the people crowding the cavernous room raised their hands and their voices in a clamor of praise. Ezzardine Clayton scooped a mic from its stand.

"One more time," she demanded, and the cheers erupted

once more. She stood solemnly on stage, surveying the scene all around her. Ty knew that expression. Present but not present. Watching and hearing but living somewhere far away. When the cheers died down, Ezzardine raised the mic again. "As you all know, I lost one of my good friends last night. My…my best friend."

Silence spread like a noxious gas, wiping smiles from faces, leaching the rhythm out of shoulders still swaying to the magic The Belles had left behind. The glitter in the air seemed to lose its shine.

"Most of you didn't really know her," she said. She was staring at the stage floor. She wasn't wearing a suit like the last time Ty had seen her – in fact, she wasn't even dressed up. Far from it. A pair of navy-blue sweatpants; a white shirt. She wore grief like a veil. "She's been traveling since she was a kid, thanks to that brain of hers. But Rosario was *from* Louisville. She grew up in our corner stores and in our summer camps and our basement dance clubs. And she was good. She was a good, good person and she had dreams that she floated on. She gave so much, even before she had anything to give."

She stopped, her mouth twitching, and Ty thought she might have been biting her lip.

"I have a lot more I want to say but I'mma just tell God." She took a deep breath. "Tonight is for Rosario. Keep her family in your thoughts. And don't listen to that bullshit they're saying on the news about her ODing. She wasn't into drugs, and it just shows how little has changed that they use drugs as a convenient way to smear people after death. We all know the who's-who never liked Rosario – you can't beat these people at their own game and expect them to love you. And Rosario never wanted their love. She just wanted to do what *she* loved. And she did."

The silence was thick – above, the glittering tightrope walker was a silver moon over the landscape of staring eyes. No one said a word until Ezzardine reached down for the bottle Ty hadn't seen her place at her feet. Water. She slowly raised it to the sky.

"To Rosario," she said softly into the mic. Barely above a whisper but everyone heard. "A good, good friend. No matter what."

"To Rosario," the crowd called back, and Ezz nodded, clutching the mic like a prayer. Ty was surprised by the tenderness of the response. No one was rushing to get back to dancing or drinking or talking, and when The Belles took the silence and filled it with "Into Each Life Some Rain Must Fall," the crowd swayed, and the tightrope walker moved slowly and somberly, sending sparkles down like metallic raindrops.

"She barely got dressed," Shavon said, her voice low with sympathy. "She's going to disappear after this, I bet. Maybe tonight isn't the best night for you to talk to her about this, Ty…"

Ty stared at Ezzardine Clayton's form on stage, shoulders rolled forward, neck bent – so different than the laughing, confident young woman from The Mahogany the other night. Some vital piece of her had been torn out. Ty knew that look. She knew that feeling.

"I know why you say that," Ty said, keeping her eyes on Ezzardine. "But I have to give it to her tonight."

She hadn't told Shavon what she carried. The urgency wouldn't transfer – Shavon hadn't seen the wildness in Rosario Vicario's eyes in her final moments, the leaking desperation as she placed the nose stud in Ty's palm. It wasn't for Ty to decide why this small object was important, she had told herself as she dressed for this evening, trying to talk herself out of going and making a fool of herself. No, it was up to her to deliver and that's all.

"I'm just saying," Shavon said. "If she's not feeling it, then you can't push it."

Ty heard the firmness in her voice, the voice of a friend; not of Ty but of Ezzardine. Ty all but winced – the message was clear:

Upset my friend and your ass is out of here.

"I won't."

But when they looked back to the stage, Ezzardine was gone. The stage bore only The Belles, the mic nested back in its stand. The swaying crowd had swallowed her, and Ty stretched her neck tall for any sign of her path.

"Usually she'd be at the gambling tables," Shavon frowned, squinting. "Winning everybody's money while listening to jazz or whatever. But I don't see her over there…"

Shavon wandered along the edge of the ballroom, Ty following awkwardly. It felt strange to be out of the barbershop and here at a party with her – she had wondered for some time if there was the possibility of friendship in their bi-weekly appointments, but this shift had been too abrupt. One moment the black cape around her throat and the next wearing a white jumpsuit, pointy gold flats. One of her few "going out" outfits. Shavon had told her that she looked nice, and she did. But not *this* nice, she thought. Not as nice as this room, as the band, as the lights that drenched the room in sunset.

Together they moved around the perimeter of the room, eyes prying at the crowd and the bars on either end of the space where guests were issued water and what looked like lemonade. A spiked option existed, Ty assumed, but both times she had seen Ezzardine she'd been drinking water. She doubted she'd be at the bar. Shavon was a few paces ahead, on tiptoe occasionally, trying to see over swells of dancing bodies. The Belles had effortlessly transitioned into wordless brassy jazz and the crowd was in full swing again. A girl Ty's age wearing a flowing red skirt swirled past them, her teeth silver in the light.

"I think I see her," Shavon said, peering up and over. "Stay right here. I'm gonna go get her and bring her back."

"But – "

Shavon squeezed into the crowd, waving a hand back at Ty,

an instruction. Ty didn't mind standing alone at a party – this wasn't middle school and she'd spent enough time being alone the last couple years that her back against the wall felt natural. But she watched the girl in the red skirt dance in a tight circle with her friends and the part of Ty's brain where loneliness had once lived twitched, coming to life. She averted her eyes, something about the girls' closeness, the sound of their laughter rising above the music, was like picking a scab. She let her gaze wander along the walls, looking for who else might be standing alone, their solitude a balm for her own. Instead she found the figure of Ezzardine Clayton opening a small door in the back corner of the ballroom, glancing over her shoulder, and ducking out into the evening air.

Ty jerked away from the wall and said "wait" out loud before she could stop herself. Two guys walking past turned to look at her curiously, as no one else was near enough for her exclamation to make sense.

"Not you," she mumbled. "Sorry."

She looked frantically over the crowd, searching for Shavon, but more and more people were arriving and the music was even louder and there were two more tightrope walkers in the air now. If Ty was going to talk to Ezzardine Clayton, she had to make a move now.

She hurried along the wall, which – thanks to The Belles – was mercifully clear. Her heart slammed in her chest, and as she approached the door, she wondered at her nervousness. Was it the looming possibility of a conversation with the magnetic woman with the saxophone laugh? Or the burden of Rosario Vicario's nose stud in the vial, slipped into the pocket of her jumpsuit? She could feel its slender weight against her leg with every step she took. She wanted it gone. She could feel the weight of Detective Segrest's eyes on her back and she needed to be free of it. Her plans didn't have space for the heat.

She pushed past the door that Ezzardine had slipped through

without a second thought, out into the cool air. She had to wait for the pink galaxy of the party to clear from her eyes – it turned the night into a haze. Inside the ballroom, the music and the lights had disoriented her, and somehow she thought she was leaving the Pink on the same side she had entered. As her eyes adjusted to the evening, she saw she was wrong.

The Pink was on a bit of a rise in the land, she found, and she stood looking down at a maze.

There were no elephants as in the front of the house. Instead there were horses. They galloped, green and shadowy, in various poses, some rearing back, some leaping. They were a wild leafy herd in the area of lawn between the house and where the maze began, a break in the foliage so smooth it looked like it had merely been erased and not cut from the branches. At the heart of the maze was a fountain, deep in the inner rings of the swirling pattern the gardened walls created. She could almost hear its falling water from where she stood. A ways to her left was a grander sort of patio with wide doors that she assumed one could access from the ballroom, but the door she had chosen to follow Ezzardine through was small and unremarkable, a sort of service door. Perfect for sneaking out for some much-needed solitude, Ty thought, and felt guilty for her determination in interrupting that peace. But the vial against her thigh pushed her onward, and she was so focused on her mission that she didn't notice the hitching warning hiss of the sprinkler system spinning to life.

"Damn," she said under her breath when the first fine mist hit her cheeks. She had wandered out into the green almost without realizing it, square between two twelve-foot horses, and half of her body was soaked before she fully realized what was happening.

She scrambled to escape the artificial rain, but in the near-dark it was hard to tell where it was coming from. Slip-sliding, she took refuge a moment later under a smaller topiary with the long legs of a colt, back hooves prancing off the ground in the dance young horses do when they're experimenting with jumping to the moon. Ty could see the color of her thighs through the wet white material of her jumpsuit.

"Shit," she muttered. "Shit!"

And then came the saxophone voice.

"It's water, actually."

CHAPTER 14

EZZ

Ezz carried a pizza box in one hand, a slice in the other. She had swiped it from the kitchen on her way out of the party. Hosting had seemed like such a good idea at the time. Noise. Sparkle. Music. People. But as the doors opened and the band began to play, she had looked around at the smiling faces crowding into her house and realized none of them were Rosario. Ezz couldn't have her, so instead she wanted peace and pizza. But now this.

"Are you lost?" she asked the white girl in the garden, who stood watching her, dripping.

"Not exactly," the girl said. "I was looking for..."

"For what? The party? Because you can't really miss it."

She used the slice of pizza to gesture back at the house. She didn't know this girl. She wanted to eat her pizza in silence.

"I was looking for you, actually," the girl said.

"What, you need a map to the bathroom?" The meanness felt good, but only slightly. Like eating a cookie when you really want cake. Or pizza. She took a bite of the slice, staring at the girl, trying to decide the best means of kicking her out. She had security for these parties, but never needed them. First time for everything.

"I'm sorry you lost your friend," said the girl softly, and Ezz's frown was so heavy she felt it in her eyes. This girl she didn't know was sorry. Everyone was sorry. Everyone had so many things to say but none of them could tell her the thing she needed to know: why her best friend had lied to her, and why Ezz had lied to herself. She had known things were strange at dinner, the way she and Rosario left the Mahogany so suddenly. But she had let Rosario tell her it was nothing. Now she would never know.

She couldn't say any of this to a random white girl in a wet jumpsuit. So instead she just said, "Yeah, well, me too."

Her pizza was getting cold. She thought about Rosario going cold. It made her want to scream and vomit at the same time. She turned away, desperate for peace, but the girl's voice caught at her.

"Wait. I don't know how to tell you this," the girl called.

Ezz felt the sensation of growing thorns, her grief making her raw and sharp.

"Tell me what? Wait, are you a fucking reporter? Are you looking for a story here? I've never seen you at the Pink before tonight, so if you…"

"No, no, no," the girl said, waving her hands, as if trying to disperse the invisible smoke that had clouded up between them. "No. I'm not a reporter. I came with Shavon. I'm a maid. I'm…"

"*My* Shavon? From Bay's? She doesn't have a maid, what the hell are you talking about?"

The girl closed her eyes tight, took a deep breath.

"No. I'm sorry. I'm not being clear. I asked Shavon to bring me here tonight. She cuts my hair. I'm a maid. At the Mahogany."

"The Mahogany," Ezz repeated. She focused on the girl now, trying to remember her. Taller than Ezz had thought at first, a shaved blonde head. Olive skin that made the white jumpsuit look good. She wore makeup like a pro, the way that Rosario's little sister Aracelis had always done Rosario's face for events. But unlike Rosario, whose eyes were always windows to a laugh, this girl's eyes were shutters. Ezz didn't think she was malicious, but there was something unnerving about her, like meeting what you thought was a cat in an alley but it turns out it's a pit bull.

"I don't remember seeing you," Ezz said.

"Cleanwork staff isn't allowed in the dining room with guests," she said. "I was...watching from the kitchen."

Ezz saw the natural blush bloom under the makeup. She was unsure of its origin, so she just frowned again.

"So what do you want?" Ezzardine said softly. She put the pizza slice back in the box, holding it in front of her like a barricade against whatever the girl had come to say.

"Rosario told me to find you," the girl said in a rush. "The night she died. As she...died."

A moment ago, Ezz could hear many things: the creak of crickets, the far-off boom and roll of The Belles, the hiss of sprinklers. But with these words everything faded. The heat of the pizza box against her palm grew cold and distant. She had said goodbye to Rosario in her private car that night, dropped off at the Pink's gate, and then never saw her again. She had barely uttered her name since the news, with no one to speak it to. But Rosario had said *Ezzardine*. Dying, Rosario had said her name.

"You were with her," Ezz whispered.

"Yes," said the girl. "I...found her."

Nearby stood the dripping leaves of Thoroughbreds, and each drop of water sounded like the tick of a bomb. Ezz felt explosive, the contents of her heart shaken and then sealed.

"I don't want to know," she said softly. "I can't. I'm going to just...I can't. No."

She turned away, even as the girl called "wait" again. Ezz couldn't wait. What would she do with this new pain? Where would she put it?

"I need to tell you," the girl cried after her. "I have to..."

"Don't you fucking dare tell me!" Ezz yelled. She marched away, toward the safety of the maze.

"She gave me something to give you!" the girl shouted, and

the words hit Ezz between the shoulders like a brick. She almost stumbled.

"What?"

"She gave me something," the girl repeated, a level below yelling. "For you. She made me promise to give it to you. I *have* to give it to you. I don't know why she wanted you to have it, but she said *they came* and then told me to hide it and she said to take it to you. I can't keep it. It was hers. It's for you."

She stopped speaking. They were both out of breath for different reasons.

"It's for you," the girl said one more time, desperate.

"What did you say she said?" Ezz said, turning slowly.

"To give it to you."

"No. The other thing."

"She said they…they came."

"*They.*"

"Yes."

Ezz didn't want it. She wanted to take whatever this random white girl was offering her and launch it into the night sky. After the death of someone you loved, one was supposed to seek closure, and Ezz knew that taking whatever this girl was offering her was akin to opening a lid instead. But the lid had already been cracked. The word *they* just threw it wide.

"Give it to me."

The closer the girl got, the more Ezz actually saw her, her features swimming into view through a glaze of tears she didn't realize were in her eyes. Ezz blinked several times and there she was, standing close, shivering a little in her wet clothes. She had a slender neck that led to a pointy chin, orb-like cheekbones. Ezz observed a single freckle above one eye – she had the sudden urge to blow it like an eyelash.

"Give it to me," Ezz said again. She put her pizza box on the ground.

The girl's hand was already in her pocket and emerged slowly as if about to perform a magic trick. When she extended the hand out to Ezz, it was bearing a slim transparent tube. Ezz took it slowly, gently, wondering if it was as breakable as she felt.

"Be careful," the girl said when Ezz opened the vial.

At first Ezz didn't see it, but then it caught the light. A red jewel tipped out onto her palm, catching a slice of moonlight.

"Her nose ring," the girl said. "She took it out. She gave it to me. I don't know why."

Ezz just stared at the ruby stud nestled in the crater of her palm, her jaws clenched.

"*Take it to her. Tell her they were looking,*" the white girl said. "That's what she said. I don't know what it means."

Ezz took the jewel between two fingers, and for a moment she thought she still might throw it into the grass, into the maze, bury it in green. But she slowly lifted it to the sky, held it against the moon staring down. She frowned. Rosario, the nerdiest girl she'd ever known. Who, the first time Ezz had spent the night when they were kids, asked if she wanted to take apart an old computer for fun. The girl who taught Ezz Morse code on a road trip just for the hell of it. Ezz stared at the stud until her eyes burned.

And then she reached for her device, scrolling down to Luz's name. She sent a quick voice message.

"Luz, can you come here real quick? I'm outside the maze."

The white girl shifted her weight as if to leave now that she had transferred the stud to Ezz's possession.

"Nah," Ezz said, pointing at the ground. "Hang out for a second."

"This is all I came to do, okay?" the girl said. "I just needed to give you this."

"My friend might have questions."

"Who is your friend?"

Luz appeared then, from the mouth of the maze. Ezz noted

that she wore black, a change from the variety of comic book shirts she'd worn every day since her arrival at the Pink. She looked like she'd been at a funeral, black dress and black flats, black shadows under her eyes. But one thing was the same: she wore her kit at her chubby waist, full of tools Ezz recognized as things she herself had procured for her resident nerd/artist. Rosario would've liked her, Ezz thought.

"How did you know I was out here?" Luz said. She merely glanced at the girl in the jumpsuit.

"I saw you come back from wherever you went," Ezz said. "I'm glad you're using the lair."

"The lair?" the white girl said, frowning. Ezz ignored her.

"You don't need it, do you?" Luz said, looking concerned. "I can move my stuff, I just…"

"Chill, it's cool. I might have a little job for you, that's all."

Luz brightened at this, and Ezz made a mental note to remind her later that her stay at the Pink did not depend on her usefulness.

"What do you think of this?" Ezz said, holding out the nose ring.

Ezz held the red jewel glittering between them, so tiny here in the garden with its giant looming horses. Ezz watched Luz squint in the dark, then draw a small object from her kit and shine it into Ezz's palm. A tiny flashlight lit up the stone, making it sparkle like hard blood.

"A…nose ring?" Luz said, frowning. "Am I missing something?"

"I don't know yet," Ezz said. "Mind scanning it for me?"

"Sure." Luz shrugged. She put away the flashlight and her hand returned with another tool, wider at one end with a slender stem. There were elements to it that Ezz couldn't see in the dark; with a clicking sound, a number of lights glowed to life along the stem.

"Hold it up," Luz instructed. "As best as you can so your hand doesn't interfere."

The jewel shone in the moonlight again, and the three girls stared at it, Luz raising her tool carefully, her hand focused and still.

"Scanning," she said under her breath. The tool emitted a low-frequency beep and she brought it to her eyes, the glow and the moon illuminating her squint. Ezz watched Luz's eyebrows lift, arching upward in a slow spread of surprise.

"What is it?" Ezz said. She kept her voice calm, but something inside her had begun to shake.

"Data," Luz said, raising her eyes to meet Ezz's. "Lots of it."

Ezz felt a centipede come alive somewhere in her body. Something growing many legs and moving steadily forward. She swallowed, and then motioned Luz toward the maze. The lid was off. There was work to be done.

"After you," she said to Luz, who nodded quickly. She moved back toward the entrance of the maze, Ezz on her heels. She was about to disappear into the maze when the white girl's voice caught her once more.

"Wait," she called.

Ezz looked back.

"What?"

"I…what about me? Can I…I want to…"

She threw her hands up, exasperated, and Ezz blinked. She remembered her pizza and stooped to get it, asking again:

"*What?*"

The girl sighed, rolling her eyes to the moon.

"I…want to help," she said. She seemed almost angry at herself for saying it, as if the words were lightning bugs escaping from a jar.

"With what?" Ezz said. She was baffled and also annoyed. Her friend was dead, the lid to that life swinging open, and her pizza was cold.

"She meant something to me," the girl said. "I've got my own shit going on, okay? But they're trying to say she ODed and it's bullshit and I found her and it's crazy and I lied to the cops and…"

"You lied to the cops?" Ezz said, slicing the tail off her sentence.

The girl faltered.

"Yeah. I had to. She told me to hide that – " she pointed into the maze, which had already swallowed the red jewel – "so I did and the detective asked me if she said anything when I found her and I said no because she said hide it, and he said he was looking for what was missing from the room and maybe I should have said something about the nose ring but she told me to hide it…"

"And so you did," Ezz said. She snapped her fingers. "Just like that."

"Yes," she said. "Yes, I did."

"For a girl you didn't even know."

"It feels like I knew her. I've seen people try to lie about someone after they're dead…" She bit something back, and Ezz watched the girl's eyes narrow. "I just want to help."

They stared at each other in silence until there was a muted crackle of leaves behind Ezz in the maze, and Luz reemerged, eyebrow arched in a question.

"Ezz?" Checking on her. Good friend to have around.

"Luz, blindfold her."

"What?" Luz and the girl both said. Ezz glanced back and forth between the two of them, unflustered.

"Blindfold her. She wants to come? Okay. Fine. Bring her."

"Do you think I just carry a blindfold around with me, or…" Ezz sucked her teeth.

"You got something in that kit."

Luz did, a black lens scarf, and Ezz watched as Luz wrapped it around the white girl's eyes, tying it securely at the back of her head.

"Do you have that Eyeball I gave you?" Ezz said, studying the now blindfolded girl.

Luz nodded, reaching again into her kit. It was a high-end security device that Luz had specifically requested, used for scanning visitors to high-risk areas. Ezz hadn't asked why she wanted it, and Luz clearly knew how to use it. She wanded the white girl's entire body, down to the pointy gold flats.

"Anything?" Ezz said.

"Just her device," Luz replied. "Works at the Mahogany. She paid for a haircut at Bay's yesterday. Isn't that where you go?"

"It's actually called a Gaze," the white girl said, correcting Ezz from behind her blindfold, her lips curving in a small smile. "Not an Eyeball. You know you can use that to steal account numbers too, if you do it right. I don't have much to steal though."

"Uh-huh," Luz said, a faint smile in her voice.

"What else?" Ezz prodded. She wanted to smile too. The white girl was calm. It was almost weird – blindfolded and wanded by two strangers, and she stood there smiling.

"Dad works at Limestone. Consultant. No mom."

The girl visibly winced. Ezz studied her.

"Your dad works at Limestone, huh?" Ezz said.

The girl shrugged. Luz frowned.

"Yeah, he used to work for a breeder," the girl said. "He was a trainer. Before horseracing got banned. I don't even know what he does there."

"Uh-huh. Okay. Can you see?" Ezz said. She raised a hand and waved it back and forth in front of the girl's face.

"No."

"Good. Come on."

She passed her pizza box to Luz and placed a gentle hand against the white girl's slightly damp back. Ezz guided her into the maze, this tall girl with a baldie; a straight back and no fear. She found herself watching the girl more than she did the path, and eventually had to ask.

"What's your name?"

The girl's painted red lips parted to impart a single soft syllable.

"Ty."

"Nice to meet you, Ty," she said. They walked side-by-side under the moonlight and when she introduced herself, she spoke it near an ear with the hair cut fresh and low around it. "I'm Ezz."

CHAPTER 15

LUZ

She was glad that Ezz and the white girl, Ty, were focused on each other. It gave her the chance to walk ahead and close the door of the first room, where she had spent the last seven hours running tests on vines, the endless formulae a worthy distraction from the thoughts that kept wandering back to the young woman she'd met at the museum. Irma. Luz shook her head. Nine days until Derby. She chanced a glance into the green room at her work before she slid the door softly shut – vines curled all along the back wall, one of them rustling softly. She smiled at it, and her head whispered a silent lullaby. *Sleep tonight*, she thought. *We'll work tomorrow.*

The next room was bright, and it was here that Ezz gently untied Ty's blindfold. Luz watched them lock eyes, and almost laughed. Love was like a strange plant, she thought, a cactus, sprouting in hostile conditions and thriving without rain, relying on something sweet and stubborn stored inside. She told herself to remember to tell Ezz this later, imagining Ezz's face contorting at the word "love." *A pretty face isn't love*, Luz knew she would say, and she had to be right, but one look at Irma made her doubt all the rules.

"So you think this is something you can do?" Ezz said. She was tearing herself away from their guest, making herself get down to business. Luz closed her eyes briefly, rooting herself as she always did. This time her mind wandered to her abuelita, back to one of the few times Luz had been in her physical presence, showing her granddaughter how to press and dry the herbs she worked with. *I'm showing you a memory*, her abuela would joke. *Who's to say time travel isn't real? We're doing it right here, right now.*

"Yup," Luz answered.

Luz's parents had other ideas about the past and the future, fears born of the very specific American capitalism. This work Ezz needed from Luz right now – the hacking, the scanning – was the kind of work her parents saw as safe. Learn to be good at something that exists in the future: learn the 1's and 0's, dot and cross the i's and t's. They were afraid not just of being dinosaurs, the kind who watched the fiery approach of the comet, but of being the kind of dinosaurs who died trapped in tar. They were stuck and wanted Luz unstuck. Luz just wanted to destroy the tar. As she sat down at one of the work benches and raised her hands to the machines to wake them, she could almost feel her mother's approval. *Okay, mommy*, she thought, *watch this.*

"Here we go," she said, turning to where Ezz and Ty had settled at the wide wooden island floating between the monitor bench and the door. The rough-hewn wood was scattered with wires and calipers, tools and comic books, things Luz had toyed with over the last hours, trying to find an angle for the puzzle in her mind. She pushed it all aside and placed a device on the tabletop.

She'd been introduced to this particular tool at Skyhorse, and when she asked Ezz to get her one for the lair, she had intended using it for her vine project. But it would come in handy now. It resembled a microscope but where one would have inserted a slide was instead a tiny C-clamp. Ezz leaned eagerly against the table.

"What's that for?" Ty said.

"Hush," said Ezz.

Luz held out her hand and Ezz reached across and poured the tiny red jewel of the nose stud into her palm from the vial. Cupping it gently, Luz then reached for a minuscule pair of forceps amid the jumble of tools and parts on the table. Gripping the jewel ever so gently, she placed it within the jaws of the C-clamp; with her free hand she turned its lever, tightening it until the scarlet stone was contained between the clamp's two edges. She withdrew the forceps and then turned the lever ever so slightly.

"Let's take a look," she said, and bent over the eyepiece. Something inside its mechanical heart whirred to life. She felt something whir inside her too – the knack of a hacker, Dr. Aldana had said of her at Skyhorse. Her parents had latched onto this: *See? You must do what you're good at. Make money. Have a life.* Only guilt kept Luz from asking, *What if I don't love what I'm good at?* She glanced down at the quetzal on her arm, imagining what it would be like to fly so free.

"What do you see?" Ezz interrupted.

"Shh," Luz said, and smiled at Ezz's good-natured grumbling. She peered through the scope, eyeing the jewel, magnified beyond recognition. But what she needed, she could see.

"There's a seam," Luz said a moment later. "I should be able to…"

She trailed off, reaching blindly for the forceps, patting around on the table until she found them. Still staring through the eyepiece, she tapped the forceps twice on the table. One end of them began to glow.

"Is the tip blue?" Luz said, not moving her eyes from the scope to check.

"Yup," said Ezz.

"Cool."

The forceps went back under the scope and this time there

was the tiniest stream of gray smoke. Luz waved it away from the scope and then made a sound of satisfaction.

"What is it?" Ezz said, leaning forward.

"Got it."

There was a gentle *clink*, the sound of the red jewel bouncing from the viewing plate to the table. Ezz jerked forward on the stool as if to grab it, but Luz waved her away.

"We don't need it anymore," she said, and lifted her head from the scope, raising the forceps – no longer glowing – alongside her face. "I have the important part."

"What is that?" Ezz said, squinting.

"A chip," Luz said triumphantly. "A tiny, tiny little baby chip. Never seen one this small – or this sophisticated. Leave it to Rosario Vicario to have it hidden in her nose ring."

She glanced at Ezz, who was gazing at the tiny chip. Her eyes were hard to look at – raw and afraid, but determined.

"It has to be something really important," the girl named Ty said. "She wouldn't have been so adamant I get it to you otherwise."

Luz nodded in agreement, studying the tiny bit of tech. She felt more of herself open, almost against her will. Getting involved in whatever this was wasn't included in the plans she had for Derby, but Ezz had done so much for her already. Doing this small thing for her felt necessary, like setting a bone.

"We're going to see what," Luz said.

"So you can open it?" said Ezz. She had yet to truly sit, instead standing rapt by the table, her hip bones pressed against it, butt hovering over the stool.

"I'm gonna try," Luz said, and turned back to her computer wall. She went to the launchpad, what looked like a plain metal scale. She placed the nearly microscopic chip on its surface and a blue outline appeared, a square inch around the edges of the chip. She turned back to Ezz and gave her what she hoped was a very frank look. "It's going to take awhile."

"Okay."

"No, it's going to take *awhile*, Ezz," she said, and gave her a long look.

"Oh," Ezz said. Then she understood. "*Oh*. You're kicking me out!"

"I mean…"

"How you gonna kick me out of my own batcave?" Ezz protested, laughing.

"I mean, you can stay, but you have to let me focus."

"So I can't ask you how it's going every five minutes."

"Definitely not."

"What about every six?"

"Ezz," Luz said, and it felt strange to laugh, but good. Like using the bone she had set. It made her want to text Mariela, to tell her not to worry, that they could be safe, as long as they kept laughing. Ezz grumbled but she returned a warm smile and settled on the stool next to Ty.

"What are all these comics?" Ty asked. "Are these yours?"

The question was directed at her, and the warmth of Ezz's smile had seeped into her, at least skin-deep, and so Luz answered.

"Yeah."

"You like Poison Ivy."

Luz found herself rolling up her sleeve, exposing the ink on her bicep to air. Her parents had rolled their eyes when she got the tattoo, but she didn't care. Every day that she got dressed and saw the fern-green skin and the blood-red hair, she felt powerful.

"How did I not know you had a tattoo?" Ezz cried, looking betrayed. "I have to bring a stranger into the batcave for you to start opening up?"

"If it was really the batcave, we would be enemies," Luz teased. "Poison Ivy tries to kill Batman like fifty times."

"Didn't she kiss him like fifty times too though?" Ty said, sounding skeptical.

"Ew, don't remind me," Luz said.

"I second that *ew*, honestly. It's fuck Bruce Wayne all day here," Ezz agreed. "All that money and all he did with it was build stuff to try to lock people up. What a loser."

Luz heard her laugh joining theirs, and all the guilt she'd been carrying from leaving her parents' house felt suddenly lighter, like two pairs of hands helping Atlas with his load. She remembered what Gina Aldana had told her at Skyhorse: *You deserve to be seen for all that you are.* She was talking about Luz making a name for herself as a coder, and shortly after that Luz stopped coming. And now she felt guilty again.

"Okay, let me get back to work," Luz said, waving them off, turning back to her desk.

"You still kicking me out?" Ezz said.

"Not if you're quiet."

"Maybe I'll organize all this junk in here," Ezz teased, gesturing at the table and its wandering armies of loose equipment.

"Don't touch my shit," Luz said without turning around.

"Maybe I'll…"

"Cállate!"

Ezz and Ty whisper-giggled, leafing through the comics. Luz felt her lungs expand hugely, comfortably, before they released. It felt a lot like being with her plants. Alone, and not alone. On the edge of something warm.

CHAPTER 16

EZZ

"So is it everything you imagined?" Ezz leveled her eyes at Ty when Luz seemed to have sunk down into her work. Ezz was determined not to bother her, and so she aimed her anxiety at her unexpected guest.

"Is what?" Ty said.

"I don't know. Whatever you thought you were getting into when you came here tonight."

"I don't think I imagined anything. I just knew I had to get this to you. Shavon said you were having a party but I didn't expect…" She trailed off.

"Expect what?"

"The Belles," Ty said with a laugh. "What the hell are they even doing in Louisville?"

"The lead singer, Nayla, she's from here," Ezz said with a shrug.

"I know, but whenever I sang at any of the clubs here and The Belles came up, they always said Nayla never came home."

"She does, she just doesn't generally perform while she's back. She likes to lay low and visit all her favorite spots and people. Be on vacation. But, wait, you used to sing?"

Ezz watched her gaze shoot downward, the way her eyes shuttered once more.

"I used to. When I was younger."

"Not anymore? Got tired of fame?" Ezz teased, trying to get closer to the truth.

"Just prefer real work."

"Art *is* real work," Ezz said. "Everybody thinks The Belles are rich, but Nayla makes about the same as a waitress."

"What? Really?"

"Why so surprised?" Ezz said. "If you used to be a singer then you know artists be starving, right?"

"Because...I don't know. There's always pictures of her online doing shows around the country. But I guess she does come *here* to hang out."

"So?"

"So there's nothing good in Louisville. What a waste."

Ezzardine felt her eyes narrow, scanning the girl on the stool, still dripping wet.

"That's a stupid thing to say."

"Don't call me stupid," Ty snapped, and Ezz felt her eyebrows rise.

"*Why so surprised?*" Ty mocked.

"I thought your haircut was the only thing with an edge," Ezz said. "But that's the work of Shavon, so I'm not surprised by that part, I guess."

Ezz looked away when Ty said nothing, turning her eyes back to Luz. *Don't bother her*, she thought. She had to clamp her mouth shut. The chip sitting so benignly on that scanner had been hidden in Rosario's nose stud. Had it been there during dinner at the Mahogany? Did it contain something stupid like her will, or maybe a letter explaining who Martha was, why Martha was allowed to know Rosario was back in Louisville and Ezz, her oldest friend, was not? But Ty said Rosario had said "them." "They" had come. Looking. For what? Ezz didn't know what was on the chip, but it couldn't be anything good. She glanced back at Ty as if to find more of the answer in her eyes, but Ty was only studying her, her eyes equally full of questions.

"Shavon says you're a patron," Ty said. "That you sponsor a bunch of people's work."

"Not a bunch," Ezz shrugged. "But some. A couple a year. Depending on what I win at the tables. Sometimes I have people stick around for awhile. Like Luz. She can stay here as long as she wants. Ellen Samudzi was here for a year."

"Interesting thing to do with your money," Ty said, and Ezz's ear caught the slant in her words. This girl had another dream for whatever money she was saving.

"It's lonely in that big ole house," Ezz said with a smirk. "Keeping it full of people keeps things from getting boring."

She wished she could have swallowed the words as soon as she spoke them. Sometimes the truth had a way of wiggling its way into jokes, and this one was too close to fact.

"How could the Pink be boring?" Ty said. "You have elephants on the lawn, for fuck's sake."

Ezz laughed at that, grateful for the convenient path away.

"The elephants are cool," Ezz said, nodding at the back of Luz's head. *Don't bother her.* "Luz did those. She has some kind of serum that makes plants grow fast. She treated some of the bushes with it and then…she made elephants."

"Yeah, Shavon told me about that," Ty said. "Do you like elephants?"

"I like animals in general."

"Including horses," Ty said, pointing upward, indicating the horses above the ground they currently sat under.

"Yeah. Horses."

"Do you ride?"

"No."

"Never?"

Ezz dodged away from the question. This truth was seated

deeper, even, than the matter of her loneliness. She used to ride, yes. Almost every day. The memory of Derbies with her parents were like mist around her; in it, her hair, still long as a child, clacking with horse-shaped barrettes. But the memory of sitting astride a horse – the solid strength beneath her, warm and rocking like the earth itself – came with other rememberances now. The warmth building hotter and hotter until it became fire. When she closed her eyes she could see a night sky turned orange, the flames like leaves of a colossal tree.

"I bet; I don't ride," Ezz said firmly.

"*Never?*"

"You sure you're not a reporter?" Ezz cried. "Damn!"

"Just curious," Ty said with a shrug.

"How long have you worked at the Mahogany?" Ezz said, desperate to change paths yet again. Now it was Ty's turn to shift, and Ezz noticed.

"Over a year."

"And now this," Ezz said, conscious of Rosario floating between them. "Do you think you'll keep working there?"

"I think so," Ty said, but Ezz could still see her dodging. "I just have to have it on my resume for awhile before I can get out of here."

"Here?"

"Louisville."

"Why do you hate Louisville so much?"

"I don't."

"You do," Ezz said firmly. "It's written all over you. You think it's shitty here."

Ty narrowed her eyes.

"Don't tell me what I think," she said.

"You already told me," Ezz shrugged. "A couple times. It's okay to not like where you're from, I guess, as long as you don't act like it's shitty for everybody and we're all too stupid to notice."

Ty didn't respond and Ezz turned her attention back to Luz – she couldn't help it. Bent over her computers, she was typing quickly, a constant clattering of muted sound. Ezz could see script appearing on one of the many illuminated screens. Boxes would appear, fill with text, then disappear before being replaced by others.

"Hacking," Ezz said softly, mostly to herself. "I was never a computer person."

"Really?" Ty said, sounding surprised. "I thought being a good gambler meant you were good with math and shit."

"Who told you I was a good gambler?" Ezz said, smiling at the floor. There was something about this girl that made her feel a little too seen. And also heard. Ty listened, sometimes hearing things Ezz hadn't even realized she said.

"Everyone," Ty laughed. "Your house."

"I inherited the house," Ezz corrected, and wondered if she still cringed outwardly when she said it, the way her whole inner self winced. Words meant things. "Inherited" meant someone died.

"Okay, everything else then. You're a benefactor, for fuck's sake. Who's a *benefactor*? At twenty-one? Is this Charles Dickens? Come on. Gambling money must be good. I heard you keep an earpod in and listen to music to get in the zone."

"I'm twenty-*two*," Ezz corrected, laughing more now. This girl was like a knife prying at an oyster. "And okay, yeah, I guess it's pretty good. Sometimes it feels like it's the only thing I'm good at."

She raised her eyes quickly from her shoes, settling them on Ty then, a vague shade of alarm sounding within her. Again she had said something truer than intended, the oyster knife sharp and somehow soft at the same time.

"My dad shits on cleanwork," Ty said. Ezz could tell she said it fast to save her. "He thinks it's ridiculous that I want to start my own business doing it. But I feel like that too. What else am I good at, besides this?"

"Lying to the cops," Ezz said quickly and – she couldn't help it – she warmed at the sound of the girl's laugh. Not reedy like some girls – richer, like a clarinet.

"I don't make a habit of it," Ty sniffed.

"Do you play cards?" Ezz said. She reached into the pocket of her baggy sweatpants and withdrew the pack that she had swiped from one of the tables in the ballroom. She had planned to eat pizza and play solitaire. Now her fingers felt itchy.

"You carry cards in your pocket?" Ty snorted. "Never know when you might need to play a game of poker at the Trolley stop?"

"She doesn't ride the Trolley," Luz said without turning around. "Ezz doesn't go anywhere she can't walk."

"*Excuse* me," Ezz said to the back of her head. "I thought you were *focusing*."

Luz ignored her.

"Anyway!" Ezz laughed. "Yes, you never know when you'll need a deck."

"I don't really play cards," Ty said.

"Spades?"

"Nope."

"White people," Ezz scoffed, and they both laughed. "Poker? Blackjack?"

"My mom showed me a game once. Texas Hold 'em, or something."

"Okay," Ezz said enthusiastically, grinning. "That's poker. We've got something to work with. Here…"

She motioned for Ty to come closer, and their stools bumped legs as they edged nearer to one another.

"You've got your hole cards," she explained, "and you get two of them. Every player does."

"No poker," Luz called from her computers, again without

turning around. "You get too loud when you start talking about poker. Can't you play something normal? Play Rummy."

"Rummy?" Ezz said, offended. "*Rummy?*"

"Rummy," Luz repeated in a low, soothing voice. "Niiice and quiet."

"Fine," Ezz said, collecting the cards again. She liked that Luz was relaxing, joking. It made her own shoulders slide down away from her ears. "The *nerd* says we have to play Rummy. Never in my damn life…"

She trailed off, glancing at Luz, whose cheekbones jutted out in a smile, even from behind.

"Okay. Rummy. We each get ten cards, right? And then…"

They played, Ezz amused by Ty's self-consciousness as she fumbled with the suits. She hadn't grown up on cards, that was evident, but in the way of immediate family, neither had Ezz. She had Shavon to thank for her introduction to Spades: Ezz had fallen in love with the riffle and the drama, had learned the rhythm of every game. She hadn't played anything but poker or blackjack in a long time – sitting and playing something as relaxed as Rummy made her breathe deep and slow down.

"Do you know any card tricks?" Ty asked after awhile.

"Man, nah," Ezz said, shaking her head.

"Lying," Luz said in her flat voice, staring at her screens, typing like lightning. Ezz stared at her back, jaw slack.

"Wait, really?" Ty said. "Do you?"

"Oh my god," Ezz groaned. "Luz, what the fuck? No self-respecting, mature gambler admits to doing card magic. It makes people think your wins aren't legit."

"Window Seat wasn't cards," Ty said.

"No, that was faith," Ezz said quickly.

"Faith in the right goddess," Ty answered.

Ezz stared at her, the utter twoness of her. In general, Ty's eyes were a pair of brick walls, the set of her jaw like barbed wire, keeping everything out, out, and everything in, in. But there was a hole in that fence with a light pouring, and it covered Ezz in its glow.

"Show me a trick," Ty said softly, and this time Ezz didn't say no; she just riffled the deck into the air, a floating arc that made Ty gasp.

"Watch this," Ezz told her, and she made cards vanish again and again, just to see Ty smile.

CHAPTER 17

LUZ

Luz stood watching them sleep, their heads cradled by their arms on the rough table, dreaming while surrounded by black cords. After midnight they'd turned one of the screens along the back wall to old movies, which had now lapsed into the news, the anchors and meteorologists shining and uniform. Luz had known this would happen, had heard the girls' laughter grow softer and softer, their conversations burning low into whisper. She'd let them sleep, setting her algorithm to run while she slipped into the room next door, working with her vines and serum, having her own whispered conversations with them. A beep of completion had drawn her back here, calling her to the screen where the data from Rosario's nose stud lay unraveled – a video file that, once pieced together, she opened and watched alone.

The cold in her heart had spread to her fingertips.

She considered not waking them at all. Telling Ezzardine she had corrupted the file. No one needed to see this, she thought, but she imagined it being buried, lost in secret and shadow, and the mere thought turned everything in her that was icy to flame. All she could think of was what the girl had said at Rosario's vigil: *They tried to bury us.* Mariela's face. This is what they'd meant.

She laid her hand on Ezz's shoulder, gently at first. Then a shake.

"Ezz," she said. "Wake up."

Ezz opened her eyes, and bless her heart, she smiled when she saw Ty sleeping next to her. Luz almost didn't tell her. She almost swallowed it all, added it to the list of things she would deal with on her own. But it was too big. She thought it might stick in her throat and choke her.

"I opened it," she said, and now they were both awake, smiles fading, the reminder of what they were all doing in this burrow settling back down over them like a veil.

"What is it?" Ezz said slowly. "Do I want to know?"

Luz didn't know what she was envisioning, what worst thing Ezz could conjure. Luz's own imagination was tainted now. She opened her mouth, then closed it, then gestured at her computer wall.

"You should see for yourself."

Ezz stood carefully, as if testing her legs for broken bones. She was preparing herself, thinking it was about Rosario. And Luz let her, because it was, even if not in the way that Ezz thought. Ty's body was tensed, and she didn't move from her stool. She allowed Ezz to approach the monitors alone, and Luz admired this restraint, the willingness to take a backseat. Soon she would wish she had never put on the blindfold to come here.

At her desk, Luz dragged the video file to a larger screen. Then she pressed play.

Darkness, moving and shifting. Shadows falling through a pale window, light from outside. Three bars on the window, cylinders throwing their shapes on the ground. The camera shifts, turns away from the window. A close, square room. Wooden walls. A bare dirt floor. The camera shudders, shifts again, and now there is a door. Wide-spaced bars in a cut-out square with another kind of light, dimmer, spilling in from beyond. The camera moves closer, swinging slightly, and finds its way through the bars. Looks right. A barn. White-painted stalls and bales of hay piled along a nearby tack room.

The camera swings to the left.

A white horse, looking back in the darkness. It peers at the camera and shivers its head, sending its mane flopping. The camera shivers then too, vibrating the picture into obscurity. And then it stops, the camera and the horse peering at each other.

"Is this...," Ezz whispered.

"A recording from a metalbred's eye," Luz confirmed.

"How the hell..."

"Keep watching."

The camera is still for a moment, the two metalbreds looking at each other. Then, behind the white horse, a sudden motion that turns its head, the eye of the camera following. Someone entering the barn, at first obscured in shadow and then emerging into the pale light as a girl, long black hair in a ponytail. She carries a toolbox, moves over to a workbench, her back to the door. The camera jiggles, the metalbred whinnying perhaps. There is no audio.

Then someone else enters the barn.

He moves quickly, like an owl swinging down from the sky. He's at the workbench in a single breath, grabbing the girl by her shoulders, wheeling her around to look at him. Their faces aren't visible. She shoves him, he grabs her again. He's whispering – he leans close, grabbing her again, pulling her in to hear him. She tears away. He snatches for her.

She runs.

She goes for the door they'd both entered through, but he grabs her hair, swings her around. She breaks away, runs toward the metalbreds, falling once then scrabbling up. Perhaps there is another door past the stalls, something the camera doesn't see. She tries so hard to escape. But he is upon her again, now mere feet from the metalbreds. The white horse watches with ears pricked forward, silent, as the man wrestles the girl to the floor. Her arms flail and one hand catches him across the cheek. He punches her, then. She weakens. Scrabbles backward in the sawdust and hay, him towering after her doggedly. They come into the light.

He's a white man wearing suit pants, a button-down shirt; she a denim shirt and shorts. She is young, maybe seventeen, copper skin. He is twice her age, older, nearly forty, but with a hairless face contorted with anger. His mouth is moving fast, speaking to her. His jaws don't strain – it's dark and he speaks softly, even now, as his hands wrap around first her wrists, and then her throat. His knee moves onto her chest. She seems to sag deeper into the floor, legs scraping sawdust, an aura of particles in the air around them.

"Oh my god," Ezz whispered.

The tears had been working their way up from somewhere deep inside Luz, and now they made their way into the soft yellow light of the lair.

The man stands a moment later. The girl has become only a shadow on the floor, his body blocking the light. He stares for a long moment somewhere alongside the camera, into the face of the metalbred, and his own face is as plain and pale as the moonlight that doesn't quite make it into the corners of the barn. He looks down at the girl, who is now just a body, and then crouches, removing something from his pocket. A bottle of spray, a white cloth. He sprays her arms, her throat, even her bare legs. He wipes her skin quickly but thoroughly, and when he stands again he's already turning for the door. He doesn't look back, he doesn't pause. The moonlight swallows him and he's gone.

Luz tapped the video shut, staring at the floor. She felt cold, and yesterday she might have kept her mouth shut and let the words freeze inside her, but something about spending the night underground with Ezz and Ty spurred her tongue into motion.

"I was there," she said thickly. "I think."

Ezz snapped her head in Luz's direction.

"What? When?"

"When this happened," Luz said. "I think I was there. The other morning when I came into the Pink early? Remember I told you I was at the backside? I saw a white man go into the barn in the dark. He came out and...and washed his hands. I think...I think it was him."

"Oh my god," Ezz whispered. She paused, running her palm down over her face. "Luz. Fuck. Did he see you?"

Luz shook her head. She closed her eyes, remembering. She had melted into shadow, something about the man's presence transforming her into a rabbit, belly low to the clover. He had not seen her, and she had been so worried about protecting herself that it hadn't occurred to her that someone was inside that barn who had not found protection. She kept her eyes closed, squeezing out the world.

"This is bad," Ezz whispered. "Really bad. Do you think he knows someone has video?"

Ty made a sound that opened Luz's eyes, and when she looked over at Ty she nearly gasped. The look on the white girl's face was like peeking through the bars at the zoo and finding the tiger's mouth full of blood. Her eyes were fixed on the screen.

"I'm sure there's not much he doesn't know," Ty finally said. "He's *him*."

Luz's heart found a sudden, unusual rhythm.

"Wait," she said. "You...you know who that is? This man?"

Ezz looked at her, eyebrows high in surprise. "*You* don't know him?"

"Who is he?" Luz said. Something in her stomach was coiling like vines.

She glanced between Ty and Ezz, both of them wearing the same grave expression now that Ty's snarl had cloaked itself. Ty's eyes had averted to the back wall of screens, where the news had glittered on. Then her gaze seemed to focus, and she lifted her hand to point.

"Him," Ty said.

Luz followed her finger. It was local news, a repeat from

sometime in the last few days. A reporter holding a microphone stood at Cavehill Downs beside a bronze statue of a Thoroughbred, a man in a neat silver suit on the other side of the horse, one hand resting gently on the arching neck. The mic was angled toward his mouth. The screen was on mute. But so had been the video from the metalbred's eye, silent and dark and revealing this same face. Here in the daylight his lips spread into a wide smile, teeth bright and even, eyes lit up with charisma. His hands, no longer wrapped around a young Brown girl's throat, gestured airily in the sunshine, empty.

Ezz turned up the volume just in time for them to catch the tail end of his interview:

"I know a little of this and a little of that," he said, flashing his grin. "Now my sister, Annie, she's the brains of the operation. I just do what big sis tells me to do. You can ask her the hard questions! That's how family business is, right?"

"Brother and sister?" Ty breathed. "I didn't fucking know that."

He joked and teased and the interviewer laughed and laughed. The block of text at the bottom of the screen told Luz who he was.

"*Brian Benedict*," she said softly. "*Chairman at Limestone Corporation*. Oh my god."

"Jesus Christ," Ezz whispered, her palms pressed against her eyes. "How did Rosario get this? Metalbreds aren't supposed to store data."

"Who was that girl?" Ty whispered.

"She's Latina," Luz said. She felt like she was standing in a field with bullets raining down around her, all of them striking nearby but none of them hitting her. Yet. "My cousin told me something happened at the racetrack. That a girl had been killed. This…this had to be what they're talking about."

"That sick son of a bitch," Ezz said, glaring at the television.

"I always knew he was a snake…you can just tell. Look at him."

Ty muttered something, but swallowed it. They all stared silently, their three heartbeats seeming to fill the room. Luz's head felt noisy. Brian Benedict chatted in his interview on the glowing screen, waving at the Downs behind him, empty for the moment but which very soon would begin to swarm for the early races in the days leading up to Derby.

"What I don't understand is how the equinibot was recording at all," Ezz said again. She sat on a stool now, eyes still wide. "Limestone models only get set to record on the racetrack in case there's a photo finish. They use the footage and then they wipe that along with everything else. But this metalbred was actively recording."

When no one said anything, she lowered her head and sighed.

"How did Rosario get this?" Ezz repeated, low.

"I had to hack the chip to get to the video file," Luz said. She sat down so her knees would stop shaking. "Maybe that's why Rosario had it. She was a hacker."

"You couldn't keep that girl out of anything," Ezz said, her voice sounding strained. "She would always find a way in."

"Do you think someone hired her to do it?" Luz said. "And maybe…Benedict found out?"

"That night I was at the Mahogany," Ezz said, going rigid. "Someone sent her a letter and we had to leave dinner early. She wouldn't tell me why. She told me everything was fine, but she was freaked out. Dropped me off at the Pink and then went off on her own in her car. That was…that was the last time I saw her. What if the letter was from Benedict? Like a threat?"

"I saw her the next morning," Ty said. "Out behind the Mahogany. She was acting strange, kind of sneaking around. That's what I told the detective. In hindsight, maybe she was scared. Watching her back. Fuck."

Luz watched Ezz squint at Ty. She knew what was coming.

"I thought you said you lied to the cops," Ezz said.

"I did. I told him she didn't say anything that night in her suite. I didn't tell him that she gave me her nose stud."

"But you told him you saw her that morning," Ezz insisted.

"Yeah, but I don't see why that matters. She was walking out to her car. In the alley."

"You told him she was sneaking around!" Ezz snapped. "That makes it seem like she was doing something she shouldn't have been doing!"

"I didn't tell *him* that!" Ty protested. "I only said that just now, not to him!"

Ezz glowered, a fog rolling in over her eyes. Luz took a deep breath, already looking ahead and seeing where this trail would lead them. She had learned that no one could think about death without also thinking about fault.

"They were after her," Ezz growled. "That's what she meant. *They came.* Limestone must have somehow known Rosario had this and sent someone to…to…"

"Kill her," Luz whispered. "Just like the girl on the video."

"You'd think they'd send a hitman or something! Jesus Christ," Ezz said softly. "Not, like…the dude himself."

"He enjoys it," Ty said flatly, staring emptily at the screen where *Chairman at Limestone Corporation* remained onscreen while Benedict chatted. Ezz looked at her, then away, and then quickly back again, and Luz watched the look in her eyes go from stone to steel.

"You," she said. Then again, slowly: "You."

"Me what?"

"How did you get this video?" Ezz said.

"What? I told you. I was there. Rosario gave it to me…"

"You were there," Ezz snapped. "Were you *there*? When he was there? When she got killed?"

"No! I came in sometime after they left, I guess. She was alone. I…"

Luz had been listening, studying Ty, when it all clicked in her head. Limestone. This was the company that entered the horseracing scene and pulled away the ladder that her parents had been trying to climb. The reason they wouldn't let their daughter anywhere near the track. Limestone swept in and cut all the Guatemalans and Mexicans and El Salvadorians off at the knees, funneling in their white tech boys from the West Coast. Limestone, whose chairman choked the life from a brown-skinned teenage girl. And now this girl Luz didn't know – Ty, who came bearing evidence of this murder – had a father who worked for Limestone.

"Your dad," Luz said, her voice rising, her anger like helium filling a righteous red balloon. "Is he part of this? Are you?"

"My *dad*?" Ty cried, angry.

"Oh shit," Ezz said, turning on her, eyes wide once more. "You said your dad works for Limestone. Does *he* know Benedict?"

Luz watched Ty's face carefully, for how it might fold or unfold, run or rear up. To her credit, it did nothing: it settled into stoniness. In her eyes swarmed a nest of hornets, but none of them left her mouth.

"I don't know anyone at Limestone," Ty said slowly. "I barely know my dad. I know we're all scared right now, but I had nothing to do with Rosario's death."

If it were Luz's house, she would kick her out. But it wasn't. She turned her gaze to Ezz, watching her taking stock, assessing the game. Ezz was a gambler – she knew about risk. Luz knew what she had decided before she even spoke.

"I think it's time for you to go," Ezz said.

"Ezz…," Ty started.

"Luz. Blindfold."

Luz withdrew the fabric from her kit again, and took a few steps toward Ty before stopping with it extended in her hand. Luz didn't want to get too close, didn't want to touch her. Everything felt sticky, as if the whole city was immersed in a substance that was being tracked from one place to another. Luz offered the blindfold, and for a moment felt sad, watching Ty's face. The girl seemed to have risen out of something in the past few hours, and now sank back down. They all had; they all did. Eventually Ty took the scarf from Luz's hand and tied it over her eyes herself.

Ezz walked Ty up to the surface, back to the elephants and the air. Luz didn't follow. She went to her green room, where her device was sitting like a stone, powered off. She powered it on and watched the missed calls from her mother fill the screen. She pressed it to her ear.

When she heard her mother's voice, she almost cried.

"Hola, mami," she said quietly.

"Luz."

The distance between them stretched, condensed, then stretched again. Neither said a word for a long time.

"What happened at the track?" Luz heard herself say. "The girl."

In the background, she heard her mother sliding her closet door open, pulling out her boots, the pair she would have repaired year after year. She was getting ready for work. 4 am.

"We don't know," her mother said eventually. "A girl is dead."

"Who?"

"It doesn't matter who. Your father and I are making plans, Luz. We are leaving this city. This state. Do you understand? And you are coming with us."

Luz's heart leapt into another strange rhythm, so fierce the room seemed to rock with it. Leaving Louisville. Kentucky. The only home she'd ever known, that which her parents had left their volcanic Chimaltenango for. Would they go back, or somewhere else? She imagined anywhere beyond what she knew as home as a desert.

"I'm not a child," Luz heard herself say. Her voice was a shaking tree with too many roots.

"No, but you are *my* child," her mother said. "Yatin wajo'."

She hung up before Luz could whisper, "I love you too."

She sat down at the table, making space among the leaves until she could spread out all her comics, Poison Ivy's face staring out at the room swarming with green. Luz slowly realized she was building a bridge in her mind. Rosario had never been just Ezz's loss – Rosario wasn't a backside girl, but the backside claimed her. Now another girl was dead. This was a garden of loss, Ezz and Luz's personal pains growing from the same rotting fertilizer. As Luz sat running her hands along her vines, occasionally turning comic pages, all she could think about was helping the garden grow legs, helping it grow fists, helping it strike back.

Maybe it would be enough to make her mother stay.

CHAPTER 18

TY

"Need a knife?"

The server at Wagner's paused by the booth where Ty sat alone hacking at a massive waffle with her fork. The knife was already extended, a look of sympathy in the server's eyebrows. Ty took the knife, muttered her thanks, and kept her eyes down.

She didn't want to go home.

It was too late anyway. By the time she caught the Trolley and got back to her house, she'd have to turn right around and come back to clock in at the Mahogany. So close to Derby. The thought led her mind to Limestone and she wheeled away internally, focusing again on the waffle at hand. She trailed the knife down the grooves the iron left behind – the grid was comforting, somehow. Orderly. She cut one cube at a time, chewing each one individually, slowly. But the sight of the knife in her hand wouldn't let her rest. Is this how she would do it? She had been planning this for over a year – what she would do when the man who killed her mother checked into the Mahogany. She knew how she would get into his room. She knew what she would say. But what would she *do*? Knowing what he could do? What he had done.

At the door, the bell's tongue laughed, admitting a group of three women, dressed for a party. Dressed *from* a party, Ty corrected, eyeing them – the smudged makeup, tired eyes, wobbly ankles. One girl had given it up and carried her shoes in her hand. Her toenails were painted bright white, like Ty's currently, and Ty was looking at them, noticing this, when the girl caught her eye, smiling. The lights at Wagner's always seemed as old as the place itself – bald white, never flattering. But this place had been here since 1922, and this was where the racetrackers came. Ty hadn't even meant to come when Ezz kicked her out – her feet had led her here, a place her mother had taken her so many times, eating biscuits and gravy while chatting with everyone who stepped foot in the door wearing shoes dusty from the track. Ty remembered studying her mother while she talked, the light showing every wrinkle, every scar. Ty liked it. The light showed a harsher version of the truth. After you left you could relax, knowing nothing was quite as bad as it had looked inside. It made her think of the police in Rosario Vicario's guest suite – the lights like this, in every corner. But leaving had not made it better. Things had only gotten worse. The girl with the white toenails kept looking, but Ty avoided her eyes.

Ty cut another cube of waffle, searching the walls of the diner for a clock. At some point since the New Derby was instated, Wagner's turned 24/7. It was now 3:21am. She would finish here and go straight to the Mahogany. Madame Richmond wasn't usually in the kitchen until 5, so Ty would let herself into an empty suite, clean herself up, put the room back in order, and then be downstairs before anyone noticed. Hopefully Camille wasn't lurking around…

"Hey, aren't you Ty? Redson? Marianne's daughter?"

Hovering at the edge of the table was the girl with the white toenails. Ty blinked up at her, at the airbrushed makeup, the red mouth. She didn't know her.

"Yes," Ty said, and that was all. When the girl was at the door

Ty had thought she was flirting, and while uninterested, Ty would have preferred flirting to this. Her vanished mother's name in the mouth of a stranger.

"I'm Irma," the girl said, moving a half step closer. "I work at the museum in Cavehill Downs. I…ran into your mom a lot when she was….you know. There."

"The Derby Museum?" Ty said. "So, what, you used to call the cops on my mom?"

"Yeah, sometimes," the girl laughed, showing beautiful teeth except one crooked incisor. Then Irma seemed to realize what she had said. Her lips froze, her eyes landing on Ty's and staying there.

"Missing context made that sound really shitty," she said. "I'm sorry. I was actually on good terms with your mom. I respected what she did – once she and Luis Funes partnered up, things really started changing. They knew it was my job to call the cops – I always waited with them until they came. They didn't really see the protest as a success unless the cops came."

Ty stared down at the remaining squares of waffle waiting to be cut. It didn't matter if they were neat and orderly, she realized. They were all going to get chewed into nothing eventually.

"Nothing is the same without them," Irma went on. "I think about something your mom said to me once when I was waiting with her: *a good movement is never just about about one person.* And that taught me a lot, you know? She used to be all about the horses. But then she gradually realized that alongside the horses were people, and that she needed to advocate for them too. She learned that from Luis, I guess, and his wife, Prudencia. I was always glad that Prudencia passed before…everything that happened. The rumors would have broken her heart, you know…"

Ty put down her fork and stood up. Irma blinked, flustered.

"Verga, I'm sorry," Irma said. "I'm sorry. I'm just talking and my mouth gets ahead of my brain. Nobody believed the rumors, okay? Let me just say that. I know that...," she coughed, "*certain people* wanted everyone to believe the whole affair thing, but nobody did. I mean, come on. Did you ever find out what happened? Was it a robbery or something?"

Yes, I did, Ty thought.

"No," Ty said. She scanned her device on the table's payment port. The server got the payment at her station, looked up, and nodded her thanks. Ty moved to leave.

"Hey, wait," Irma said. "Look. I'm sorry. I really am not usually this idiotic. I've been out all night for a work event and I don't even like my coworkers." She nodded toward the table where her group was sitting. They didn't look up. "I just saw your face and...and you look so much like her."

Ty grimaced as if Irma hadn't spoken but spit. She could hear the kindness in her words but couldn't wring the pain out of them – the video she had seen in Ezzardine Clayton's lair tonight ripped every stitch out of her deepest wound. That face. Brian Benedict, snarling over the face of a dead teenage girl.

Two years ago, she had seen Brian Benedict standing over the body of her mother, pieces of her skull joining with Luis Funes's. Ty had watched Brian Benedict wipe the gun and place it just so in Luis's palm. Had watched him spray the arms that had once belonged to her mother with fluid from a bottle he withdrew then slipped back into his pocket. She had watched Brian Benedict disappear.

"It was an honor to know your mom," Irma was saying. Ty hadn't heard what led them here. "I just wanted you to know how sorry I am and, you know, if you ever need anything...you know where I work."

Ty swallowed, feeling a scream scratching somewhere in her throat. Now was not the time, not when she had so much to do before Derby. She had to smile. Normalcy.

"They're keeping you busy around Derby, huh?" Ty said.

"They've got us going out every fucking night," Irma said, shaking her head. "My feet are killing me."

"Cute shoes though," Ty said, nodding at them dangling from her hand. Irma laughed.

"Yeah, just not on human feet. Excellent for mannequin feet though."

They both laughed, followed by the inevitably awkward pause when the land ahead has not yet been pioneered.

"Well, I've got to get to work," Ty said at the same time that Irma held up her device.

"Take my number," Irma said, quirking one side of her mouth almost apologetically. "I know we don't know each other, but…if you want to talk, like, for real…about anything. I don't mind."

Ty took her number at the same time that one of Irma's coworkers started to stare in their direction.

"Good luck with them," Ty said, waving her hand at them. The woman staring had her lips pursed. A boss. A boss who thought she was a parent, an owner. The worst kind.

"Bye," Irma smiled, and tip-toed barefoot through the restaurant back to the table. She waved once more when Ty reached the door of Wagner's, and then their evenings split apart, sending Ty out into the night, where the street sweepers were beginning their rounds before rush hour. She had many blocks to walk and she didn't have earpods to drown out the thoughts that filled her head. All she could picture was Brian Benedict's face, grinning from every streetlight.

The Mahogany was silent when she approached the staff door. She made herself go right in, scanning her fob quickly without pausing to linger, thinking about the last time she had entered these doors, watching Rosario move through the garden to her car alone. What if Brian Benedict had been driving it? What if, what if, what if?

"Stop," she whispered to herself, going to her locker.

The locker swung open and she stared at its contents. Her kit, which she had left here after going straight from work to meet Shavon. She'd been reluctant about leaving it, even behind the security of a lock, but all was well. From the hanger, like Peter Pan's unstitched shadow, hung her black cleanwork uniform. Time to re-shadow, re-cloak.

She took the stairs so the hum of the elevator wouldn't draw any attention, up to the third floor, where all the suites were thankfully shut, guests either sleeping or still partying. Ty stopped at the cleanwork closet, unlocked it, and slipped shampoo and bodywash from the guest stores, using a towel as a pouch. Clutching it with her uniform, she walked to the end of the hall to 8, which she knew to be empty, conscious that it was the room beneath Rosario Vicario's. Would it always be Rosario Vicario's? The room with a stain, even when the carpet was spotless again? She threw the static robe from her kit around her body, raised the hood over her bald head to trap any fibers, and entered Suite 8.

She stopped there and leaned her back against the door for a moment. It was empty now, but in a matter of days Brian Benedict would be checking in. Ty squinted through the dark at the outline of the bed, imagined him snoring softly while she stood over him, revenge in the form of a silver point. A hammer. She could feel herself sinking into the fantasy.

"Later," she whispered, and crept around the perimeter of the room, determined not to leave tracks of any kind on Hilda's carpet. She went straight for the bathroom, leaving the lights off, and started the water – cold, so that the mirror wouldn't fog.

"This is going to suck," she whispered, unwrapping the tiny organic soap, mentally preparing for the ice bath. She took several deep breaths, hopping from foot to foot, and then stepped in.

At home she would have cursed long and loud, but at home she wouldn't have any room to step away from the water stream in the tiny cell shower. At the Mahogany, however, the glass walk-in was large enough for three people; she could dodge out of the many cold jets, lathering with the basil-infused soap, then dodge back in to rinse. She washed her hair quickly – not much to wash: a quick scalp rub – and then her body. No exfoliating, which would mean more skin cells left behind to retrieve. Quick rinse. Tone. Water off.

She stepped out, sighing in relief. She wrapped herself in the towel, so white it seemed to glow in the dim bathroom, and sighed at that too. No strings at the edges, no patches where the material thinned. An absorbent fur that covered her from her shaved head to her painted toes. She stared at the toes, thinking of Irma at Wagner's. Maybe Ty would text her. She didn't know what they would talk about aside from comparing the size and scope of their Marianne memories. Maybe that was enough.

Once dry, she dressed quickly, cursing that she hadn't grabbed the micropress. Yesterday's dirty clothes on today's clean body felt like a specific kind of blasphemy. She swept the static robe over the top of it all. It would catch whatever was loose, she decided, and turned to her kit to return the bathroom to its previous state of unusedness.

She was buffing the last of the shower walls when a slash of lamplight from the suite stained the dark floor of the bathroom.

"Here we are," came Madame Richmond's soft voice. "Here is your key. If you need anything at all don't hesitate to ask me or my staff. We're here to make you comfortable."

Shit. Ty snatched up her kit, buckling it silently around her waist and taking one long step to hide behind the door. She didn't dare look through the crack, imagining Richmond's sharp gaze sweeping every detail, looking for fuzz, shadow, flaw. Ty stayed against the wall and tried not to breathe, wondering who the hell was checking in in the middle of the night. Benedict, her heart screamed. A few days early. She was fucked. So was the plan.

"Thank you, Madame," a man said. There was the slide of his shoes against the clean, clean carpet, the light *thunk* of his luggage finding a place to rest. Ty could feel him surveying the room. "Just beautiful. This is what the races in New York don't have. Everything is too stylized. Nothing hometown about it. Nothing that feels like the history."

Ty held her breath, listening hard. It didn't sound like Benedict. New York?

"We're proud to make history part of the Mahogany's appeal," Madame Richmond said. Ty could hear the beam of her smile. "All of the wood paneling you see is original. The artwork is unchanged since the house was built in 1899."

"Beautiful, just beautiful."

"I have to say, Mr. Darden," Richmond went on. "I'm always pleased to hear that Kentucky leaves an impression when it comes to the races. Especially for someone by way of Saratoga Springs, like yourself."

Definitely not Benedict. Ty would have relaxed, but the man laughed, a boom that filled the room. He had moved closer.

"All these years," he said, "and New York and Kentucky still have that rivalry, huh? It outlasted the horses themselves."

"I wouldn't call it a rivalry," Madame Richmond purred. "Just good business."

"Which is why I'm here," he said. He had moved to the window.

"Oh?" Richmond said expectantly. Ty rolled her eyes at the wheedling. Still, the woman was good at it.

"It's hardly a secret that Kentucky racing has made its way to the top with the help of Limestone," he said. "No one to blame except the CEO's parents, really. Why couldn't Annie Claybelle have been born in New York, damn her?" He laughed a less convincing laugh. "But really. With the factories in Kentucky and two major racetracks in Kentucky, well…the money just floods in. And we'd be fools not to look for a way in too. So when Ms. Claybelle's people at Limestone called and asked me to come down for a meeting, well…! How could I refuse?"

There was the rustle of Madame Richmond shifting, leaning against the doorway perhaps.

"How nice! A partnership?"

"Perhaps," he said. He moved toward the bathroom and every inch of Ty's body turned to cold, still porcelain, trying to blend with the spotless walls. His hand entered the doorway, flipped on the light. If the mirror over the sink were four inches to the right he would be staring directly at Ty's reflection. Any moment now he would step through and scare her out like a rabbit from the brush, sending her off into the forest of unemployment. Maybe jail. Instead he flicked the light back off and returned to the suite.

"I'm not the dealmaker," he said, yawning. "So calling me was an interesting choice. I'm the ground-layer. I get the call when there is ground that needs to be smoothed before the deal is even discussed. But it means Ms. Claybelle might see a deal on the horizon so…hell, I'll smooth whatever she wants! As long as those metalbreds keep running – and maybe a shiny new factory for 'em in the north eventually – we can all stay rich and friendly."

He yawned again, louder and longer.

"You should get some rest, Mr. Darden," Madame Richmond said. Ty could hear her backing out the door. "I'm serving breakfast in a few hours, so once you've caught a little sleep after such an early train you can come down and eat something."

"Kind of you," he said, and there was the squish of him sitting down on the bed, not even waiting for her to leave. Ty's muscles twitched. As soon as that door closed, the rabbit would be trapped.

"Sleep well," Madame Richmond trilled, and the door whispered shut. A moment later the light went off. Ty trembled, every breath like a foghorn in her ears.

The bed creaked as Mr. Darden rose, and Ty knew he would be coming to the bathroom to unpack, to piss, to brush his teeth, something. She heard the slide of fabric. He must be getting undressed, she thought. Now he would be naked when he found her, which would make everything worse. For both of them.

Instead she heard the distant click of a device unlocking as he slid his finger across its surface, and a moment later he began to speak.

"I made it down. Yes. Just checked in at the inn. Not sure where they'll call the meeting – could be at the Downs or Limestone. Hell of a time to have a meeting like this, the bastards. Right before Derby. The city's crawling. Nope, no problem. The Limestone people are just so busy with all this shit going on. Uh-huh. Do some snooping if I can. Hard with this much security. It's different down here – they did a police funding separation back in '23. The street boys are still in pocket, but the investigators are a little harder to persuade. They've got one giving them a hard time right now apparently. Huh? No, am I complaining? If they didn't need a fixer I wouldn't have a job!"

He chuckled then paused for awhile, listening. Then the boom of his laugh.

"Well, you know me. I can fit in just about anywhere. Plus these Kentucky people aren't hicks like people used to say. Maybe they never were. Uh-huh. I'm meeting with Benedict at 10 am. He's who Claybelle mentioned. I'll let you know how it goes. If I do well with him, maybe he'll let me at Annie to talk about deals. For now, I need to sleep."

He muttered a few more words, and then Ty heard the click of the device being placed on the nightstand. The creak of the bed again as he hefted himself up, then the sound of the light switch that sent everything into darkness. It blanketed the room in a buzzy silence. Ty imagined her breathing rattling through the chamber to his ears, drawing him out to find the source of the racket. But all she truly heard was his own breath, deep sighs at first as he settled himself. Then deeper, longer. Ten minutes – an eternity – later, the rumble of a snore. Her father was like this – three minutes after a screaming match he would be strolling peacefully through dreamland while her mother paced the kitchen for hours, flaming. Ty peeked into the suite.

All was dark. The shades were drawn, sealing the room into near darkness. The crack of light from the hallway was the beacon her feet followed, only daring to move during each long snore. She crept through the dark wearing the static robe like an invisibility cloak, and when she reached the door she was almost shocked to see the light illuminate her feet. She reached for the knob.

"Who's there…" His voice cracked through the still air like a whip, and her lungs seemed to collapse. She froze, looking over her shoulder where Darden sat up in bed, the pale of his skin catching the minimal light and rendering him ghostly. He was propped up on one elbow.

Ty didn't move a muscle. Her black uniform and the gray robe would help, but surely he was looking right at her, and soon her face would swim through the shadows to become a lightbulb in the dark.

"Six thousand on Gemini Dragonfly," he muttered. "Seven thousand. Cash. Cash, you fucking bitch."

She didn't dare breathe. She couldn't make out his eyes in the dark, only the general shape of his features, all of them seeming smeared with sleep and dark. She pretended to be a piece of furniture, imagined herself as still, bloodless wood.

He collapsed back onto his pillow, snores rumbling into the air before he was fully still. She breathed as if through a straw, and after ten more snores, reached again for the door, her fingers trembling.

She opened it only a crack and inched one arm out, then one leg. She took a deep breath. When he snored again, she slipped the rest of her body through and then closed it the way a spirit might – soft and silvery, a plume of smoke. Safe on the other side, her hand rested on the doorknob, shaking.

"Well done," said a voice behind her, and Ty might have screamed if she hadn't still been held in the cloud of silence that carried her through to escape. She leapt away from the door, spinning around, and found Camille Richmond standing in the open door of the cleanwork closet, watching her carefully.

"Camille, what the fuck are you doing!" Ty hissed.

Camille tilted her head, widening her eyes for effect, and then used both hands to make a little gesture of presentation, indicating Ty as the true recipient of such a question.

"I…got stuck," Ty said, feeling stupid.

"Were you stealing from him?" Camille said flatly.

"What? No!"

"What then?"

Ty squeezed her eyes shut, rubbing her temples. She realized she was still wearing the static robe hood and lowered it slowly. She would rather have been caught in the suite than this, she thought. Fired for using the facilities and not because the boss's daughter tattled about a fictional theft.

"I needed to take a shower," Ty admitted. "I didn't go home last night. So I used the only empty suite and then…that dude checked in early."

"*That dude* helps run the second-largest racetrack in the country," Camille said.

"I gathered, okay? Saratoga Springs. I didn't do it on purpose. I thought the room was empty. It was when I went in. Who the hell checks in before dawn? And isn't –" She stopped before her question could find light: *what about Benedict's reservation?*

"…the dude who helps run the second-largest racetrack in the country checks in before dawn," Camille repeated. "You think Madame was passing that up? She'd wake up early for $10."

"That was the last room," Ty said, trying to find a way to ask about Benedict without saying his name. "Is he staying through Derby?"

"Yes," Camille said.

Ty had to maintain her mask. Something inside her was slipping.

"Whoever was originally in Suite 12 canceled," Camille went on.

Ty knew who was supposed to be in Suite 12.

"So, are you going to snitch?" Ty said, refusing to let everything fall apart. Not here.

"About what?" Camille said.

"I don't know, about me being in there. You thought I was stealing."

"I *hoped* you were stealing," Camille said, sniffing. She closed the supply closet door. "I saw him when he checked in and he had like a thousand in cash in his wallet. I was going to tell you you could buy me lunch."

Ty stared at her, incredulous. The absurdity of it clashed with the fear that had sunk its fangs into her skin at the sound of Benedict's name, spoken in the dark by Mr. Darden. Camille didn't give her any time to ruminate.

"Anyway, maybe next time," Camille said. She went to the staircase and began to make her way down. "I'm glad you weren't in there to kill him or something. The Mahogany has had enough murder."

Ty nodded. But inside she thought, *Not quite.*

CHAPTER 19

TY

Ty crouched on her hands and knees, massaging a special oil into a section of the rich wood siding of the Mahogany's stairwell. Every section she polished came out looking like a freshly groomed horse trotting in sunlight. She hated that everything always came back to horses.

Ty had once been a horse girl – the girls with horses on their T-shirts and a net full of plush stallions at home. Maybe they owned a real one if they were rich, maybe they dreamed about them if they weren't. Young Ty would look over the pasture fence at Joelle's horses next door and could name every marking, every shade. Bay, chestnut, blaze, bald-faced…she memorized it all, she breathed horses, pined quietly for them. Her mother loved horses in a different way – out loud and carrying signs. She marched outside Cavehill Downs and eventually Limestone headquarters. She interviewed backside workers and typed up what she learned, emailing pages to the local news. And when she rode on the weekends she would take Ty with her, and for a long time this was the feeling horses filled her daughter with: fullness, sun-gold Saturdays astride a trail horse, rocking through the woods behind her mother.

And then it was all gone. Now when Ty thought of horses, there was only a void, a feeling of being stretched to the point of snapping. She polished harder, willing the wood before her to be wood only, trying not to hear the sound of the parade beginning on the street outside. She watched the walls begin to glow, and she focused on murder. This was how she liked it.

"Parade started early," someone called from the front of the house. It echoed from room to empty room. Ty closed her eyes and sighed. Eight days until Derby, and her plan had been pulled out from beneath her.

"Which is it today?" Ty called back.

"Everyone's in pink. Must be Breast Cancer Day. I remember when you only wore pink on Oaks Day."

Pink. Ty couldn't help but think of Ezzardine, her lavish home filled with even more lavish people, the way the music had hit the walls and dripped down like rose syrup. She could almost feel herself still standing in the room, Ezz's silhouette on stage like a patch cut out of space that Ty wanted to fall into. She *had* fallen in – at least halfway. Until she'd been spat back out at the end of the night, back into the life that felt loose around her after the close air of Ezzardine's lair. She returned the polish to her kit and wandered to the front of the Mahogany for distraction. Most of the staff was doing the same, some of them venturing out onto the wide warm porch that overlooked the street. It looked strangely empty now without the press clustering there along the short iron fence, hoping for a glimpse at the body of Rosario Vicario. Today was a normal day. No police, no death. Just the streets filled with metalbreds and already inebriated tourists clapping and singing as bands marched by with brass blaring.

"Are those horses last year's models?" Cayenne said. It was she who had called back about the parade – she was new to Louisville by way of Las Vegas and was still enthralled by the equinibots.

"Probably," Ty said. "Putting them through the parades before retiring them."

"It would seem sad if it wasn't also so environmentally friendly. I read that no piece goes unused. It's not like cars, hundreds of thousands of them stacking up all over the world. It's just these few thousand, recycled over and over."

"Probably still sad to the horses," Josie laughed, stepping out beside them.

"Nothing is sad to them," Cayenne said. "They don't remember anything, don't feel anything. Must be nice!" She laughed a shrill, sarcastic laugh.

The door swung open behind them and the eldest two Richmond sisters appeared, eyes as bright and quick as the parade itself. They took in the pink procession, the metalbreds draped in fuchsia.

"They're prettier every year!" Caroline Richmond cried. "Look at the steel, Christine!"

"That one must not have made it to the Derby last year," her sister answered. "I would've remembered. So pretty, like, oh my god."

"I remember the first year they looked like horses, but there was still something mechanical about them. Not the way they walked or ran, but something about the way they moved their heads…"

The ears, Ty thought. It had been the ears. She knew from her childhood the way a horse's ears could tell so much about what they were thinking, feeling, if you knew to watch them. Pricking forward, pinned back, one tilted one way and the other tilted another. She had watched her mother's ears sometimes, wishing they would tell her something about the maze inside her head, if she felt about her daughter the way she did about her husband. Why she didn't trust her daughter enough that night to answer Ty's question: *Where are you going?* And so Ty had followed to see for herself.

"They have it now," Caroline nodded enthusiastically. "A few years of trial and error and they are exactly like the real thing. I don't think I could tell them apart at this point."

"They've got all those ranches out west now," Christine said. "All the retired racehorses. The *real* ones. Rescues from tracks that tried to keep running after the ban. I wonder what those herds would do if you put a metalbred in there. Would they even notice?"

"They'd notice," Josie said.

"They'd probably tear it apart," said Cayenne. "It would probably freak them out."

"I don't think they'd mind," Christine said. "They'd probably want to help it. Horses were so sensitive and empathetic."

Were, Ty thought derisively, as if they were extinct. She felt defensive about this for a reason she couldn't quite place. In her mind her mother was one of the horses, a wild thing cut loose from a life she had once loved but that had grown to hurt her.

Ty watched the ears of the metalbreds – they *were* better now, it was true. Some pricked forward in interest at what lay ahead; others tilted forward and back as if to take in the music that swelled around them. They were ridden by people waving at the crowd, barely holding the reins and not needing to – uniformed Limestone handlers walked here and there among them – carrying signs or buckets of candy and coins that they tossed to the spectators.

"The metalbreds have that *something*," Ty said out loud, leaning against a beam. "There's something that all horses have and they have it. It's hard to describe, it's just…"

"There." Camille finished her sentence, appearing on the porch in her usual spectral fashion. The door was cracked open behind her, indicating that she had actually come through it rather than materializing out of thin air.

"Camille," Christine said to her sister, amused. "You know

we live in the same house and I haven't seen you in six days."

"Success," Camille yawned.

"It's really impressive," Caroline agreed. "You never leave the house and still you're also never here."

"I'm very proud," said Camille.

Ty imagined Camille curled up in her secret kitchen hideaway or folded up under a bed reading in the dark and smiled. She wondered how many other hiding places their little sister had that they didn't know about, how many were right under their noses.

"Did you see the mail that I left for you?" Caroline said. She was fanning herself as the heat started to set in for the day. "The party invitation?"

"Yes."

"Are you going to go?"

"No."

"Christ, Cammy, you're so boring. You're not even agoraphobic – why don't you ever *do* anything?"

Christine stepped back away from the rail to assess her youngest sister in more detail.

"I see you're still having cute clothes delivered," she said, pointing to the flowy black top Camille wore over slim Bermuda shorts. "What's the point?"

"I dress for myself, not the Louisville masses," Camille said.

"Oh, come on," Caroline said, rolling her eyes. "We dress for ourselves too. The masses just happen to like seeing pictures of us at events."

"Is it really dressing for yourself if they send you outfits along with the invitation, and you have wear the outfits if you want to get in?"

"Sure," Christine shrugged. "They have good taste. They know what we like. Did you even look at what they sent with your invitation?"

"No."

"They give options now. Like three or four outfits you can choose from!"

"I get to keep them either way," Camille said, smiling thinly.

"Afraid if you wear something that's not monochromatic people won't realize how deep you are?"

Camille rolled her eyes.

"Oh relax, sensitive little house plant," Caroline clucked. "If you want to wear black and stay inside all the time that's up to you. Oh look, maybe that girl is in your coven."

Caroline pointed a long, polished claw out at the street, indicating a young woman dressed mostly in black, camera in front of her face, taking photos of the parade. She was chubby and pretty and wearing a DC Comics shirt, long black hair pinned atop her head in a precise bun. She drew the eye amid all the pastel of the Derby tourists, but there was something about her that held Ty's gaze after the conversation had moved on. When she lowered the camera, Ty got a full view of her heart-shaped face – a mouth shining black and perfect, the lipstick applied with a steady hand.

Luz.

Luz had the same focused look that she wore in Ezzardine's underground study, fixed on something either too far or too complex for the people around her to see or understand. She wasn't there for the parade, that much was obvious to Ty, and Ty studied her, watching the purposeful angling of her hands bearing the camera, pointing it at the passers-by in the street.

Ty began to notice a pattern. Facing Luz as she was, she could see the quick black eye of the camera lens blink every time she took a photo. The band passed, then two metalbreds. A gaggle of children throwing candy. The camera didn't move. But when the light blue uniform of a Limestone handler passed by, Ty's eye caught the quick snap of the lens, Luz's mouth a tight knot of concentration. More children. A brigade of baton-twirling preteens. A Limestone employee. *Snap.* Miss Kentucky on a pedestal. A second brass band. A Limestone employee. *Snap.* The parade was moving on down the street and many of the watchers moved on with it, surging in from the sidewalks to trail the procession and dance in the street, scooping up candy and streamers. But Luz stayed put, snapping pictures until every blue-suited handler had passed. Then, with the wraithiness of Camille, she sank back into the crowd, swallowed by fuchsia. She was gone, leaving Ty to sweep the street for her shadow.

"Something wrong?" Camille said when she noticed Ty's frown.

"No," Ty said, and wasn't sure if it was a lie. "I just…thought I saw someone I know."

"Madame's back," someone called from inside the house. No one moved for a moment – gone were the days of an employer's presence registering as spur against rib. But everyone knew they'd had their break and drifted back indoors, everyone except the Richmond sisters, minus Camille, who had vanished back into one dark corner or another.

Ty was the last employee inside, looking back over her shoulder at the street for a final glimpse of Luz and her camera. But she was gone, having gotten whatever it was that she came for. Without calling it forth, the image of the girl on the video, a pair of hands around her throat, came twitching back into Ty's mind, jumbling with memories of the mist of red that had haloed Ty's mother's head in the breath before her body met dust. Above them both, the same hairless face: Benedict. He was supposed to be staying at the Mahogany on Derby night. Now that had changed, and Ty's plans had come unraveled. But Rosario had put the small red jewel in Ty's palm and shown her another murder, another needle piercing through the stillness of her life. Ty suddenly imagined herself as a piece of thread, slipping through the needle. Its shining end pointed back toward the Pink.

CHAPTER 20

EZZ

I t was the first time since the beginning that she considered canceling a party.

This had been her thing since she inherited the mansion: in the weeks leading up to Derby, she hosted party after party at the Pink. She hired local femmes to put money in their pocket, caterers of color, artists of color…it was her own personal affront to the white hurricane Derby had become. Her parents would have loved it. But this year Ezz's head was full of loss, and as she watched the décor company redecorate the ballroom – rose lights turned gold, the tightropes replaced with hundreds of gilded orbs – she had the sudden urge to tell everyone to go home. By the time the ballroom had filled with guests, she had squirreled herself away in the kitchen, crouching over a bowl of Froot Loops while the caterers moved in and out. She would have stayed there all night if Shavon hadn't appeared.

"Annnd…you're still wearing the same sweatpants as last night," Shavon said, teasing, but her frown was real.

"I've been busy," Ezz shrugged. Shavon was family, blood or not. But there was currently a line between what was in Ezz's head and what was in her heart. It wasn't just the loss of Rosario – now there was another death. Two murders, as far as she could tell. She couldn't put this burden on Shavon.

"I can tell," Shavon said, picking up the box of cereal and shaking it, the sad sound of three hoops echoing in the emptiness. "Busy eating these Froot Loops."

"It's comfort food." Ezz scowled down into her bowl.

Shavon nodded, leaning her hip against Ezz's shoulder.

"You're going through it, cuzzo. I understand. Is there anything I can do to help?"

"Get all these people out my house?" Ezz said, raising her eyes.

"Give me something I can actually do," Shavon laughed. "You know people love the Pink. They'll only leave if you tell them to."

"I'm just not feeling it tonight," Ezz said. The bass of the band carried through the mansion's thick walls, the buzz of the guests filling up the ballroom's dome. Usually all the hoopla helped to fill the hole in her chest, but tonight it only made her feel lonelier. All she could think about was Rosario, and now the video Rosario had sent from beyond the grave. And, annoyingly, the girl with the shaved head who had brought it here.

"Remember what my Uncle Reggie said when Auntie Angela passed?" Shavon said. "Grief is like any other wound: you have to deal with it, or it will fester just like anything else. I'm sorry you're hurting, Ezz. I think listening to the fact that you're not feeling like partying right now is good. So tomorrow…cancel the party. Take care of you for once. You're always out here taking care of everybody else. You haven't really even stopped to grieve since your parents…"

"I have the means," Ezz interrupted. She didn't want to hear the rest. She stared at Froot Loops fattening in milk to ignore the itching feeling in her eyes. "I can't just pause everything while I make myself feel better. It feels selfish to make it about me."

"Healing isn't *making it about you!*" Shavon cried. "You lost your parents. And Rosario was your best friend. Since you were

166

like ten. You are allowed to feel pain."

Ezz nodded. But she thought of the girl on the tape. *It wasn't just Rosario*, she thought, but she couldn't tell Shavon. She couldn't. The angle of Ezz's face made it easy for a tear to slide down the side of her nose and drip into her cereal.

"Gross," she whispered, and Shavon laughed.

"It's not gross," Shavon said.

"Salty cereal is gross."

"Well, if you want to hear something that will *really* make you salty," Shavon said, and the shift in her tone raised Ezz's eyes. "Remember that white girl you kicked out at the last party?"

"Ty?" Ezz said quickly. "How did you know I kicked her out?"

"Because she's in the ballroom right now and she told me."

Ezz half stood up, the embarrassing twinkle of eagerness extinguished by a flame of irritation.

"What? What the hell is she doing here? I told her not to come back!"

"I know," Shavon nodded. "She told me that too."

"What did you say to her?" Ezz snapped. "You should have dragged her ass to the door!"

"I told her I've been cutting her hair for two years and have gotten to know her a little bit, but this was some very Caucasian shit she was pulling at this moment. And she agreed." Shavon laughed. "That girl is stubborn. She said she needed to talk to you. Something important."

"I don't give a damn what she said," Ezz said, pushing away her bowl of cereal. She stalked away from the table and toward the kitchen door. "I told her not to come back."

"That's what I told her you'd say!" Shavon called after her.

Ezz side-stepped a pair of caterers and moved down the hallway that connected to the ballroom. The gold light flooded over her when she emerged into the party, the music from the stage rolling over her in gold waves. The ballroom was even more packed than the night before, which would have transformed her into a butterfly on another night. Not tonight.

But then she saw her.

Standing halfway between the stage and the entryway, wearing a red dress that brought out the olive in her skin, she looked like a burning candle. But Ezz was determined not to notice this. She made her way through the crowd, getting stopped every five feet by people wanting to dap her up or give side hugs and condolences. She wasn't in the mood. Ty was at the end of her trajectory like a planet waiting for an asteroid. Ty saw her coming, Ezz knew she did: she could feel Ty's round brown eyes on her. But she just stood there, and when Ezz finally locked eyes with her twenty feet away, pushing through the pulsing crowd, she saw that they both knew the same thing: Ezz was going to kick her out.

And then Ty turned and ran.

As fast as one can run through a crowd, anyway. Ezz stared after her, frozen with surprise. At first Ty appeared to be making a straight line toward the exit, but then she paused, her face hidden by a couple dancing. She appeared to be undecided, then her back straightened and she veered toward the stage.

"What the hell are you doing?" Ezz whispered, watching her, just beginning to follow.

Ty made it to the stage just as The Belles brought one song to a close, and Ezz watched Ty scale the black curtained steps just as the drummer – her hair shaved like Ty but dyed silver – started to tap out the rhythm for the next song. Ezz recognized it. Not a cover, as so many of the others were, but a Belles original that Ezz knew well. In the gold spotlights that swam across the stage, Ty almost looked like she belonged, and when the lead singer, Spectra Santos, began to croon the first words, Ezz pushed closer to the stage's edge, planning to climb up the same stairs and cuss Ty out before showing her the door. Spectra began to sing.

"Running out of time and running out of breath
I saw you behind the mustang and I stood at the edge
Of something shining like a falling star, the whole world in my
mouth,
You tell me I can stay but listen girl I'm going to have to follow
you out..."*

Standing so close to Spectra, Ty must have said something, must have done something, because from where Ezz watched on the floor she saw Spectra turn in Ty's direction, lowering her eyebrows before breaking into a broad smile. She motioned Ty closer while Ezz stared, frozen – when Spectra opened her mouth for the next lines, she motioned Ty closer to share the mic, and Ezz heard Ty sing for the very first time.

"I'd follow you into the dark but baby you should know
That there are worse things than getting lost in shadows
When white light spills through the crack in the door
I'll be holding your hand when you ask what more can be done...
The sound of horses galloping will be the thunder when we run
When we run
When we run
Beyond the light is darkness and wouldn't it be fun
If we made it all the way and stood behind the sun..."

Ty's voice was like the color magenta, deep and sweet and glowing. Around Ezz everyone was swaying and grinding and smiling but she felt like a violet planet knocked out of orbit, spinning slowly and silently in a universe shining with gold. All she could do was stare. Ty looked out of breath, sweat making her face shine, and Spectra sang the next verse alone, her voice carrying up into the cathedral ceiling and floating before crashing down in the last lines of the song. Then Ty joined her one more time:

"When we run, when we run
I'll follow you through white light and I'll meet you past the sun..."

Ezz vaguely heard the party-goers clapping – most of them went on dancing, whoever was singing onstage not the feature of their evening – but Ezz did not. She slowly made her way through the crowds, trying to net her thoughts. She was a few feet away when one of the black-suited security guards she paid to have onsite approached Ty, who was cautiously making her way down the steps. Shavon must have called him.

"It's alright, Mr. Kau," Ezz said, finally approaching. "I've got it."

He glanced at her, then glanced again, and Ezz was embarrassed by the knowingness on his face, as if he saw a flower growing there that she hadn't intended on planting. He left them alone, and the two girls just stared at each other, Ty still slightly out of breath. Ezz didn't trust her own face – she knew it looked like melting ice. She didn't know whether she wanted to be cold or soft. Ty didn't move, didn't speak, waiting for her to decide.

"What did you say to Spectra?" Ezz said over the music. "To make her let you sing?"

"I just said I needed to make you smile," Ty said, almost too soft.

Ezz could feel herself folding like the deck of cards in her pocket. She reached out her hand. Ty flicked her eyes from Ezz's palm to her eyes. Ezz twisted her lips, tilted her head. When Ty intwined her fingers with Ezz's, Ezz imagined the ground beneath her feet gradually softening until she was treading air.

They made their way through throngs of guests. Straight ahead were the front doors – and for a moment Ezz still considered kicking her out. But when she reached the thickest part of the crowd, everyone swaying as Spectra's voice turned air to velvet, Ezz paused. She still had Ty's hand held in hers, dry and warm and solid. She looked over her shoulder, eyeing Ty, weighing, measuring. Ty stared back.

"I know I shouldn't be here," Ty started.

"But you are."

"Yeah. I am."

Ezz's palm, a rogue entity, decided something before she did. Before her mind had truly decided, Ezz was pulling Ty forward again, closer into her chest, her other hand rising to rest on Ty's waist.

"Let's dance," she heard herself saying, her lips also turned traitor.

In a breath they shared breath, dancing close. They swayed, and the feeling of Ty's lower back under her hand felt like the earth itself, the warmth and realness of it drawing Ezz back down from the cold, distant place she'd been living for the last few days. Together they ceased to be people and instead became a song, while onstage Spectra and The Belles turned the scene blue with a new melody that sifted slow like moonlit sand. It was a cover. "Sway My Way." Spectra sang, and Ezz felt each word run like rain down Ty's spine.

"Why did you come back?" Ezz said. She felt a little dizzy. It was as if the two of them stood at the tip of a mountain together, tipping forward and back.

"I had to talk to you. About –" Ty paused. Whatever it was, she didn't want to say it. Saying it would be the slash of a knife through the perfect trembling bubble that encased them. But she had to say it, Ezz knew. "About Rosario."

Ezz felt her palm stiffen against Ty's back. There was outer space again – sucking the warm air out of her lungs.

"Tell me," Ezz said.

"I was at work yesterday," Ty said. "At the Mahogany. And I snuck into a suite to take a shower. While I was in there, a surprise guest from Saratoga Springs – you know, from the competing race tracks up there – checked in. He talked about…" Ezz watched her swallow. "Brian Benedict. Apparently Limestone invited this guy down as a fixer. For a deal. He said Benedict has a mess he needs him to clean up."

She said this all close to Ezz's ear, and Ezz didn't know if she actually moved, but deep inside, something flinched. Her heart was an open wound. Ty had come to the party bearing salt.

"Who was the dude?" Ezz said eventually, when she could.

"Darren. No. *Darden*. From Saratoga Springs."

"Saratoga Springs…"

"Do you know the name Darden?" Ty asked.

Ezz paused, thinking.

"No," she said. "But if he's from Saratoga Springs and is doing a deal with the Downs…and Limestone is involved…well. That's very interesting."

"Interesting how?"

"Smells like money," Ezz said. "And that kinda money almost always smells like blood."

Ezz again wanted out of this shining gold room. She pictured the dead girl on the floor of the barn, her face replaced with Rosario's. She started to release Ty's back, already envisioning her path back to the lair, back under the cool gaze of Luz. But Ty was gripping her, keeping her from pulling away.

"I want to help," Ty said. She drew her face away just far enough so that they could look each other fully in the eye. One could mistake it for thirst, but when Ezz really studied her, she saw only a sort of hunger. It made Ezz feel inexplicably nervous.

"How do you think you can help?" Ezz said. "And why?"

"I'm in the Mahogany. I'll hear things. From Darden. I can hang around, see if he says anything."

"What, like a spy?" Ezz said doubtfully.

"Yes, exactly like a spy," Ty said. "I don't know why you even said it with tone. You *need* a spy. You may be rich but I don't see any other way you'll be able to stay close to a guy like him."

"You'd be surprised," Ezz said, and frowned, but she was also amused again. Every time she thought the girl was soft, she showed something sharp.

"I probably would," said Ty quickly.

They went on staring at each other. They were still half-swaying, some part of each of them not ready to let the dance go. Spectra's voice hung in the air around them like fireflies, hovering, ready to drop off into darkness. Ezz pulled her in close again.

"How can I trust you?" Ezz said softly, cheek to cheek so she could avoid Ty's eyes. She was listening instead, searching for the truth with her ears.

"I'm here," Ty murmured. "I'm already doing what I said I'd do and you haven't even asked me yet."

"One thing I *did* ask you to do is not come back though."

"I'll apologize again if you want me to."

"Apologize again."

"I'm sorry."

"Mhmm."

"I saw Luz today," Ty said after a moment. "*She's* helping you. Let me help too."

"You saw her doing what?"

"Taking pictures. Outside the Mahogany."

The song's notes were fading. As the last breath of the music quivered out over the swaying crowd, Ezz's hands seemed again to find their autonomy, guiding pressure on Ty's palm and lower back. She twirled Ty in a small, gentle circle, watching as the hem of Ty's dress went still just as the song did. Ezz decided.

The crowd cheered and hummed and Ezz leaned into Ty's neck.

"Meet me at the backside in the morning. 4:30 am. Goodnight."

Then she turned, let the band's brass swallow her up, escaping into the night. She wouldn't go to the lair – she would find an elephant's embrace, sit in the leafy dark and think. What had Luz been doing outside the Mahogany? Ezz hadn't asked her to go. And Ty…she pretended that their plans were the same, but Ezz was learning that the girl's words were like a fragment of iceberg. Could a girl with eyes like razors be trusted? Outside, the night air licked cool when it blew. But the place on Ezz's shoulder where Ty's hand had lain was warm.

CHAPTER 21

LUZ

Luz hadn't slept, awake running another round of tests before the sun rose. Even in the lair she could feel the thrum of the party like the heartbeat of a massive, distant animal. But eventually it had slowed, then stopped, and she was considering going to bed when she heard Ezz pass her green room for the tech lab.

"Luz?" Ezz called, searching. Luz glanced at her device – 3 am.

Luz hurried to open the green room door, slipping out and closing it behind her. She moved toward the lab just as Ezz reemerged from it.

"Oh, there you are," Ezz said. She looked better than she sounded – Luz had expected undereye circles to match her own. She must have left the party early. "I figured you'd be awake."

"You figured I'd be awake at 3 am?" Luz said.

"I've never seen you sleep," Ezz shrugged. "I think I've just started assuming you're nocturnal."

"Something like that," Luz said. "Why are *you* awake?"

"I'm going somewhere," Ezz said. "But I need your help getting there."

"Okay, but I don't know how to drive either," Luz teased, following her into the lab.

Ezz smiled, but she seemed impatient, and Luz raised an eyebrow.

"No, no, I need a press pass," Ezz said. "Or something. Something that will get me into the backside at the Downs. You're familiar, right?"

Luz felt a bit of her smile fade. She thought of the days of visiting the backside in secret, stopping by after school to fit her hands through the bars and stroke the noses of Thoroughbreds and, later, metalbreds, her parents coming out of the barn to chase her off. The horses always made Luz think of her abuelita, even if in Chimaltenango, her abuelita said, the only horses were skinny and sharp, so unlike the towering Thoroughbreds of the racing industry. As always, mention of the backside put a velvety feeling of nostalgia in Luz's bones, but now there was a hole in the velvet, a stab of fear.

"Why do you want to go to the backside?" Luz said, going to a stool by her screens and sitting down.

"I just want to poke around," Ezz said. She held up a small photo and Luz winced to see the still face of the girl from the video, a screenshot from the moment she turned to find Brian Benedict alongside her in the barn. "Ask some questions. A barn the size of the one in the video…plus what your cousin said…the chances are high that this girl worked on the backside. There has to be someone who at least knows her – the horse industry is big and small at the same time. You know how Louisville is – everybody knows everybody and their business. Rosario had that video delivered to me for a reason. I can't just sit here and act like I didn't see it."

Luz studied Ezz, aware of the feelings battling in her chest. Pride, for having a friend like Ezz, so full of duty and honor. And then, beside it, the purple swell of ever-present guilt. She had been at the backside while a girl was being murdered. She had known nothing, done nothing.

"Are you sure you want to do that?" Luz said quietly.

"Yes," said Ezz. No changing her mind. "So can you do it?"

Luz looked at her for a moment longer before nodding, turning to her screens, opening the program. It would be easy to do, and hard to hand over, knowing what she was making was akin to fire, maybe sending Ezz off into a tinderbox. She sighed as she worked, clicking, dragging, typing.

"What's wrong?" Ezz said, watching.

"You have to be careful."

"Careful won't solve this thing," Ezz said.

"No, but it will keep you alive."

They were silent while she finished. Luz glanced at Ezz, the photo of the dead girl clutched in two fingers like one of her playing cards. This was a gamble. It all was, including the things Ezz didn't know. Luz imagined herself as a hermit crab – settled in the welcome aquarium of Ezz's home, Luz hiding her plans in the secret shell she carried on her back. She imagined the vines snaking out of the lair and creeping all the way to the Downs. But what about the backside? Even if she took Cavehill Downs apart brick by brick, where would it leave her parents? She thought of what Irma had said: making a new table, the old one just kindling.

"I'm coming with you," she said to Ezz.

"What? Are you sure?"

"No," Luz sighed.

"You can print two?" Ezz said, peering.

"Yes."

"Print three then."

"Three? For what?"

"One for Ty."

Luz looked at her sharply, a question on her lips, but Ezz was bashful and waved her hands.

"Don't ask, okay? I just…I think I trust her."

Luz pursed her lips to hide her smile. She printed three documents.

"Let's go."

Ty was waiting at the gate, yawning, when Luz and Ezz approached. Ezz had told her to dress like a member of the press, and Ty could probably pass: jeans and a white blouse. Luz, however, had asked Ezz for a hat to tuck her long hair up inside, and all she had was a flat-brimmed Cardinals fitted. It didn't exactly scream "journalist," but it would work if she hoped to walk around the backside and not be immediately recognized by her parents from afar.

"Good morning," Ty said. "Is 4 am considered morning?"

"It is to the backside," Luz said, lifting her chin to indicate the scores of workers and trainers and tourists already swarming beyond the security fence of the backside.

"If you want to seem like a local," a tour guide called to her group, leading a small, tired clump of tourists nearby, "you need to say it right. *Back*side. Not back*side*. Back*side* is a horse's rump. This is the *back*side. The side not everyone sees."

The girls allowed the group to pass by, and then Luz moved toward the gate, manned by a uniformed security officer.

"How are we going to get in?" Ty whispered.

"Luz has the key to everything," Ezz said.

"I don't *have* them," Luz corrected. "I *make* them."

The security guard was eyeing Luz the way one would a candy apple – a round look, full of hunger. She ignored his stare and held up the passes of her own creation.

"Press. Here for hot walker interviews."

"You got it," the uniformed man said. He didn't give the passes a second glance, instead eyeing Luz's cherry lips, her round waist.

"Maybe I can take you to a game sometime," he said, nodding at her hat.

"Maybe," she said, making her mouth smile, a mask. She imagined herself as Poison Ivy, hips and lips camouflaging her intent.

The guard scanned the passes eagerly and the gate blinked a bright, obliging green. A moment later Ty, Ezz, and Luz were within the boundaries of the backside, standing aside as a towering metalbred was led by a boy no more than thirteen, tiny beside the massive copper-shine animal. As always, Luz had to remind herself it was a machine.

"Here we are," she said softly to herself, and tried to wipe her feelings from her face, into what her mother always called her "study face." *You* are *here to study*, after all, she told herself.

"They really do get better every year," Ezz said, and even she looked impressed. "Look at the muscles. It's just a machine, but the printing tech has advanced so much that the interior structure has printed veins. No blood in them, but the veins are there."

"It's so busy here," Ty said, taking in the whole bustling scene, metalbreds being led to and from the track, people walking in and out of the immaculately kept barns.

"I used to come back here with Rosario," Ezz said. "But never during peak season. She was always too busy."

Luz stood very still, her eyes sweeping over the rows and rows of barns, the shedrow with the heads of metalbreds poked out and swinging. The sound of Spanish being spoken rose up with the clip-clop of hooves. Laughter that could have been her father's tumbled from the stalls. The nearby jangle of Norteñas. Luz soaked it in, saying nothing. A girl had died here, while Luz hid in shadow. And that wasn't the only grief in her heart – the forbiddenness of the backside was always like an ache in her heart. Ezz glanced at her.

"You probably could give us the tour, huh?" Ezz said softly, and Luz found herself smiling a little in spite of that ache. This was her parents' kingdom, not hers. But it still felt like home.

"The metalbreds still need a lot of the same things horses did, just for different reasons," she heard herself saying. "The hot walkers," she nodded at a group of preteens speaking Spanish, returning from the track, "used to cool the Thoroughbreds down after exercise. They needed to be walked until their coats cooled, otherwise they could get sick. Now it's a little different – the hot walkers help with the metalbreds' exercise, and still do cool-downs after they've been breezing, even if any 'sickness' is now technical malfunction. Metalbreds need lots of maintenance – the only folks that had to switch tracks were the farriers, really. The grooming and hoof-picking still happens because they're constantly looking for glitches or breaks in the printing material. Stuff that, unnoticed, could cost them the race when it comes down to it."

"I know you want to avoid your parents," Ezz said, "and that's your choice. But is there anyone else you know here? People we could talk to? Ask them stuff?"

Luz kept her face averted, allowing the questions to strike her like hail, then bounce off. How to say: her parents had kept her away from the place that they loved, afraid that their love would infect her? How could she answer: *They wanted something brighter and shinier than their own lives, and so their own lives became strangers?* Her parents – the separate world they walked in, that Luz had watched from afar, through a microscope.

"Not really," she said simply.

Ezz merely nodded, and Luz was grateful.

"Then we'd better get started," Ezz said, and it sounded like she was almost hoping someone would disagree. But Luz swallowed, nodding, and moved toward the closest barn.

"Let's go," she said, and Ezz and Ty followed close behind.

Inside the barn only a few metalbreds were outside their stalls. Instead, various handlers and hot walkers and jockeys were within the close spaces reserved for equinibots racing in the Derby in just over a week. The floors were hard-packed dirt mingled with sawdust, swept neat. Luz knew what a barn was supposed to smell like, and this was not it, the ghost of the real thing hovering in a shaded lane of her brain. The smell of manure was the obvious missing piece, but there was also the absence of the hot, sweet smell of animals' breath. There were only humans here, and they didn't emit sun and grass the way horses did. She happened to glance at her companions, and Luz was surprised to find it was like looking in two mirrors – in Ezz's face, a flash of longing and violet grief. The same with Ty, aside from the spark there at the center. Rage. They reached an open stall and Luz was glad for the excuse to look away.

Inside, a towering chestnut metalbred stood with its haunches toward the door, a jockey crouched by its neck, plugged in with his kit and tweaking different parts of the equinibot's programming.

"Just like horses," Ezz said in a hushed voice. "What worked last week can change overnight. They're sensitive. Like flowers, Rosario used to say."

The next stall was open too, and they almost passed by until the sign on the post caught Luz's eye. *Horse: All's Well. Jockey: Rosario Vicario.*

"Oh," she said softly, and she wished she hadn't, because then Ezz was looking too, and Luz watched Rosario's name sink into her friend's eyes like a stain.

"This was hers," Ezz said softly.

The stall was empty, the floor just brushed sawdust and straw that had floated in. The air had the shimmery quality barns always have, dust floating and catching the light. In the corner of the stall was a scruffy spotted dog, curled up, asleep. Luz stared at it, afraid to look at Ezz.

Ezz stepped back sharply, away from the stall and the emptiness.

"It's not right," Ezz whispered. "We're going to figure this out, Rosario."

Luz said nothing, but ventured to squeeze her bicep, and Ezz nodded, blinking back tears.

Someone was coming, a boy walking down the wide center aisle of the barn, tech kit in hand, whistling a quiet tune.

"Let's ask him," Ty whispered, and Luz nodded in agreement. She squeezed Ezz's arm one more time and then stepped over to intercept the boy, praying he didn't recognize her.

"Perdón. ¿Reconoces a la chica de esta foto?" she said. He paused, features pleasant, to peer at the photo Luz's hand extended.

The photo, taken from the metalbred's eye, was only a glimpse of the girl's face, expression blank in the moment before terror had set in. Even this photo, magnified and sharpened for clarity, was slightly blurry, but Luz watched the boy look, and see.

"No," he said quickly. "No la conozco."

He hurried away toward the daylight of the backside and it wasn't until he reached the doorway that he chanced a single glance over his shoulder. He made a sharp right and was gone. Luz's stomach curled in on itself.

"Is it just me, or did he switch it up when he saw the photo?" Ezz appeared at Luz's shoulder, frowning.

Luz nodded once, definitively, then looked around, uneasy. The boy clearly knew the girl's face, so the theory that she must have worked here seemed to stick. It made Luz feel sick. If the girl had worked here, Luz's cousin Mariela might have walked past her at some point. The girl might have exchanged words with Luz's own parents – 'Buenos días' with a smile, or '¡Aguas!' when a metalbred was malfunctioning, or any number of small interchanges that came from swimming in the same ocean, avoiding the same sharks. It felt sharp and heavy, this losing someone you hadn't known, but might have soon. Horses in stalls watched with what looked like bright curiosity – so many, and this just one barn. It would be impossible to ascertain which metalbred might have recorded the footage of the murder. Even so, Luz thought, knowing *which* wouldn't explain how it was able to start recording while not on the racetrack in the first place. Had a jockey been present, controlling it the way one would a security camera? Luz continued down the middle aisle, this time approaching a girl who was just affixing a lead to the halter of a chestnut metalbred.

"Perdón," Luz said, approaching the girl. The equinibot was just stepping out of the stall and the girl paused it with a soft touch of her hand on its muzzle.

"Yeah?"

Luz took a deep breath and held up the photo once more.

"¿Reconoces a la niña de esta foto?"

The girl stared at the photo, and Luz could see her eyes studying the shadows on the face captured there. A similar shadow now appeared on the girl's face. Her eyes lifted from Luz's hand and wandered to the barn door. Luz turned and looked. The boy she had first asked was peering in, and two or three other workers were clustered at his side, all watching. The girl's eyes darted back to Luz.

"No," she said loudly, and with a gentle tug on the bridle, led the metalbred fully out into the aisle. Luz felt her stomach sink as the huge machine stepped out, and she watched the girl who, in another life, she could have known, raise her arm, ensuring the bot exited the stall cleanly. It wasn't until the girl was turning it, the shining body between her and the barn door, that Luz heard her strained whisper: "Pregúntale a Elena. 2B."

And then the girl was moving off down the aisle, the muscular grace of the metalbred beside her languid in a way that her own steps were not – quick, nervous. When she reached the barn door, she paused as the other hot walkers and grooms leaned in to whisper, and none of them moved until Luz started down the aisle in their direction, when they all suddenly had somewhere urgent to be. She almost called after them: *Do you know my parents? Otto?*

Shery? Do they ever talk of me? Do I exist when I enter this place? But her tongue felt like a clot, and by the time she and Ezz and Ty reached the barn door, no one remained.

"She said to ask Elena. 2B," Luz said softly.

"Not much of a clue," Ezz frowned. "No one wants to talk."

"It's not about *want*," Luz said, impatiently. "Someone is dead and people are scared. Do you know how much rides on their ability to fly under the radar?"

Ezz nodded apologetically, and Luz swallowed, trying to keep down the explosive feeling that had been growing in her like vines since she stepped past the gate. On her first night under Ezz's roof, Luz thought maybe her mother kicking her out was a good thing – she would find her own story, find her true self. Maybe she would find a path away from the backside after all. But now, feeling the fear that pulsed through the air like radio waves, she could only think of what Irma had said in passing at the museum – how Limestone wielded ICE like its own private army, how this was a world spinning on the finger of people like Brian Benedict and Annie Claybelle. *This* is what her parents wanted her away from. And this is why she couldn't turn away.

"These assholes," Ty said, and Luz looked up. Ty was gesturing at a jockey wearing a sleek tech kit walking between two or three people dressed in clothes that gave off the unmistakable sheen of wealth. They laughed the way diamonds might – hard and bright. "These people don't seem like they care about the fact that one of their colleagues just died. Rosario has only been gone for a few days."

"Those are the owners," Ezz said, squinting at the suits of snake and sharkskin. "The real money. The jockeys make a lot, but the owners and breeders have the real coin. Some things have stayed true: jockey income is based on the races they win, experience, and networks. Guess what the networks of the highest paid jockeys look like?"

Ezz gestured, and Luz knew she was motioning to the whiteness, the maleness, the suits. As it so often did lately, the Poison Ivy tattoo on her arm seemed to itch. Ty, on the other hand, didn't even look, her attention elsewhere, and Luz watched Ezz watching Ty, annoyance rolling off her. Luz could see the bar being set – Ty had let Ezz down once, in her mind, and now Ezz was daring her to fuck up again.

"Are you even listening?" Ezz said then, nudging her. "You're the one who wanted to help, right?"

"There," Ty said, ignoring Ezz, prodding Luz. Ty's finger rose, pointing past the metalbreds and their glamorous jockeys and the dusty uniforms of the young brown-skinned workers who moved with such ease between the hooves and the boots. Ty indicated the yellow-brown buildings just beyond the backside perimeter. From where they stood Luz could see three separate stairways, each with a sign and a flickering light. The backside living quarters. The center building read 2B.

"Of *course*," Luz repeated. Her satisfaction felt bitter. "Let's go."

It wasn't hard to slip out of the backside bustle and through the gate. The people who lived here for the season weren't considered as valuable as the animals they tended, Luz thought. The bitterness sharpened.

"Back in the day people slept right in the barns, in rooms over the stalls," Luz said as they walked. "But they built these to accommodate workers before the ban, before Limestone. I don't know why I didn't think of this before."

"People live at the backside?" Ty said as they approached the crumbling building, and Luz nodded, vaguely remembering. The stuctures had the feeling of being old since the moment they were built, the corners dulled by wind and time, not a sharp edge to be found. Luz didn't know if the memories she had of this place were actually hers, or culled from her parents' stories. They'd lived at the backside until she was four, until her parents had moved into the apartment they'd lived in for the last seventeen years, her home. Was it still?

"Yes," Luz nodded, stepping decisively out of her head. "Seasonal and migrant, mostly, but some long-time workers. They made it a little smaller after they expanded the parking lot –"

"Displacing hundreds of people," Ezz cut in.

Luz nodded, letting her eyes sweep over the people walking to and from the buildings – mostly uniformed, some standing and talking, smoking, eating, laughing. Here was the overlap of many lives on different paths, resting in the current circle of this galloping Venn diagram. The yard of the apartments was clean and shady, oak and elm making the ground cooler than the backside itself, where all was exposed to the sun and media. Near one of these trees Luz glimpsed a girl, around seventeen, leaning against the smooth bark of a single white birch. She was in uniform, her eyes and hair as brown as the material but for a blue stripe in her bangs, her chin sharp and her cheeks full. Luz looked away when the girl's stare caught on her face like a thorn. Ahead, Ezz was already addressing a cluster of girls.

"Hi," she said. "Hey. Can we ask y'all a question?"

The girls had appeared out of the 2B staircase, also dressed in the brown-and-white backside uniforms. They were whispering, solemn, eyes shooting over Ezz's shoulders, scanning the yard. Luz glanced up, looking for the blue-haired girl by the birch, but she was gone.

"Hey," Luz said to the group, drawing even with Ezz. "Donde vive Elena?"

The girls froze in their tracks, big-eyed and nervous like a band of colts. Their whispers faded, regarding Luz and her company with guarded frowns.

"Who are you?" said the boldest, a short girl with hair in two braids going back along each side of her head. "Por qué quieres saber?"

"Soy un amiga."

"Estás seguro?" The girl's skeptical eyebrows were matched by her posse.

"Yes, I'm sure," Luz said patiently.

"No le digas nada," one of the quieter girls warned, and the short girl shushed her. Her eyes swept over the yard one more time before landing heavily back on Luz.

"Just there," she said, pointing up the stairs, at the door at the very top of the landing.

"Gracias," Luz said, and moved for the stairs, Ezz and Ty tailing her. The other girls stood watching, silent, until they got to the top. By the time Luz raised her hand to knock, the group downstairs had vanished like smoke. Luz felt breath hush from her in a long sigh, thinking of how so many girls in the world were half ghost by the time they reached thirteen.

It took three knocks and a long time for the door to open. The sound of multiple locks were like knuckles cracking to unfurl a tightly curled fist. When the door inched open, a sliver of a face appeared, the eyes red, raw as oysters with their pearls recently plucked out. A woman stared at Luz and then Ezz and then Ty, her gaze empty. Finally, she uttered one word.

"Yes?"

"Are you…Elena?" Luz said. She felt her voice soften into an offered palm. The wrong word could send her fleeing.

"Yes," the woman whispered.

"We were told…," Luz started, softly.

"You are not the police," Elena said. The door inched open, enough space for an extra breath but no more.

"No," Luz said.

"You were told what?" said Elena.

"That you might know…"

"I know nothing."

"You don't know what I'm asking yet," Luz said gently.

"No necesito saber cuando no sé nada," Elena hissed.

"You don't need to know," Luz repeated. "But can I at least come in? Ask you some questions…"

"What could you ask?" Elena snapped. The door cracked open an inch wider and Luz's eyes sprang past the woman's rigid shoulders into the dim apartment beyond. Thin purple curtains over the single window lent the room the air of a bruise. Elena stood in a tiny entranceway, photos on the wall at her back. In the frame of the largest stood Elena herself, each arm around the shoulders of two almost-twin girls. One, older: tall, smile like a banquet of teeth. The other was younger, smaller, serious. Brown eyes like tunnels over the shy light of her smile, with a stripe of blue highlight in her bang. Sisters. Luz knew both faces.

"About this girl," Luz pressed, trying to lift the photo, but Elena's hand was a cobra. It slapped Luz's hand with such speed and ferocity that Luz cried out, the photo spinning to the floor, fluttering down two stairs.

"What is there to know?" Elena said, her voice like a gash. "Except that she is gone?"

The door slammed, forcing all three girls back a step with its force. From inside the apartment came the sound of shattering glass, and the ragged cry of the equivalent human shatter. Luz and the others stood numb, not looking at each other.

"This was a bad idea," Luz said softly.

"Not bad," Ezz said. "Just…"

She trailed off.

"Let's go downstairs so we can talk," Ty said, already three steps down. She bent to retrieve the photo from where it lay, but Luz rushed to intercept her, some internal buzz like a swarm of wasps called to protect it. She used two fingers to brush the dirt from the dead girl's cheeks. She didn't want to look at it too long; it would interfere with the snapshot she'd taken in her head.

She knew what she had seen. Now, as they walked silently

back down the stairs, she felt as if she were tip-toeing a tightrope over a canyon. At one edge of the chasm were her vines and the hopes she had for them, her own twisting, green design. At the other edge was the face of the girl, preserved in life in the photo in Luz's hand, her mother's thick grief like mist around her.

"Did you see the photo?" Luz said when they reached the bottom.

"Yeah, when she smacked it out of your hand," Ezz said.

"Not this photo. The one in her apartment. Behind her."

Ezz peered at her, Ty paying rapt attention. "What photo?"

"It was a photo of Elena and two girls. One of them," Luz said, holding the printed photo aloft for Ty and Ezz to see, "was her."

"Her daughter," Ty said. Her face looked gray. "Fuck."

"Yes," Luz said. Her voice sounded like it was being drawn out with pliers, and she swallowed before speaking again. "Her eyes. We should have known right away – the same."

"That woman lost her kid and we were up there in her face asking about it," Ezz said, rubbing her temples. "I don't see her answering our questions anytime soon."

Luz stared down at the photo in her fingers, still balancing, teetering. Eventually she slipped it into her pocket.

"Let's get out of here," she said softly, and when Ezz stood waiting, hesitant, Luz waved her along with Ty. She wanted to walk alone.

She plodded on, creating a cocoon of her emotions. Through the fence at her left, metalbreds made their way to and from the track, hot walkers and grooms revolving around them like tiny planets around glowing chestnut suns. Any of them could be her parents, a world away. They used to be this girl. The sun was actually rising now, glinting in her eye, rendering them all invisible for a few blinks. When she looked again, someone caught her gaze.

A serious brown stare. A stripe of blue in her hair. The other sister, who Luz had first seen leaning against the birch tree. Her eyes, her cheekbones carbon copies of the sibling she lost. Those eyes watched Luz until she realized Luz was looking back, and then she turned away, vanishing behind the flank of a metalbred, there and then gone. Luz looked and looked but did not see her again.

CHAPTER 22

TY

Ty watched as her mother sat backward on a motorcycle, the engine's roar drowned out by the laughter bawling from her mouth like a foghorn. It wasn't her laugh. It wasn't even her mouth. The lips were wrong, the teeth. Ty stared in horror as her mother's face lengthened and stretched, mutating hideously, the nostrils flaring and the eyes growing huge and round, glassy. By the time her face had become a horse's, the laugh coming out of her mouth had transformed into a scream.

Ty came awake on the porch with a start, almost slipping off the swing onto the concrete. She caught herself on the chain, pinched her hand in it, and cursed.

"Excuse me?" the letter carrier said, hand paused where she was dropping mail in the box by Ty's front door.

"What?" Ty mumbled. "Oh. No. Not you. Sorry. I…I was sleeping and…nevermind."

"Not a bad day for a porch nap," the woman said, forgiving her instantly. "I might do the same when I get off. Might skip the parade altogether. Day like today you just want to enjoy the breeze."

She waved and Ty nodded, groggy. Her device told her it was well after two, which meant she'd been asleep on this swing for almost three hours. Her father had come home from work to find her eating the cereal she had purchased, which he insisted was his. When he'd asked to see the receipt, she poured the entire box in the trash and came out here. He didn't like to fight in public. Yelling three inches from his daughter's face painted outside the lines of the careful nice-guy box he invented for the world.

Ty was off work. She had nowhere to be. The kind of day that opened up before her like the mouth of a giant cat, a slow yawn shining with teeth. On another day she would've found an excuse to go to the Mahogany, show her face, smile, pretend to be normal. Create her alibi. But she had lost her grip on what was certain – that Brian Benedict would be staying at the Mahogany – and now everything important felt out of reach. Besides, today all she could think about was Luz, and the way her face had folded in on itself when she thought no one was watching, the way the dead girl on the tape was like a signal calling Luz out of a cave, from which she came lumbering with a sword. She thought of Luz, and she thought of Ezz. All of them feeling different kinds of loss. All of them pretending to be whole.

Her device vibrated and she felt a green sprig of hope spring up – Ezz?

Not Ezz. Shavon.

S: What are you up to?

T: Are you sure this was meant for me?

S: Why wouldn't it be?

S: Ohhhh hahaha because I snitched on you at the Pink?

S: What, are you crashing *another* party right now? Should I hit you later?

T: Oh please. WTF Shavon, you NARCed me out last night.

S: I sure the hell did. Ezz is my people, you're a chick whose hair I cut. But Ezz hit me up after the party and said you're cool. So I forgive you.

Ty laughed out loud and then checked over her shoulder to

make sure her dad hadn't heard her through the screen window. Then she leaned back over her device.

T: YOU forgive ME for almost almost getting me hemmed up by security?!

S: Yup. You're welcome. Now, what are you doing today?

T: Nothing. Was kind of wondering if I'd hear from Ezz…

S: Forget Ezz today, I want you to go somewhere with me.

Ty raised her eyebrow at the screen.

T: ???

S: Yup. My cousin's having a BBQ today and it turns out you already know her.

T: I do??

S: …….you know Joelle Simms, right?

Ty let the hand holding her device flop down on her lap and her back thudded against the porch swing. Nostalgia was like a pitcher of cold sweet tea poured straight into her many cups of memory. They all seemed to overflow at the memory of Joelle – the girl standing on the bottom rung of a peeling white fence, knobby knees sticking over the middle slat as she beckoned Ty to come pet the horses. The two of them had spent many afternoons in the hay loft of the Simms barn comparing scars and freckles, watching sparrows scratch in the dust. Joelle always close enough to touch.

T: Yes.

It was all she could type. It was as if her heart were attached to fishing line, a catfish yanking the other end, dragging her back into the past. Before her father lost his job and things went from bad to worse. Before her mother disappeared. When Ty could still look at horses and feel something as soft as their noses.

S: Come with me. It will be fun.

T: What can I bring?

S: Anything but potato salad.

T: Very funny.

S: Yes, but I'm also very serious. HA. Bring lemonade.

T: Okay. What's the address?

S: She lives in the same place.

T: Wait, she does? Tarrington Farms?

S: Called Murphy Farms now. But yes. I'm assuming you don't need the address!

T: No.

S: See you at 4.

The elevated Trolley only went so far in Louisville. Mayor Gardner had pushed it through just after the city had nearly collapsed into the century-old sewer system that every climate change expert had been warning about for three decades. After that, the Trolley was the next logical step in moving the city into the future. But the future stopped just a little way past Floyds Fork and so did the Trolley. From there Ty took a bus the rest of the way to the place she had once lived, and with every mile into the thick green country that she went, she felt her heart sinking into the past, a rabbit wandering into a thicket. She could get lost in these clover-sweet memories. As she walked up the shady lane to the house she grew up beside, she warned herself not to dive too deep.

It helped that her house wasn't there.

She stood in the front yard of Joelle's house – a new paint job, robin's-egg blue, a new extension added to the side of the building, and a new sign: ISAAC MURPHY PASTURES – looking at the place across the smaller field where her own home used to be. Gone. Flat grass, a scrubby tree or two revealed by its absence. Even the fence that had once separated the two plots was gone, moved back an acre. Ty stared, open-mouthed, scanning the photographs of her memories, looking for a smudge that told her she misremembered.

"My parents bought it the year after y'all left," a voice called.

Ty knew the voice. It was older now but still sounded like cricket song.

Joelle stood on the porch, grinning. She was tiny when they were ten, but time had lengthened all of her but her hair – 5'9" at least with long, strong limbs, hair coppery brown, cut as low as Ty's.

"I guess Shavon is your barber too!" Ty called, running to her. In the bag that hung down at her side the lemonade jolted, sweet.

They hugged and Joelle laughed and it was strange to Ty that they had never hugged as children but were now and that it was normal and good. Joelle smelled like straw and maybe woodsmoke. When they pulled away, Joelle cupped Ty's cheeks, gazing at her. The coolness of her hands made Ty realize how warm her own skin was, a sudden flush she'd barely noticed.

"My Ty," Joelle smiled. "We're grown, isn't that wild? Come on, Uncle Reggie is on the grill and it's looking nice. You remember Uncle Reggie?"

The backyard was different than Ty remembered, a stone patio and a tiny pond with a fountain, trellises that covered the chairs with ivied shade. A wave of "heys" went up when Ty joined the gathering, and she waved generally, smiling, before spotting Shavon.

"You made it!" Shavon cried, standing up for a half-hug.

"Where should I put the potato salad?" Ty said earnestly.

"Oh my god no you didn't."

Ty pulled out the lemonade and grinned as Shavon clutched her chest in mock relief. They all cracked up and Joelle walked them over to the tables by the grill where buns and condiments huddled next to brown compostable plates.

"This is my Uncle Reggie, if you don't remember." Joelle tapped the person at the grill on the shoulder, a man of about fifty with a salt-and-pepper beard. He wore loafers and sunglasses, and while Ty didn't recognize his face, the gap-toothed smile that he beamed down at her told her he knew her.

"You probably don't," he grinned. "You were just a little thing when your family moved and I only came around sometimes. But I remember seeing you over there running around, always with your eye on the horses. You and Joelle both had that same look. Horse girls."

"Horse girls," Joelle repeated, laughing, but she was nodding. "People always joke about that concept. But I have a theory."

"What's that?" Uncle Reggie said.

"There's so much pressure on girls," Joelle continued. "For everything. I feel like when we're young, if we were raised right, we think we have so much power. And then the world starts realizing we're girls and it starts closing in, trying to make us act the way it thinks we're supposed to act. And horse girls – or, whatever, the girls who become horse girls – are the ones who somehow remember what the power felt like. And the world tells us we can't be that, so we almost…transfer that imagining onto something that can. Does that make sense? We identify with horses cuz they're huge and strong and fast and free. Or they should be, anyway. Like us."

Ty shifted, suddenly not wanting to look at any of them. She remembered what it had felt like to look out the window and watch the horses moving across Joelle's land while the sound of her parents' shouting rose through the floor beneath her.

Joelle followed her gaze, seeing what was no longer there, and touched Ty's arm to bring her back.

"After my grandma passed, my parents bought the land next door," she said. "They demolished the house that used to be yours so the animals would have more room to roam."

They all turned to survey the long stretch of green, and Ty was surprised by the lack of concern she felt about the thought of her childhood home being bulldozed. Her room had been tiny and wallpapered in pink floral, which her parents claimed they could do nothing about. She had plastered it with posters of horses and girl-bands, but she was always looking out the window anyway. In that way, nothing had changed when she stood looking at the fields she ran as a little girl. Green-blue grass, and the slowly wandering legs of Thoroughbreds. When she scanned the field as a child, there were only four. Now she counted eight without trying.

"I'm so glad you still have horses," Ty said, and then was embarrassed by the eagerness in her voice, a horse in itself, galloping away before she could catch it.

"Once a horse girl, always a horse girl," Uncle Reggie said as he flipped a veggie burger, his cheeks raising up his sunglasses when he smiled.

Joelle took the lemonade from Ty and placed it on the table, then tugged on her sleeve.

"Come on, I'll give you the tour. Shavon, you wanna come?"

"Y'all catch up. I don't have on bug spray. Y'all and these animals…" She waved them off, grinning, and Joelle led the way down a paved path that snaked away from the robin-egg house and toward the gleaming red barn. In Ty's memory it was black and chipping, and the new coat of paint gave everything a dream-like quality, threads of familiar and unfamiliar weaving together to create something new that felt more like déjà vu.

"Different, huh?" Joelle said, watching her. "We needed more space when we decided to open the rescue. It was just a personal hobby for our family at first, you know. We had two and then got two more – retired racehorses that had various injuries or bad track records that no one wanted to buy or breed. So we took them. And then after horseracing was banned and Limestone came on the scene…well. You can imagine. There's a lot more horses out there that need a soft place to land. We stable nineteen here. My aunt in Mississippi has twenty more."

"A rescue," Ty said. They'd reached the fence and, just like when they were little girls, immediately stepped up onto the bottom rung, elbows hooked over the top. They glanced at each other and laughed. "That's amazing. Nineteen. Holy shit. No wonder you needed more space."

"It's amazing work," Joelle agreed. She smiled out at the acres of green and goldenrod, a perimeter of tall slim trees bordering the land that seemed to go on and on. "These animals used to be superstars. Some of them, anyway. But you know how it was. The industry got so ugly. They were all doped up. People made millions coming up with new hormones and drugs that wouldn't be detected in the tests. I know a lot of people were upset when the ban came down, but if I'm being real, I was relieved. These animals weren't signing up for the shit humans were putting them through. They just wanna run. Be horses."

"Look at them!" Ty cried, standing on her toes on the fence. A few hundred yards away two bays kicked up dust in an impromptu race, tossing their heads. When they slowed, they moved through the field languidly like copper jellyfish, the bluegrass a swaying ocean contained by far-off fences. Up close the wood was clean and white before stretching off against the afternoon and blurring orange where the sky bled down onto the ground. Ty felt her skin warm orange at the sight of it, the memory of being barefoot and half-cold in the grass before the dew started to gather.

"They're just how I remember them," Ty sighed, and she could hear the orange sky in her voice now, filling her throat with a thick nostalgia.

"Some of them actually are the same," Joelle said. She pointed at the black mare nodding up along the fence line. "Remember Baeza? She's 16 now. Same girl. Remember when you were freaked out by her night eyes?"

They laughed, and Baeza, dapple gray, rubbed her forehead

on the fencepost, playing coy when Joelle reached her hand out to stroke her neck. Then Baeza stepped forward eagerly, and at her rump a companion snorted, stepping around her, vying for affection. Ty watched her own hand snake out, run fingers down the horse's mane, between the twitching ears. She looked into the honey-warm eye, the thick lashes that batted slow and easy, studying her. He was a massive Palomino with a build like a Thoroughbred, his handsome face carrying a white blaze. The hairs that fuzzed the gentle nose were a forest of sweet bristles.

"What's his name?"

"We're calling him Johnny," Joelle said. "John Doe. Our newest. He's only been here for a few days, actually. Someone did emergency drop-off with him – that happens sometimes. Less often these days, but still. Racing ban or not, there's always somebody who's going to be shitty."

"People are sick," Ty said. She used both hands now, stroking the strong cheek and jaw.

Joelle studied her, watching Ty's hands and Johnny's eyes.

"He's beautiful, isn't he?" Joelle said.

"So beautiful. It's been so long since I was this close. Horses used to be such a big part of my life. You know how it was with my mom: always going to protests and horse events. So weird how everything can…" She stopped, swallowing. She'd wandered down a path she hadn't intended. "Can change so fast."

"Too fast," Joelle said, still watching her. "We get knocked off course, and have to find our way back. Or maybe never back – just the same path in a different direction."

"Maybe," Ty said, frowning. She could see her own face reflected in Johnny's eye.

"You miss your mom?" Joelle said, and there was a snag like barbed wire in her tone. Ty glanced at her. It had been a long time since she had been around someone who actually knew her. Who had known her mother. Who knew they weren't close, not the way Ty always wanted.

"I guess so," Ty said. Her tongue felt dry. "Feels weird to not just say *yes*. More than missing her, I'm angry she's gone. Does that make sense?"

"Yes," said Joelle, and nothing else.

Ty fiddled with Johnny's forelock.

"We never got along. She cared more about horses than she cared about me, if we're being honest. But," she paused, staring into Johnny's eyes, "who can really blame her?"

"I don't think that's true," Joelle said. "But I know what you mean. From what I remember, she was gone a lot. That's why you hung out with me."

Ty nodded slowly.

"Hard to miss someone that you didn't...really know."

They were silent a moment, and Ty was conscious of Joelle watching as Ty rubbed her palms up and down Johnny's neck. Joelle remembered Ty's mom not being around, always so eager to leave her kid for the stables or the protests. Ty felt both embarrassed and vindicated.

"Can I tell you a secret?" Joelle said softly.

"Yeah. Of course."

"I used to tell you all kinds of secrets," Joelle smiled. "Remember? You never told me any though."

"I guess I didn't have anything to tell."

"Me neither," Joelle said. "Not really. I was ten."

Like sunlight filtering through the cracked ceiling of the barn, the days in the hayloft glimmered again through Ty's memory. Joelle's face close to hers and smiling, lips moving in a whisper. Another kind of secret.

"But you do now?" Ty said.

"Kind of."

"What is it?"

"You see Johnny?" Joelle nodded at him. He glanced at her,

stomped a fly off his withers. Joelle's face was serious now, guarded.

"Yeah?" said Ty, taking him in.

Joelle paused, as if still considering. Then her lips parted and she said, almost a whisper:

"He's a metalbred."

"What?"

The corner of Joelle's mouth turned up in a careful smile.

"Johnny. This pretty boy right here. He's an equinibot."

Ty slowly withdrew her hand, rubbing her fingers together. She felt the silky coat of dirt between her fingertips, velvety horse residue. Johnny stomped off another fly, idly reached his muzzle in her direction for more rubbing. Ty stared at him, at the twitching ears, the relaxed shift of weight from one hip to the other.

"Impossible," she breathed.

"You'd think so," said Joelle. "But when we took him in and gave him a full check-up to see if he needed any treatment, we realized he didn't have a heartbeat. He's got the thrum, you know?"

"Thrum?"

"Machine thrum. Put your hand right here."

She directed Ty's hand to Johnny's chest, just past it. Joelle scratched while Ty tentatively let her hand rest, feeling. The subtle warm vibration wasn't a heart. It was chilling to feel it, under the warm convincing skin and coat. She withdrew her hand as quickly as she could without snatching it.

"How?" she said. "Who would get rid of a metalbred? That's not even legal, is it? They have to be accounted for or recycled every year."

"No idea. And no, it's not legal. But we have no idea who dropped him off."

"Have you contacted Limestone?"

"No. But we think something is broken with his system, otherwise they'd have already tracked him down."

"You could ask a jockey to come take a look," Ty suggested. She was afraid to touch the thing again.

"We would've asked Rosario Vicario, but…," Joelle said.

She let her voice fade, and Ty didn't ask any more questions to draw it out again. She pictured Rosario's face again, the blood like lace around her lips. She wondered if Rosario's parents believed she overdosed the way the police were saying, if they suspected anything at all. She wondered how well Joelle knew her, if at all. She didn't want to ask. The weight of knowing something – even if it wasn't everything – seemed suddenly unbearably heavy. But she didn't know where to put it down.

Just then, Baeza snorted and trotted back toward the open grass, Johnny's head turning like a graceful sailboat and following. They moved shoulder to shoulder until Baeza broke out into a gallop, and then they were off, the wind carrying their manes back like celebrations as the powerful bodies moved forward in the golden light.

"Do you think Baeza knows?" Ty said softly.

"I don't think she cares," Joelle said, finally smiling again.

CHAPTER 23

EZZ

I t was 10:55 am and Ezz was standing outside the Mahogany, pacing. She had messaged Ty twice already with no response and now loitered across the street watching the windows on the upper floors, hoping Ty might pass one. She knew she couldn't knock – if Madame Richmond answered, she wouldn't be able to answer her questions. *Why do you want to come in? What do you mean, you need to go into the room where Rosario Vicario died?* She needed Ty.

Finally her device vibrated and she snapped it up to eye level.

Ty: What's up?

Ezz: Look out on Oak.

Ty: ???

Ezz waited impatiently, shifting her weight from foot to foot, eyes leaping from window to window until, on the third floor, the black-clad form of Ty appeared, hand raised to withdraw an earpod from one ear. Ezz couldn't make out her eyes from here, but she could tell she was searching the street out front before her gaze came to rest on Ezz. Ezz lifted her device in greeting.

Ty: What are you doing here??

Ezz: Is your boss there?

Ty: No, why?

Ezz: I need to come in.

Ty: In here?? Why? I'm working!
Ezz: I'll tell you when you let me in.

Ezz watched the uncertainty of Ty's body language, the reluctance. The desire. Ezz knew she would soon be inside. She sent one more message.

Ezz: I'll meet you in the back.

Up through the window, she watched Ty throw her hands up, annoyed, giving in. She flashed Ezz her middle finger through the glass, and then disappeared.

Ty: Fine.

Ezz trotted down one alley, then turned into the other, waiting at the gate that barred the world from the back of the Mahogany. Beyond the gate, a garden sprang green and hungry within tidily organized plots. Ezz studied it while she waited for Ty – it was different than whatever it was that Luz worked on in the lair: down there underground were vines that twitched when Ezz peeked in, leaves that seemed to unfurl too fast. Maybe it was just the shadows.

Beyond the garden, a back door to the hotel cracked open and Ty's shaved blonde head popped out. Ezz felt herself be seen, and Ty made her way down the garden paths, expression guarded. She was a lot like Luz in that way, Ezz thought. Frowning girls and their secrets.

"I need you to get me into Rosario's room," Ezz said as soon as they were face to face.

"Wait, what?" Ty cried. "Are you being serious? I can't sneak you in!"

"Why not?"

"It's a *crime scene*, for starters."

"And? Do they have a guard?"

"No. But it's taped off!"

"Tape," Ezz scoffed. "It's probably not even locked."

"It's absolutely locked."

"And you absolutely have the key," Ezz pressed.

Ty didn't answer.

"See? You have the key," Ezz confirmed. "I need you to do this for me, Ty."

"Why? They swept the whole place. They had whole teams full of people in here."

"That's what I need to see."

Ty stared at her and Ezz stared back, trying to look focused and unfazed. She needed to do this, and she needed Ty to make it happen. But she had never seen Ty in her work uniform, and there was something about it that felt like a layer had been pulled back, an element of a disguise wiped away. Ty looked on edge, as if there were something inside the Mahogany that would leak out if she opened the door, and part of Ezz wanted to ask what it was that turned Ty's face into barbed wire. But part of her needed to get into that building. Now.

"Get me up there and I'll explain," Ezz said quietly. "I promise."

Ty studied her, and Ezz, who had walked out of the house wearing baggy camo pants and a white T-shirt, suddenly wished she had worn something that would keep Ty's eyes on her a little longer.

"Come on," Ty sighed, and turned toward the hotel.

Inside, they took the stairs. Ty didn't want to risk running into any of the cleanwork staff on the lift, she said, but she still paused at every corner, peering and listening.

"I thought you said your boss wasn't here?" Ezz said.

"Yeah, but she has a daughter," Ty muttered, "and that girl is like a ferret. She sneaks into the weirdest places, always popping up..." She trailed off.

"Where is everybody?" Ezz said when they reached the third-floor landing and had seen no one. "I kind of thought you sneaking me in would have to be...sneakier."

"Derby parties," Ty said. "Luncheons. Parades. Day clubs. You know how it is. All these people are in Louisville to spend money. The hotel is the last place they want to pass the day."

"Even one as nice as this," Ezz said, eyeing the shining wood archways.

"Your house is way nicer than this," Ty scoffed.

"Maybe," Ezz shrugged. "But it's empty."

"So you fill it with the family you choose," Ty said, not looking at her. Ezz glanced at her sharply, then away, aware of a feeling like a fish hook being lodged in her sternum. Then Ty stopped, pointing. "That's it."

The crime scene tape was like stripes of siren at the end of the dim hallway. They screamed silently at the two girls, who stood gaping as if at a mirage. Ezz found herself staring at the door hard, as if by looking long enough it would all just disintegrate. A trick. A hallucination. She had told herself coming here would be no big deal if she focused on the mission. She was wrong. She blinked three times in rapid succession and by the time her vision focused, she was seeing Ty's back moving away toward the room. Ezz hurried to catch up.

"Go ahead," Ezz whispered when they stood at the door.

Ty held up the hand wearing the ring fob and took a deep breath. So did Ezz. She knew when she entered, everything she had imagined would be thrown out and replaced with a sharper, more painful reality. Her mind had been a maze of inventions since Rosario died, creating scenes she didn't ask to see. Now she would know exactly what the carpet that Rosario had died on looked like. She would know what curtains had been closed to keep the paparazzi's eyes off her body. She would see blood, maybe. The bed where Rosario had spent her last night, the secrets she kept from her best friend beside her on the pillow.

"Got it," Ty whispered, and Ezz swallowed. The door opened.

The drapes were all closed, not even cracks around each window allowing in daylight. The officers had hung up canvases over each large window, covering even those spare cracks – just in case journalist drones got clever with their angles and leaked a corner of an ink stain, a sliver of a bedsheet. A bedsheet could spur an entire new fleet of lies and rumors. The only light in the room came from the violet-blue hologram rotating along the back wall – the index registering the staff who had entered the crime scene and when. This is what Ezz had come for.

But she couldn't make herself move toward it. She stood at the door, her back almost against it, as if stepping into the room would be stepping into a pit of giant squid, tentacles dragging her down and down.

"This is it, huh?" she heard her voice say, ragged and low.

"Yes," said Ty gently. Ezz wondered if she could feel the tremble in Ezz's limbs even without touching her. A horse half-wild and ready to bolt.

"It's so unfair," Ezz said. "It's just…not right. And whoever did this is out there walking around, like it was nothing. I won't stand for that."

"Is that why you're here?" Ty said. She sounded cautious, as if she were gauging Ezz's answer to compare it to some internal blueprint of her own.

"Yes." Ezz's eyes raised from the floor then, resolving to stop looking for Rosario's ghost. She scanned the walls and then came to rest on the softly glowing hologram rotating on the wall, the slow switch from face to uniformed face. She stepped resolutely away from the safety of the wall and into the deep water of the room where her best friend died.

"The detective said this is everybody who has had access to the crime scene," Ty told her. "Like a face log."

"That's what Luz said they would have," Ezz nodded, crossing the room slowly, picking her way around debris. There was an empty place in the middle of it all, and the sight of it made Ezz swallow. That's where Rosario had lain – she didn't need to ask. She glanced at Ty to see if she was watching her, and found her crouched near that empty spot, head dropped to peer under the heavy cherry wardrobe.

"What are you doing?" Ezz said, pausing.

"Nothing," Ty said, and stood. "Thought I saw something. So you're here for the hologram log. Why?"

Ezz crossed the final span of the room to stand before the rotating faces, sliding her device out of her back pocket. A moment later, Luz's face appeared on the slick black screen. She was perched on her chair in Ezz's lair, the many monitors on the wall lit up with other faces. They rotated faster than the ones of the hologram.

"Ready?" Ezz said quietly.

"Ready," said Luz, and Ezz held up the device, flipping it around so Luz could see the hologram herself.

"What's going on?" Ty said, watching with narrowed eyes.

"We thought of something yesterday when we left the backside," Ezz said. "Luz was really upset so we went to go get donuts and of course there were cops up in there. Or, you know, *Special Police* who are really just living that cop fantasy. And we were thinking about the fact that Rosario had footage of the murder – but she didn't go to the Special Police with it. And she didn't ask *you* to give it to them. So she must have known that the cops either wouldn't believe her or they were in on it."

"I mean, it's Brian Benedict," Ty said, and Ezz noted that her voice had that peculiar quality that it sometimes got, when it turned into a rusty sword. "He probably has at least some of the Special Police on his payroll. Detective Segrest is independent, but I wouldn't be surprised if Benedict owned him too. We can't trust *any* cops."

"Yeah, well, exactly," Ezz said, looking back at the hologram, tilting to see Luz's face on the screen of her device. "So we thought, we need to go to the crime scene. See their log. Not likely that we'd see Brian Benedict himself show up on it, but if we're going to try to expose this whole thing, we need to know the players."

On Ezz's screen, Luz was aiming some kind of scanner through the screen – almost a camera but not, trained on the revolving holograms.

"So," Ezz went on, a grim confidence growing in her stomach. "Luz hit a few high-profile Derby parties last night using her fake press pass, scanning faces of people hanging out with Limestone folks. We want to see if there's any crossover to who might have been at Rosario's crime scene."

"Is this what you were doing at the parade?" Ty said, aiming her voice at Luz. Luz glanced out at the device and Ezz watched her carefully.

"What parade?" Luz said.

"On Oak Street. I saw you scanning faces of Limestone employees."

"I'm building a database," Luz frowned. "Ever since we saw the video of that girl...well. It's fucked up. I know Limestone is behind this and I want photos of everyone who might be involved. So I was scanning for faces and data."

Noted, Ezz thought.

"Data?" Ty said.

"Yes. The way Rosario had the video file in her nose ring? It's more and more common for people to keep sensitive data in personal accessories. Keep it close."

"And did you find anything? Any personal accessories, I mean," said Ty.

"Yes. I found that a lot of Limestone employees carry data in their cufflinks."

"What kind of data is it?" Ty pressed.

"I don't know," Luz said. "My devices just show me *where* it is. I can't look at the data itself unless I get my hands on the actual cufflinks."

"What all have you found?" Ty said, and Ezz glanced at Ty now, noting the sound of a shovel in her voice.

"Nothing major yet," said Luz, turned back to her screens. "Just that Limestone employees sometimes end up at the same parties as off-duty cops. Nothing linking them to Rosario or the girl in the video."

"Keep running your database," Ezz said, turning back to the holograms on the wall, bracing the hand holding the device on the inside of her elbow. "We'll see what we see."

She turned to Ty just in time to see a scowl pass over her face – her eyes fixed on the wall. Ezz twitched her gaze to the hologram to find the face of a white man staring out, blue squinty eyes and a light brown beard.

"Was that your detective?" Ezz said, and Ty's eyes shot back to her. "The one you said you lied to?"

"Yes," Ty said.

"You heard anything else from him?"

"No. He said he'd be in touch if he needed to talk to me, but I haven't heard from him."

"He hasn't come by the hotel?"

In the hologram on the wall, Detective Segrest's face peered out at them before being replaced by a stocky Asian woman noted as the coroner. The next face was a slim white guy, young. He could have been college-aged if it weren't for the uniform. He stared out at the room with an expression of reluctance, as if he wasn't sure his photo would turn out right. A heartbeat later, Luz's voice rang from Ezz's device.

"Him."

Ezz hurriedly turned the device around and in her chest her heart began to gallop. She bent her head close to the device, Ty following suit, to see Luz pointing at one of her screens, device angled to encapsulate her and it.

"Look at that," Luz said, triumphant. "This cop was partying at the Carousel party last night. I didn't notice him while I was there, but he's in my footage. There he is at the back, see?"

Ezz did see. The reluctant young officer whose face had, a moment before, been illuminated blue in the room where Rosario died, was paused on a screen above Luz's workbench, frozen with a big sloppy smile on his face, drink raised and wearing an almost-nice suit. Ezz recognized the expression – relieved gratitude, just happy to be there.

"The Carousel," Ty said. "You were at the Carousel?"

Luz made a face as if she'd been reminded about a particularly unsavory meal she'd been forced to eat. Ezz snorted. For Derby-goers with money, there was Millionaire's Row. But there were some people too rich for Millionaire's Row, and they partied on the private event circuit, the Carousel, the location of the party revolving each night. Unmarked doors – Ezz didn't even know where the venues were, only that it existed. Tight security. Celebrities and socialites. Masquerades.

"Yes," Luz said. "There was a special event last night: Limestone and horse industry people only. They were only letting in a few press people so I got there early."

"So why would a cop be there?" Ezz mused. "Rubbing elbows with rich-ass horse people?"

"Not on duty," Ty said, pointing at the suit. "He was there to party. Look at him."

"Maybe he did them a favor," Luz said, her frown deepening. "And so they did *him* a favor in return."

"What kind of favor?" Ezz said. She raised her eyes to the rotating hologram, as if hoping one of the faces might answer.

"We're going to have to ask," Luz said, sounding grim. "Another party tonight. At the Carousel. We need to be there."

"Jesus, how many parties *are* there?" Ty said, disgusted.

"Every night leading up to Derby," said Luz. "You know how it is."

"So wait," Ezz said. "I hear you saying we'll go and ask him. Is that the plan? Just ask him what the hell he's doing? That doesn't seem like it would be...effective."

"Okay, maybe not just *ask* him, but nose around," Luz pressed. "See who he talks to. See what we can overhear."

"Blend in and ear hustle," Ezz said, pondering. "Hmm."

"How do we know he'll be there tonight?" Ty said.

Luz pointed at her freeze frame of the drunken cop.

"Purple ribbon," she said, indicating the small emblem on his lapel. "Full pass. With all the free drinks and supermodels at these parties during Derby...where *else* would he be?"

"True," Ezz agreed. "But you're forgetting one piece, Luz. You've got your little fancy press pass or whatever. What about me and her? How are we going to get in? You said they're only letting a few press in, and I'm not letting you go alone again. Shit is getting real."

Luz scrunched her lips, thinking, and Ezz was going to keep brainstorming, but then the floor beneath her feet shuddered ever so slightly. She glanced down, surprised, then back up at Ty. Ty's eyes were wide.

"Shit," Ty said out loud, and gripped Ezz's elbow. "We have to go."

Ezz followed without protest, hanging up on Luz immediately. She stood silent and still as Ty cracked the suite door and peered out into the hallway. She could hear muffled voices below, spiraling up the polished stairs. But no one was climbing, and the elevator was hushed.

"Let's go," Ty whispered, and they snaked out into the hall, not speaking until Ty had swiped them into what Ezz realized was the cleanwork elevator.

"Boss home?" Ezz said softly as they shuddered downward. They were only inches apart and Ezz could almost feel Ty's thundering heartbeat traveling across the brief space.

"Maybe," Ty said. They landed with a muted thud, and Ty peeked through the elevator bars, Ezz peering out over her head. Two young women, twins, sauntered out into the dining hall where Ezz had eaten her last dinner with Rosario. The twins' arms were laden with snacks and shopping bags. Ty and Ezz waited until they went out back, garden bound, and then Ezz allowed herself to be tugged along toward the front door, feet like whispers. Her blood felt carbonated until they reached the front door, Ty flipping the locks and throwing it open. Ezz expected a quick exit, but Ty grabbed her by the shirt, drawing her close, a smile creeping across her face like the slow spread of spilled wine.

"What?" Ezz said, confused, hyper-aware of the feeling of Ty's fingers tugging at her clothes, exposing an inch of stomach.

"I know how we're going to get into the party tonight," Ty said, and to Ezz, something in the girl's eyes felt like a tiger that didn't know if it would roar or purr. Ty let go of Ezz's shirt and Ezz stumbled out into the afternoon beyond. "I'll meet you at your house at 9. Make sure you dress up."

CHAPTER 24

TY

The Richmond twins were lounging in the concrete circle cut-out in the center of the back garden, a Tupperware container open between them, out of which they fished miniature chocolate muffins. Ty peeked through the Venetian blinds at them, and she was 99% sure Madame Richmond intended the muffins for this evening's guests. But Ty's plans relied on the twins remaining in the garden, eating muffins and smoking weed, a joint of which Caroline was rolling messily in her lap. Ty waited for the green-brown flakes to burst out one more time before turning back to the kitchen, where the hallway up toward the Richmond quarters loomed like a dragon's violet throat. She knew her ring fob would work. Josie, who was assigned to clean the Richmonds' level, had asked to use Ty's fob once when her own had malfunctioned. Any cleanwork ring would get her inside, but she had no idea what to expect once she made it in.

As it turned out, the door opened onto a carpeted stairway leading up into a separate level of the Mahogany, the old brickwork of the antique building covered in fresh drywall. Ty took each step cautiously; knowing Madame Richmond wouldn't be back for an hour wasn't enough to mitigate the flinching she felt in her bones every time her feet produced a squeak. She couldn't relax, even when she reached the top and found herself in a wide parlor with carpet that felt like walking across a herd of alpaca. She took three steps into the wide parlor and had to pause, breathing in and out three times, as if preparing to dive into deep water. In a way, she was. If she were found here, she would not only lose her job but probably risk jail time. She'd never work in Louisville again, not after the rumor of her as a thief made its way through the cleanwork circuit – and she would never be able to kill Brian Benedict. Although even that plan was spinning out of her grasp. But that was exactly why she had to do this, she thought, as she padded forward: her window at the Mahogany had closed. She had to make a new window, and working alongside Luz and Ezz seemed the best possible route.

Ty knew the twins would have tickets to a Carousel party. They received tickets to everything, especially during Derby. It wasn't even that they were so wealthy as to have earned their place on the socialite court – they were just the kind of young white woman that event organizers loved to have grazing in the fields of Louisville's nightlife. Tall, blondish, the right shade of spray tan. They had agreeable laughs and no political opinions. Ty crept down the hallway of the Richmond manor – it was smaller than she had expected. They used the kitchen downstairs in the Mahogany, so what Ty found herself in now was living quarters only. Sparsely decorated, everything in shades of white and light gray, it felt like a waiting room. It felt like the Richmond women were hung up in the closets somewhere, waiting to be put on and puppeted down the stairs.

The first room down the hallway out of the living area was a gym. The hum of electronic workout equipment surprised her, scared her almost with its mechanical anxiety. She inched the door shut and moved down the hall, past an actual bathroom, and then past a door that was locked firmly. The door at the end of the hallway she knew had to be Madame's – Ty could smell the Dior from a mile away. But the room before it was unlocked and open, and the wafting scent of a citrus beach told her this was where the twins slept.

She was right.

She poked her head inside the door, peeping around. Canopied beds. Two big mirrors over two glowing vanities. Glass (or maybe just transparent plastic) tiers displaying armies of make-up and perfumes, fluffy faux fur rugs draping the floor. It was the sort of room Ty didn't like to admit she coveted. Her own room was so far from this soft landscape of excess that confessing she liked it would admit just how far out of reach it was.

She crossed to the vanities, made herself ignore the glittering vials and bottles. Her eyes swept the surfaces, but aside from discarded cosmetic pads and various charging docks, she didn't see anything that looked like an invitation. She moved to the curving white dressers placed against the small windows – the windows were the only things she didn't like about the room. Like squinted eyes. The light that came in felt like leftovers.

Nothing on the dressers but bras and books. Condoms. Candy. She stared at the drawers. Would she open them? She thought of someone entering her room and that was bad enough, but imagining them sifting through her underwear – even in search of something stupid like tickets – made her feel cringey.

"If you're looking for money, it's in the music box."

Ty spun around, throwing her back against the dresser as if she would magically become part of it, sink into the wood and disappear before whoever was in the doorway grabbed her, dragged her out in cuffs.

But there was no one in the doorway.

She stared, heart thudding, then took a tentative step toward the door, thinking whoever it was had stepped back out into the hall. She imagined them dialing the police.

"I don't think they have any real drugs – they're out back

smoking mild stuff. But I've never seen you high, so maybe that's not what you're after."

The voice was right in the room with Ty. She looked around, realization dawning on her, too slowly to calm her pulse right away. She moved to the bed closest to where she stood, slowly crouched down, and peered underneath.

Camille. She lay flat on her back, a glowing reading device held over her face, which was tilted sideways to stare at Ty. She grinned, her teeth shimmering like the Cheshire cat's in the close white light.

"What the hell are you doing?" Ty said.

Camille made a face.

"You're asking *me*," she said, then waved her hand in a shooing motion. Ty shuffled backward and stood, making room for Camille to scoot out. Once out, she placed her device on her sister's bed and stretched. "What are you looking for?"

Ty stared at her, searching her face for clues of what might happen next, and inwardly cursing herself for forgetting about Camille. First she'd caught Ty coming out of Darden's room – now this.

Ty decided to take the honest route.

"I'm looking for tickets," she said. "To the Carousel party tonight."

Camille blinked at her, long and slow as if readjusting her lens.

"Oh. Well. You could've just asked me," she said. She scooped her device up and loped out of the room. It didn't occur to Ty that she should follow until Camille paused at the door, raised her eyebrows meaningfully.

The locked room in the hall was Camille's. She fished a key out of her bra and slipped it into the lock. The doorknob emitted a light click, and then they were stepping inside.

It was as if she and the twins were from different planets, and

Camille's planet was oceanic. Everything was blue. The walls, the bedding, the lampshades. There were no curtains, but blue silky scarves were draped over the curtain rods. Ty felt as if she had been transported into the bedchamber of a mermaid princess. The only thing similar to the twins' room was her dresser – the same white curving piece. Camille had painted the drawer fronts aquamarine.

"Wow, your room is…really pretty," Ty said, a little taken aback. It was pretty. But, like Camille, it seemed to emerge out of the shadows, unexpected. She had expected a room like a bruise, black and maroon and maybe a little foreboding.

"Thank you," Camille said, flopping on her bed and scooching across on her belly to reach the cobalt nightstand on the other side. "It's relaxing."

"So…why were you hanging out in your sisters' room then?" Ty ventured.

Camille withdrew an envelope from a drawer, craning around to look at her.

"It smells nice in there. Didn't you notice?"

"I mean, sure, but…"

"I like being where I'm not supposed to be," Camille said, sitting up. "When you're somewhere you're not supposed to be, you see things you're not supposed to see." She scanned Ty from head to toe. "Case in point."

"I'm not a thief," Ty said, and tried to sound the way she felt when she was turning over a guest suite. Neat. Straight-edged. Sanitized. "I'm just…working on something. And I need to be at the Carousel tonight to do it."

"I didn't see you for the Derby party type," Camille said. She held the envelope in both hands, letting it rest on her lap and stroking it like a teacup poodle. "You don't seem like a party girl at all."

"I'm not," said Ty flatly. "I told you: I'm working on something."

"On what?"

"An…investigation. With some friends."

"Friends such as…Ezzardine Clayton?"

Ty squinted at her, at the ripple of a smile that passed over her lips before being swallowed by the look of polite curiosity.

"How did you know?"

"I saw her come in a little while ago. Does Madame know she was here?"

"No."

"Oh, good. I love when my mother doesn't know things. It's rare."

"Does she know you spy on everyone in the house?" Ty snapped.

"It's a family trait."

They stared at each other for a long moment, but Camille's smile was back, and it drew the tension out like a toxin through a syringe.

"What are you trying to do at the Carousel?" she asked. "Does this have to do with Rosario Vicario?"

"Why would you say that?" Ty said quickly.

"Come on," Camille said, quirking her lips. She let her eyes wander the floor, as if looking through the layers of mahogany between where they stood and where Rosario's body had lain. "You'd never laid eyes on Ezzardine Clayton until that night, and now you're spending time together and trying to crash a Carousel party hosted by Derby muckity-mucks. I'm not stupid. Something's up."

Ty stared at the envelope in Camille's hand, trying to decide if the truth was worth what was inside it. It was. They needed to get inside a Carousel event and be where they didn't belong so they could see what they weren't supposed to see. But trusting Camille felt like trusting a bridge Ty couldn't see the end of, the other side obscured by mist.

"Look," Ty said slowly. She decided to tell the other side of the truth. "Yes, it has to do with Rosario. But I can't tell you what or why, okay? Not only do we...just not know anything, I don't know *you*. All I know is that you're my boss's daughter and that you're good at disappearing. But I don't *know* you, know you. And I can't jeopardize this...project."

"You mean you can't jeopardize your budding romance," Camille said, eyes glinting.

"That's not what I mean," Ty said, blushing. She swiped a hand down over her buzz, as if to tamp down the feeling of steam that arose whenever she thought of Ezzardine.

Camille studied her for a moment, grinning, before finally speaking again.

"Look," she said. "I'll give you the invitation. But only if you don't mind me coming with you."

"Wait, what?"

Camille tapped the envelope on her lap.

"Good for *me*...plus two," she said, looking teasingly mournful. "Sadly you won't be able to get in without me being there. Consider me your chaperone."

"But you never leave the house," said Ty, struggling to find a way around or out of this new development. "You never go to parties."

"Yes, well, I know a good cause when I see one," she said. "I need a good girls' night."

"When is the last time you *had* a girls' night?" Ty said, baffled.

"Never," Camille grinned. "So this is good timing."

She popped up from the bed and moved to the closet door, which Ty hadn't noticed, draped as it was in scarves of many shades of blue. She half-expected water to come pouring out, but instead found an immaculately organized closet, also containing a full-length mirror which showed Ty gaping at Camille's back.

One side of the closet was lined with black and gray and white, which Ty was accustomed to Camille being suited in. But the other side was ablaze with color: lush green satin and blazes of yellow, a section of crimson and scarlet.

"What is all *that?*" Ty said, taking a step forward without meaning to, a hand outstretched. She was a magpie being drawn toward a nest of silky glowing objects.

"This is all the stuff they send when they deliver invitations for parties I never go to," Camille said, running her finger down the row. "Jumpsuits. Suits. But mostly dresses. Sometimes they send shoes too. I don't know who the hell told them my shoe size. I'm convinced all the entertainment circuit people are former CIA."

Ty had drifted into the closet, reluctant at first but drawn by the heady feeling of *want*...the colors and textures were so vibrant she could almost taste them. All the pieces still had tags dangling from their sleeves and necklines. Some of the prices were enough to pay a mortgage.

"Jesus...," she murmured.

"A clothes horse," Camille said, amused. "I wouldn't have predicted that either."

"I'm not," Ty protested, then ran her open hand down the line, the different fabrics imprinting on her fingertips. She sighed lovingly. "Not really, anyway."

"Try this one," Camille said, pulling a fiery orange gown out of the fray. "A tall neckline is just the thing with your haircut."

"I didn't think you were into fashion either," Ty said, doubtful.

"I am. Just not *this* fashion. What do you think I look at all day?"

"I don't know," Ty said. "I thought you were reading, like, serious tomes and shit."

"Well, that too. But also *Vogue*. My runway just never sees the light of day."

"But tonight is different?" Ty said. Camille was pressing the dress into her hands and Ty found her fingers opening for it, closing on it. The fabric was so smooth and cool and Camille's smile was warm and real. Ty had done this once with her mother: trying on outfits for a party she ended up not going to. Taking off and putting on clothes had been the best part, standing in the mirror and trying on the costume of different smiles, postures. She had experimented with different futures by standing in different shoes. The future she ended up with hadn't occurred to her at the time.

Ty slid out of her uniform, and the way Camille watched and didn't watch was like slipping on old socks. It had been so long since Ty felt like she had friends, the warm familiarity of sisterhood. Ty watched herself try on the orange dress and become the sun.

CHAPTER 25

LUZ

L uz stood nestled in the leafy embrace of a topiary elephant, her sparkling dress covered in twigs. She had been making her way out to where Ty would soon be arriving to take them all to the Carousel when her device had buzzed with an incoming message from her father.

You're breaking your mother's heart.

Luz wasn't sure if it was her shoes or the message that made her feel unsteady. She stared at the words and wondered why they didn't make her cry. Her mother's broken heart should make her feel something, she told herself. And it did, but the "something" was nothing new. The guilt that ached between her shoulder blades was as familiar as a birthmark by now. She was twenty-one years old and, until she started working in the greenhouse, had never strayed from the path her parents imagined for her. Now that she had...there was no going back. She felt she would suffocate if she did. The thought made her fingers move across the screen, typing words she would never say out loud to her father:

What about my broken heart, papi?

She almost wondered if he wouldn't write back, and then:

You are too smart for the racetrack. Too smart to plant flowers. You could run your own business. You could make something.

She felt her cheeks flame, her fingers flying.

There's technology in the greenhouse too, papi. We analyze the soil, we blend plants together.

She sent the message, her heart full of vines, and almost typed "I *have* made something," but she bit her lip. Not yet.

We want more for you. We want the world to see you, mija.

She stared at the message for a long moment before she replied.

Then we want the same thing for each other.

Beyond the green embrace of the elephant, she heard Ty and Ezz exclaiming over each other's outfits. It was time. She pushed out through the branches, swiping twigs and leaves off her dress, and then crossed the short distance to the gate. Ty saw her first.

"Your dress!" Ty exclaimed, and sent a chef's kiss skyward. She wore an emerald green sheath that showed her thigh, and her warm smile was a balm on the cold that had swept over Luz's skin. Luz looked down at herself, at the black gown Ezz had brought her, the slit even higher than Ty's. She picked off a stray leaf.

"Thanks," Luz said, pleased. "You look nice too."

Beside Ty, Ezz's suit was black at first glance but revealed its gold and green undertones in the glow from the streetlight. She looked like a dragon from an underground realm, rising up from volcanic rock. Luz glanced slyly at Ty, watching something in those hard eyes thaw slightly, and felt her own smile widen, pushing back the thought that her father had not written back. Tonight was business, yes, but also this could be…fun. Maybe she deserved fun.

They all piled into the car, and Luz gasped when she realized someone was in the six-seat cab with them. Luz hadn't even seen her at first – she seemed to melt into the shadows, swathed in a wraith-like dress the color of cobwebs.

"This is Camille," Ty said. "She's the one who's getting us in tonight. Tickets."

"Camille Richmond," Ezz nodded, holding out her hand, which Camille took readily. "I've never actually laid eyes on you. Nice to meet you."

"Likewise," Camille said. "Thanks for allowing me along."

"Well, it sounds like you're the key to the door," Ezz said. "And the key is always welcome."

Luz watched Ezz's eyes swing over to Ty, taking in the emerald velvet. Ezz said nothing, but the amber in her brown eyes seemed suddenly brighter, following the green fabric of the dress up to the slit. Luz looked away, taking in the night beyond the window, smiling, listening to them talk. She thought again of the woman she had met in the museum, Irma. Maybe when this was all over she'd go back, ask Irma to give her a real tour.

"I thought you were going to steal some tickets," Ezz teased Ty. "Not much of a thief?"

"Not much of a thief," Camille answered. "But a good friend, I think."

"Whose car is this?" Luz said, glancing up toward the black partition. She couldn't see the driver's face and it made her a little nervous.

"My family's," Camille said. "He can pick us up too, if necessary."

Luz nodded, continuing to look out the window. Ezz didn't live far from all the Derby action, and the car had slowed to wind around people reveling in the street. It was only 9:30 pm and the slightly precarious feeling of after midnight had already spilled out into the evening. People were on their way to parties, bar crawls, and nightclubs, the sidewalks glittering with costumes and bottles of alcohol. The streets of Old Louisville, with their metal fleurs-de-lis on every porch and fencepost, were dappled from streetlights and glowing drones that shone through the maple and magnolia lining the sidewalks. Neon figures wove between them. The days of strict seersucker at noon were gone – Derby had swallowed the idea of Mardi Gras and put a saddle on its back.

But the sidewalk where Camille's driver rolled to a stop was bare of neon, and quiet compared to the throngs of masked revelers they had just passed through. Peering out, Luz thought it looked almost residential: gray stone, iron gates, windows with shades drawn closed against the night. She could see the glow of Cavehill, just a few blocks away.

Camille lowered the partition.

"Are you sure this is it?" she called up to the driver.

"Yep." He pointed at a red door. "That's the one. When should I pick you up?"

"Give it two hours. If you haven't heard from me, make it three."

"You got it."

The four young women climbed out, cautious as bunnies. Once on the sidewalk, Ezz glanced at Luz.

"Is this right?"

"I don't know," Luz shrugged. "It's the Carousel, remember? Revolves to a different location every night. Last night I was clear over in the Highlands."

"Let's hope the cop we're looking for got the memo," Ty said.

Luz marched up the stairs, eyeing her companions. They were all figuratively dressed to kill, but with Ty it seemed to veer toward literal. Her eye caught on Ty, the steel that rarely seemed to leave her eyes, as if she had once been something soft that had melted and been remolded into a weapon. Luz turned away. The red door was unmarked. No sign, no knocker, no peep hole. Beside her, Camille knocked twice, and the sound was unexpectedly loud on the quiet street.

"Are we sure this is the right place?" Luz said, looking around.

Camille slipped the invitation out of her purse, peering down in the yellow light offered from an arching lantern.

"It says Number 56," she said. "This is 56."

"Let me see." Ezz extended her hand and plucked the gold-foil invitation from Camille, holding it closer to her face.

"It says *password: gallop* at the bottom," she read, then lifted her chin to peer at the door. She paused, then opened her mouth and shouted: "GALLOP!"

They all stared, but the door merely stared back.

"Did you really think yelling *gallop* at a closed door was gonna work?" Luz muttered.

"It says it's the password!" Ezz protested. "What did you do at the last Carousel party?"

"I got there right as they were letting another group in," Luz frowned. "So I just walked in behind them and then they checked my press pass."

"Wait, wait...," said Ty, and Luz could tell by her voice that she had caught onto a thread of something, was pulling it, wondering. "What if..."

Ty raised one hand to the door, and then two. She placed both knuckles against the door, took a deep breath, and then beat out a rhythm. It was a sound Luz knew from birth, close and far at the same time. Against the door, Ty knocked out the sound of a horse's hooves, as if creating a sound effect for a cartoon.

The door opened so fast she almost knocked on the face of the man who'd been behind it. He stood grinning, wearing a red tuxedo.

"Welcome," he said, "to the Carousel."

The entryway was an elevator, and Luz expected to be borne down into a basement, where they'd be swallowed by black lights. Instead she felt herself being carried upward, one short level. When the doors opened, the man in the red tux beamed and said, "Follow the music."

The four girls stood in a long, dim hallway, many doors on each side, the cracks at the bottom dark and silent. All but one. A thin gold line, the distant sounds of laughter snaking under the door and reaching their ears. Luz was listening for the thump of bass as a musical indicator, so it took her a moment to catch the delicate tremble of violins.

"Well, this isn't exactly a puzzle," Ezz said.

"I'm just glad I'm not by myself," Luz frowned. Violins echoing down a hallway didn't seem like a party to her – it felt creepy.

"I don't think the red tux is giving off the impression that he hoped," Camille said, turning to scowl at the door. "It was like Satan chaperoning us to Hell's gates."

"Exactly!" Luz cried. "I should have worn sneakers instead of these stupid heels."

"At least we came up and not down," Ty offered as they moved slowly down the hall.

"Oh, I feel so *much* better now," said Ezz.

They were three feet away when the doors swung open, and a woman in a violet ballgown stood before them. Luz could only see her eyes, deeply blue, peering at them from the slits of a mask of peacock feathers. The hem of the gown and the height of the feathers gave her the impression of a giant, and Luz was almost afraid to flash her press pass. Would it be used against her after she was murdered – an indication that she had chosen to be there? People's favorite thing to look for when a girl was killed was why she deserved it. But the woman waved her press pass and Camille's invitation away.

"No need," the woman said, her voice rising above the violins. "You've made it this far, so you must belong here. Would you like a mask?"

"Yes," Luz said eagerly. She felt like a soft-bodied animal caught in the meadow, bare with moonlight. The mask would feel like camouflage, and they each took one, all made of the same shimmering gold sequins.

The peacock lady stepped aside and swept her arm wide, allowing them entrance, and the four of them stepped into the swell of violins.

Luz had thought they might be overdressed. They weren't.

The room was draped in red velvet, the air thick with the breath of instruments and wine. There were more people in tuxedos than dresses, but the shining marble floor was still obscured by the sweep of ball gowns, some swaying to music and others moving from circle to circle of conversation, gossip, laughter.

"Did they invite anybody that wasn't white?" Ezz whispered as they made their way into the party. Luz grimaced, her blood filling with bees.

"Is anyone staring?" Camille said, indignant. "I'll file a complaint if they are."

"We need to keep a low profile," said Ezz, shaking her head. "Going all *let me speak to the manager* isn't going to help with that."

Camille made a soft huffing sound, and the group of them sought refuge behind an eight-foot charcuterie table. Grapes and olives shone like dark marbles, meats and cheeses piled high alongside golden crackers.

"Luz, do you see any familiar faces?" Ezz said, glancing at her.

"No," said Luz, allowing her eyes to rove the room. "Not yet. The masks don't help, but at least it's mostly women wearing them."

"We should split up," Ty said. "Work the room. See what we see. And hear."

"I'm staying with Camille," said Ezz, shaking her head. "All these white people? It's only a matter of time before somebody asks me what the hell I'm doing here. I'm sticking close to the invitation."

"Good idea," said Luz, before Ty could answer. "I have my

press pass. So me and Ty can walk around and see what we see."

"Let's do it," said Ty, reluctantly. Luz glanced at her, trying not to smile. Ty had been imagining herself dancing with Ezz in a room heavy with blue shadows. Maybe once the work was done she'd still get her chance.

Together they moved out into the crowd. Dressed as they were, slinky dresses and thigh slits, Luz thought they looked like they had stepped onto the set of a spy movie. It felt that way too. She didn't mind it. It felt more powerful than the truth – a girl with a heart full of grief and a head full of vines.

"Tell me if you see any faces you recognize," Ty said as they squeezed past a group of men who paused their conversation to glance silently after the two of them.

"I will," said Luz. "But right now they all look the same. A bunch of white dudes with horse money who don't care about how Derby actually works."

"Agreed on the white dudes. But what do you mean by how it actually works?"

Just then, a murmur of pleasure spread through the room, starting in the corner by the great arching windows that Luz hadn't even noticed until that moment. Just beyond them were the illuminated triple spires of Cavehill Downs, piercing up through the night toward the moon. Everyone in the Carousel was arching their necks toward the corner, and Luz bobbed her head back and forth to see.

"*Mira*," she said. "This is my point."

The crowd parted for the metalbred. It was the current model, taller than Secretariat and a shimmering chestnut that looked fiery in the low light. It moved slowly through the crowd, led by a young Latinx person wearing a brown uniform. They kept their eyes on the floor, gripping the braided lead rope tightly as the partygoers made way, sometimes reaching out and touching the Limestone animal and exclaiming to their friends.

"Like I said, if it weren't for Latinx people," Luz said in a low voice, not taking her eyes off the young person, "there would be no Derby. We've always been horse people – in some of our home countries we are jockeys, trainers. But here they prefer to keep us as groomers, hot walkers, sweeps. It was this way before the ban, and even worse since. They don't care that that they – " she pointed at the young person leading the metalbred – "knows more about that animal than all the owners in this room. We make their party run smooth and that's all they want from us."

Luz watched the young woman leading the horse, the way she laid her hand against its shoulder here, the way she gently tugged the halter there. And Luz knew that the metalbred was a machine, but the tenderness of the girl and the way it bent its head toward her voice made Luz wonder if there was something the two of them understood that the rest of the world did not.

"I'm a former horse girl," Ty said, drawing Luz's attention back. "Plus I do cleanwork, and there's tons of Latinx people in my field. I get it."

"But that's exactly my point," Luz said. "All my years of loving and living around horses. And no one ever called me a *horse girl*. They just called me the help. And now a bunch of white people – people like you – are maids, and suddenly it's called *cleanwork*. My abuela, and indigenous women like her, have been cleaning houses in the capital of Chimaltenango since before you were born. This work had dignity before people like you came in and made it trendy. And still they suffer. You get a salary."

Luz saw the way her words landed on Ty like a bucket of cold water, wilting her, but she looked away. She didn't have space in her head to fill in Ty's blind spots and also scan the room for clues about the girl who Luz knew only as "daughter of Elena." Luz turned away from Ty, intent on doing the latter, just in time to lock eyes with a tall, handsome man who was closing in on her with an expression like a dog sighting unaccompanied steak. And any other day she would have let her disgust show all over her face – but this time she didn't. He was tall, slim, white...and had a Special Police tattoo peeking above the collar of his almost-nice suit.

The cop.

CHAPTER 26

TY

The party had swelled and Ty lurked at its edge, eyes roaming between Ezz across the room and Luz at its center, her hips swaying under the palms of the off-duty officer they had come to find. But he had found them. Ty watched his lips moving, always smiling, and she ached to hear what was being said. Was this a trap? Did the cop know why they were here?

Two men passed in front of her, eyeing her, and she realized that her position by the windows was like a deer mid-meadow. She moved toward the bar while still glancing at Luz every few steps, afraid to lose sight.

The smell of mint hit her in a wave. There was a whole planter of it surrounding the bar, both aesthetic and ingredient. Ty used to drink. When she was seventeen and singing at shows she would have a few – why the hell not? No one said no, and she'd barely had to ask. But her desire for alcohol, even weed, had vanished along with her mother. She ordered ginger ale and stared at the mint leaves while the bartender poured it, and allowed her ears to catch the things around her that alcohol would have blurred.

"I'm not betting this year," said a man's voice.

"Still mad about last year?" his friend laughed. "That's what you get for betting on the name alone. A good name doesn't make a fast bot!"

They moved off, Ty watching their backs from the corner of her eye. They were replaced by a heavyset man in a flat black suit, no tie. He held an unlit cigar. On his other side was a companion Ty couldn't see.

"Finally ready to enjoy the city, huh?" the companion said, a man. "You haven't relaxed since you got into town!"

"I didn't come here to relax," said the man closest to Ty. His fingers twirled the cigar. "I came to do business."

Ty knew his voice.

"Ever heard of multitasking?" the friend laughed, and the man chuckled. Ty paid the bartender and turned away from the bar to face the party, in the process taking in the two men next to her. The one next to her was Darden, the fixer from Saratoga Springs. He and his friend hadn't bothered with masks.

"What do you think this is?" Darden said, waving the cigar. He motioned to the bartender while Ty surveyed the party.

"The Carousel is supposed to be recreation," the friend said. "See, even the Police aren't in uniform."

"Mhmm – that's who I'm here to talk to."

The friend lowered his voice. Ty only heard the tail end of his words:

" – thing taken care of?"

"Not quite," Darden muttered. Ty could hear the scowl in his voice. "An incomplete equation."

"I failed math," the friend laughed, loud, drunk.

"Let's just say I'm missing a variable."

"You thought cops were smart?" The friend was all smiles, oblivious to Darden's glower. "They sure weren't thinking of us when they made detectives independent. You know how many times I've tried to slip those guys something and they got all self-righteous?"

"The detective is out of the question," Darden said. "But I've got my guy."

Ty dared to glance at him, found his eyes fastened the same place hers had been – on Luz and the cop. Luz was talking now, a smile on her lips. If she was talking to the cop, maybe she was getting information. The look on Darden's face said that he was going to interrupt any minute.

"Didn't I see you at the track?" Ty said, turning to Darden. Her words came out rushed, the decision made in her mouth before her brain caught up. If it weren't for the sequined mask she wore, she wouldn't have spoken at all.

Darden looked almost startled, the eyebrows reflexing toward anger before he realized she was a pretty girl. Then his expression went lax, dismissive for the same reason.

"You probably saw everyone here at the track," he said.

"You look like you know what you're doing," she said, and realized how poor she was at this kind of pretense, how the fact that Luz slipped it on so easily meant she had survived a different world than Ty. "Maybe you can give me some tips."

"You don't look like you're even old enough to gamble," he chuckled, and so did his companion. He nodded at her glass. "What's that? Ginger ale?"

His laughter was like a scaling knife. She felt raw. Every tooth in her mouth yearned to become a fang and sink into the hand holding the cigar. Her eyes went to Ezz across the room, watching her. Making a scene would only fuck things up. Part of her wanted to fuck things up.

"If my guy can't get it, I'll do it myself," he said to his friend, Ty forgotten. "I'm right down the hall, after all."

They both laughed at that, and Ty went on staring at the party. The idea that Darden's plans within the Mahogany remained while hers had been shifted – Benedict doubtless moved to accommodate Darden, the fixer; or maybe to avoid the scene of the crime – made her eyes sting. She watched Luz, she and the cop moving in a slow circle, not far from where they started. Ty felt she wasn't far from where she started either, somehow.

"You look familiar," Darden said, touching her with the back of one finger, his smile saying he would do her the favor of addressing her again. "Even with the mask. Familiar…"

"Do I?" she said, sipping her drink.

"Maybe you *did* see me at the track," he said, still smiling, but his eyes going slightly unfocused, trying to remember. He had looked this same way that night in his suite, sitting up half asleep, and Ty threw back her head to swallow the rest of the ginger ale.

"Or maybe from a dream," she said.

CHAPTER 27

LUZ

She was having trouble keeping the cop's hands at her waist.

"Don't you love this song?" he said, leaning in so she could hear him.

"I *do* love this song," said Luz. Out of the corner of her eye she could still see Ty, watching from afar. It made her voice stronger.

"I love this dress too," the man said, and Luz knew this look, the hazy expression in the eyes. He wasn't seeing her – he was seeing the illusion he'd been spinning in his head. *Sexy Latina. All chili pepper and salsa. Spicy. Hot. Caliente.* Taco Bell-ified versions of her humanity. It took everything in her not to dress him down when he asked her to dance, but instead she blasted him with what she hoped was a sexy smile, shining it on him like a heat lamp on a coiled snake. She made her hand soft to stay in his grasp as he moved her slowly around the dance floor.

"Didn't I see you at the other Carousel party last night?" he said, slightly slurry, and she frowned inwardly. She wondered who else might have seen her, if it jeopardized her plans, and her frown must have surfaced on her lips because he mirrored it.

"What?" he said. "Don't tell me I'm getting you confused with someone else. You're one of a kind."

"Must be two of a kind," she said. "This is my first time to a Carousel party."

"The Carousel," he repeated, mocking her soft accent, and she frowned visibly now, a red prick of anger sparking like a slow flame. "I like your voice. Did I see you come in with a press pass?"

"Don't miss much," she said.

"I'm Special Police, it's my job," he grinned.

"Are you working tonight, or just coming to party?"

"Celebrating," he said, his grin growing.

"Celebrating what?"

"I'm getting a promotion," he said, eyes trying to sparkle behind the dulling veneer of alcohol. "It's about time."

Luz turned up the wattage of her smile – he was too drunk to notice how fake it was. Or maybe just too male.

"Been putting in some overtime?" she said. "Finally got them to notice you?"

"You could say that." He was trying to be sly but in the end his need to preen overcame the need to be coy. "They asked me to fix a problem they had, and I fixed it."

Luz raised her eyes to the room, wishing Ezz and everyone else were birds on her shoulder, listening to whatever might come next. Had this man clutching her waist killed Rosario? His face wasn't on the horse eye's tape, but the hologram said he was at the crime scene in Rosario's hotel room, and now he was here, bragging about being rewarded. Luz's eyes quickly swept the room and found everyone distracted – Ezz appeared to be mock-arguing with Camille, who seemed to be eating the display flowers of the charcuterie table rather than the meat and olives. And now Ty, off by herself, appeared to be in conversation with a bald man wearing a suit that was so expensive it seemed to glow.

"Somewhere you'd rather be?" the cop she was dancing with said, squeezing the hand he held in his own. Luz brought her eyes back to his with a snap, ready for the glint of rage that could appear at any moment. Not yet. So far he was still teasing.

"Just taking in the costumes," she said. "What problem did you fix?"

"I can't tell you that," he grinned, relieved to be returned to the stage of her gaze. "Otherwise *you'd* be a problem I'd have to fix."

"Say no more," she said, and averted her eyes again. And again he squeezed her hand, drawing her back.

"Put it this way," he said, lowering his voice, but barely. "There was something that was left at…an important place. And I was able to retrieve it."

Luz's brain whirred. His badge and face were registered at the crime scene. That must be the important place. Nothing else made sense. But what did he take?

"What was it?" she said, trying to make her voice sound like sliding oil. "Something that locked up the bad guy?"

She thought his grin might falter, but it grew only wider.

"Once you get into my world," he said, "you see that it isn't so much good and bad. It's people who are powerful and people who aren't."

"And *you're* powerful?" she crooned, wanting to break his fingers.

He didn't reply, only smiled and smiled, swaying to the music.

CHAPTER 28

EZZ

The party was growing like a blister, and Ezz watched Ty move away from a man in a black suit, cufflinks she could see from across the room. Ezz stared at those cufflinks, wondering if they were the kind that Luz told them about – the kind that carried data. The man had been talking to Ty, laughing and then serious, and she had stood before him like she hadn't yet decided to sink or to fly. But he'd been distracted by a friend, and now Ezz watched Ty edge down the bar, where a woman with a glittery beard served glass after glass of bourbon. Ty paused there, as if considering, then continued picking her way through the crowd. She was carrying a storm: even with the mask Ezz could see that, and it was as if a bow was being drawn across strings in Ezz's gut, a sound of warning. She watched Ty draw closer, watching her bury the storm with every step, a conscious, precise practice of concealment. Ezz wondered for the first time if she should be afraid of her.

"Your friend is eating the display flowers," Ezz said when Ty arrived.

"What?"

Ezz pointed at Camille, who stood nibbling a dainty blue blossom.

"What the hell are you doing, Camille?" Ty said.

"They're borage flowers," Camille said, not taking her eyes off the party. "Beautiful and excellent for decoration. Also edible."

"You know there's cheese though," Ezz said. "And meat. And, like, anything else."

Camille didn't answer, and Ezz exchanged a glance with Ty. *Nervous*, Ty mouthed, and from what Ty had told Ezz about Camille, Ezz figured she must feel like a mouse leaving her safe hole full of books for a room full of cats.

Then Camille let the flower drop.

"Oh no," she said, and when Ezz followed her gaze, she saw two of the room's cats heading straight toward them. Twins.

"Her sisters," Ty muttered into Ezz's ear. She was closer than she ever had been, and Ezz glanced at her, surprised. Part of the storm inside her hadn't yet been tucked away, and it seemed to have made her bold. Or maybe she'd had a drink after all.

"I recognize them from the tabloids," Ezz said, sizing up the two women. Their eyes brightened with the kill as they closed in on Camille.

"Sister," said Christine Richmond as they swooped in. "Doth my eyes deceive me?"

"They do not," said Caroline Richmond, gasping dramatically. "The third wheel of the Richmond sister tricycle...out in the moonlight! It's twenty 'til twelve...you're not going to turn into a pumpkin, are you?"

In the same way Ezz had watched Ty transform herself as she made her way down the bar, Camille stripped off her nervousness like press-on nails.

"A fairy godmother who would only give Cinderella until midnight is a fascist," Camille sniffed. "I'm my own fairy godmother, obviously."

While the sisters conversed, Ezz leaned in toward Ty.

"Who was that dude you were talking to?"

"What dude?" Ty said, and her eyes remained on the

Richmond sisters, but Ezz saw the line of her jaw pulling tight like a tripwire.

"The guy in the suit with the cufflinks. He seemed intense."

"Just drunk," Ty said, still not looking at her. Ezz didn't know her well, but she knew liars well, and Ty had just become one. Ezz kept watching her until their attention was drawn by the abrupt departure of the Richmond twins. Camille mockingly waved a napkin in farewell, only allowing herself to scowl once they had fully retreated.

"Fucking molerats," she muttered. Then her eyes zeroed in on something else. "Ty, isn't that Darden?"

Ezz followed her gaze and her eyes found, again, the man in the black suit.

"Darden," Ezz repeated. "The Saratoga Springs guy staying at your hotel?"

Ty hesitated, then nodded, shifting.

"What did he say to you?" Ezz said, nudging her sharply. "Why did you just lie?"

"He said he recognized me," Ty said, still staring across the room at Darden. "I didn't want you to freak out."

Ezz felt herself stiffen.

"Did he? Recognize you, I mean? Did he start asking questions?"

Ty shook her head.

"No. I don't think he actually knew who I was. Just vague recognition."

"Did he say anything else?" Ezz felt sharp with sudden distrust, as if she needed to poke a thousand holes to get one answer.

"No," said Ty. "Did you see who Luz was dancing with?"

"The cop," Ezz nodded, still frowning.

"Yeah. That's two people here who have at least set foot in the Mahogany since Rosario was murdered," Ty muttered. "Him and Darden."

"Not too surprising," Ezz said, "given the season and the location. But I wonder what Darden is up to."

"Covering something," Ty said. She still seemed faraway somehow, her mind split.

"Hopefully Luz is getting something with that drunk-ass cop," she said.

"Darden's groping the waitress," Camille said, staring across the party. He was.

"Jesus Christ," growled Ty. Ezz looked at her just in time to see her snatch up a block of cheese and shove it into her mouth.

"Damn!" Ezz said, aghast. "There's like little mini-tongs and shit right there you're supposed to use!"

In response, Ty grabbed another block of cheese and shoved it into her mouth before snatching up a paper-thin slice of prosciutto and stuffing it in after. She stared Ezz in the eye, chewing aggressively. Ezz gaped at her, horrified, before bursting into laughter.

"You're really nasty," Ezz said, still wanting very much to be mad. "Wearing that gorgeous dress and doing all that. Just nasty."

"You like it," Ty said, mouth full.

Ezz just shook her head, mad at herself, and she reached for a piece of cheese to keep from reaching out to Ty and resting an arm around her waist in the blue light.

Blue.

Ezz's gaze caught on a stripe of blue in a young woman's hair, in the corner of the room by a curtained door. She wore the black pants and white shirt of a server, but something about her looked familiar, snagged on Ezz's vision like a burr in her sock. Suddenly Luz was rushing up to them, through the crowd, her eyes wide and a trail of people she had pushed aside behind her.

"That's her!" Luz snapped, pointing. "The dead girl's sister! From the backside!"

"Is that where I know her face from?" Ezz said, unconvinced.

Beside her, Ty's gaze was a knife.

In the crowd behind Luz, the cop she'd been dancing with was pushing his way through gowns, wearing an expression of irritation. Ezz knew that face: a man who wanted an explanation he wasn't owed.

"We need to talk to her," Luz cried, and their collective gaze must have been magnetic in its strength; across the room, the blue-haired girl's eyes drifted toward them, then locked: seeing Luz's pointing finger, seeing her face, and knowing her. She took a step backward.

"She's going to run," Ty said, low. Something about her voice pulled Ezz's eyes, and she found Ty staring intently at the blue-haired girl. Through the holes of Ty's mask, her eyes looked raw, exposed.

Across the room the girl was backing away; her fear was like a tank of gasoline laid on its side, chugging slowly onto the ground. She would be empty soon, but one glance at Ty told Ezz she was fire and the look in the girl's eyes ignited her.

"Let's go," Ty said, just as the girl turned to run.

CHAPTER 29

TY

Part of her wanted to make a scene. She wanted to make everyone look at all the things that were invisible: the sister of a vanished girl, and she, the remnant. Ty, too, felt like a remnant, and she thought that to make everyone see would help her feel less lonely. But there was still more to conceal before the exposing could begin, and she moved through the crowd as silently as a bat through the night. It wasn't until the girl with the blue streak of hair shoved past the black service curtain that Ty broke into a run.

Ty sprinted through the curtain after her, Ty managing to stay in her heels as they ran through the service kitchen; even as they clattered down the stairs – the girl with the blue hair always ten feet ahead – Ty managed not to break her ankles. But when they exploded outside into the night air, Cavehill like three glowing fangs inverted in the sky, Ty kicked off her shoes. The two girls were crossing grass now, and the spikes stuck in the soft soil. Ty was already losing her, and the knowledge made her panic. She put on an extra burst of speed, hearing the seam of her borrowed dress tear a little at her thigh. Behind her she thought she might have heard the sound of her name being called, but she pressed forward.

"Wait!" she cried, her breath ragged, but the girl did not wait.

She was running out of gas too, but was angling toward the fence, rows and rows of barns and shedrow on the other side. If she got through, Ty would never catch her.

A blur of black-gold sped by, the comet of Ezz rushing past Ty and after the girl.

"We're not the cops!" Ezz shouted. "We're just trying to help!"

In flat shoes, Ezz closed the gap fast and was only three feet from the fence when the girl slipped through a hole. Then her pants pocket caught on a barb and, as she turned to wrench it free, Ezz skidded to a stop, hands out as if facing a spooked horse.

"We're not here to hurt you," Ezz said, breathing hard. "We know what happened to your sister. We're friends of Rosario. Rosario Vicario! The jockey who died! Do you know about her? We're trying to…trying to find who killed her. Maybe whoever did it…maybe they hurt your sister too!"

The girl stood on the other side of the fence, the metal bars gripped in her fists. She stared through at Ezz with wild, wet eyes.

"She was chasing me," she said in a choked voice. She was pointing at Ty, and it made Ty wince, the fear in those eyes aimed at her.

"She's not the cops though," Ezz panted, then turned and shot Ty a venomous look. "She's just stupid as hell. She didn't mean to scare you."

"I didn't mean to scare you," Ty repeated, wheezing. She sensed that Ezz was the one who needed to do this particular negotiating and remained motionless, hands on her knees as she caught her breath.

"How do you know my sister?" the girl said. A tear finally escaped one dark eye and she quickly swiped it away.

"We don't," Ezz said. "We just…we know what happened. We know someone killed her. We know who. We just don't know why."

"You know *who*?" the girl said. Her body turned electric again, ready to flee.

"We saw a tape," Ty said. She couldn't stop herself. "We saw him do it. We know he's Limestone."

"Then you know why I can't talk to you," the girl said. Ty watched the fear in her eyes grow leathery wings, taking to the sky as helpless rage. Then it plummeted down and more tears squeezed out. She pressed her hands to her face.

"I know," Ty said. "I know. You're up against fucking giants. But they won't get away with this. We won't let them."

The dark cloak that had swept around Ty's mother and whisked her death into the shadow of rumor and scandal was being used here too. The power of men in suits – white men in suits – welded into a hammer and brought down on the heads of women. *Fuck that*, Ty thought. Her grief felt suddenly too strong, too sharp, like it might burst out through the flesh.

The girl was still crying, but when she looked at Ty this time, Ty didn't see the fear. Not for her. She believed her. Now Ty had to believe herself.

"Martha was a jockey," the girl whispered, and Ty felt herself moving closer now, to the iron fence that separated them. From the barns echoed the faint stomp and swish of metalbreds.

"Martha?" Ezz whispered, and her tone drew Ty's eye. She knew the name somehow, her eyes were suddenly wet.

"She was good," the girl went on. "Martha was so good. She taught herself the coding – finishing her work on the backside and then going to ride and code. Sometimes..."

She paused, and her eyes wavered between Ezz and Ty, a sparrow of uncertainty still fluttering there.

"It's okay," Ezz said, her voice sounding ragged, as Ty nodded encouragingly. "We're not the feds. We're trying to help."

"Sometimes...," the girl said, and swallowed. "Martha would work on metalbreds she wasn't supposed to. She had to, you know? They've made it so you pretty much have to be rich and white to have access to the equinibots at all. They closed the door behind Rosario Vicario, but by then she was already in the game. Now everybody else is locked out. You see? So Martha would sneak and sometimes do jockey work on metalbreds she was hot-walking. When no one was around, you know. And she was getting good. Really good. She'd been working on a Derby frontrunner."

Ty glanced at Ezz and saw her eyes widen.

"She was tinkering with the pros," Ty said.

"Yes," the girl snapped. "And doing it better than some of the pros who had the connections with rich white owners. She did it all herself. Learned it all alone. At least until she met Rosario. Rosario helped her; they were working on a project together for awhile. Martha was planning to go to Limestone's career fair and everything. She was so excited. Up until...until the night before she died."

"What happened the night before she died?" Ezz pressed.

"I don't know," the girl said, hanging her head. "I wish I knew. I'm not into equinibots – I'm just working here until I'm 18 and then I'm going to be a stylist. Make real money to send to my family in Mazatenango. So when Martha would talk about metalbred builds and things, I would mostly say 'whatever.' You know? I loved her, but I don't love the backside work. But that night she was all excited about something she had found while she was working on a Limestone model. She rushed in all dirty and said 'Rebeca, he hecho un descubrimiento!'"

She squeezed her eyes shut, as if repeating the words made her sister's voice echo.

"*Rebeca, I've made a discovery,*" Luz translated, appearing between Ty and Ezz. Her voice sounded like she was delivering a eulogy. Martha's sister Rebeca opened her eyes and stared hard at Luz; Ty watched something pass between them, a shared grief, an understanding borne in the bones.

"The next day she was dead and the metalbred was gone."

"Gone?" said Ty. "What happened to the bot?"

"I don't know," Rebeca said. "People are spreading rumors that she tried to steal it and that's why she's dead. But Martha was not a thief."

"And she wouldn't have stolen a million-dollar equinibot if she was trying to get a job at Limestone of all places," Ezz frowned. "Your sister sounded smart and only an idiot would do that."

"She was the smartest person I knew," Rebeca sniffed. "And so good with real horses too, even though she preferred machines. She would come into the barn and hold their bridle and scratch in just the right place and whisper '*Patience, girl*,' and just like that, the horses would settle. And now...and now she's dead. Gone."

"I'm so sorry," Ty said. The moonlight covered them all in a silver veil. She couldn't help but think this was exactly the moonlight she remembered from the night her mother was murdered.

"We just have to move on or make our own justice," Rebeca said. "No one cares. The Special Police won't investigate – we already know they don't care because Martha was undocumented. She said Limestone would've helped her get citizenship with the discovery she had made."

"You said she was going to an event?" Ty said. "An interview or job fair or something?"

"Yes. But it doesn't matter now. Limestone didn't want someone like her working for them. They probably stole her discovery and killed her to hide it, just like this country has done to people like us forever and ever."

"They probably did," Ty agreed. "They would do anything to stay rich. Do you know who she was going to meet with?"

"Raymond Salt," Rebeca spat. "Piece of shit."

Ty shut her mouth, then looked up at the moon. She felt as if she were standing in the center of a circle that grew smaller and smaller.

"What's wrong?" Ezz said, studying her. "You know that name?"

It was a long time before Ty could speak, swallowing the lava of rage that bubbled up hot in her throat.

"Yes," she said slowly. "That's my dad's boss."

CHAPTER 30

LUZ

The Downs museum closed in 28 minutes, but Luz went inside anyway. She'd been pacing the entranceway for a half hour already, ping-ponging between the two bronze horse statues that pranced on either side. Time and moisture reacting with the copper had turned the bronze green, and she felt a little green herself as she pushed through the gleaming double doors. She didn't know how to flirt. Anxiety always made her tongue clumsy and stiff. But she had done things lately that hadn't seemed possible before. She had left her parents' house; she had lived with someone new. She had gone to a party and danced with a stranger, in the pursuit of truth. Maybe this was one more thing she could do.

The museum was clearing of people, white tourists making their way toward the doors with children clutching plush ponies from the gift shop. They barely looked at Luz, which both relieved and annoyed her. People flocked to this place with its three fangs biting the sky and gladly handed over their money, knowing nothing about Limestone and all the bloody strings they pulled from backstage. Was it ever possible to truly know all the places your money went, leaking down like sewage runoff? Maybe that was why she was really here, she thought as she stalked along the edge of the exhibit, not yet approaching the desk. Because she couldn't get Rebeca's words out of her head, more of the truth about the dead girl in the barn – and now she had a name: Martha – coming slowly to light. Love and rage swirled together in her heart, combining into one blinding firestorm.

She tapped the single earpod she had in and the voice of one of the security guards filled her head. She couldn't see him, but she could hear him, patched into the security network of Cavehill Downs with the frequency recordings she'd deciphered after her last visit.

Rotate posts in three minutes, the voice said. She imagined him patrolling somewhere on the upper floors of the Downs, oblivious to her listening ear. *Post 2, check on that gate by the catering tunnel. They were supposed to fix it today.*

Through the buzz of security in her head, Luz watched the young man working the desk answer what must have been a ringing phone she couldn't hear. They were closing soon – he was the only employee in sight. No Irma. The disappointment made her wobbly before embarrassment stiffened her again. The sinking feeling was too much for a girl she had met only once, who had probably forgotten her the moment she walked away. Then she realized why she had come here: she was looking to be defused. Or maybe blown out. A place for her pain and anger to be reflected, then held softly. That same pain and anger made her feel like a campfire creeping toward dry brush – the letdown of Irma's absence was a stiff wind. She yanked on the door that would take her back outside and slammed straight into a person coming in. Luz's single earpod fell out, clattering to the sidewalk.

"¿Qué chingados…?" the person exclaimed, and Luz cried out an apology, part of her irrationally hoping to look up and find herself apologizing to Irma. It wasn't Irma, but Luz did know the face.

"Luz!" the girl said, and Luz did a frantic search of her mind for her name. Luz knew her from Skyhorse, but had seen her more recently as well.

"Zarita," Luz said. "Wow. Hi. I think I saw you at Rosario's vigil."

Zarita nodded, her black hair rippling around just past her chin, pink at the tips. She carried a sleek silver drone under her left arm, the remote sticking out of her back pocket.

"I thought I saw you there too! I was going to say hi, but you left pretty quick."

Luz tried to scoot around her to reach the outdoors, as aware of her own awkwardness as she was of the curiosity in Zarita's eyes.

"Yeah, well...," she started, but Zarita just smiled gently.

"Still don't love the crowds?"

Luz shrugged the question off, embarrassed. If Zarita, who she had barely spoken to at Skyhorse, knew this about her, what else did she know?

"What are you doing here?" she asked instead.

Zarita let the door close between them and the museum, but pointed through it at the young guy at the desk. He was watching them and gave a little wave.

"Meeting my boyfriend," Zarita said, hefting the drone. "Dave. He gets off work soon. We're gonna go fly this over the waterfront. Take some pictures."

"Oh."

"What are you doing here?"

"I was...looking for someone else," Luz said. "This girl who works here."

"Who?" Zarita said, raising an eyebrow. "I know them all. Rachel? Irma?"

"Irma."

"¿Es neta?" Zarita said, her lips twisting with disbelief. "You're friends with *Irma*?"

Luz's cheeks felt hot.

"No, not really. Why?"

"Ella es una fresa," Zarita laughed. "So full of herself. Why were you looking for her?"

"Um, just…working on a project," Luz said.

"A project, huh?" Zarita said. "Well, you always did keep busy, didn't you?"

She wasn't going to press her, and Luz was grateful. Then Zarita looked down and saw the earpod Luz had forgotten about in her surprise.

"Here," she said. "Let me get this for you. What does Luz Cabo Trejo listen to while she's brooding, huh?"

Before Luz could stop her, Zarita popped the earpod into her ear, grinning.

"Wait," Luz said, reaching, but her hand froze halfway. She could tell by Zarita's face it was already too late, the grin fading.

"¿Qué es esto?" Zarita said softly, eyes slightly unfocused, listening.

"Es nada," Luz said quickly. "Es nada."

But she could see it becoming something in Zarita's eyes, watched them lift over Luz's head to look at Dave where he closed the register at the end of his shift. Then they darted back to Luz.

"Luz," Zarita said slowly. "What the fuck are you into?"

"Es nada," Luz repeated.

"¿Nada? No suena a nada. It sounds like *something*. It sounds like trouble."

It had never been discussed with Ezz and Ty, but there was an understanding that what they were digging through was meant to stay among the three of them. But Zarita had been at the vigil, had spoken about seeds being buried, about justice. And besides, what Luz had planned on her own, her own Poison Ivy dreams, was just that: her own. These thoughts led her to open her mouth and allow a leaf of truth to taste the air.

"I'm going to take Cavehill apart brick by brick," she said. "Stone by stone."

Under Zarita's eyes, Luz felt what a metalbred must feel, if it could feel: assessed, diagnosed. Zarita didn't smile, and Luz couldn't speak. She just waited.

"Why?" Zarita said eventually. "For Rosario?"

"For all of us," Luz said softly.

The smile across Zarita's mouth was an oriole, a flash and then gone.

"What if I told you somebody was already taking care of that?" she whispered.

Luz could only stare at her.

"What? Who?"

"Me," she said. "But not me alone. Me and some other friends. People you know. And some you don't."

She looked meaningfully over her shoulder at Dave.

"What, him?" Luz said. "What, he's like…an inside man?"

"He's able to give us information about how the board talks, what their plans are," Zarita said. Then she held up Luz's earpod. "But not this. How did you get this?"

Luz shrugged, her head spinning.

"What are you going to do?" Luz said. She felt suddenly, unbearably thirsty.

"We're planning a huge demonstration on Derby Day," Zarita said. "At Limestone. We have a huge inflatable rat, bullhorns, sleeping dragons, the whole nine yards. We're going to camp out for as long as it takes them to break up their board and establish something new that includes…us."

She grinned at Luz for a moment, offering her back the earpod, but the expression on Luz's face brought the oriole of her smile swooping back to earth.

"What?" Zarita said, frowning. "Wait, what did *you* mean? When you said brick by brick? Stone by stone?"

Luz knew her lips were moving, and she knew that no words were coming out, all of them tangled in a green mass at the back of her throat. All she could think about were vines. The fact that

Zarita had a plan, one that would force the wheel of change, should have felt like the defusing she had been in search of when she came here. Instead she only felt her fire climb higher, the Poison Ivy tattoo on her arm itching. She envisioned the three spires crushed in a leafy embrace. Some of this must have made it into her eyes, because Zarita's widened.

"¿Y la gente que?" she said. She pointed at the quetzal inked into Luz's bicep. "What about the people, Luz?"

"I want us to be seen," Luz heard herself say. "I want to do something they can't look away from."

Luz took the earpod from Zarita's open hand and turned away, down the flower-lined path and toward the street that would carry her back to her green room and its rustling vines. She didn't look back when Zarita called after her.

"Who cares about them?" Her voice carried on the wind. "¿Pero qué hay de nosotros? What about *us*?"

CHAPTER 31

TY

Her hair was freshly bleached and her clothes micropressed. She had actually taken the time to paint her nails – stark white, contrasting sharply with her all-black pantsuit. Her lips were red. The entirety of Limestone headquarters was mirrored, and as she walked up the stone stairs to the Limestone Derby party, she saw herself coming and thought she looked a little dangerous.

Good, she thought.

Then her father entered the reflection, jogging up the stairs after her. He'd dropped her off and parked the car and was now catching up, and the sight of him beside her made her hands tighten inside her pants pockets. She could only do this by his side but everything in her wanted to walk faster and faster until he was a smudge in the distance.

"I can't believe you actually decided to come," he said, more to himself than her. He was clutching the invitation they had fought about the last time they'd argued in the kitchen. She had always intended on going – she'd originally imagined learning more about Benedict, his weaknesses. Now her scope had widened.

"Excited?" he said, and she still didn't bother to reply. He was eyeing himself in the mirrored face of Limestone, straightening the tie of his rented tux, saying empty words. She was an accessory on his evening as he sought to rise in the company. He was here for one purpose, but that was okay, she thought. So was she.

They both had to remove their jackets for security, leaving her in the thin-strapped jumpsuit while the navy-suited guards first wanded her and waved her into the Oculatum security orb, its transparent walls lined with microscopic sensors and cameras. She'd only seen security this high tech in the state capitol when she'd visited on a field trip as a child. She was waved through and stood waiting for her father on the other side, where flocks of tuxedoed guests were already being escorted down the long marble hall toward the reception. On this side of security, she could gaze out the huge windows at the endless fields of bluegrass that encircled the Limestone campus. Empty, not a horse or a metalbred in sight.

"Your jacket, miss," a security guard said, and held it up for her to shrug on. Her father joined her then, glancing at her sidelong.

"You could've worn something a little more feminine," he said when the guard stepped ahead to escort them.

"Is red lipstick not feminine enough?" she snapped.

"Most of the women are wearing dresses."

"And?"

He shrugged then, not because she was right, but because his attention was elsewhere, scanning the scene for his boss, for his colleagues, people at whom he would need to aim the shotgun of his smile. A moment later, the rifle was cocked.

"Dr. Salt!" he beamed at a man walking toward them with his hand out, ready to be shaken. They both smiled the same plastic smile. "Unchained yourself from the desk?"

"Red," the man said, and Ty rolled her eyes. The nickname her father had given himself. Tyler Redson. He'd insisted on naming his daughter after himself, but when people shortened his name to Ty, it suddenly became *her* name, a girl who wasn't the girl he'd dreamed of: pigtails and frills. So he became Red, the new name like an exit ramp. Ty thought there was nothing sadder in the world than a person who nicknamed themselves. "They must just be letting anybody in here nowadays! But who is this? You must have had to pay her to come with you!"

"This is my daughter," her father said quickly, and Ty knew it was to protect his boss from further embarrassment, not her. "Ty, this is Dr. Raymond Salt."

"Pleased to meet you," she said, and studied him, wondering what his exact role was in making Martha disappear. She tried to ignore the growing buzz in her belly, reminding herself that the only thing anyone knew about her here was what she let on. She cleared her throat. "I've heard a lot about you."

"Your father's a talker, isn't he?" Salt said, smiling. "Good at his job though. Half these engineers have never been around a real Thoroughbred. The knowledge that people like your dad have is indispensable."

"Are there no engineers who have horse experience?" she said. Everything Rebeca had told her pulsed in her head.

"Oh, sure, I suppose," he said. He adjusted his watch and her eyes dropped down momentarily to his wrists, where cufflinks glittered. She raised her gaze back to his face smoothly. "It's just a different crowd, you see."

"West Coast guys," she nodded, as if in agreement. "It's funny, I remember being told something about how an influx of Latinx immigrants from the West Coast changed horseracing way back in the old, old days. And now a bunch of white West Coast guys have changed it again."

His two hands found their way to his pockets.

"Ah...alright." He wasn't annoyed yet, just confused. Ty pushed on, ignoring the warning look her father was aiming in her direction.

"I heard that Limestone said at some point that they wanted to hire more Latinx people. Grooms and stuff."

He brightened at this, an opportunity to brag about Limestone's diversity initiatives.

"Yes, we have an excellent mentorship program in place. We help younger people who want to work their way up and learn about the industry."

Ty cocked her head, trying to keep her eyes empty and innocent.

"But don't they already know about the industry?" she said. "I know some people have worked on the tracks since they were little kids."

"I...," he started, his eyes beginning to narrow.

"Ty," her father said, bordering on a growl.

"What if I knew someone?" Ty said, swallowing her nerves. "Someone who knew a lot about the industry and, like, metalbreds and stuff? Do they apply straight to you?"

He eyed her the way someone eyes a costume on Halloween – a little kid dressed as a monster, or something real to fear?

"Yes, you can send them to me," he said.

"Just to you?" she said. "No one else?"

"Just to me," he said, irritation lacing his voice.

A security guard appeared at his elbow and Ty's heart dropped, wondering if someone had zeroed in on her. But instead the man in the suit leaned in and said, "The keynote will begin in ten minutes, sir."

Dr. Salt thanked him and then turned back to Ty and her father, casting a look of cool relief over the both of them.

"Duty calls," he smiled. "Enjoy the evening, folks."

As soon as he was gone, Ty's father turned on her, bending close to her ear.

"What the fuck is wrong with you?" he gritted.

"I'm thirsty," she said, and stepped away before he got louder, following Dr. Salt into what she had heard her father describe at home as the Crystal.

Unlike the outside of Limestone, every inch of which was reflective, the entirety of this inner core of the building was transparent. They stood at the bottom of what seemed to be a shining cube, four different sets of open-air stairways rising three stories, the floors of which seemed to float above them like heavenly platforms in the clouds. Here, too, the bluegrass fields outside the glass walls of Limestone spread around them like a whispering ocean, and the not-quite-sunset tinged it all pink, a soft palette drifting into this colorless space and washing the man-made with the natural. Men in suits stood everywhere, soft music coming from nowhere, and here and there throughout the loose crowds were dotted motionless metalbreds, some vintage models with the necks lacking the natural slope that moved the newer models so close to realism. The sight of them, sleeping and stiff, their eyes as dark as a screen powered down, made Ty want to run out into the grass and not look back.

"Miss Redson, I think?" said a voice at her elbow. She turned and looked into the cool gray eyes of Detective Segrest. Like the other men in the room, he wore a tux, and she knew with one look it wasn't rented.

"Detective," she said, surprised. "What are you doing here?"

"I was invited," he said, studying her. "As a friend of Limestone, my invitation said. And you?"

"My dad works here," she said. Then, coldly: "Or don't you remember that? I guess I can't expect you to remember the details of every case."

He frowned, and if she didn't know better she'd think he looked sad.

"I remember," he said slowly. "For some reason I thought maybe he would have...retired."

She snorted.

"He's only 48," she said. "He wants to die in this place."

"I see," he said, then hesitated. "How is he holding up?"

He was talking about her dead mother. It felt like he had drawn a red circle in the air that settled around her neck and tightened like a noose.

She found her father in the crowd and stared at him. He was laughing with a colleague.

"He's fine," she said.

"I see," he said, and followed her gaze with his. "What does he do here again?"

"Equine imitation specialist," she said. "He'd love to tell you about it."

"He makes the metalbreds seem like Thoroughbreds," he said, watching her father. "All those things locked into the programming that the jockeys can't change. The ear twitches. The slow blinks. He advises the Limestone engineers."

"You know a lot about it," she said, raising her eyebrows. "Are you a cop or a horseman?"

"Hmm," he said, and if he weren't a cop she would've told him that *hmm* wasn't an answer. "I'm glad to see you, actually. I was going to stop by the Mahogany and ask you something, along with the other cleanwork staff."

"Ask us what?" she said, feigning distraction. Raymond Salt was moving toward the stage and she wished he would hurry the fuck up so Segrest would stop talking.

"Do you use bleach?" he said. "In your cleanwork kits, I mean. I understood it to be a bit of an outdated substance in your field."

"Bleach?" she said. "No. A place like the Mahogany doesn't allow it – too harsh, smells bad."

"Not even in the bathrooms?"

"No."

"And so never in the guest suites?"

"Never," she said, gazing back up at the stage, her heart pounding. Salt was moving toward the microphone, smiling.

"Interesting."

"Why do you ask?" she said. But she knew why. This was a shared curiosity.

But then Raymond Salt was speaking, his voice booming over them, and Segrest gave a polite smile, moving away. Ty stared after him, frowning. Her father turned to look for her, and she moved reluctantly to his side.

"Good evening," Salt boomed into an invisible mic. Like her father's, the man's smile was false. But the material it was constructed from was different – not plastic. Something harder. It burned out of his thin face now as everyone attended to him. "Welcome to Limestone's annual Derby celebration. You are standing in the eye of our headquarters, and it's filled with cameras, so it's a good thing you all look so beautiful."

Light laughter followed, and he delved into his welcome speech, which, Ty quickly realized, was mostly statistics about how much money Limestone had made since its inception.

"From $2 billion to $10 billion," he droned on. "People were tired of seeing animals used and abused. The whips, the drugs, the broken legs. We've single-handedly transformed the racing industry and put Kentucky at the top of the heap, as it should be, with a wreath of roses around its neck."

"Amen!" her father said loudly as he clapped; around him, other employees beamed. Ty swept her eyes over the sparkling crowd, everyone drinking in the dollar amounts as if the numbers, too, were champagne. Her mother would have hated this, she knew, and the thought made her feel heavy and sick, as if her ghost were watching Ty without context, and would think her a part of all this.

"I need to pee," she whispered to her father, who shot her an annoyed look then looked away. She turned and cut through the crowd, smiling apologies.

The bathrooms glowed green at the side of the room, but she hadn't quite reached them when someone toward the back caught her eye. The back of someone: a white man in a navy-blue suit, a good haircut with wavy chestnut hair. He was standing close to a woman near the bar, which was nestled against one of the glass walls. Ty paused, just in time for the man to turn slightly to better see Dr. Salt on stage.

Brian Benedict.

After Ty had finished dressing for the evening, after she had applied her makeup, she stared in the mirror, mentally applying another veneer. Cool. Untouchable. A mask of ice. At the sight of Brian Benedict fifty yards away, not on a screen but in the flesh, the mask melted under a wave of heat.

On the stage, Dr. Salt was extolling the virtues of a post-rider Derby. A projection had appeared behind him in the air, graphs that climbed up and up. Like Ty, Benedict barely watched. He was too busy engaging in low converstion with the woman at his side – a white redhead wearing a powder-blue gown. Annie Claybelle. Ty had seen her before on TV, but her face held Ty's gaze because, like Ty, she appeared to be wearing a mask. She was smiling, calm and cool, as she stared ahead at the projection. But in her eyes and in the tightness around her mouth, Ty saw fury.

Ty stayed close to the wall as she made her way toward the bar. Everyone had moved toward where Dr. Salt gave his speech, and a glance at the bartender told her that his eyes, too, were fixed on the presentation – no one to notice her as she spidered along. Claybelle and Benedict both spoke in low voices, and even when she reached the end of the bar, Ty could just barely make out their conversation. She crouched – glad she hadn't worn a dress – and allowed the bar to obscure her as she listened.

"This isn't the place I want to have this conversation," Claybelle hissed.

"You could have at least looped me in, Annie," Benedict said.

"I thought he was the police when he came to my office asking questions. I looked like a fucking idiot until he finally told me who had sent him."

"You're whining again, Brian," Annie said. Her voice was like an icepick. "You know I hate when you whine."

He muttered something Ty couldn't hear, and then:

"He says the cop didn't get the whole thing. Just the needle."

"I know," said Claybelle. "Now stop talking. Later."

But Benedict went on whispering.

"So what the fuck are we going to do now? That detective is here right now and was asking –"

"Stop looking around like that, Brian. You look like a goddamn seagull."

"Okay, fine. But what do we do? Send our cop back to get the rest? What if someone has picked it up already?"

Ty stared at the floor to keep herself from peeping up over the bar – she so wanted to see their faces during this exchange, to drink in the panic she heard in Benedict's voice.

"A problem you created," Claybelle said, low.

"You're the one who said we –"

"I keep hearing 'we' from your mouth," Claybelle drawled. "Your expectation that I get you out of the mess you created is really getting old, Brian. How many fucking times…"

But he cut her off.

"It *is* our mess," Benedict snapped. "You think I…" and he whispered something Ty couldn't hear, "…because I just *wanted* to?"

"Wouldn't be the first time," Claybelle snapped back.

"This was different," he growled. "After the meeting with Salt…"

"I meant for you to hire someone," Claybelle said, her voice low and pointy.

"You should've called Conrad then."

"You don't think I *didn't*?" she retorted. "He was the first person I called, but he couldn't get near this. I would think my own brother would be competent enough to –"

"I *did*!"

"But you left…" Claybelle's voice dropped too low to hear. "*And* fucking blood? This is why I called New York."

Then there was another voice, this one coming right down on top of Ty.

"Miss, can I help you with something?" the voice said, and Ty's ankles nearly folded under her. She looked up slowly, and found a dark-suited security guard staring down at her. Nearby, of course, Claybelle and Benedict both fell silent.

Ty blinked up at the guard for a moment, the world seeming to spin, and then snapped out of it.

"I…I dropped my bracelet somewhere over here," she said, hearing her voice soar high into lying mode. Her mother would have known she was lying. But her mother wasn't here. "Do you see it anywhere?"

The guard frowned and looked around.

"Uh, no, I don't see it. Would you like me to check Lost and Found?"

"That would be lovely," Ty said, forcing herself to smile. "Thank you so much."

He walked away, and she could feel the eyes of Claybelle and Benedict on her back like shovels. She turned, tried to offer a slight casual smile, and then let her eyes drop to the floor, still hunting for the nonexistent bracelet.

"Must be around here somewhere," she muttered, and didn't dare look back up, afraid of what they would see, of what *she* would see.

"But I know what you're really here to see," said Dr. Salt from his transparent podium, and Ty looked toward his voice eagerly, taking a slow step forward. Claybelle and Benedict were still

266

watching her, their eyes as powerful as gravity.

"You're here to see the *real* Limestone," Dr. Salt proclaimed. "You're here to see the stone at the heart of the fruits of our labor. And I'm going to show it to you."

On cue, the clouded-glass windows at the edge of the party swung open and everyone in the small audience began to shift, necks craning, lips parting to murmur. From the corner of Ty's eye, she could see Claybelle and Benedict lean close, whisper. Ty moved toward the crowd. She picked out her father, his head swiveling as he searched for her. For once she was glad. She threw her hand up and waved dramatically, if only for the audience of two at her back.

"They're ready for us," Dr. Salt said, and swung his arm open, a general directing his army. A cluster of Limestone employees had appeared and began to usher the guests forward when a piercing whinny rang out from whatever was beyond the doors. The effect was immediate: the swish and click of tuxedo pants and high heels intensified, the crowd moving toward the mystery beyond. Equine or equinibot? Real or not? Ty suddenly realized that's what they all had come to see: the real, whatever it was. Ty's father motioned for her impatiently, and when she joined him, she had to force herself not to look over her shoulder. The whole crowed moved into the next room.

Dr. Salt lectured from the rear of the procession as they were herded into the inner sanctum of Limestone. The invisible mic made his voice godlike and it boomed out around them even as they moved out of the Crystal and into – her father whispered into her ear – the Paddock.

"If you've ever wondered how a metalbred is born," Dr. Salt announced. "Here's your answer."

It was not a paddock. It was a multi-level research pavilion with a soaring ceiling and shining metal walls. Screens and floating three-dimensional dioramas of sub-sectioned horses filled Ty's eyes; instead of the smell of manure and sun-baked grass, all she smelled was the lingering scent of coffee, no doubt drunk by the many technicians who stood idly by in jeans and sneakers, some wearing ties and shirts needing a micropress. Tech guys, Ty knew. She'd heard her father talk shit about them, and knew from experience that the shit was envy in disguise for the men who had been in the tech world before the horse world had collapsed into it. Men who looked at her father and saw nothing but an old-fashioned hick – his superiors.

"In the center is what we call the showroom," Dr. Salt went on, and everyone's heads turned, as hungry and eager as baby hawks. Their eyes ate up the room and landed on what they should have seen from the beginning: a metalbred, the massive and shining new Secretariat model, 16.5 hands of illuminated chestnut. It stood on a circular, elevated pedestal at the center of the cavernous space, Dr. Salt gesturing up at it. "This is where we place a model when it's been through inspection and is ready to undergo a final pass by our equine imitation specialists."

"That's me," her father said, a poor attempt at a whisper. It was hard to imagine him in this room, Ty thought, gazing around. It was a place full of delicate and serious equipment, a room that looked like it required some restraint to exist within, and her father wasn't careful a single day in his life. With anyone or anything.

Dr. Salt had moved toward the pedestal that bore the metalbred, talking the whole way about the process of the bot build, the lessons Limestone had learned over the years.

"...the perfect specimen. The programmed competitiveness and grace of a Thoroughbred, situated in a machine that feels no pain, no fear. The answer to the racing industry's prayers. It's a lot quieter on race day now," he said with a wide smile. "Nothing for protestors to protest anymore! Perhaps they've gone on with life, and found new hobbies."

This drew a few chuckles from the audience, and Ty shot a look at her father, whose face remained unchanged. She felt her palms grow damp. Her mother had been one of those activists. Showing up on race day dressed as a traditional jockey, smeared with blood. Ty and her father had to pick her up from jail once, and Ty had heard the jokes tossed around by the police as her father posted bail. The insinuations that she was sleeping with Luis Funes, the way Ty's father's ears reddened to a shade they would never have taken on if Luis Funes had been named something like Raymond Salt instead. This had helped her father take Limestone's side, Ty thought poisonously. She didn't know if he truly believed the rumors, but it didn't actually matter. In his mind, one flowed into the other. His wife had "slept with Mexicans," and in a way that's what made her dead to him. Ty found herself staring at him instead of the presentation, wondering how her revenge might spread, like a damp cup placed on tissue.

"I'd like a volunteer, if anyone is feeling brave!" Dr. Salt called from the stairs of the pedestal. "Step into the shoes of an equine imitation specialist and join me for a check of all the things that make a Limestone horse a horse!"

She should've seen it coming, but when her father's hands braced against her back and shoved her forward, it took her completely by surprise. If she'd been wearing heels she would have fallen, but she caught herself as well as she could and then looked around to see if anyone had noticed her father's forced "volunteer."

Everyone noticed. Including Dr. Salt. He stared down at her over the top of his glasses, his expression one of indecision. Remembering her interrogation, she knew. Wondering if she was trying to make a fool of him. His eyes darted around, as if looking for alternatives, but around Ty people had begun to clap encouragingly, and he forced on a smile.

"Ah, Mr. Redson's daughter! Red – trying to get his legacy into the business!"

He stage-chuckled, and behind her Ty's father chuckled, and the people who knew "Red" chuckled, and Ty could feel the part of her that might have laughed along to smooth things out shriveling, a worm shrinking under a sun of rage. She was tightening her fists, flexing her jaws, preparing for the "no" she was about to deliver and the fallout it would earn. Her father hated her, and she hated him. She realized this suddenly and without regret. It was what it was, and she wouldn't go along with his plastic laugh and the graveyard of emotions behind it. Not anymore.

But then, as he beckoned her, her eyes landed on Dr. Salt's cufflinks once more.

From where he stood near the pedestal, the towering metalbred motionless beside him, the bald white lights hovered over him like the beam of an alien ship about to bear him skyward. In that same white light glittered the presence of a cufflink on each of his wrists. In Ty's head was the clamor of a thousand scales clattering back and forth as she made up her mind. Luz said tech folks sometimes carried sensitive data close. Necklaces. Nose studs.

Cufflinks.

"I'll try," Ty announced, to applause, and stepped forward, hoping she looked meek. If she got caught – and she might: she'd stolen makeup and groceries before, but had never been a pickpocket – playing shy might help. She approached the glittering metal staircase, gazing up at Dr. Salt, who now grinned down at her, gladdened by her mildness. With the light reflecting white in his glasses he didn't look quite human.

She climbed the stairs, and together they stepped up onto the platform where the metalbred stood still and shining.

"The machine is in sleep mode," Dr. Salt informed her and

the audience. "Go ahead, touch it."

Ty watched her hand rise and cross the space between her and the equinibot. She felt a trembling in her throat. Would horses always be an open wound in her heart?

"Soft, isn't it?" Dr. Salt smiled. "A combination of synthetic materials inlaid with sensory receptors. The wind blows and the machine 'feels' it, but only so that it's able to sense how much power is needed to push through the resistance."

"It *is* soft," Ty murmured. Almost like the real thing. Almost. Too soft, actually. She wondered how her father let this sort of thing pass inspection – an imaginary version of the way a horse felt, missing the subtle coarseness their nature demanded. Probably metalbreds weren't designed with touch in mind, and people like her father never really loved the animals anyway. Not the way her mother did.

"We debated on whether to give them tails," Dr. Salt went on for the audience, and Ty cut her eyes at him. "They wouldn't need them to swat flies. Flies don't bother bots! But in the end we decided that it was best to imitate the actual horse as much as possible. People were resistant to the idea of equinibots at first. Do you remember? It seems so long ago now, doesn't it? The sign of something visionary – when you can't remember what life was like before it!"

Nods from the crowd, and all Ty could do was dart her eyes down at the cufflinks shining at Dr. Salt's wrists. It distracted her from the burning feeling in her palms, the desire to swing one against the side of his thinly-bearded face.

"A solid piece of machinery," he went on, tweaking the bot's ear, running a rough hand down the crest of its arching neck. "A hardware flexible enough for the jockeys to customize, with plenty of hidden loopholes for them to exploit if they know what to look for. Secure enough in its foundational code so that no one can turn a metalbred into a Ferrari. Predictable and unpredictable all at once. A new sport created for the new breed of jockeys, but reviving the old sport for the people in the stands. Two races in one, you could say, with Limestone – and America – at the center. You remember what it used to be like? Half the horses spoke Spanish!" He laughed heartily. "Horseracing has evolved, and Limestone made it possible."

He gave the rump of the metalbred a sharp pat for emphasis, a look of supreme smugness on his face. He probably gave this speech a dozen times a year for wealthy white investors, enjoying being on the pedestal with the thing he helped create, looking down at his audience and drinking their awe like bourbon. Ty again imagined slapping him, imagined his spectacles spinning off into space as he fell back under the force of her hand.

But she didn't move. So when Dr. Salt went reeling backward, it took her a moment to realize that it was because the horse had kicked him.

"Oh my god!" someone shouted from the crowd, shrill, the awe leaking out of their voice and replaced with panic. Ty stumbled sideways as a blur of wind and motion sent her spinning. Beside her, the equinibot was whirling on the pedestal, a faint huffing sound coming from somewhere inside it, and the crowd shrank back away from the showroom, their backs seeking a door their eyes refused to turn away to locate.

"What the fucking hell…!" Ty heard Dr. Salt say through blood. The blood made his voice thick, covered the pedestal in it. Ty wasn't sure if he'd been kicked in the face or if his face had connected with the handrails, but she threw herself back against them, blinded by the white examination lights. The metalbred was oblivious to her, and to Dr. Salt. It seemed interested only in finding a way free of the height, the lights, perhaps the whole building.

"Shut it down!" she heard someone yell from the crowd. Perhaps her father. Dr. Salt was cringing, frozen, his face a mask of wet red, his hands splayed across his mouth and nose. Yes, he had hit the rail – Ty could see the place on the pedestal where his face had connected. Blood. A white bit of tooth that looked silver on the reflective platform.

Silver. His cufflinks glittered in front of his face, spectacles gone just as she had first imagined. Ty ducked under the rail that ringed the platform, narrowly avoiding a wild kick from the metalbred, which was huffing louder, snorting. She caught a glimpse of its eyes, which a moment before had been as hard and still as a river in winter. The ice was broken now: the eyes rolling and roiling, whatever was inside them rushing wild. Ty inched her way along the outside of the platform to where Dr. Salt clung, cowering.

"Here, sir," she said, loud over the clatter of hooves and the huffing snorts. The tail that Dr. Salt had considered removing from the Limestone builds whipped by as the metalbred whirled, catching her on the cheek. It stung, but missed her eye, and she held her hand out for Dr. Salt.

Through the blood he saw her, recognized her, reached out, his hand red and slick. It was easy to grip his wrists instead of the bloody, slippery fingers. Easy to hold them tightly, to slip a little in the chaos, to drag him over the rail with her, his feet sliding in his own blood. It was easy to guide him to the stairs, still holding one wrist, to deliver him into the waiting group of security guards. On the platform, the Secretariat model pawed the air with its front hooves, the eyes still wide and wild. Ty's father reached her a moment later, dragging her toward the exit while the engineers struggled to shut the robot down.

"The Aristidean component is malfunctioning!" one of them shouted.

"Again?!" yelled someone else.

Ty let herself be dragged to the door, her face stiff with the mask of fear. Behind it, she felt smooth and tight. Just like her hand, inside which was gripped a silver cufflink.

CHAPTER 32

EZZ

Ezz stood waiting at the entrance to the maze, eyes prying at the darkness for Ty. She felt torn as she paced – eager to see the tall bald frame cutting through the shadows, but also not. Ezz's head was full of Rosario. Rosario and Martha. Friends. Both dead. The girl Rosario had never told Ezz about – but who Rosario's parents clearly knew – had been working alongside Rosario on the backside. They were both gone, murdered, and so Ezz was ashamed of the helpless anger that flooded her when she thought of Rosario and Martha bonding over horses and coding, spending hours in barns just miles from Ezz's front door while Ezz believed Rosario to be traveling. She imagined Rosario telling Martha, "Oh, I had a friend I used to be close with. We grew up together, but we grew apart. She says she loves horses but she doesn't even ride anymore. Can't remember the last time she saddled up…"

Ezz rubbed her fists into her eyes. *You can't be angry at the dead*, she told herself furiously, but…she was.

"Hey," came a soft voice through the shadows, and Ezz looked up to find Ty striding toward her over the dark, damp grass. She felt the familiar pang that swarmed in her belly at the sight of her. Ty was dressed neatly and pressed for cleanwork, probably headed to the Mahogany in a few hours. Watching her approach, she realized she'd never seen Ty in anything but party clothes and her work uniform. She wondered if there was an in-between. She caught Ty's eye and was about to ask about this middle Ty, but Ty was already opening her mouth to speak.

"Just us?" she said, scanning the area for, Ezz realized, Luz. Then her eyes wandered to the edge of Ezz's shirt, where the border of her sports bra peeked out near the neck. Ezz waited for the return of eye contact, for the blush that would inevitably spring up on Ty's cheekbones. And there it was, a field of poppies Ezz knew almost by heart at this point.

"Just us," Ezz nodded.

Ty closed the rest of the distance between them, stepping into the glow of the fairy lights hidden in the leaves of the topiary beasts. Luz had put them in at some point, completing the transformation of Ezz's garden from empty green to sculpted magic. Now Ezz could see Ty's face fully, the way her two arching eyebrows knitted together in an unexpected expression of worry.

"What's the matter?" Ezz frowned.

"I'm…fine."

"You don't look fine."

"I am. The event at Limestone was just…stressful."

Ezz didn't reply, waiting. In the manner of gardens, Ty was always a bit of a cactus. Looking at her now, the thorns seemed weaker. Ty sighed in the silence, then finally said:

"I hate my dad. Like, really. It was fucking terrible being around him for that long, especially in a place where he felt like he was in control. And they were talking shit about the activists who used to picket the Derby. My mom, before she… You know. She would do that. She loved the horses, had grown up with them. These people don't give a shit about horses. And they want to talk all this racist shit about Latinx people. Even at the height, horseracing was always white as fuck and there was a reason for that. And now Limestone got to start over with a clean, white slate.

And make people like my mom and Luis Funes out to be the real villains."

"Who's Luis Funes?" Ezz said, and was surprised by the look that crossed Ty's face in response, a look like a deer, surprised at being caught out in moonlight.

"The one..." Ty started, but stopped. "A friend of my mom's. He's dead."

She took a deep breath, her nostrils flared like a Thoroughbred after a race. She kept her eyes down, refusing to look at Ezz. Ezz decided to have mercy.

"They had to turn her and people like her into nutjobs," Ezz said. "To protect their industry. Meanwhile, the people inside were abusing those horses and pumping them full of drugs. Letting them break down. Letting them die. I think the original jockeys, the original racers, I think they would have been disgusted."

"Are they all like that?" Ty said, looking up at the sky now. The hum of a far-off plane reached their ears and Ty looked like she wished she were onboard. "Today's Derby people, I mean."

"No," Ezz said quickly, then stopped abruptly. She felt suddenly adrift, unsure of how she had continued working in the horse world – even just as gambler – after the loss of her parents. How had she gone to the track day after day, how had she walked down the shedrow getting glimpses of the ranking metalbreds, chatting with jockeys, looking for hints that signaled a winner? She had done it all, with her parents tucked away in a separate room of her mind, but now the door was swinging open. Had Ty opened it, with her dead mother? Or did a locked door only keep grief out for so long? She swallowed. She could smell her parents' barn. Manure and ash in her nostrils. "Like, even though the old industry was full of people who hurt their animals, abused them, there were tons of people who cherished their horses. Took care of them. Loved them. The same is true for the new industry.

Rosario was an outlier, but not unique. This industry is broken, but it can be fixed. We have to flush the money. Put the industry into the hands of people who care about the animals."

Ty shrugged, nodded once. Ezz stared at her for awhile, thinking of the word *broken* in the same speech as *Rosario*. Had Rosario been trying to fix it? Or burn it all down?

"What did you find?" Ezz said finally, lifting her chin, then dropping it. She was so curious it felt like hunger. Ever since Ty had said she was going to the Limestone event with her dad, Ezz had stalked the floor of her lair, eyeing her device. But nothing had come through. Luz had spent the evening trying to assure her that Ty hadn't been arrested, and if she had, there was nothing they could do. Ezz had been ready to prepare bail when Ty had texted saying she was on her way.

"Something," Ty said, and the smile that spread across her mouth felt like an antidote to the swarm of anxiety in Ezz's stomach.

"*Something*, huh," Ezz said. "Well, let's get that something down to Luz."

She turned, but Ty didn't follow, paused at the base of the elephant. Ezz turned, eyebrows questioning, and then it hit her.

"Oh. Nah, I'm not going to blindfold you. Unless…do I need to?"

Two pairs of eyes, locked on each other as if stuck in honey. Ezz was remembering the way Ty had masked herself at the Carousel, the slow cold roll of a façade as she moved down the bar. Ezz was still suspicious, wondering what such a mask could conceal. But here, under the fairy lights of the garden, everything felt honest. They were two girls who had lost something, and they were searching the same ground.

"Do I need to?" Ezz repeated when Ty didn't answer.

"No," said Ty, and when she smiled it was like a bird fluttering out from her face and into Ezz's cupped palms. Ezz led them into the labyrinth.

In they went, the green shadows swallowing them. Ty walked close, their knuckles brushing. Just when Ezz was considering taking her hand, they reached the place in the leaves where the doorway was buried. She held her arm out. "After you."

Down they went. Past the open door where Luz had been working all night on things Ezz didn't ask about. The green, earthy smell wafted out into the hall, and when Ezz glanced in, she was surprised by the masses of vines that she found curling onto the floor. Surely they hadn't been that long, that thick, when she went upstairs? They seemed to have appeared from nowhere. But next to her, Ty smelled as she always did – like linen, like lace – and she thought that in her eagerness to reach that smell above ground, she must not have noticed the vines. She kept walking, but Ty had paused.

"What *is* all this?" Ty said, calling after her.

"Luz's stuff," Ezz said. "She does her computer stuff in the other room and her garden stuff in here."

"Looks like kudzu," Ty said, studying the green-purple leaves, and Ezz stepped closer to look. Kudzu was called "the plant that swallowed the south" and was known to grow extremely fast, covering cars and houses in a matter of weeks if left unchecked. But not this fast.

"Looks too purple to be kudzu," Ezz said, peering through the gloom. "But it does look a lot like it. Maybe a hybrid."

"Why would she make a kudzu hybrid?" Ty said, raising an eyebrow. "I thought everyone was always trying to get *rid* of kudzu."

Just then, Luz poked her head out into the hall from the room ahead, the glow of screens illuminating the back of her hair. Her eyes seemed to narrow at finding them at the door to her room of green shadows, but when Ezz met her gaze the expression was gone.

"Did you get anything?" Luz said, looking past Ezz at Ty.

Ezz watched Ty reach into her pocket, and she held her breath. When she withdrew her hand, she was holding a cufflink up to catch the light. Luz's grin burned like a torch.

"I can't believe it," Luz said, when they were all huddled around it on her workbench. "How did you get it? That had to have been some slick finger work."

"Luck of the draw," Ty said. "There was a…diversion and I saw my chance."

"What kind of diversion?"

"A really scary one, actually," Ty said. "They had a metalbred model there for exhibition and it…freaked out."

"Freaked out how?' Ezz said, frowning. *Freaked out* wasn't a term she would associate with a machine.

Luz's eyes raised from the magnifying scanner she was firing up.

"Yeah, freaked out how?"

"Wigged," Ty shrugged. "It was in sleep mode and all the sudden it…wasn't. Kicked Dr. Salt, made him fall. Acted like a wild stallion."

Luz shifted back in her chair. "That's intense."

"I heard someone say it had a glitch in the Aristidean component," Ty said.

"Could make for an interesting Derby if we're this close to the race and Limestone is having model issues. I wonder if the buyers know," Ezz said, thinking of Rosario. Ezz had been behind the scenes for a couple Derbys with her friend, and despite all the pomp and brass, it was a pretty straightforward affair once you'd walked the red carpet. The jockeys went to their booths and when the gate slammed open, they did their work. A system glitch was not straightforward.

"They made us all sign NDA's at the door," Ty said. "Just to cover their asses, I'm guessing. There's no way they knew this was going to happen. I'm sure they're ready to sue our asses into oblivion if we speak a word about it."

Luz was examining the cufflink Ty had handed over through the lens of the same device she'd used to scan Rosario's nose stud. Ezz could feel herself holding her breath, but Ty looked even more nervous. As if whatever Luz might see through the delicate lens would reveal something else instead, a confirmation of something held in secret up Ty's sleeves.

Luz raised her eyes from the scope.

"We've got data."

Ezz clapped her hands once, loud, in celebration and Luz grinned, spinning her chair around to face her wall of screens.

"Hell yeah," Ty emphasized, slapping her thighs with both hands, and Ezz was relieved to watch some of the metal fade from her eyes. Ty was glad, truly. But Ezz was starting to wonder if the reasons why were less straightforward than she had thought. She stood and went to Luz's shoulder.

"Do you think it will tell us anything?" Ezz said, hovering. "About Rosario? About Martha?"

"No way of knowing," Luz said, squinting as she fired up her processes. "It will definitely have sensitive Limestone data that's probably worth a lot of money. But that's not our aim. And it's going to be hell decrypting this fucking thing."

"Are you sure you can do it?" Ezz said, overwhelmed by the lines of code that Luz's flying fingers threw up on the wall, the matrices and diagrams. Luz glanced at her and sniffed.

"Bitch please. I'm a genius."

Ezz laughed and went on watching, she and Ty passing a bag of pretzels that Ezz had procured from a drawer back and forth over Luz's head. A few loud crunches later and Luz was oscillating a glare between them.

"Don't y'all have something to…I don't know…*do*?"

"Yes," nodded Ezz. "Help you."

"Help me," Luz repeated, blinking.

"Yeah. You know. Moral support."

"You two crunching these stale boquitas in my ears isn't helping me. Why don't you go back down to the backside? Take Martha's mama that money."

"What money?" Ty said.

Ezz was suddenly very aware of their eyes on her; she looked down, absorbing herself in choosing the perfect pretzel from the bag.

"I raised some money for the family," she said, eyes in the bag. "You know. Funerals are expensive. And you know Cavehill ain't helping."

"She *raised* like a hundred of it," Luz said, typing busily. "The rest is her money."

"Hush," Ezz said, and bundled the pretzels away. She stood, suddenly eager to be out of this room and out of this conversation. "Fine, you want your nerd space, whatever. I'm going to go to the track and drop it off. Maybe her sister, Rebeca, will talk to us again."

Luz wheeled around again to study her seriously.

"Do not bother that girl, Ezzardine," she said. "Okay? If she wants to talk, fine. But do not badger her."

Then she swung her eyes over to Ty.

"And you. Try to curb your most Caucasian impulses, okay? Maybe don't chase a scared teenage girl through the dark this time."

Ezz choked down a laugh.

"It'll be daylight by the time we get there," Ty countered, and Luz rolled her eyes.

"I'm serious," Luz said. "Chill."

"I will," Ty said, serious now too. "I'm sorry about the other night...I...I don't know. Sometimes it's like I'm chasing too many things at once. I lost track of what it was in that moment."

Luz stared at her, and Ezz watched something pass between them, an understanding as sharp and mutual as broken glass falling across both their backs. She was surprised by the feeling of isolation she was suddenly bathed in – she, after one thing. The two of them...something more.

"Fine," Luz said, and the spell was broken. She spun in her chair to return to the screens. "Scram."

"Have that shit cracked when we get back!" Ezz said, pointing.

"Or what?"

"I don't know. No more snacks."

"You couldn't stop snacking if your life depended on it," Luz sniffed.

Ezz moved out into the hall and once again she looked back to find Ty reluctant, awaiting invitation. How could she not know that Ezz had begun to expect her at her side, that the path felt uncertain without her glowing certainty? Ezz didn't say this. Instead she just called,

"You coming?" and the small winged flock of Ty's smile was back again, carrying them through the door and back out into the dawn.

CHAPTER 33

TY

The backside had been awake for hours. Ty felt it when they slipped in through the gate using the fake press passes, the way the air felt warmer the closer they got to the barn, the dust stirred up and the dew trodden down. From the direction of the racetrack they could hear the steady gallop of robotic hooves being analyzed by hot walkers and owners. Five days until Derby. The smaller races had begun and the tension around the track was like a thick wire, strummed by an unseen finger and vibrating hotly.

"I don't see Rebeca," Ezz said after they had done a sweep of the barns and shedrow. "This is prime time. She should be here, right?"

"Let's try the workers' residences again," Ty said, already moving toward the gate, but she held back when Ezz hesitated.

"Luz said not to bother them," Ezz said. "People always think they're doing the right thing when somebody loses family. But a lot of times folks just want to be left alone."

Ty heard the blue around the edges of Ezz's words. She wanted to say: *I wouldn't know. The only person around after my mom died was my dad,* but she bit it back.

"We can leave them alone…," she said gently, "after you give them the money."

"True," Ezz said slowly.

The gate was open as it had been before, and the yard of the residences empty. They encountered no one on their way up the stairs to the door, and still didn't, even after knocking for five minutes.

"I don't think they're home," Ty said, glancing around.

"Or just not answering the door," Ezz sighed. "Probably see us through the peephole and don't want to even fuck with us. I can't blame her."

Ezz paused and then raised her voice a little.

"If you're home, we promise we don't want to bother you! We just want to give you something. To help with Martha."

The sound of a door opening jerked both of their eyes to the crack, but it was the neighboring door to the left, creaking open and then shut, emitting a short muscular man with a neat gray beard. He glanced at them as he went to the stairs, then paused at the top.

"You are looking for Ms. Rodríguez?" he said.

"Is that Martha's last name? The girl who died?" Ty said, ignoring Ezz's disapproving look.

"Yes," he said sadly. "That was Martha's name. You are her friends?"

"Sort of," Ty said. "We're looking for her mom. We wanted to give her something."

"Ms. Rodríguez is gone," he said, shaking his head.

"Gone?" Ezz said, stepping forward. "What do you mean, gone?"

"She left. Last night. Late."

"Where did they go?" Ty said.

"I do not know," he said. Ty knew he was lying, at least in the way that even if he did know, he wouldn't tell anyone. "They just had to leave."

"Are they coming back?" Ezz insisted.

Olivia A. Cole

"They took all their things," he said. "I think no."

"Damn," Ezz said, and Ty watched her deflate. "We were…we were trying to help. After what happened to Martha."

"Are you part of Skyhorse?" he said, paused there at the top of the steps.

"Skyhorse?" Ty said. "What's that?"

"Luz used to go there," Ezz muttered. "She's talked about Skyhorse."

"The school," he said, smiling. "For backside children. They're trying to give horses back to the Guatemalan people, the Mexican people, the Puerto Rican people. And not just us," he nodded at Ezz. "Black people too. The original American jockeys. You know about this? This industry has been bad for so long: keeping us as hot walkers and groomers, so rarely as trainers. Forget about owners! People pointed to all the Latino jockeys to say 'See? No problem!' But even the Latino jockeys, as far back as Braulio Baeza and Victor Espinoza – the white people called it 'an invasion.' Like ants. Termitas. Tried to stop us from speaking Spanish to the horses. You know. They built so many things to keep us from racing before, and now again with metalbreds, but Skyhorse is trying to build a tunnel under the wall."

"A tunnel under the wall," Ezz repeated softly. Ty thought of what Rebeca had said about her sister's talent, the way she was teaching herself and learning the work alone to break into racing. Limestone had collapsed the tunnel on top of her.

"You've worked with Thoroughbreds and metalbreds?" Ty said just as the man turned to leave.

"Yes," he said. "To me they are the same. They want the same things. So do we. We all want the same things we have always wanted."

Something in Ty felt like it was stretching – equinibots and horses existed in separate pastures in her mind. It was how she had comfortably judged the sections of her life with her mother: the

285

before, when her mother picketed for humane treatment of horses; then the increasingly strange and scary *after,* when the ban came down, and the robots were introduced. Her mother had pivoted to picketing for people, and Ty had assumed this was because her mother understood the bots were not real. Ty's father insisted that her mother wasn't happy unless she was complaining, that she thought of herself as a white savior, and Ty had absorbed some of this without fully realizing it. Hearing this man link the two kinds of horses made an equation solidify out of chalk dust; that perhaps her mother had understood something Ty and her father did not: that the people who could best advocate for the horses – flesh or metal – were those who knew them the best.

"But they're not real," Ty said, mostly to herself, but the man laughed, then leaned down and lifted the very bottom edge of his brown uniform pants, revealing the shiny silver of a bionic leg.

"Dime, ¿soy real o no lo soy?" he chuckled, then let the pant leg fall as he turned to go to work. "Am I real enough? Sometimes I still feel my leg, the one I was born with. Coded into me somehow. I wonder if the metalbreds have the wind programmed in their hearts somewhere. They might remember it the same way."

He carried on down the stairs, only the slightest limp in his step.

"Thanks for your help," Ezz called.

"Yo no ayudé," his voice came from the bottom. "You want to help, go to Skyhorse."

They stood outside a shabby blue building off Southern Parkway, a Pegasus mural adorning the wall, wings stretching from corner to corner.

"How long has this been here?" Ty said, studying it.

"Dunno. Paint is at least crisp though. We could ask Luz."

"They painted the mural last spring," a girl's voice said, and they turned to find her watching them from the three steps that led to the front door, backpack over her shoulder. She was a little younger than them, wearing a U of L hoodie and track pants. "Or were you asking about Skyhorse?"

"Both, I guess," Ezz said.

"I've been coming here since I was twelve," the girl said. "When we first came to the States. And Dr. Aldana had already been running it for awhile when I got here."

"Is Dr. Aldana the owner?"

"I guess you could call her that. She runs the place. Do you want to come in? I can introduce you."

Ty and Ezz exchanged glances, shrugging.

"Sure, thanks," said Ty, and they followed her up the three steps with the clean white paint, vined plants in pots narrowing the walkway. The welcome mat featured a faded rainbow border, the words *Don't Rein It In* printed in the center surrounded by hoof prints. The door opened, and the sound of a drill whined out in welcome.

"Come on," said the young woman with the backpack, and stepped away, waving at a tall thin woman with light brown skin, ink-black hair tied back at the nape of her neck. Ty felt the woman's gaze scan them like an x-ray, sharp eyes placed above even sharper cheekbones, her tight skin pitted with old acne scars, a golden hoop in her left nostril. If Ty were twenty years older she knew she'd be falling at her feet.

"Aniela?" the woman called to the girl, striding across the room. The drill sounds came from behind her, where two long tables full of various youths curled their necks over wires and circuit boards, some over glowing screens. Another group teased strangled sounds out of a few instruments – a French horn and two clarinets. The woman seemed to be placing herself between Ty and Ezz and these young people, as if the two of them might be wolves in disguise.

"They're here to meet you, Dr. Aldana," the girl called Aniela said.

"Can I help you?" the woman said, openly suspicious.

"Um, maybe?" Ty said. "We were just over at the backside and got sent your way."

"Oh? By who?"

Ty was a little taken aback by her tone – wrapped with wire, as full of sparks as the circuit boards behind her. She stood squarely in front of them now, gray T-shirt dipping low enough to reveal two silver clavicle piercings.

"We didn't catch his name actually," said Ezz, and Ty could hear from her voice that she had caught the tone as well, and little sparks of her own were starting to kindle.

"We're here for Martha," Ty said quickly. "Martha Rodríguez."

It was as if a bucket of water washed over the circuit of the tall woman's eyes, a wildfire hushed by rain. She frowned sadly at them now, searching their faces.

"Were you her friends?"

"We're her friends," Ty said, hoping this lie could be forgiven. "And we raised money for her funeral. But we just found out her mom and sister left town."

"Oh no," Dr. Aldana said, one of her long-fingered hands rising to her cheek. The gesture was unexpectedly tender and Ty felt her heart squeeze. "Poor Elena. They lost their father two years ago and now Martha. Elena is probably losing her mind."

Nearby, Aniela with the backpack lingered, trying to listen. Dr. Aldana turned and shooed her off.

"You'd better step into my office," Dr. Aldana said, motioning. Ty checked her device. She still had time to make it to the Mahogany for work. She couldn't leave now – not when Dr. Aldana was offering a conversation, and, potentially, answers.

Her office was small and warm with only one chair aside from her own. Ezz motioned for Ty to sit down and then leaned against the wall behind her. Ty was intensely aware of her nearness, and focused hard on Dr. Aldana's deep brown eyes.

"How did you know Martha?" Dr. Aldana asked when she had settled into her chair. Her desk and the narrow walls around her were covered with photos and framed certificates – one was a degree from MIT, Ty noticed. The photos were of Dr. Aldana standing with children holding medals, or crouched over circuit boards and three-dimensional coding modules. Hackathon Winner of the Year, several plaques read – four different times, Ty noted. She felt Ezz shift, and Ty realized quickly that she was in the driver's seat, so to speak, because she had commenced the lying. *Go ahead and drive*, she could feel Ezz commanding.

"From the backside," Ty said. "She worked there."

"I know," Dr. Aldana nodded. "Her sister too. Rebeca?"

"Yes," Ty said. "But she's gone now too. Ms. Rodríguez took off last night, like we said. That's why we're here. We're hoping we can find someone who knows where they might have gone. Or why."

"Why?" Dr. Aldana said, raising her eyebrows. "We just established that the woman lost her husband and her child in a span of two years. Why would she stay in a place with so many painful memories?"

"Sure," Ty nodded, hoping she didn't sound callous, but the need to press forward felt like a charging bull just under her flesh. "But the timing...doesn't it seem like she's...watching out for something?"

Something shifted under Dr. Aldana's gaze, like a salamander sliding half into the water.

"Women like Señora Rodríguez are always watching," she said seriously. "Watching for violence in her home country. For ICE thugs in this country. She has two daughters, so she is always watching for men who think no one will care if a Brown girl is hurt or goes missing. Watching her boss to ensure she isn't being cheated, and even if she is, what can she say? She is always watching for opportunities, for herself and for her children. She is watching for people who call her a hard worker but never pay her for the work. Her children become watchful too. Martha watched for opportunity, and found Skyhorse."

"Is that all she found?" Ty said quickly. The way a bloodhound follows the dead, her nose was leading her somewhere else.

"She found opportunity, as I said," Dr. Aldana said. She sat back in her chair, crossing her arms, the steel returning to her eyes. "Why are you here?"

"We're trying to help Martha's family," Ty said. This was the truth, even if it was a small part, a tiny bone in a skeleton half-buried in mud.

Behind Ty, Ezz stayed silent, but Ty could feel the tension emanating from her like steam from a horse's coat. Dr. Aldana surveyed them from behind her desk, all the children she had mentored surveying them from the walls like a silent jury.

"I've been teaching immigrant kids robotics for fifteen years," she said, unmoving except for her eyes, which wavered between Ty and Ezz. "Trying to give them a leg up in a country that fights like hell to keep them out and down. My family emigrated to Louisville when I was just two, so it feels like home to me. When I finished school, I came back here to start this program. I've worked with hundreds of youth. And out of all of them, Martha was the most talented."

Ty's heart felt like it was pumping a thick sludge of oil instead of blood. In her mind was the video of Benedict with his hands around Martha's throat. All of her talent and promise and the care her mother had taken to keep her safe floating up and bursting like leaden bubbles.

"I knew this was going to happen," Dr. Aldana said slowly,

her voice becoming heavy. "She was so bright, so ambitious. And working at the backside just made her even more hungry. Can you imagine? Seeing jockeys make hundreds of thousands of dollars doing something that you're better at?"

"Her sister said she was more talented than all the jockeys," Ty said, and then bit her lip, hoping this didn't give her away as a fraud. But Dr. Aldana just nodded.

"I teach orchestra too," she said, and pointed up at another series of photos, children and teenagers lined up on a football field and at Cavehill Downs. "Every year on Derby Day we perform. Sometimes the music kids will practice here while the robotics kids tinker, and it drives them crazy. Can't focus. But not Martha. She would get in the zone – nothing could distract her. There'd be cymbals crashing right by her head and she would just go right on. She'd only been coming to Skyhorse for a year, but she caught on so fast. She was born to do this."

She sniffed then, the sternness in her eyes cracking open.

"Do you know why someone would kill her?" Ty said quickly, softly, before she could stop herself, before she could tell herself it was heartless. Dr. Aldana didn't flinch, nor did she try to stop the tears squeezing from her eyes.

"People have been talking," she said slowly. "A Limestone frontrunner is missing. They're saying Martha stole it."

"We've heard that too," Ezz said over Ty's head.

"It doesn't make sense," Ty and Dr. Aldana said at the same time. Dr. Aldana leveled her eyes at Ty once more.

"It *doesn't* make sense," the woman repeated. "But I don't know any other reason someone would have to take her life. She was young, innocent, brilliant, never hurt a soul. Wanted to be a jockey like Rosario Vicario."

Behind her, Ty heard Ezz make a small sound. Something between a sigh and a half-spoken curse. She made a mental note to ask about it later.

"Why would they kill her over a bot?" Ty went on. "If anything, they'd just put her in jail. Make an example of her."

"I had a friend," Ezz said, and Ty almost flinched, knowing she was talking about Rosario. "She always talked about the owners and how much rage a lot of them have. Martha didn't say anything about pissing anyone off? One of the owners, maybe, who didn't like Martha working on the metalbreds? Could someone have felt threatened by her talent?"

Dr. Aldana frowned deeply, and Ty could tell by the look on her face that she was imagining this; Martha on the other side of rage and entitlement. She hadn't seen the video. Ty was glad.

"You know how they are," Dr. Aldana said, these words for Ezz. Ty was aware that she was not part of this conversation, and kept her mouth shut. "Two's a party, but three's a crowd. One too many of us and suddenly they feel like we're taking over. For us, Latinx people, they always said all the same basura: *Oh, they're small people, they're short and light, it comes naturally.* Never because we worked hard, because we studied. That's why they make it so hard for us now – and Black people too. Anyone of any size can be a jockey now, so they say. You just have to be good with the machines. What lie will they lean on about us now? How do they explain Rosario Vicario, in the world of their myths? Martha would have just been too much."

She laughed a short, harsh laugh, then rubbed her eyes.

"So you don't think she stole a horse," Ty said. "Do you think they were just trying to keep her from being the next Rosario?"

"I…" Dr. Aldana paused. She bowed her head. "I don't know what I think. I just don't know what she thought she would do with a stolen Limestone model," Dr. Aldana said, rubbing her forehead. "She told me all about the one she'd been working on – it was an unusual-looking model. It's not as if she could have taken it to run in another race! Cloud Parliament – the bot she told me about – had a Palomino coloring, hard to reproduce on an equinibot; once it's set, it takes weeks to undo. Martha was brilliant but she would have had trouble undoing it all by herself. A Palomino with a blaze? It would be recognized immediately. You can't just spirit that away."

"What did you say?" The oil in Ty's heart suddenly turned to water, slipping fast through the valves. "Did you say a Palomino? With a blaze?"

"Yes," Dr. Aldana said, dropping her hand. "I'm sure you know the one if you worked in the shedrow with Martha? That metalbred was all she talked about in the weeks leading up to…up to…the event of her death."

"Yes," Ty said. She was standing, and didn't remember standing. Her hand was gripping Ezz's forearm and she didn't remember doing that either. "Dr. Aldana, we have to go. We're so sorry but we have to go right now."

Dr. Aldana was half-standing too, confusion and grief fighting for position on her face.

"I…I wish I could help you," she said. "I wish there were something I could do."

"You did," said Ty, towing Ezz to the door. "You did."

Outside Skyhorse, with the traffic whizzing by, Ezz wrenched away and Ty let her, power-walking toward the Trolley. She had her device out, texting the Mahogany. She was going to be late. Very late.

"Where the hell are you going?" Ezz called. "What's going on?"

"The horse Martha supposedly stole," Ty shouted over her shoulder. "I know where it is."

CHAPTER 34

EZZ

Ezz recognized the sound as soon as they approached the egg-blue house: the whinnies of horses being brought in from pasture, the promise of grain luring them in from the grass soaked gold by the late afternoon. She had paused then, feeling shivery, memories like spiders spinning webs around her feet. These sounds – horse sounds – were threads that led down to the yarn of her soul, attached to something soft and essential that she had once worn like a sweater and had, for years now, refused to put back on. The realization came suddenly then, standing in the front yard of a stranger's house: this is why she kept gambling, even as her parents' barn still smoldered in her memory, they and the horses inside. The metalbreds were not real. And that meant they were safe. The memory of her mother and father coated in steel.

Her device buzzed in her pocket, and she pulled it out, expecting and finding a text from Luz. She felt a swell of hope until she opened the message.

L: I can't crack the cufflink. I've been trying for hours.

Ezz stared at the message, embarrassed by the anger that sprang into her mouth like blood from a bitten tongue. She started and erased three messages, all laced with poison, until she finally forced herself to say, **It's okay. Keep trying.** It wasn't Luz's fault,

Olivia A. Cole

she told herself, but trying not to blame someone when there was so much out there needing blame was like trying to keep hands off a poison ivy rash.

"Coming?" Ty said, turning, curious. Ezz could only nod, and then follow.

Ty had spent the entire train ride on her device, arguing first with her father, who demanded to know where she was, and then the Mahogany, where Madame Richmond took her plea for an off-day with nothing less than acrimony, demanding she come in that night. But Ty seemed determined to bring them here, waiting an hour for the Trolley, silent as they then took the bus to this pretty, blue house. They crossed the front yard toward a vibrant red barn, where Ezz could see two people with lead ropes, waiting for horses. Ezz glanced at Ty, trying to gauge what was happening behind the dark spin in her eyes. Ezz felt more and more like they were walking toward something sticky, like the truth was a patch of darkly spreading amber, she a mosquito trapped inside.

The visualization made her reach for Ty's elbow, tugging her to a halt.

"So are you going to tell me what's up?" she urged. "You've been silent for like two hours, dragging me out here without even telling me what the hell's going on. If I'd known we were going this far I would've called a car or something."

"I always take the Trolley," Ty said, and Ezz was relieved by the smile there, a slice of sunlight through the concentrated clouds on her face. "Don't be a brat."

"A brat?" Ezz cried.

"Yes," Ty said. "Always in a rush. Sometimes a slow journey is a good one. Gives us time to think."

"And what did you think of?" Ezz said. "Between yelling at your dad and your boss?"

"I wasn't *yelling* at my boss," Ty said. "And I haven't really thought of anything."

295

She paused then, looking annoyed – at herself, Ezz thought – before carrying on.

"We're just going to have to see how this plays out."

"I'm following your lead," Ezz said. "You'd better not be getting me into something you can't get me out of."

They made their way down the light slope of the hill. They were in full view of the barn then, and Ezz didn't get the feeling that they were sneaking. Two people, around Ezz and Ty's age, one of them a slender Black girl with hair as short as Ty's, jeans and T-shirt spotted with dirt and grass stains, oil stains along the cuff of one pant leg. A horse girl, Ezz knew immediately. She also knew immediately that the girl was half in love with Ty. Or had been.

"Hey, you," the girl said, walking up to meet them, eyebrows raised in surprise and delight. She had a doll-like face, smooth brown and freckled, front teeth jutting out ever so slightly. Her eyes took in Ty like well-loved clothes from the line, ready to take her in her arms and smooth her out. "What are you doing here?"

"Joelle," Ty said, and Ezz glanced at her, wondering if she was in love with this tall, freckled girl with muscles that stood out from her arms in gentle slopes. Ezz had never worried about being short until now. She was suddenly glad she was on the hill. "Sorry to drop by like this."

"You had a long trip out here," Joelle said. "Couldn't let me know you were coming? I'm glad I was home!"

"Me too," Ty said. "I was on the phone on the way out, sorry. My dad. Asshole."

Joelle nodded, and then darted her eyes curiously at Ezz, who stood watching silently. Ty glanced between them and then back again.

"Oh! Sorry," she said. "Joelle, this is Ezz. My...my friend. She knows your cousin Shavon. We've been working on a kind of project together. Ezz, this is Joelle. She and her family own this farm. I grew up next door."

Ezz cast her eye across the seemingly endless green, searching for a home beyond the blue one just up the little hill.

"When there *was* a next door," Ty said, noticing Ezz's searching look. "It's all part of their rescue now."

"Nice to meet you," said Ezz, trying hard to keep the edge out of her voice. It had felt like a ripple inside her at first, but as she spoke and the words rolled up from below, it gained momentum until it felt like what could become a tidal wave. She swallowed.

"Nice to meet you too," Joelle said. "This is my cousin Marcus. We were just bringing some of the animals in for medicine."

Ezz let her eyes wander away from Joelle's face and over the fence, taking in the horses. As always, she felt the familiar ache at the sight of them, a nostalgic filling of the senses. Summer-warm. Her mother's laugh. "Is this what you rescue? Horses?"

"Yep," Joelle nodded. "It was my nana's farm first, and then we gradually converted it. She was the only Black-owned farm out here for the longest, but that's changing now."

"Not gonna lie," Ezz said. "I'm mad relieved right now. Ty said she was taking me out to see a friend and we got farther and farther from the city and I was getting kinda nervous. She didn't tell me y'all were Black."

Joelle threw back her head and laughed, showing all her teeth. Ty too, embarrassed.

"Sorry," Ty said. "I guess I was on autopilot."

"You thought she was bringing you out to the boonies to see some rednecks?" Joelle chuckled. "Like I said, not too many Black horse people out here, but we're out here."

"We're out here," Ezz agreed and then Joelle took a second glance.

"Wait, I know you!" she cried, a spark of recognition in her eyes that Ezz knew well. "I knew I recognized you. You're Ezzardine Clayton! You were friends with..." she trailed off, and Ezz could see Rosario's name turning into smoke in the girl's mouth.

"Rosario Vicario," Joelle said, quietly, as if she had tried to stop herself from saying it and failed.

"She was my best friend." Ezz still almost choked on *was*.

"I'm so sorry for your loss," Joelle said, mouth creasing into a frown "I heard how she died and..."

"She wasn't an addict," Ty said quickly and Ezz knew Ty said it so that she wouldn't have to. The desire to hold her hand came over her like a sudden sweat.

"I know," Joelle said just as quickly, and then they all stared at each other, something awkward sprouting up among them.

"Did you know her?" Ezz said.

"We crossed paths now and then," Joelle said, and turned toward her cousin. Marcus, who had said nothing and only offered a nod in greeting, was now gently untying the lead rope of a horse from a post.

"How did you know her?" Ty said.

Joelle still didn't look at them. She turned to the horse Marcus was seeing to, stroking its cheek. "You know how it is. Horse world is a small world. Especially since Limestone."

Marcus stood back now, watching the conversation unfold, eyes squinted slightly. Ezz thought he gave the impression of a German Shepherd listening from its doghouse, awaiting a signal. Ezz's vision felt suddenly narrow, homing in on Joelle, her hands; Marcus, his feet, set squarely on the earth. Next to her, Ty was standing very still. Whatever was in the air, Ty smelled it too.

"Bringing them all in?" Ezz said, nodding out at the horses in the pasture.

"A few at a time," Joelle said. "Vet coming today to check everyone out. We've got one with a cough and one that came in with cracked heels. Hoping we can get another grant soon to help care for all these babies."

"At least you have one that you don't need to worry about with that stuff," Ty said. "That one won't even need feed, right? He doesn't even need real food."

Ezz felt the heavieness in Ty's words, even without knowing what they were weighted with, and she watched Joelle's eyes dart over to Ty. There was a spark of something quick and sharp skittering through them, and Ezz felt it in her own eyes too.

"You're talking about the bot I told you about," Joelle said. Ezz felt like she was skinny dipping after dark – the water dim and her skin dangerously exposed. But she said nothing, shooting a look at Ty, looking for a sign about what the hell they were doing here and what bot Joelle was talking about. When she glanced back at Joelle, the girl's eyes had just left Marcus. Ezz had already missed whatever expression they'd exchanged.

"Ty didn't tell me you keep metalbreds too," Ezz said when no one spoke.

"Did you find out where it came from?" Ty said. Ezz could hear her making an effort to keep her voice level, and Ezz forced her face to stay neutral too, but internally she was scrabbling at every detail, snatching them up and examining each one. "The bot, I mean. With a face and physique like that, I feel like it would be easy to track down if you didn't know where it came from."

"Someone dropped off a bot with you," said Ezz, trying to sound like this was a fact she already knew. She was thinking of Rosario, of Martha, of loose threads waiting for a needle. "You have to spend another million if you want to take a metalbred out of rotation...who would do that just to drop it off at a rescue?"

"What are you doing here, Ty?" Joelle said, lifting her chin in Ty's direction once, sharply. She ignored Ezz, and Ezz let her.

"Just came to see you," Ty said. "You said we should get together again soon, right? And I've just been...thinking."

"About what?" Joelle said. The three girls stood alone now – Marcus had gone, leading the horse into the barn. Joelle and Ty stared at each other, Ezz watching them both closely.

"When I was here the other day and you were telling me about the horses and you told me someone had dropped off a metalbred, I didn't really think anything about it. My mind was on other stuff, I guess."

The rest of the horses were plodding up to the fence now, ears pricked forward, eager for whatever it was the humans might offer, soft nickers uttered to draw Joelle's attention. But Joelle kept staring at Ty.

"But today I met someone who had been working with a backside girl," Ty went on. "They told me that this girl had been working on a Limestone model, a frontrunner. And it went missing. No one knows where. An equinibot worth that much money...the police have been searching the underground tracks, assuming someone wanted to put it in races against retired horses, make some money. The Limestone models have trackers built in, but no one has been able to find this one that went missing."

Ezz's stomach had transformed into a dark lake – every word out of Ty's mouth was a pebble dropping from the sky. She saw the ripples in Joelle's eye, in her flexed jaw. Behind her, the horses had all gathered at the fence, one or two velvet noses stretching across the top board to nudge her. Wires were lining up slowly in Ezz's head, a lightbulb flickering.

"The person I met today told me about the missing metalbred," Ty said. "Said its name was Cloud Parliament. Blaze-faced palomino, like a white fire spreading across. Kind of like..."

Ty paused, then raised her finger, leveling it at one of the muzzles reaching across the fence.

"Kind of like that."

Ezz stared, waiting for it to make sense. There's no way that the animal Ty indicated was a metalbred. There wasn't a jockey in sight, so it would have to be on an autosaddle setting. But Ezz knew from Rosario that autosaddle didn't include what she was seeing right now: the neck stretching in that way that horses do when they're confident, playful, when they know you and your scent and what they can get away with. Ears relaxed, tail swishing at flies that may or may not be buzzing. This was a *horse*. And yet the look in Joelle's eyes, walled off, told her that Ty was telling the truth.

Joelle didn't look at the horse. When she took her eyes off Ty, it was to glance at the barn, where Marcus was emerging from putting the horse away.

"Remember when I said you never told me your secrets when we were kids?" Joelle said.

"Yeah," said Ty, and Ezz's blood felt like a buzz again, bubbles swimming through her veins at the idea of the story Ty and this girl may have shared.

"Usually I wouldn't want to share my secrets with someone who didn't tell me theirs. I don't like one-way streets. But with you I didn't mind. You know why?"

Ty just stared at her, and the bubbles in Ezz's blood seemed to all be rushing toward the same destination: a place in her gut where they were forming into something solidly anxious.

"Because you just accepted them," Joelle said. "I would whisper things in your ear and you would nod, and I know you would hear me, but you would never say anything. You held my secrets. You didn't even ask questions."

Ezz stared at her. A shoe had been lifted and taken a step. She was waiting for the other to drop now.

Joelle rubbed her temples in slow circles. "You never asked questions. I don't know why you had to start now."

Then she was nodding at her cousin, and Ezz heard Ty's curse before she saw the reason for it. She darted her eyes to Marcus and found him standing squarely on the path from the barn with a shotgun leveled at them.

"What the fuck, Jo," Ty whispered.

"I don't know why you had to come over here with this shit," Joelle sighed.

"You stole a fucking million-dollar metalbred?" Ezz cried. She took a step forward but then so did Marcus and the gun. She stepped back again, scowling.

"Why?" Ty said. "What can you do with a metalbred? Sell it for parts?"

"How'd you even disable the tracker?" Ezz said. She was afraid of the gun being pointed at her chest, but mostly she was angry. She had been trying to find out why Rosario died, and then tell the world. Make sure it never happened again. And now this. "You must have a hell of a jockey on staff at your lil dusty-ass rescue."

"I didn't have to disable shit," Joelle said, glaring. "Cloud Parliament's tracker is disabled because he disabled it himself."

"What?" Ezz snapped. "What the fuck are you even talking about? You're trying to tell me a robot disabled its own…"

But Joelle cut her off, raising her hand to signal Marcus.

"Nobody can find Cloud Parliament because he disabled his tracker," Joelle said. "And now nobody is gonna find y'all either."

CHAPTER 35

LUZ

L uz woke up under a bush, the sensation of something crawling across her cheek bringing her to sudden consciousness. She slapped her face, too hard, wincing as the bug flew off unharmed – a firefly. An early-bird, the sun not yet set. *Kentucky*, she thought. She unlocked her device, the glowing line of missed calls from her mother reminding her why she hadn't powered it on all day. Her mother wanted to leave Kentucky and take Luz with her. How could she leave this place, where the bugs glowed gold, where the grass glowed blue?

She sat up, groggy, leaves swiping across her cheeks. She remembered, then, how the atmosphere of the lair had seemed to become thick with her failure, the way the screens had started to burn her retinas. She had gone to the green room, seeking comfort, but had found none. Vines. Leaves. All she could think about was the look on Zarita's face. *What about us?* Words that had, in a heartbeat, sent Luz's steady plans swirling into mist. She'd told her mother she wasn't a child, but she felt like one. She came up into the sunlight, and the sunlight put her to sleep. Like a child.

She ignored the missed calls from her mother and opened a new message to Ezz instead.

Are you coming back? How did things go at the backside?

Did you give Martha's mom the money?

She stared at the screen until it went dark. Soon Ezz would be back and Luz would have to tell her that the cufflink was unhackable. Ezz would come back with hope in her eyes and grief on her lips, and Luz would have to show her the empty screen, the impenetrable shield someone had built for the data inside. The only thing Luz had been able to force open was what looked like a signature code – twelve-digit sequences that she assumed were tied to Dr. Salt's personal access point to the Limestone database. But it was like finding an address on an envelope in a lockbox. The lockbox was good. But she needed to open the vault beyond it. Rosario Vicario could have done it. But Rosario Vicario was dead.

"¡Jueputa!" she shouted at the sky, slapping at the tears that spilled hot down her cheeks. If she had stayed in Skyhorse like her parents had wanted, she thought, she could do what needed to be done right now, could uncover the thing that would prove who killed Rosario. It was the proof that made her dig her nails into her palms – she had seen Brian Benedict at the backside on the night Martha was dead, and that was a fact. But Rosario...logic said that these deaths were connected, and Luz spoke the language of logic. And what wasn't logical was the idea of Benedict acting alone. A billionaire who liked to kill for fun? It wouldn't be the first time, Luz reasoned, but there had to be more. Who pulled the strings of a billionaire?

"Jueputa," she said again, whispering this time.

Then she was tearing out of the bushes, tripping over a root and falling flat, barely feeling it, before sprinting back toward the maze. She felt a hot momentum thrumming through her, and she didn't want to lose a single second. She found her way through the labyrinth and through the leaves and down to the lair, where she passed her green room and went straight to the lab.

She didn't bother to sit. On the main screen, she swiped aside the little she was able to hack of Salt's cufflink – Ezz would be disappointed, but maybe there was something better. She had already been poking around in Limestone's databases, looking for access points to Salt's data. She had even done a cursory combing of Benedict's files. Finding Annie Claybelle's was only the work of a moment, and as Luz dug deeper through the layers of security, like prying up digital floorboards, she remembered the interview she had seen of Benedict – *Now my sister, Annie, she's the brains of the operation. I just do what big sis tells me to do.*

"And just what did she tell you to do, Brian?" she whispered, blue light from the computers flooding over her fingers.

It was like an egg cracking, messages and data and payments leaking out of the screen and into her eyes. Emails to donors, mostly innocuous. Texts to her brother and someone who appeared to be her mother-in-law. Board meeting notes. Strategy sessions. Documents requiring Claybelle's signature, which generally had another layer or two of security that Luz hacked without much trouble. This is what Gina Aldana had meant about the knack of a hacker: the feeling she got as she dug deeper and deeper, an unknowable feeling of knowing when she was getting close to something, whatever that something was. It felt like tunneling through the crust of the earth, closer and closer to the hot mantle.

Hours passed, but she didn't notice in the isolation of the lair. She paused only to stretch her fingers when they began to cramp. She burrowed through event itineraries and wedding invitations. But it wasn't what was there that Luz was looking for – it was what wasn't there, and she had to go far and deep to find deletions, past backups into echoes of backups. Limestone's server had a way of dis-integrating data. A flaw, Luz knew, from Skyhorse and from common sense. Someone had gotten lazy, had built the system to protect itself from outsiders, but not from itself. Luz wrapped herself in Limestone access keys and plunged into the last layer of Limestone's underserver.

And that's when she struck magma.

CHAPTER 36

TY

"What, you're gonna kill us?" Ezz said. Her laugh was a cold snake twisting through Ty's ears. "In front of the horses? Bury us out in the bluegrass? What the fuck is going on here?"

"You work for Limestone," Joelle said, her voice low. She motioned Marcus closer with a jerk of her head.

"The *fuck* we do," Ezz snorted.

"Why the hell would you think that?" Ty said. Her heart was beating so fast it seemed not to beat at all.

"I was bartending at the ball Limestone threw the other night," Marcus said. His eyes were on Ty, and she felt the coldness in his stare seeping through her like a thrown drink. "At their headquarters. I saw you there with your dad, chatting with all the executives and shit, standing next to Claybelle and Benedict."

"He said you rescued Dr. Salt's worthless ass too," Joelle said. The girl Ty had once known, had run barefoot across this very grass with, was gone, replaced with stony eyes and a steel jaw. "When he told me what he saw, I thought maybe there was a misunderstanding. But here you are now. Bet they promised to make you Employee of the Month."

"I do *not* work for Limestone," Ty said. She was embarrassed by her voice, so unlike Ezz's. Her own was a rabbit tearing across the field before hounds.

"Bullshit," Joelle countered. "You're there rubbing elbows with their executives and then you show up here asking some very specific questions about Limestone property? You're either Limestone or you're the feds. Either way you've got to go."

The click of the gun's safety was like a crack of lightning, amplified by more than Ty's fear. Louder was the echo of something more complex. More piercing than "stay alive" was the refrain of *but we're not finished.*

"I was working at Limestone that night, yes," Ty said, loud. "But not *for* Limestone. I was there as a spy."

"Excuse me?" Joelle said, her eyebrow arching up in a way that indicated more irritation than curiosity.

"My dad works there, that's true." Ty's voice shook less with the truth bolstering it. "But I was using him. I was there to get information about Dr. Salt. And I did."

"Fucking *spying?*" Marcus said, almost laughing. "Yeah, right. For who?"

"For *me,*" Ezz said.

"So *you* work for the feds," Marcus answered, sarcastic.

"No. I work for myself."

"You're rich, we know," Joelle said, rolling her eyes.

"It's not about that," Ezz said, rolling hers right back. "This is about finding out the truth. About how Rosario died."

"And what do you know about that?" Joelle said.

"I said she was my best friend," Ezz snapped.

"That doesn't mean you know how she died!" Joelle said, almost shouting.

"But I do," Ty jumped in. "I was there when she died. In the hotel she was staying in. I was with her. She basically told me she was murdered. And that's what me and Ezz are doing together" – she blushed saying *together*, in spite of herself – "trying to find out who killed her. Athough we have a pretty fucking good idea."

"And why," Ezz added.

"One thread led us to the backside, so we followed that," Ty said. "And then another thread led us to a girl who got murdered there, and then…"

"Martha," Joelle said, and if she was stone before she was diamond now, so stiff and sharp she could pierce through Ty and Ezz both with one sweep. "How do you know about Martha?"

"How do *you* know about Martha?" Ty demanded.

"Can you put the goddamn shotgun down now?" Ezz yelled at Marcus. "I think it's pretty obvious we're on the same side. Or in the same shape. Or some shit. But we're not the feds and we're sure as hell not Limestone."

Marcus cast a look at Joelle. Joelle stared Ty in the eye for a long time, and behind the honey brown of her irises Ty could almost see the memories playing out – the golden sparkle of hayloft sunlight, of bare toes with grass shooting up between each one. Then Joelle made a clipped sweeping gesture with her hand, and Ty couldn't help but wonder what else about her childhood friend had changed, how many times that hand had waved and the outcome meant something else. In any case, the mouth of the shotgun yawned at the ground now, and Joelle had turned to the fence line, where the horses eagerly lipped at her empty palms.

"What do you see?" she said, raising her voice so it flowed backward toward Ty and Ezz, neither of whom moved any closer. The charge of uncertainty had not yet left the air – both of them were still electrified by it.

"Horses," Ty said. "And a bot."

"Only because you *know* it's a bot," Joelle said. "Remember your first day you came back to visit? I had to tell you – and looking back I should've kept my fucking mouth shut – but you wouldn't have known if I hadn't said so."

"I would've known," Ty said, reflexively, and Joelle glanced back at her, amused. "Eventually."

"Yeah? How?"

"I would have noticed that it doesn't eat. That it doesn't drink."

"Maybe," Joelle said, turning back to the animals. Cloud Parliament stood between two others, hip to hip, the brown eyes blinking slowly now and again, tail twitching when a horsefly explored its golden rump. The Palomino's ears tilted to catch Joelle's voice, then turned sideways again, relaxed. "But is that what makes a horse a horse? Eating? Drinking?"

"That's what makes something alive," Ty said, frowning, standing still.

"Kind of," Joelle said, and laid her palm against the metalbred's forehead. Cloud Parliament blinked a slow, contented blink, eyelashes fluttering when she began to scratch with barn-dirty nails. "But is that *life*?"

"What are you trying to say?" Ty said. "That you think this thing is…real? That even though it's a machine, it's…what? Sentient? Alive? *Alive* alive?"

"You think this goddamn equinibot has a soul?" Ezz added. "Is that what you're trying to tell us? Just because, what, it glitched and its tracker was disabled?"

Joelle turned and stared at them, her eyes as brown and serious as the horses'.

"No. I'm trying to tell you that *all* of them have souls. Every metalbred that Limestone ever made."

Ty laughed, incredulous. Limestone had made their billions off the very opposite of this claim. Equinibots, metalbreds – the saving grace of horseracing. Metal shells that look like the real thing, but are no different than putting an engine in a very expensive tuna can. No whips or steroids or spirit to consider. Just nuts and bolts and ones and zeroes that, when arranged properly and coded correctly, could run a race and then power down until the next one.

"Bullshit," said Ezz. "*Bullshit.*"

"Prove it," said Ty, shaking her head.

"I don't have to," Joelle said. "Martha Rodríguez already did."

She clipped a lead rope onto Cloud Parliament's halter and then motioned for Ty to step out of the way, swinging the gate open when the way was clear. She clicked her tongue for the metalbred and Ty held her breath as the massive creature moved leisurely through, inches from her body. Something more than her heart felt like it was stuttering – a soul-deep shudder, the questioning of enormous truths. She watched her hand raise in spite of the sharp desire not to, and her fingers trailed along Cloud Parliament's side as he stepped past. The gate swung shut behind them, and it wasn't until they got to the open door of the barn that Ty caught hold of everything inside her running away. As she stood looking after them, the sound of dry hay blowing across the swept dirt floor reached Ty's ears in the instant before Joelle's voice did.

"You'd better come with me," Joelle said, almost wearily, then turned to disappear inside the barn. "I'll show you."

Ty took a step, then stopped. She turned to Ezz, who she had almost forgotten, and found her already looking back. They said nothing, mirrors to each other's uncertainty. But looming up in the reflection, large and clear, was the need to *know.*

"We have to," Ezz whispered.

"For Rosario," Ty agreed.

"Fuck," Ezz said, shaking her head. Ty nodded, and they followed Joelle.

She led them to a tack room, the walls lined with bridles and bits and saddles. Ty took one step inside and her whole body turned gold with a flood of nostalgia, the smell of hay and animal and sweet feed entering her brain through her nose and twisting into a labyrinth of memories. She felt herself beginning to wander through the little room, remembering the first time Joelle had brought her here to get handfuls of grain, both of them ten and sweating. Ty had already known she liked girls, and she had felt the same unnamed something in the way Joelle had regarded her, the lingering smile, the way they seemed to have grown from the same seed.

"Through here," Joelle said, and reached for a red bridle hanging from a nail. As she tugged it there was a click; the wall covered with hanging equipment shifted almost imperceptibly until Joelle pressed her fingers against it. Under her guidance, it withdrew an inch or two and then slid sideways.

"Nice." Ezz nodded approvingly.

"What the fuck," Ty grumbled. "Why does everyone have a secret lair but me?"

"I don't have a secret lair either, if that helps," Marcus said.

"No, just a secret gun," Ty said, rolling her eyes.

"We're country folks," Marcus shrugged.

Joelle stepped through the revealed doorway and into a large bright room, leading Cloud Parliament in with her. The bot didn't seem bothered by the strangeness. Once Ty would have thought it was because metalbreds were only bothered by those things they were programmed to react to – that is, nothing. But the easiness of the bot's step, the way it leaned into Joelle's neck scratch while she waited for the others to enter the room… Down was up. Marcus closed the doorway behind them.

"Was this always here?" Ty said, gazing around. "When we were kids?"

"Yes," Joelle nodded. "But I didn't know about it until a few years ago. My grandma had it installed to help hide undocumented folks when ICE would come around. I added the equipment once I met Martha."

"Your grandma was legendary," Ty sighed. Joelle nodded, smiling.

As Joelle moved to one side of the room, Ty and Ezz stood shoulder to shoulder the way the horses had. Ty pushed down the thrill that shuddered through her at the neighboring warmth. She focused instead on Joelle's face and Marcus's hands, but the cold look seemed to have passed from her old friend's eyes, and Marcus's hands remained empty. The gun leaned against the wall, the safety clicked on again. It didn't make Ty feel any better. The cold gray nearness of it was enough to keep her on edge, even as Joelle spoke to them in the voice Ty had come to know: soft and slightly rumbly, like a box of kittens purring.

"I met Martha at a place called Skyhorse," Joelle said. "It's an organization that teaches Latinx folks robotics and –"

"We know about Skyhorse," Ezz cut in. "We were just there."

"Then you probably know Dr. Aldana," Joelle went on. She had a workbench similar to Luz's, Ty noted, though less fancy. She fiddled with a control on the dashboard. "I met her at a planning session for the Urban League when they were trying to figure out ways to diversify Louisville's horse scene. My parents had offered to let some of the Skyhorse kids come and see real horses. It's a privilege, you know? A lot of the most successful jockeys are able to do what they do because they've had access to real horses. Know how they run, about their bodies, temperaments. Poor Brown kids didn't really get to see Thoroughbreds *before* the ban, you know? Let alone now. Martha and some others came to the farm; she and I hit it off right away."

Ty raised her eyebrow, remembering how she and Joelle had hit it off so many years ago, and the mark it had left on her heart. Joelle caught the look and seemed to hear her thoughts, shaking her head.

"Not like that. Martha wasn't really interested in dating. She used every second to focus on her jockey work and making the most out of her proximity to the metalbreds. Then she got assigned as a groom to the bot in the stall next to Rosario Vicario,

312

and they started chatting sometimes. Rosario would give her tips and stuff like that."

Joelle clicked something on her dash; in the center of the room a pale blue diamond appeared, three-dimensional and rotating slowly in mid-air. It enveloped Cloud Parliament, but the bot stood placidly.

"Martha wanted to do what Rosario did," Joelle said, tapping away on one of the smaller screens. "Take the world by storm. Know everything there was to know. And she was doing a damn good job. So fucking talented."

"Dr. Aldana at Skyhorse told us how gifted she was," Ty said softly.

"*So* gifted," Joelle said, her voice a damp flower. "She just had a spark. And the jockey she was assigned to knew it too. Martha started out walking hots and then the jockey started letting her do more and more, fixing tiny glitches and stuff."

"Good of them to let her learn like that," Ezz said, impressed. "A Limestone model isn't usually a test course for people learning to do what they do. Worth too much."

"He was mostly lazy," Marcus said, leaning against the wall. "And had a powder problem. I think he was too high to tell a horse from a mule half the time."

"Which is why what happened, happened," Joelle said.

She tapped something on the screen and in the center of the room appeared an equinibot schematic. It overlaid Cloud Parliament's body, like an X-ray that showed the mechanics just below the surface of the synthetic skin and hair. Ty had seen schematics like this on the news sometimes – a sneak peek offered after the races had been run that revealed a rare insight into what jockeys contended with when working on a Limestone build. A horse-shaped blueprint with seemingly endless code points, extending from the horse's body like acupuncture needles. This was a map that only jockeys could read; though Ty was illiterate in this particular language, she took in the complex schematic with the awe it commanded: here were all the moving parts, both tiny and massive, that made the eyes blink, the legs move in congress, the head swing – Limestone's foundation, and all the extra specialties that the jockeys added with their unique expertise.

"What do you mean, *what happened?*" Ezz said.

"The accident," Joelle said. "This horse, Cloud Parliament, was in training with the jockey and owner when it shorted out. Not sure why – probably the jockey's neglect of running ported tests every day. In any case, Cloud Parliament shorted, and that led to a system failure. They had to cart the whole build back to the barn to be fixed. Martha had messaged me telling me the jockey did a quick fix and then went to party; she said she was going to take a look herself. These are the messages she sent me."

Alongside the schematic appeared the blue text of a device conversation, M and J indicating Martha and Joelle.

J: You sure you want to be poking around in there?

M: Nothing I haven't already done! The owner won't even notice.

J: What if you turn the bot purple? I'm pretty sure they'd notice that.

M: Very funny. I'm looking now. It looks like the Aristidean component got fried. The jock did a shitty job of fixing it.

"The Aristidean component would have to be repaired by Limestone," Ezz said, reading. "Jockeys aren't really able, let alone authorized, to do that."

"That's what Martha told me next time we spoke in person," Joelle nodded. "Her theory was that the jockey didn't want to get in trouble for frying it in the first place. If the owner found out, he'd probably be fined for having to get it replaced, and possibly have the metalbred pulled out of the race. This close to Derby? The jockey could lose his paycheck, and the owners would probably sue his ass."

"So what happened?"

"Nothing," Joelle said. "Not right away."

"But…?" Ty said. The feeling of something hovering over them in the room was like the shadow of a pterodactyl.

"Awhile later she sent me this," Joelle said, and tapped her device.

The metalbred schematic disappeared and the sound of laughter filled the room as a video began to roll, blurry at first and then clearing as whoever was holding the device steadied their hand and aimed it where they intended. A horse came into view – Palomino with a blaze, trotting along the fence line at Cavehill. Cloud Parliament.

"Watch him go," said a voice, and a corner of Martha's face appeared in front of the lens, her arm visible where she held the camera to capture herself and the bot. Ty's heart squeezed at the sight of her, at the sound of her voice. A person who Ty had only ever known through a video of her last moments captured in gray-white light. In this footage, though, she was bathed in sunshine, shiny pink gloss on her lips, hair in a messy bun. Her eyes were bright, reflecting the green of the Downs' infield, empty but for waving grass. She dodged out of the frame then, focusing again on Cloud Parliament.

As the equinibot trotted along the fence line, right away Ty could tell something was different. The legs were looser, casual, and something about the equinibot's gait was easier. Carefree.

"Watch this," Martha said, and in front of the lens appeared the jockey control unit that came with Limestone models. Ty didn't know how it worked, but to her it always seemed to be like a complicated remote control. She watched Martha type in a quick line of code. "Instructing model into a gallop," she said in the video.

The lens flicked back to Cloud Parliament, who appeared to pause for a moment as if interpreting an unseen signal. Ty waited for the muscles to bunch, for the mechanical surge that she had seen from the starting gate at every Derby since the ban. The replacement of horse with h0rse, the steel lunge.

Instead the metalbred slowed from a trot to a walk.

"What the hell?" Ezz whispered.

"Uh-huh," Joelle said. "Keep watching."

"Instructing model to stop," Martha's voice said offscreen.

Cloud Parliament didn't even pause. This time, at the moment Martha issued a coded direction, the equinibot stretched out its neck, reaching for something Ty couldn't see. Martha couldn't see either – the video's vantage suddenly tightened, zooming in on whatever had caught the horse's attention.

A butterfly.

The orange-and-black wings of a monarch fluttered just beyond the equinibot's muzzle, a blur of soft color, and Cloud Parliament was delighted. While it should have been stopping in response to the mechanical imperative issued by the jockey remote unit, instead the bot kicked up its back hooves in a coltish display of pleasure, dust circling up and around as it finally broke into a gallop, surging forward and then wheeling around a few yards later.

The horse stood on the track, where its program demanded it obey, and it disobeyed with joyous abandon.

"Holy shit," Ty said softly. She barely heard herself, scarcely dared to raise her voice.

The video went black abruptly. Ty almost jumped.

"That's not all," Joelle said seriously, staring through the bluish glow that emanated from the schematic. "There are also memories."

"Whose?" said Ty, still thinking of her own, all the things in her mind that standing in this barn uncovered.

"Cloud Parliament's. This bot has been storing memories," Joelle said, staring into Ty's eyes. "The Limestone models are only supposed to store the finish-line footage. Everything else gets wiped when they melt them down for the following year's models. But this machine has tens of hundreds of hours of footage that it has selectively stored in its apparatus. Martha couldn't find any rhyme or reason for any of it. There's good, there's bad. It's just…horse memories."

"Like what?" Ezz said, her mouth hanging open. "What does a horse choose to remember?"

"Chasing the butterfly, for instance," Joelle said. "A good memory. There are other things it kept…the jockey hitting it with a broom is one we saw when going through the files."

Something was simmering in Ty's brain, bubbles rising to the surface from water thick with algae.

"Martha's murder," she whispered.

Joelle was looking her right in the eye.

"You've seen it," she said.

Suddenly some of the threads in Ty's mind were pulled taut.

"You gave the file to Rosario," Ty said slowly.

"Yes," Joelle said, and Ty glanced at Ezz in time to see her eyes widen. "I knew Martha had reached out to Rosario when she discovered that the metalbred could no longer be considered just a piece of machinery. They figured out the truth together. The night Martha died, her sister Rebeca called me. You know Rebeca? Yes. When I found out what happened to Martha, I sent Rosario a note right away so we could figure out what to do."

"I was with her," Ezz said. "When she got a note. At dinner. That was from you?"

The pain on Ezz's face was so acute Ty could barely stand to look at her.

"Yes," Joelle nodded. "She went straight to the backside but the cops were there canvassing the barn where Martha died – they'd had all the bots moved to the other barn. Together Rosario and Rebeca stole Cloud Parliament and brought him here. We opened his schematic, and that's when we found the memories. Including what happened to Martha."

Joelle stared at the metalbred standing in the center of the room, its brown eyes staring back. Ty felt a sudden prickle run from scalp to spine – Cloud Parliament had seen Martha die. And remembered. Was remembering the same thing as storing data? If he was alive, *how* alive? Did the machine understand what they were saying? What else did he understand?

"He loved her, I think," Joelle said sadly. "Martha took care of him. Maybe I'm humanizing him, but he probably felt like she was the only one who knew him. The only one who cared. She knew the truth and she died for it."

"The truth," Ty repeated, the implications of it still like meteors hurtling through the spaces of her brain, not yet striking ground. "I'm still...I don't know. What *is* the truth?"

"That the metalbreds are...horses," Ezz said slowly. "Or something? Something that can *feel*."

"Yes," Joelle said, her frown a canyon. "And the truth is more than just what Martha and Rosario found out – it's what happened once they did. The truth is that Limestone *knows* and is using the Aristidean component to keep the animals' sentience hidden."

"I always thought the Aristidean component was like a brain, but really it's like...a lock on a brain," Ezz said shaking her head.

Joelle nodded.

"Rosario started looking into other metalbreds housed at the backside," Joelle said. "And she found that they are *all* stockpiling memories, but with the Aristidean component in place, they're unable to act on their own impulses, despite feeling fear, joy, and even pain."

"How can they feel pain?" Ezz protested, sounding near tears. "They're made of metal! Synthetics!"

"Pain is just an impulse that happens in the brain," Marcus

said, speaking for the first time. "It's an interpretation. They can do that too, even if they feel it differently."

"Jesus Christ," Ty whispered. Her eyes prickled, the enormity of what Joelle was saying washing over her in waves.

"The same thing that led to horseracing being banned," Marcus said, shaking his head. "Happening again to what replaced it. Humans not giving a fuck about the things they're responsible for in the name of greed and power."

"This would shut Limestone down if the public knew about it," Ezz said. At some point her hand had come to rest gently on Cloud Parliament's withers, and seeing it there made Ty shiver. Ezz's hand somehow became her mother's; this proximity to horses made her feel she was standing watching a gun lifted to her mother's skull. *This would shut Limestone down.* That's what her mother had come to want. What had she known that Ty had not?

"And *that* is why Rosario and Martha are dead," Joelle was saying. She closed the schematic with a click, leaving only the shifting form of Cloud Parliament between them, its hidden parts hidden again. Not flesh and blood, but something else. Something alive.

"Because they knew," Ty said. A web in her heart was spreading. At first only her mother and, by extension, Luis, had been stuck there in its strings, but then Ty had seen the video of Martha's murder. Now the thing that had been lurking in the corner of her mind crept fully into view: the man who had killed her mother, the same man in Cloud Parliament's last memory of Martha…that same face had likely hovered over Rosario the night she died. Ty looked at Ezz and knew immediately that the connection between Rosario and Martha had turned solid in her mind too. She looked like she might vomit.

"Because they knew," Ezz repeated.

"And because they were going public," Joelle nodded.

Ty felt what was left of the blood in her face drain away.

"They were? To the press?"

"The plan started as a presentation to Limestone," Joelle said. "From what I understand, Martha had developed a virus, with Rosario's help. Martha inititally built it as a demonstration. She thought she could go in and present it to Limestone as part of a way to open up a greater path for backside workers. Like, *Hey, look what we can do if you let us!* The virus would fry the Aristidean component of every metalbred it encountered. Martha thought Limestone would see that she had uncovered a major vulnerability in their business model and might offer her a job. But they were shitty to her, basically kicked her out of the office. That's when Martha and Rosario decided to take a different tack: Untether the metalbreds. Show the world. No clue how they were going to deliver it to the bots, but Martha told me the day before she died that that was their plan."

"Jesus Christ," Ty said, her fist pressed against her lips. She stared at Cloud Parliament, the relaxed angle of its ears. It swung its head slowly to look at Joelle, doe eyes blinking. Ty imagined every horse in the Derby chasing butterflies, out of the jockeys' reach, enjoying the sun and being free to run when they pleased and not when a line of code demanded it.

"So where's the virus?" Ezz said. Ty could hear the swell of grief in her voice, so close to the hulking truth that killed her best friend. She had wanted to know why, and now she did. Ignorance was a knife, but the truth was a bullet.

"We don't know," Joelle said, her eyes on Cloud Parliament. "The day before she died, Martha said she and Rosario had it hidden. And now they're both gone."

CHAPTER 37

LUZ

Luz was watching Ezz destroy an elephant.

She observed from the mouth of the labyrinth, certain that if Ezz saw her, she would stop the obliteration of the thing Luz had created with hours and sharp shears, and Luz felt to the soles of her feet that this decimation was something Ezz needed to do. She would let her. The truth was, watching something she had created be destroyed branch by branch felt something like a relief. When she would carve the bushes into something lifelike, there was always the looming threat of when it would grow back into what the bush preferred to be, a slow erasure. This was not that. This was the Big Bang.

Armed with a glittering pair of shears, Ezz stalked around the topiary garden, hacking at the thick greenery, wine-colored now in the sunset that inked its way across the ground. Luz could hear bits of her voice carrying across the grass.

"I don't know what I thought," Ezz said. Clip. Snap. "What...I was going to solve ...murder...make everything better? The answers don't change the... She's dead. And now I know why it had...and it doesn't change a fucking thing."

Luz remained silent, biting her lip. She knew she should be offering comfort, not lurking in the shadows like something with fangs and a forked tongue. But what she had uncovered in Annie

Claybelle's files was just that – monstrous – and she had come to the surface again seeking air. Instead she had found Ezz, and it seemed they both needed a moment. Then Ezz swung her arm back, gripping the clippers one-handed, abandoning the blades and resorting to using the whole instrument as a blunt weapon. Luz saw what was about to happen and stepped forward, too far away to stop it.

One foam handle swung down and caught Ezz in the jaw, sent her staggering sideways. Luz broke cover and ran to her then, out into the moonlight from the shadows, monster transformed into silver unicorn. She grabbed the clippers from Ezz before she swung them again, maybe catching the blade. Ezz gasped, then seeing it was Luz, broke into tears.

"Fuck," Ezz sobbed. "Fuck."

Luz tossed the clippers away and, without thinking, enveloped Ezzardine in a tight hug, squeezing her when her host's body jerked against her grip.

"I don't know," Ezz said about nothing, about everything. "I don't know."

"It's okay," Luz said, still squeezing her. "It's okay."

"It's not okay," Ezz cried. "Nothing is okay. Rosario is dead and Martha is dead and we all know who did it but we can't prove it and –"

"I can," Luz said softly. The words felt like smoke from her lips. "Kinda."

Ezz pulled away, her eyes shining.

"What did you say?"

"I think I can prove it," Luz said.

"The cufflink…" Ezz started but Luz cut her off with a shake of her head.

"Something else," she said. "Look."

She held up her device, where she had sent the bundle of files she'd extracted from Limestone and Claybelle's underserver. She swiped through to a few simple screenshots of emails and call logs.

"Do you see this?" she said to Ezz. Her throat felt dry and cracked after hours of silent staring. "These are dates when ICE raided the backside. And this? These are phone calls that Annie Claybelle had with Conrad Miller."

Ezz blinked at the name.

"Who?"

"The chief of Louisville's ICE squad. Every time there was a raid in the last two years, it was preceded by a phone call from Annie Claybelle. And after the phone calls, Claybelle made a payment – sometimes up to $100,000 – to a company called Louisville Leathers."

Ezz looked baffled.

"What the hell is Louisville Leathers?"

Hearing it all out loud, conjuring it outside her head, Luz's words flooded fast and hot. She held up her device, showing everything to Ezz.

"It's a company that sells riding leathers from an online shop. It barely cleared $200,000 in revenue last year. It wouldn't have even come close if it weren't for these payments by Claybelle."

Ezz stared, waiting.

"Conrad Miller owns Louisville Leathers," she said, triumphant. "It's a shell company. Annie Claybelle was paying Conrad Miller to use his ICE forces to raid the Cavehill Downs backside! Like her own personal fucking army."

"What the…," Ezz whispered, but Luz plowed on.

"*And*," she said. "I cross-referenced these raids with social media posts of when the workers – people like this girl Zarita I know – were organizing to demand equity. The phone call from Claybelle always came the same week as a workers' rights event."

Ezz was nodding, her tears dried and gone.

"So what happened to Rosario?"

"I don't know exactly what triggered it," Luz admitted. "But the day Martha died, Claybelle called Conrad Miller. Except this time there was no money transfer. I couldn't find any preserved audio files, but my guess is she tried to put a hit out on Martha, and the dude refused. Maybe too obvious even for scum like him."

"So what then?" Ezz said, looking like she might cry again. "Annie Claybelle went and killed Martha?"

"Not quite," Luz said, and skipped to another part of her data bundle. This time she stared down at two simple text screenshots. She held them up. "What do you see?"

Ezz squinted.

"Says it's to Brian," she said. "I'm guessing Benedict, her brother? All I see is she sent him a thumbs-up emoji and he sent her one back."

"The day Martha died," Luz said, then skipped to the next screenshot. "What do you see?"

"The exact same thing," Ezz said. "Thumbs up from her, then thumbs up from him."

"This is from the day Rosario died," Luz said. "The very next day. Then Claybelle deleted the messages and, after that, deleted the backup. I had to get it from their underserver. I think Claybelle tried to put a hit on Martha and Rosario, was turned down by her usual thug, and called her brother to handle it."

"Jesus Christ," Ezz said softly.

"But I don't know why," Luz cried, staring at her device. "I still don't know *why*. Like, clearly Claybelle had no problem subjecting backside workers to violence and deportation – not to mention human trafficking, which fucking Conrad Miller is rumored to be part of – but for her to straight out put a hit on two girls…well. There had to have been something even bigger at stake than workers unionizing. I just don't know what."

Ezz turned away, moving toward the ruined elephant, sinking down at its base. She looked ten years older than when Luz had said goodbye hours before.

"My turn," she said, sighing, and then Luz listened to the events of the day spill from her mouth. Listening to Ezz talk, explaining the whys, Luz realized that there was an animal in her heart, and with every additional detail Ezz provided, the animal added legs and fangs and claws until it was a beast, salivating for justice. She only softened at the mention of Dr. Aldana and Skyhorse, the place her father had once walked Luz for the first time, leading her inside where kids worked on robotics alongside kids practicing the cello. Luz had eventually followed the call of the roses, but still Skyhorse was a sweet, sad spot in her heart. It was what her parents wanted, on the map they deemed safe. Except Luz knew for sure now – no map was safe.

"They knew each other," Luz said softly. "I guess I should've known. Maybe if I had stayed at Skyhorse, I would've known her too. Maybe I could've…"

She couldn't finish. She felt Ezz's eyes on her, wondering, and Luz just shook her head. Wishing she could protect a girl who she didn't know, who was already gone. Invisible.

"She found out the truth," Ezz said, her head in her hands. "She and Rosario. Limestone killed these two girls who never hurt a soul just because they might've…what? Lost money? That's what it comes down to."

"It's more than money," Luz said, staring up at the torn branches she had once crafted so carefully into trunk, tusks. She wasn't surprised to hear that the metalbreds had something of a soul – she knew firsthand the way 1's and 0's could come alive, the way plants, given the right tools, could grow something like legs and thank you for them. How strange was it that the horses who had been programmed to look like life, had eventually found their own version of it? "They've made something they can control. People like the ones at the top of Limestone will always do whatever it takes to keep control. Martha and Rosario weren't just a threat to the money. They were a threat to an empire."

"I hate this world sometimes," Ezz said. "You and me and Ty been running around trying to solve this, and the answer was what the answer always is: some rich white people decided their money and power was more important than the lives of human beings. Especially Brown girls."

"I just wish I could have cracked the cufflink," Luz said after a moment. "Who knows what Dr. Salt is keeping? Because all the shit that I found between Claybelle and Benedict is damning, but not damning enough. And what do we do with it? Give it the Special Police? Una broma. As if. Now that I see the guy who runs ICE here has a shell company, who knows how many officers Limestone has on their payroll?"

"I just can't believe this…," Ezz said, covering her face. "And Rosario never said a word. If I had been there instead of Ty, maybe I could've…I don't know. Something."

"Something else is on your mind too," Luz said. "What is it?"

"Nothing."

"I haven't been your roommate for very long," Luz said. "But I think it's been just long enough to notice something changing since…"

"Since what?"

"Since you met Ty."

She watched Ezz cover her face with her hands again.

"It's complicated," Ezz said softly. Luz just nodded. Of course it was. Everything was.

"Do you like her?"

"It's complicated," Ezz repeated.

"Make it simple."

Ezz dropped her hands, then stared at their palms.

"It's like…eating ice cream when you already have a toothache. Even if it doesn't hurt, you know it will soon. Or you wonder if it doesn't hurt because it's numb."

"You feel numb?"

"I feel everything and nothing all at once."

Luz knew this feeling – to walk around the world like an exposed nerve, like a bare hand in a blizzard. The two girls were silent again, staring at the night sky through what was left of the elephant.

"Were you going to hack it down into nothing?" Luz said after awhile. She curled her hair around her finger.

"I'm sorry," Ezz whispered.

"It's okay. I'm going to turn it into an armadillo," Luz said, reaching up and pulling off a leaf. "Or a rabbit. Something that hides. A chameleon. People will come to see a topiary garden and all they'll see is bushes. And I'll just be like, *Oh, they're chameleons. They're blending in. You don't see the chameleons? It's* art!"

Ezz smiled weakly, then grimaced.

"It's going to take them forever to grow back. I'm such an idiot. I'm sorry."

"It's okay," Luz shrugged. "I'll just do some work on the seeds and they'll sprout back in like two seconds…"

Ezz didn't say anything at first, and Luz could feel her words hanging in the air, sinking into Ezz's ears slowly. Had she heard her? Had she known that Luz was offering her something adjacent to the truth, in exchange for her toothache confession?

"I saw the vines down there," Ezz said, not looking at her. "I wasn't going to ask."

"It's your house," Luz said. "You can ask."

"I wasn't going to."

"Ask."

"No."

"Why?"

Ezz just shrugged in reply, then rubbed her temples.

"What have you been working on, Luz?" she said quietly. "If you want me to know, I want to know. But only if you want me to know."

"Revenge," Luz said quickly, before the blossom of truth could close again. "I've been working on…small revenge. It feels stupid now."

Ezz lowered her hands, casting a sidelong look in Luz's direction.

"What kind of revenge, small or otherwise, has leaves?" she said.

"My kind."

"Can I see?"

"Not yet," Luz said. She felt like she had unleashed a flash flood, then dammed it with a mere twig. It wouldn't hold the curiosity in Ezz's eyes for long. She stood up. "I've got other work to do right now."

"Like what?" Ezz said, watching her.

"Like working on Salt's cufflink."

"Even if you could, I don't even know if there's a point, Luz," Ezz said, sounding disgusted. "You've already done so much finding out what Claybelle is part of – and we don't even know what to do with *that*. They've already killed two girls. We open that shit and who knows, maybe we're next."

"I think knowing what we know, we're on the list either way," Luz said. "It's only a matter of time. Maybe we were born on the list of something like Limestone."

Luz stood up. She felt jittery, as if letting someone in on her secret – even just a single leaf of it – was a puff of a first cigarette. She wanted to sit next to Ezz, but she also wanted to be back down in the lair. She also wanted to be at her parents' house, sitting on the couch while her mother folded towers of laundry. She also wanted to be in the greenhouse at Cavehill, tending thorn and blossom in the sunshine. She had been spending so much time underground. When she saw her parents again, would they recognize their daughter, girl-turned-rebel, turned mole? Poison Ivy without the spandex outfit? Would they see her? Would they want to?

"Stay," Ezz said, looking up, but Luz could see a shadow crossing the topiary garden, and despite the shiver in her bones, she knew it wasn't Limestone walking toward them, but someone more familiar. Big hips, bald head.

"I think it's a good time for me to head down," Luz said, pointing at the shadow, turning back toward the maze as Ezz turned to look.

"Hey, Ty," Luz called as she slipped into the maze.

"Hi," Ty called over the shrub before joining Ezz. As Luz slipped into the maze, she smiled at the way their voices blurred together, rising into a hum almost like the sound of bees on tulips.

CHAPTER 38

TY

"I thought you were supposed to be at work," Ezz said. Ezz wasn't looking at her, but Ty still felt as if she were twitching under a microscope.

"Nice to see you too," she said. "I'm off. By the time I got there from Joelle's, there was only so much I could do with some of the guests asleep."

"Did you learn anything else about Darden?" Ezz asked.

"He wasn't there. And Richmond was all on my ass since I didn't come in for the start of my shift. Not much else I could really do. Did Luz crack the cufflink?"

"No. But she learned something else."

Then Ezz began to speak, and everything she said was like standing in front of a firehose. As she listened, Ty felt increasingly drenched, the truth sinking into her, making her feel sodden and heavy. She wondered at the heaviness – where was her sparking rage, the thing that had kept her going since she witnessed Brian Benedict kill her mother? It felt buried, sunken; the weight of the truth just too, too massive. What does one do with a truth so huge?

"Well…fuck," she said when Ezz had told her everything – the shell companies and the text messages.

"Yeah," Ezz agreed. "That."

Looking into Ezz's eyes felt too painful – for both of them.

The look on Ezz's face told Ty she felt equally overcome. Although part of Ty wanted nothing more than to say *Me too; he took someone from me too*, she couldn't bear to say it, couldn't bear to see Ezz hear it. So she studied the ruined elephant topiary instead, gazing up into its branches. She had seen trees hit by lightning, the white crack through the trunk like a slice by an invisible hatchet. This wasn't that, unless the lightning was many small hatchets, flurried and weak. She eyed the loppers at Ezz's feet, the slight swelling along her beautiful jaw.

"Did you get in a fight with the plant?"

"Fuck you," Ezz said, and Ty gauged from her face that she was as surprised to hear it come out of her mouth as Ty was.

"Wow," said Ty. She had planned to sit next to Ezz but now she stayed standing. She thought she should cross her arms, raise her eyebrow, do something to indicate she was pissed. But she couldn't quite muster the energy. She was burned out on rage. Today was the day Benedict should've checked in to the Mahogany. He did not. Instead she had cleaned Darden's room, opening every drawer and finding nothing, unzipping every pocket of his suitcase and finding nothing. Benedict should have been in that bed, and she had thought for over a year about killing him; instead she had to dust the bureau of the man hired to clean up the mess of the one she wanted to kill. She'd closed the door and buried her face in a pillow someone had slept on, germs be damned, and screamed until her throat was raw. Yes, Ty was burned out on rage.

"Sorry," Ezz said, still not looking at Ty when she said it. She too stared down at the loppers, and Ty could see that something in her was emptied out as well. Whatever had leaked from her took the form of the slashed branches that carpeted the area around the topiary.

"Care to share?" Ty said, then winced. This was something her mother used to say, always a little sarcastic, always treating

331

Ty's tears as an anecdote in a parenting book she had only skimmed. They came out of Ty the same way, and if the words were fire, whatever was left in the bucket of almost-empty Ezz flared up like gasoline.

"No, I don't," Ezz snapped. "Why would I tell you any fucking thing? You almost got us killed today!"

"*I* almost got us killed?" Ty repeated, incredulous. "Pretty sure it would've been a shotgun that did that. Not me."

"We wouldn't have been there if it weren't for you!"

"We wouldn't have been there if it weren't for *you*," Ty fired back. She had a little gasoline left in her bucket too, it seemed. "You and this Scooby Doo bullshit!"

"You're the one who said you wanted to help!" Ezz shouted. "You could've just given me Rosario's nose ring and then fucked off. Or better yet, you could've just kept that shit to yourself instead of crashing my party that night!"

"Fuck you and your Cinderella balls," Ty said. She knew how not to shout in a fight like this. She knew how to turn her voice into a blade, knew the ribs to slide it between. "You *need* people to crash your parties to feed into your Oliver Twist bullshit – the orphan and her faithful band of friends."

Ty was surprised when Ezz laughed, something her father never did when she went for blood. She hated that it still sounded like a saxophone.

"You think you're so tough," Ezz chuckled. "You're not tough. You don't scare me with your act. You went through something, you felt something terrible, and you think you're goddamn Batman, girl. Grow up. You're Baby Bruce. And you're too broke to be a superhero."

That one hurt, Ty realized. They had laughed over Batman, she and Ezz and Luz, with her Poison Ivy tattoo. It had felt like a portrait of what was possible, and now Ezz drew a red slash through the center.

"Batman?" Ty snapped. "Batman doesn't even kill anybody and you have no idea…"

"What?" Ezz mocked. "No idea what? What you'd *do*? Clearly you have your own grudge against Benedict. You don't think I noticed? You think I'm stupid or something? You're so typical. Going after the *one person* who hurt *you* and not the system that supports it."

Ezz laughed again, and Ty laughed then too, bitterly, forcing herself to savor the meanness that had sprouted up between them. She had a feeling it would be over soon, whatever this "it" with Ezzardine Clayton was and had been, and she felt hungry for one more memory to store in the icebox of her heart.

"Why do you act like this toward me?" Ty said. "We'll be getting along so well, and then other times you're like…this."

"What is *this*?" Ezz spat.

"Cold," Ty said simply. "Far away. You feel like Antarctica."

"*I'm* Antarctica?" Ezz said, shaking her head, and the disgusted look on her face made Ty want to flare up again, but instead she just threw up her hands. "*You're* Antarctica. Talk about distant? Like we don't see how much you hold back?"

"I'm real with you about what matters," Ty said, swallowing. "Why can't you just be real with me? Would that be so hard?"

The boiling look on Ezz's face roiled for a moment longer, her eyes locked with Ty's in a way that made Ty's heart flutter like the elephant's leaves. And then the heat seemed to falter, the boiling settling down to a stir, and then still. Her eyes were soft, and it made Ty's hands clench against her thighs to keep from reaching for her.

"You know how you can associate people with things?" Ezz said quietly.

Ty stared at her, not answering.

"You know," Ezz said, rubbing her eyes, as if searching for the words in the stars the rubbing produced. "Like, you smell a certain smell – cedar, maybe – and it reminds you of something specific? Or sometimes someone? Like I smell cedar and I think of my granny, a long, long time ago, and helping her put away clothes for the winter. I see a cardinal and I think of the first time I walked the grounds of this house, when the For Sale sign was still in the yard."

Ezz turned to look back at the pink mansion, its peaks jutting up against the violet sky.

"It was right after we moved in, and I left my room at dawn and walked around. Before it really felt like home. If it ever has. They died before we could even unpack, before we had made any real memories. Even in this big year, the white people on this block couldn't believe that a Black family was moving into this huge-ass house. We paid cash. It still didn't feel real to me either, and I was walking around by myself before the sun rose, getting used to it. And then I saw a cardinal sitting on a branch – it was all just trees and bramble then, you know? Wild, tangled. I felt like that cardinal. This splash of something that felt too bright in the middle of all this chaos. Scared and hopeful. And two days later, my parents are dead. Now I see a cardinal, and all that comes rushing into my brain. I think of all the horses that died with them. I think of the way the ashes smelled. I think of how I haven't ridden a horse since. All that. Just because of one bird."

She squinted at the trees, and Ty could see that she was remembering how it had looked, every branch and feather like stone in her memory. She had been chipping it all away.

"And you associate…what with me?" Ty said. She didn't want to hear the answer. She could almost smell what it was going to be.

Ezz looked back at her, and the soft expression of apology in her eyes made Ty look away before she even opened her mouth to speak.

"Rosario's murder," Ezz said. The word *murder* was like a

cardinal across the back of Ty's eyelids. "I saw she was dead. And I was walking through minefields in my head, like every memory was waiting to blow up in my face. And I was figuring out how I was going to live with it. And then you popped up at my party telling me she was murdered. It was like a bomb falling from the sky while I had been so busy looking at my feet for landmines. Does…does this make sense?"

She let go of a long breath.

"When I see you," Ezz said, "I see a bomb."

Ty couldn't look at her, but she could hear her, and she nodded. It did make sense, even if it hurt. She remembered running into Irma, the Derby Museum girl, at the diner – how the mere sight of someone who had once known the sound of her mother's voice, her sneeze, the sound of her nails clicking together when she was distracted, was like a lit match pressed against skin.

"Yes," Ty said eventually. "I get it."

"It's not your fault," Ezz sighed. She leaned against what was left of the former elephant, its leaves in wild disarray.

"No, but it still…sucks," Ty said. She remained standing there in the shadowy grass like a sad, still tree, and something told her she should probably go now, uproot herself and be gone.

"*Memories* suck," Ezz said eventually.

Ty nodded. She still couldn't make herself leave. Memories did suck, the way a vortex sucked, the way the drain in a bottomless sink sucked. She had the feeling that if she left this spot, she would go spinning down that drain into the void that her mother left, and every warm thing that had sprouted inside her since she met Ezz would wither. Maybe withering was what had to happen. She didn't need Ezz to continue down the path she was walking – Derby was in two days. Her plan at the Mahogany had fallen through, but she knew Benedict would be at Cavehill for the race. She would find a way to close the open circle in her head, Benedict at its center.

"Memories suck," Ty echoed. "But at least we can make new ones." That was what got her to pick up her feet finally, to turn away. "The metalbreds were doing it, right? Making memories. And they shouldn't even have been able to. We were born being able to remember things – sometimes it feels like the worst gift in the world. But it's a gift, either way."

She turned away, toward the path that would wind her around back to the road.

"I feel bad for the elephant," Ty said, a parting joke. "I don't know what you were trying to make, but maybe next time try something simple like a dog."

She moved down the path, the silence behind her more painful than the feeling of scar tissue being torn open, a new wound planted in its place. She put one foot in front of the other, determined not to look back, determined to make it to the road and be swallowed by the swell of Derby season traffic.

But then she heard her name.

Had she? She paused, unsure. And then Ezz said it again.

"Ty," Ezz said, and Ty couldn't put a bridle on the leaping hope that erupted in her chest. But when she turned back to Ezz, the expression on her face wasn't what she had expected. Ezz's eyes were wide, swimming with realization. Her hands were hovering near her mouth, as if they might either cover her lips or cup around them to shout.

"What's wrong?" Ty said, unnerved.

"A dog," Ezz said, her voice shaking. "You said a dog."

"Yes…?" Ty said.

Ezz's hands tightened into fists, still held up by her face.

"We gotta get to the backside," Ezz said, low. "Like *right* now. We gotta go."

"What? The backside? Why? Martha's family is gone and…"

"Come on," Ezz interrupted, rushing past her and grabbing her hand in the process. Ty was too stunned to really notice the warm wave that coursed up her arm. "I have a feeling. We've gotta go."

"We?" Ty managed to choke out.

Ezz glanced at her for just long enough for Ty to realize that her eyes were soft, Antarctica close and thawing.

"Yes."

CHAPTER 39

LUZ

This time, Luz didn't go back to the lair. She had spent too much time underground. Now, with Derby so close and any plans she had spun in her mind still far out of reach, she needed to be in the air, high. High enough to see, to breathe. She chose the tallest tree in Ezz's vast, closed yard, and climbed it branch by branch.

She hadn't climbed like this since she was a child, and maybe not even then. Her parents guarded her life like a secret, and would've shouted her down after six feet. But nothing stopped her now. She imagined herself as moonlight, allowing that feeling to lift her now, carrying her up into the highest branches. When she was high enough to make herself dizzy, she settled herself on the branch, close to the trunk, and looked down.

The Pink didn't glow as it did on party nights – only one light was lit: the kitchen, where Ezz spent all her time. Ezz had given Luz a bedroom in the Pink, of course, but like Ezz, she never used it. Luz had a home already, she thought. She wasn't here to live, she was here to work. But what about Ezz? If this wasn't home, where was?

Luz eyed the mansion's grounds, much of it gone wild since Rosario's death. There were people who would come cut the grass, but Ezz hadn't made the call to summon them. So the grounds

Olivia A. Cole

grew, following their own order. From here it was easy for Luz to sink into the fantasy of herself as Poison Ivy, perched on a skyscraper, urging the plants into rebellion. But despite her imaginings, the plants didn't look rebellious. They looked comfortable, relaxed. Luz imagined horses wading through. Would Ezz ever ride a horse again? Or would grief grow taller and wider, keeping her from it forever? Luz's parents had all but forbidden her to ride – they knew how it was. Once you learned to move with an animal beneath you, to understand one another and walk through the wind together, there was no going back. It was like Sleeping Beauty's parents removing all the spinning wheels in the kingdom for fear of the power of the witch's curse. Luz's parents had forbidden her, and now Ezz forbid herself.

Pressed between her hip and the tree, Luz's device vibrated. Clinging to the trunk with one arm, she awkwardly pulled it free. It wasn't a text, it was a call. From her mother.

"Hola, mami," she said, when she answered. She was so high, she felt she could see her mother from here, sitting on the front porch the way she did when she called Luz's abuela.

"Mija," her mother said. "Where are you?"

"I'm…" Luz paused, wondering how specific she should be. "I'm in the backyard at my friend's house."

"The same friend who is keeping you from your family," her mother said.

Luz sighed.

"No one is keeping me from anything," she said. *Except you and papi keeping me from what I love*, she thought. But her mother was calling her. Her voice was in her ear. The guilt swept against Luz like a stiff wind. "Are you okay? Why are you calling?"

"Are you telling me I can't call my own daughter?" her mother said, huffing the way she always did. "At least now you answer."

"I've been kind of…busy," Luz said.

"I'm worried about you, mija," her mother said abruptly. "You have heard about the girl? At the backside? Your cousin said she saw you and told you."

Luz's stomach clenched.

"Yes," she said.

"That girl was even younger than you," her mother said. "She was a baby."

"I know."

"*This* is why we tell you to keep away," her mother burst out. "*This* is why, Luz! Por eso! Already they have moved on, acting like it didn't happen. We walk through the barn where her body lay, and we're supposed to pretend she never existed. I can't let that happen to you."

"But what does staying away really change?" Luz said. Her voice rang out from the tree, startling a pair of pigeons. "Look at Rosario Vicario! She and Martha…" She stopped, swallowing. She couldn't say *worked together. Were friends. Were uncovering the truth.* So instead she said something else true: "…were the same. And it didn't matter one bit. I can't just look away."

"Something has to matter," her mother said. She was crying, and the guilt in Luz's heart grew tentacles that wrapped her up and squeezed. "I wanted you to go further than your parents. Subir más. But you're so stubborn. Fine. Bueno. You can plant flowers, you can study your soil samples, you can do whatever you want, but I need my daughter safe. We are not staying in this place. I don't know where you are. You could be anywhere. You could be in a barn dead."

"I'm not in a barn dead, mommy," Luz said softly.

"I need you safe," her mother repeated.

"Where would we go?" Luz said. "Where is better?"

"Chicago, maybe," her mother said. "Your Tía Ladira lives there now. She could help us find work, a place to live."

"Is there a track there?"

"Luz!" her mother scolded. "We can't –"

"But what if we could, mami?" Luz interrupted. "What if…there was something we could do? To weed out what's bad? Keep what's good and plant more?"

"Always your weeds and plants," her mother scoffed.

"I'm serious," Luz said. "What if I told you…what if I told you…"

"Told me what, Luz?"

Luz sighed. What she knew was like a virus – it was catching, and right now she couldn't protect her mother against it. And the actual virus that Ezz discovered Rosario had created with Martha was nowhere to be found. For so long she'd been imagining her vines crushing brick, and she hadn't yet let go of that dream, but now it felt bigger. So much more than brick needed to be crushed. She had seen murder planned, had watched that murder leave a screen and transform into actual blood. She kept this all to herself.

Her mother sighed at her daughter's silence, long and heavy, the same as the breeze starting to move the branches around her.

"These people are always going to do what they want," her mother said. "They don't see us, what we do, what we know. I don't know if we can make them."

Luz gripped the tree a little tighter, letting her gaze wander past the boundaries of the Pink, across the city to the not-so-distant glow of Cavehill's triple spires.

"But what if we did?" Luz said softly.

"Come home," her mother said. "We can talk about Chicago. We can talk about your roses and your tulips. But come home, mija. I need you safe."

"Soon," Luz said. She trained her eyes on the lights. "But, mami, do you have Zarita Moreno-Mendoza's number?"

CHAPTER 40

EZZ

"It's almost 1 am," Ty groaned. "What the fuck are all these people doing here?!"

Ezz didn't reply, but she was groaning internally from where they stood outside the backside. The epiphany that had sparked in her was like a tiny, wavering flame, and she'd been so focused on getting here that she hadn't thought of what they'd do once they arrived. Two days before Derby – less – and the place was crawling with tourists.

"I should've gone down and grabbed the press pass from Luz," she said, rubbing her knuckles across her bottom lip. "How the hell are we going to get in there?"

She glared at the crowds of tourists – from where she and Ty stood just beyond the dome of light that the barns and track were encased in, she could hear the clip-clop of hooves, the shuffle of feet, the creak and slam of stall doors. Alive and awake – equinibots didn't need to sleep. Or did they? She shook the thought away. Focus.

"We should go back for the press pass," Ty said, but Ezz didn't answer. She worked through plans better in silence. Strategy. She eyed the fence. She could probably climb it, but not without attracting a lot of attention. The area was too well-lit, lights at every fencepost. It reminded her a little of a prison, now that she thought about it. She stared through at passing metalbreds, led by hot walkers and the occasional jockey. The equinibots moved as they always moved – elegantly, realistically – but somehow their gentle steps now took on a deep sadness. In every movement she searched for a consciousness she could now discern. That sparkle that she once thought was all metal and reflection was something else. A whirring soul trapped in a steel box.

"Can't go back," Ezz said finally, to distract herself. "We're here."

"You still haven't told me what we're looking for," Ty said, glancing at her. Ezz sized her up – something about the backside put Ty on edge, she could see that. Now wasn't the time to ask.

"I don't want to jinx it," Ezz said. "I just have a feeling."

"And you needed me to come...why?" Ty said. She was fishing now and Ezz knew it, looking for an apology, an admission, a reversal of all the sharp words spoken in the garden. But before Ezz could offer it, Ty was interrupting herself, grabbing Ezz's arm, pointing.

"Look!"

She was indicating a group of people wandering from the track, some of them swaying a little drunkenly. They were led by a young woman wearing a headset that glowed white, which the group followed like moths through the night, her voice floating out over their heads.

"And now we are approaching the backside," the woman drawled. This must have been her hundredth tour of the day: her voice was raspy and bored. Ty grabbed Ezz's arm and towed her toward the group.

"What the hell?" Ezz protested, pulling back, confused.

"We have to get to them before they get to the gate," Ty said, ignoring her.

"Why are you...? Ohhhh." Ty's intentions sank in then, and

Ezz couldn't believe she was suddenly walking quickly beside her, towed along toward what could become a Trojan horse if they played their cards right. "This is some real white shit, Ty. Do you see those people? I don't exactly blend in."

She watched Ty scan the group, taking in their whiteness, their cocktail party attire. She didn't flag. She seemed to settle her gaze on something and then barrel forward.

"Them," she said without pointing, but Ezz saw them immediately regardless: two people near the center of the group, arm-in-arm. They whispered to each other, their smiles bright and crooked from alcohol. They were a little more casually dressed than their fellow guests, and young. Ezz could see Ty's plan forming, dots connecting in the air.

"Follow my lead," Ty said excitedly. "Green dress. Link her arm and I'll talk."

"Jesus…," Ezz whispered, but she strode ahead and together they pierced into the group, smiling and excusing themselves to the people on the edges, who barely noticed, some still carrying half-full drinks. Ezz took a deep breath and then linked her arm with the woman in the sparkly green dress, sections of her blonde hair escaping from the ballerina bun at the crown of her head. She turned and, finding Ezz on her arm, barely looked surprised.

"That dress," Ezz said meaningfully. Ty linked onto Ezz's other arm and allowed the group to close around them, craning her neck to join the conversation.

"Stunning," Ty added, but the woman was looking at Ezz, a half-smile on her mouth.

"You like it? He doesn't like it," she said, letting her head loll in the direction of the man on her other arm.

He leaned forward to see who had interrupted his evening.

"I just said with your eyes, blue would've been better," he protested.

"Did you know I don't even know him?" the woman said.

"Well, you don't know me either, but I can tell you he was wrong," Ezz said.

"I thought I was going to do the talking," Ty whispered.

Ezz elbowed her in reply.

"I *don't* know you," the woman agreed. "But maybe I'd like to."

"I don't see why," the man on her other side said, pouting. Ezz ignored him, darting her eyes to the guard ahead, as the tour guide approached him with a tired wave. The gate was swinging open – Ezz braced herself but the gate stayed wide. The guard nodded at the tour guide, the two of them sharing the weary smile that Ezz knew well – two people doing their jobs and sending the silent communication that the people they did it for were idiots. Ty and Ezz slipped inside the perimeter of the backside, enveloped by the tour group, Ezz chatting amicably with the woman in the sparkly dress while her former date looked on sourly.

"Here we have some jockeys preparing for some last-minute training," the tour guide said. Ezz couldn't see her face, only the white halo of light emitted from her headset. "They're gathering now to pay respects to one of their own, jockey Rosario Vicario."

The group moved on, but Ezz and Ty extracted themselves from the ranks. Ezz felt like she had developed a second pulse since her best friend's murder – it wasn't her heart that throbbed as she drifted by the backside's main paddock, where a photo of Rosario had been erected amid swaths of red roses. It was a substance that seemed to have leaked out of her heart and coated the tunnels of every artery in its thick, sad paste. Tomorrow was Oaks Day, Ezz remembered, looking at the roses, what often felt like the official start of Derby weekend. Rosario would have been racing. She may have made Limestone look like fools, and some jockeys were resentful that she had taken the industry by storm, but as Ezz looked around at the faces clustered around her picture – jockeys and grooms and hot walkers – the grief and love were as vivid as the red of the roses. Rosario may not have grown up on the backside, but she belonged to them.

"Un-fucking-real," Ezz murmured, and she turned away before the tears could fall, before Ty could say anything comforting, before any of the jockeys could see her and say, *Weren't you her friend? Weren't you close? Where were you when she died?* She could answer those questions, but the last one would always be a splinter in her throat. *I was at home. And I didn't even know she was in danger...because she never told me.* Ezz was racing against her tears, moving so fast toward the barn that Ty had to run to catch up, and even then Ezz didn't slow down until the stillness of the barn's wide aisle required it.

Only a few hot walkers were inside, sliding stall doors closed after metalbreds. Ezz noticed they avoided her and Ty's eyes as they passed. Had word spread? That two girls had come asking questions? She wondered if these questions were part of what drove Martha's mother and sister to pick up and leave. A weight of guilt dropped in her stomach.

"Do you think Limestone threatened them?" Ty said softly from just behind her, as if reading her mind. "Martha's family, I mean? I hope they did."

Ezz turned on her, intending to ask her what the fuck she meant by that, but Ty was shaking her head.

"I meant, I hope that's why they're gone. That they left to stay alive. That they're not already...dead."

"They probably didn't need to threaten them," Ezz said, continuing down the aisle. "They already killed one of them, you know? The message was sent."

"What if they start harassing Skyhorse too?" Ty said.

"What do you mean?"

"They're the pipeline for more Rosarios, you know? More Marthas. If one self-trained jockey could expose their secret, another one will. What if Claybelle pays ICE to go after them next?"

Ezz's pace slowed for a moment, her brow furrowed. She'd seen it over and over, growing up as one of three Black kids in a private school – the way intelligence and curiosity could paint a target on a girl's back, especially when she wasn't white.

"Bastards," she said, but then they had arrived at the stall that was once Rosario's. *Horse: All's Well. Jockey: Rosario Vicario.* The sign had not yet realized that Rosario was gone, that the metalbred was gone, reassigned. Ezz stood staring at the open stall, at the shadowed doorway; if her brain wanted to be here, her legs did not. They trembled, as if the swept sawdust inside might be stained with blood, as if the murder happened here and not at the Mahogany. But it was empty. When she turned to look at Ty, she found her eyes already on her, an expression of damp knowing in them.

"I know that look," is all Ty said.

"What look?"

"The one that sees a ghost even outside the haunted house," she said.

"How do you know?

Ty just shrugged.

"I'm just so…" Ezz started, then stopped. "I'm angry. I keep trying not to be, cuz eventually anger is exhausting. But I'm angry, because I'm always going to…wonder. Rosario had been home for a week before she called me to have dinner. She lied to me. Turned out she'd been hanging out with Martha, doing all this. Engineering a *virus*. Even your friend Joelle knew this shit. And Rosario never told me. She never breathed a word. I'm always going to wonder why I didn't know any of it. Why Rosario didn't trust me to help her carry it. I was her best friend, and she kept it all to herself."

She stopped, her throat starting to swell with emotions she'd been burying. But she'd buried them using sand, not good, heavy soil, and the sand just shifted with every step she took. She could feel Ty staring but couldn't bear to look back.

"Maybe she thought you had enough burdens," Ty said softly, and Ezz thought this was how Ty knew about seeing ghosts. "This was something she didn't want you to carry. She was protecting you."

"But I could've helped her," Ezz cried. "She was my best friend. And she died with me on the outside of her life."

Ty said nothing, and as much as Ezz didn't want her to offer empty comfort, the silence was terrible, because it was Rosario's silence too.

She couldn't speak, so she moved instead, stepping into the stall where her best friend had spent so much time fiddling with the inner workings of metalbreds. Empty.

"What were you hoping to find?" Ty said from behind her.

"I just thought…I had a feeling…that maybe she let me in after all. But…"

Empty.

She turned slowly, rotating on the spot to take in every corner of the place that had been a sort of home for Rosario Vicario. She felt as if she were sinking into deep water, remembering the first time Rosario had brought her here, the last time. She wished she could remember every time. Ezz had almost turned in a full circle when she saw it, and she leapt back with a stifled cry.

A dog.

It was curled up in a tight ball in the corner of the stall to the left of the doorway, its brown-and-white fur almost blending in with the straw and sawdust. Its snout was tucked in under one hind leg as it dozed peacefully in the abandoned stall. It was just as Ezz remembered it from the first time she and Luz and Ty visited the backside, sleeping then as well, but in a different corner.

"You again," Ezz said, surprised, relieved. Not a cadaver. Not a ghost. Just a dog. She moved toward it. Ty's voice caught at her back.

"I thought you didn't like dogs?" she said.

"How do you know?" Ezz said, glancing over her shoulder. She watched the blush hum across Ty's cheeks.

"I…the night you visited the Mahogany with Rosario. I was listening. You said you didn't like dogs."

"And what did Rosario say?" Ezz said, turning back to the dog.

"Huh?"

"Do you remember what Rosario said?" Ezz was inches away from the dog now, her hand outstretched.

"You said you didn't like dogs…," Ty said slowly, remembering. Ezz wished she could have been watching, listening that night too. To have a picture of her and Rosario together in her mind. "But Rosario said they're man's best friend…"

Ty paused, and Ezz wasn't looking at her but she knew Ty was feeling what she felt: realization spreading over her like a cool rain.

"You said her dog bots were too real…," Ty said.

"Yes," Ezz nodded. "They were."

She slowly, slowly laid her hand on the dog's scruffy head; her fingers shaking, she began to scratch it gently behind an ear.

The dog lifted its head, strange blue eyes opening and taking Ezz in with a blink. Its tail thumped against the hard-packed floor. Ezz wet her lips.

"*They keep all your secrets,*" Ezz said, her voice trembling as she echoed Rosario's words that night at the table.

The dog's head cocked sideways, the way any dog's would, its eyes deep and curious. But then its mouth opened, and from somewhere down its throat came the recorded voice of Rosario Vicario.

"*Voice token…confirmed. Hello, Ezzardine Clayton. I have something for you.*"

CHAPTER 41

LUZ

uz Cabo Trejo didn't much care for dogs, but she took one look in Ezzardine's eyes when she walked into the lair cradling the shaggy mutt and knew this was different. Five minutes later the dog was hooked up to the scanner. Ezz refused to let the bot off her lap.

"It's storing a huge amount of data," Luz said, scrolling. The data had filled her screens as soon as she connected it, and she turned to the dog with a new awe. Its pink tongue hung happily from its mouth; staring at it, Luz wondered if it too had evolved the way the metalbreds had, if that joy was real or programmed. What was real anyway?

"I know," Ezz said. "I knew as soon as I saw it. It's storing that virus."

"The one Rosario and Martha made?" Luz said. "How do you know?"

"I just know," Ezz said. "What else could it be?"

"She left it for you," Ty said. She sounded as convinced as Ezz. "She knew something was going to happen and she left it for you to find. She trusted you to figure this out."

"Yes," Ezz said, staring down at the dog in her lap as if it were made of gold.

"It's going to take me hours to hack it," Luz said, rubbing her temples. "I've been working nonstop on the cufflink, Ezz. I'm tired as hell…"

"I thought you said she couldn't open it?" Ty said to Ezz, standing up, but Luz waved her back down.

"Don't get too excited," she said. "Like Ezz said, I was only able to open part of it, to Salt's personal key. But…I did find something else."

She looked at Ezz, and was rewarded with a gleam like a fleck of diamond in her eyes. For a moment, the dog on her lap was forgotten. Luz turned to her machines, grinning.

"I had already hacked into Limestone's underserver," she explained. "When I was poking around in Claybelle's files. So I did the same for Dr. Salt and accessed the computer he keeps at work."

"You were able to hack into *Limestone*?" Ty said in disbelief. "I mean, Ezz told me what you found out about Claybelle and her shell company, but it still just seems…insane? That one person was able to access one of the biggest tech companies in the state."

"That's the thing," Luz said, spinning in her chair. "I couldn't have…if somebody else hadn't already done it first."

"Come again?" Ezz straightened her back.

"Someone else already hacked Limestone before me," Luz said gleefully. "And Limestone doesn't even realize it: the hacker covered their tracks so brilliantly that I barely noticed I was in a pre-dug tunnel at first. But using what they had already opened, I was able to find…*this*."

She pointed at her largest screen, where she had dragged the unremarkable white folder to the center.

"This is Dr. Salt's *just in case* file," she said.

"His what?" Ty said, squinting. Her intensity seemed to roll off her in waves of smoke.

"He has a file of secrets that he keeps in fragments throughout his Limestone data. I'm not a good enough hacker to figure it all out – I guarantee the fact that the metalbreds are conscious is somewhere in there – but check this out..."

She opened the folder, where two little files were nested. Her grin almost hurt. She clicked the first, and a white document filled the screen, filled with a few innocuous lines of text.

"Okay…," Ty said, still squinting.

"These are tax codes for Annie Claybelle's shell companies," Luz said triumphantly. "I searched each one, and they all are tied to companies that she owns and I suspect either launders money through or makes payments to people like Conrad Miller with."

"Holy shit!" Ezz said, whistling. "Why does Salt have them?"

"No idea," Luz shrugged. "But he's keeping a record. If we ever find a cop we can trust with this shit, Salt would be the one to sing like a canary. The perfect snitch. Which brings me to exhibit number two…"

She closed the first document and opened the second file. A video file immediately leapt to fill the screen, Claybelle's face large and Salt's small – a call recorded from his device. Annie Claybelle's voice rang out clear and cold:

" – done your part, Raymond. I'll take care of the girl."

And then it snapped into black.

"Where's the rest?" Ty said quickly.

"That's all there is," Luz said. "Like I said, he fragmented it all, and if I had unlimited time and a little more skill, I could probably piece it all together but…this alone is pretty damn good."

She spun in her chair again, and jumped in suprise to find Ezz right behind her. Ezz had placed the dog on the ground and stood facing Luz, where she placed one hand on either side of Luz's face.

"You…are…fucking…amazing," she said, staring her in the eyes.

Luz blushed under the palms of her friend, casting her eyes down.

"Don't be so extra," she smiled, shrugging away. "I appreciate that. Thanks, Ezz. I mean, it's all shit that would send that bitch to jail in ordinary circumstances, but it doesn't help us since we know going to the cops isn't an option…"

"What about the eye?" Ezz said, glancing at Ty. "The private detective? Does he seem legit? The Special Police wouldn't be blocking him if he was crooked, right?"

Ty shrugged, and Luz had that crackling feeling that Ty sometimes gave – the feeling that a wire had been cut and flailed loose just beneath the skin.

"I don't know if we can trust him," Ty said.

"Okay, fuck all that anyway," Ezz said, returning to the dog, who sat wagging where she'd placed it. "We'll get to that. For now: the pooch."

Luz shifted, a familiar guilt spreading.

"It's amazing that you found this, Ezz, but…it's gonna take me hours to crack and I haven't had much sleep…"

"That's the good news!" Ezz interrupted, her eyes glowing. "I don't think you're going to have to hack it at all. I think I know the password."

Luz perked up. Hacking a bot that Rosario Vicario, one of the best jockeys who had ever lived, had coded would have been mind-wrenching. But she very much wanted to see what was inside.

"Really? You're finally bringing me something that I can just…open?" she teased.

"We'll see," Ezz said, and patted her leg for the dog. Its tongue lolled out in a smile before it hopped up and trotted over to meet her outstretched hand. Ezz scooped it up again and presented it to Luz, who wrinkled her nose.

"It looks so much like a real dog," she said.

"Wild, right?" Ezz said, shaking her head. "The worst. What do you need to do? Power it off?"

Luz stared at the dog with a curious expression on her face.

"What if it's like the metalbreds?" she finally said out loud. "What if it's...?"

"Real?" said Ty. "I was thinking the same thing."

"Yeah. Or...I don't know. Like us. Half the time I don't know if I'm real either."

They all stared at the dog, and Luz wondered if this was a moment the dog might remember if, in the future, robots lay the human population to waste. Three human survivors who had once been kind to a dog. Luz guessed she could live with that. Eternal third wheel.

"Don't shut it down," Ty said quietly. "Just plug it in. Or whatever."

"Will that work?" Ezz said.

Luz nodded. She barely took her eyes off the dog when she reached for the cable. A moment later the bot was plugged in; one of Luz's screens immediately filled with a request for a password. Luz shot her eyes at Ezz.

"Frankfort," Ezz said without hesitation. "With an O."

"*Frankfort?*" Luz said.

"Yeah. That's where Rosario and I met for the first time. Class field trip."

"You're sure?" Luz said doubtfully. "I don't know how many tries I get."

"I'm sure. She left this for me. I know that's what she was thinking. This was her way of letting me in."

Luz turned and slowly typed the letters into her computer, leaving no room for error.

As if a floodgate had been opened, the monitor began rapidly filling with code and schematics, the lines growing and expanding faster than Luz could follow.

"Holy shit," she said, stepping closer to the screen, her eyes racing across the surface. "This is intense."

"What is it?" Ezz said, leaning forward over the dog's head. "Is it the virus?"

Luz's breath felt somewhere between shallow and nonexistent. This was really happening. The idea of finishing Rosario's unfinished business – business that aligned so closely with Luz's own plans – made her feel trembly. Rosario could never have known, but her plan, this virus, might be the other side of a die that Luz had been spinning in her pocket, waiting for the right moment to cast.

"I think it is," Luz said, and saw the smile begin at one corner of Ezz's mouth before spreading across the rest. She didn't look at Ty, afraid of what she'd see.

"How long do you think she was working on this?" Luz said.

"She didn't tell me about it," Ezz said, and Luz felt the pain in these words, even if she didn't know why they hurt. "Rosario was brilliant, though. She probably did it overnight."

"She and Martha both died for this," Luz said softly, and knew that behind all their eyelids played the video file that Cloud Parliament had kept. A memory. As if the metalbred itself had hoped to uncover the truth, drag the shadows cast by Limestone into the light.

"*We* have to do it," Ezz said, loud. Her voice echoed in the mostly empty room.

"We don't exactly know what Rosario and Martha had planned," Luz said, turning from her screens. "Delivery, I mean. If their goal was to damage the Aristidean component and release the metalbreds from their programming, then that's only part of the process. We have to *deliver* the virus first."

"Is there nothing in the file?" Ezz said. "Did she leave any notes? Breadcrumbs that we can pick up?"

"As far as I can tell," Luz said, turning back, "it's just the virus itself. A massive file that has been uncondensed. And wait..."

She paused, squinting. To anyone else, everything on the

screen would look like chaos, but Luz's eyes were scalpels cutting through the mess down to the meat. She knew what beginnings and ends looked like, and she did not find the latter here on these screens.

"It's not complete," she said, scarcely able to say it out loud.

"What?" Ezz leaned forward, eyebrows low.

"It's not done," Luz said, pointing. "See there? Rosario and Martha were missing some foundational code. Just a few dozen digits, from what I can tell. Maybe even letters. It looks like a keypoint. Something that's supposed to correspond with the Limestone code. The virus won't actually communicate with the metalbred build unless the foundational code has been plugged in. If we fed this to the horses right now it would error out."

Ezz didn't speak, not even to curse. She stared at the screen the way one stranded on an island might watch a receding boat. It made Luz sink.

"She was so close," Ezz said softly.

"Limestone must have known just how close they were," Ty said, even softer. "Dr. Salt told Claybelle what Martha had discovered and called her hitman. When she he turned her down, she was desperate, so she called her brother. And even though I'm convinced Benedict simply enjoys killing people, this was different. He moved fast and messy. He knew Martha and Rosario were onto something that would have brought the whole fucking thing crashing down. I wonder if my mother…"

Whatever it was that would've come next, she bit it back. Luz wasn't sure she'd even said it at all.

Ezz squeezed her eyes shut.

"You're *sure* it won't work, Luz?" she said.

"I'm sorry," Luz said, unable to keep her voice from dropping. "Right now it would be like putting an envelope in the mail with no stamp."

"Right," Ezz said. "Right."

But then Ezz's eyes flew open.

"What did you say?" she said, almost shouting, and Luz jumped.

"What??"

"It would be like…," Ezz said, staring holes in the wall beyond Luz.

"Like putting an envelope in the mail with no stamp."

"*Envelope*," Ezz said.

"What?" Luz demanded. "What the fuck, yes, I said an envelope and… ¡Jueputa! Oh my god, *an envelope*!"

"An envelope," Ty said loudly. "I can say that too! ENVELOPE. Let's all say 'envelope'! What the fuck are we talking about?"

Luz ignored her, a grin appearing on her mouth that materialized on Ezz's like a reflection, like two mirrored sunrises.

"Jesus Christ, *what*?" Ty said desperately.

"Wait, just wait," Ezz whispered. "I don't wanna be wrong."

Luz's fingers flew across the keyboard, the screen coming alive and flashing between windows of code. She already knew. She knew. She could see the code in her mind – the way it had seemed like such a useless fragment, a direction of a throw with no object being thrown.

"Here it is," she said to herself. "The cufflink data. Just an envelope, I didn't think it could be anything…"

They stood watching her and she tried not to notice. She didn't want to let them down, but she already knew she wouldn't.

"Close out, refresh, reopen…," Luz said to herself, her voice fluttering like her fingers. "An envelope with an address is useless without something inside. But if you already have what's inside and you just need the address…"

Her fingers were like brown horses galloping across the keys. She never made mistakes, never had to backspace. On the screen, letters and numbers soared. And then just a white box. Simple and seemingly empty.

"Magnify," Luz whispered.

The line of code was fifty digits and would look like nothing special to anyone else. But Luz's shoulders had begun to rise and fall as her breath quickened.

"Overlay," Luz whispered, and leaned far over to tap a button on the keyboard of the screen bearing Rosario's virus. One of the larger screens between them illuminated suddenly, like an eye blinking open. The cufflink data and the virus data suddenly shared a white, empty pasture, the galloping of Luz's fingers still filling the silence.

"Maybe…?" she said softly, so softly no one else heard. It was a prayer, a delicate thing with feathers that fluttered up to the ceiling and looked down on the three girls, waiting.

The screen looked like a bomb ticking down or up, a spinning combination of numbers that rolled on faster than the eye could follow. There was no sound in the room except the hum of the machines. Luz didn't dare breathe.

And then she screamed.

She vaguely heard Ty scream too. Ezz didn't make a sound, just stood motionless with her fingers splayed on Luz's desk. Luz turned slowly to face them.

"It. Fucking. Worked," Luz hissed.

Ty shrieked again.

"You're lying!" Ezz shouted, grinning. "It did? For real? How?"

Luz turned gleefully back to the screens.

"Rosario and Martha must have been the ones hacking Limestone," she said. "The pathways I was talking about – I mean, who else would it be? They had a lot of the metalbred foundational code set up already, with their own virus attached to it. Parasitic code. They were just missing this last piece: Dr. Salt's signature code. Has to be because he wrote a lot of the foundational code, and so they needed his key. My program extracted it from his

Olivia A. Cole

cufflink envelope." She darted her eyes at Ty. "Good fucking work, Ty."

"I could kiss you," Ezz said, grabbing Ty by the shoulders, and for a moment Luz thought she actually would, and she watched every inch of Ty's skin lighting up in anticipation. It had been so long since Luz herself had been kissed, she didn't even know what it would feel like. And just like that, Irma appeared in her mind unbidden. In the end, Ezz's gaze was drawn back toward the screens.

"What's wrong?" said Luz.

"You really think they got the foundational code by hacking Limestone? Rosario was a hell of a jockey but not much of a hacker. Different skills, right? Unless that was another life I knew about."

"True," nodded Luz. "I'm good as hell at this but I could never program an equinibot. I doubt Martha was at this level either. I mean, it's possible, but..."

"Is there anything in the code that shows where it comes from?" Ty said. "Is that even how it works?"

"Not really," Luz said. "Maybe for another kind of framework, but not this. Rosario didn't build it inside the dog bot's framework – the mutt is just a vessel like the cufflink. Did Martha's sister, Rebeca, say anything about her being a hacker aside from a programmer?"

Ezz shook her head, middle finger pressed against her lips, thinking hard.

"No," she said. "And as talented as Martha was...foundational code from a billion-dollar enterprise? This would be like...genius-level hacking."

"Do we need to know where it came from in order to use it, though?" said Ty. "Like, it's complete, right? We can use it?"

"We can use it," said Luz, turning back to the screen. "It's just a matter of figuring out how to deliver it. I don't know how

359

Rosario and Martha had planned to do this aside from sneaking into every stall on the backside and plugging them up..."

Her voice trailed off as she studied the screen.

"What?" said Ezz, eyes searching Luz's face. "What's wrong?"

"Not wrong, exactly," Luz said slowly. "Just...weird. I'm looking at the file type and I was expecting an .exe or something like that – a program file. But when I put it into my translator...," she paused, gesturing at the code on the screen, tapping a few keys. "It says it's an .ogg?"

"Put it in *my* translator now," Ezz said. "Girl, what?"

"It's an *audio* file," Luz said, tapping the screen. "A series of tones at a higher pitch than our ear can even pick up. What the hell? I've never heard of a virus you can hear."

"Except we can't," Ezz said excitedly. "Our ear can't pick it up. But I bet you a metalbred's can."

"What did Rosario plan to do?" Luz cried. "Walk around the barn with a boom box?"

"What's a boom box?" Ty said. Both Luz and Ezz both paused to roll their eyes but didn't respond.

"She had to have had a plan," Ezz said. "If Rosario made the virus an audio file, she made it that way for a reason. We just have to think like her. How would *she* have delivered it?"

"Thinking like her won't help us if it was Martha's idea though," Luz countered.

"Can you play it?" Ezz pressed. "What does it sound like?"

"Yeah, but it's likely just a series of tones that wouldn't make sense to us anyway."

"So she could've played it in the barn and nobody would have even noticed," Ty said.

"Right. Pretty sure, anyway."

"But not all the horses are in the stables on Derby Day," Ezz argued. "They're warming up, they're getting tuned up, they're filing through last inspections by the track...there's no way she could have played it so that every metalbred would heard it. Not in the barn."

"She'd have to have done it at the starting gate or something," Luz shrugged. "When they're all in one place. She'd have needed a microphone or something. And maybe something to distract the audience, in case someone could actually hear it for some reason..."

Then Ezz and Ty were staring at each other, and Luz could see a realization glinting at first like the wink of a firefly and then growing in brightness and intensity until it was as if a small inferno blazed between them, alight with epiphany.

"*What?*" Luz said. "What is it?"

"A microphone," said Ty.

"A distraction," said Ezz.

"Do you think...?" Ty ventured, then paused. "No way. Do you think...she knew?"

"She had to have helped," Ezz added, eyes wide.

"Who?" said Luz. Then it all came bubbling up from the depths of her brain, as if someone had turned on the heat. "Rosario would have needed a hacker, somebody who knew her and someone she trusted."

"And maybe someone with an orchestra," Ty said.

"Holy shit," said Ezz, and then they all spoke in tandem:

"Skyhorse."

CHAPTER 42

LUZ

D r. Aldana was not exactly the kind of woman who could blend in easily, and Luz saw her well before Dr. Aldana saw them. It gave Luz time to bite back the guilt-shaped lump that had come to be in her throat. Here was the woman who had taught her to code, who had led Luz by the hand into the field she had staked out precisely for girls like Luz. And Luz had turned her back for…what? Roses. Dirt. Why did doing what you love have to mean disappointing other people? By the time Luz and Ezz made their way through the crowd to approach Dr. Aldana, the final parade before Derby Day was in full swing, confetti raining down on their heads, and Luz had swallowed the lump and focused on the matter at hand.

"Luz," Dr. Aldana said when she laid her eyes on her. A moment before those eyes had been as smooth and cold as a pocketknife, but the steel folded away when she took in Luz's face. "I have been thinking of you so much. Why didn't you come see me with your friends the other day?"

Her eyes flashed up over Luz's shoulder, where Ezz stood silently, waiting. Luz could see the barbed wire in Dr. Aldana's eyes. They had purposefully left Ty behind since she'd done the bulk of the lying when they had visited Skyhorse.

"I wasn't expecting to see you again after you rushed out of my office," Dr. Aldana said to Ezz, sour.

"Um…sorry about that," Ezz said. "Ever since Rosario and Martha died, it's been…kind of hectic."

"Oh, you're still doing that," Dr. Aldana said. Her head lolled sideways, exasperated.

"Doing what?"

"Pretending that you actually knew Martha," she said.

Luz intervened.

"Dr. Aldana, it's complicated, okay? We didn't know Martha but…"

"But *you* could have," Dr. Aldana said. If it had been her voice on the phone, maybe it wouldn't have felt the way it did – fingers across a guitar's strings, playing a sorrowful note. But her face with the words, pinched with regret, was almost too much. "Luz, why did you stop coming to Skyhorse? You just disappeared one day. Your parents came expecting you to be there and I had to tell them I didn't know where you were! And then months passed, a year. Almost two."

"I just couldn't keep pretending," Luz said. "My heart is in the greenhouse. Why can't anybody see that?"

"Luz," Dr. Aldana said, softening. "I know you're angry. It seems like everyone is trying to keep you from what you want. But your parents don't want you working at Cavehill for good reason. They want something better for you…"

"Better according to whom?" Luz cried. "According to the people who tell them that what they do isn't good enough, that what they *are* isn't good enough. Fuck that, Dr. Gina. Fuck that. We don't all have to be robotics engineers or fucking astronauts. Some of us want to work with the soil, with the animals. That work is beautiful and honorable and important too. There is dignity and expertise in what my parents do. In what my abuela does! I'm tired of this – our lives and work can matter without walking on the damn moon!"

Dr. Aldana opened her mouth as if to speak, and then closed it again, pressing her lips together the way she did when she was thinking. Luz knew this face. Something she had said had gotten through, but Dr. Aldana wasn't willing to admit it yet. Instead her gaze moved back to Ezz.

"You and your friend – the white girl – came to my office under false pretenses," Dr. Aldana said, eyes narrowing. "You lied to my face about knowing one of my mentees. And now you want me to tell you more about her – this girl you didn't actually know – in order to…what? What exactly is your motivation here?"

Her arms uncrossed and her long-fingered hands came to rest on her hips, her face bright with anger. Luz had only seen her look like this once before, when ICE had come sniffing around Skyhorse a few years before. Looking back, Luz wondered if Claybelle had sent them. Dr. Aldana had stared the agents down, holding her birth certificate in their faces like a cross against vampires. She wouldn't let them inside, and they'd been forced to say they'd come back with warrants. They hadn't, of course.

"A virus," Luz said quickly, applause almost drowning her out. "That's why Ezz and Ty came to see you – trying to track down what happened to Martha and Rosario. We know they were working together on a virus that would expose Limestone for what it is."

Dr. Aldana's hands dropped from her hips, and Luz wondered if she was aware of the clues her own body gave.

"At this point I need some proof," Dr. Aldana said slowly.

"Proof of what?" said Ezz.

"Proof that you're not working for Limestone, for one. And proof that you're not out here trying to do more damage to those girls' memories than has already been done. So tell me what it is that you know about a supposed virus and I'll decide if you're trustworthy enough to know what I know."

Ezz looked helpless, but Luz had been expecting this. Dr.

Aldana protected the Skyhorse kids like a lion would her cubs.

"We know the metalbreds have souls," Luz said, and Dr. Aldana shifted.

"What did you say?" Her eyes flickered over Luz's face like two searchlights.

"We don't *know* that," Ezz said quickly. "Souls may not even be..."

"They have free will," Luz went on. "So whatever that means as far as a soul goes. Inside their heads, they're free. And the Aristidean component that Limestone implements in all the horses keeps them bound. They're, like, trapped in there."

"That's what Rosario and Martha's virus attacked," Ezz said. Luz could feel Dr. Aldana giving in. "It damages the Aristidean component and sets the horses free from the programming."

"This is what Martha was trying to tell me," Dr. Aldana said, and everything hard in her went soft again, her shoulders slumping. One hand went searching backward in space, finding the short wall bordering the sidewalk. She sank down onto it, as if the memory of Martha was too heavy. Other parade goers surged into the spot she had just occupied. "Before she died."

Luz and Ezz said nothing, waiting. To press her seemed cruel, Luz thought, and this was all cruel enough already.

"She came to me," Dr. Aldana said, raising her eyes but not her head. "She said she had made a discovery."

Ezz nodded.

"She told her sister Rebeca the same thing. From what I understand, she went to Limestone and told them, hoping to get a job and support her family – apparently she met with Dr. Salt, the chief engineer. But Limestone gave her the brush-off." Luz nodded, listening. All true. "While Rosario and Martha were planning the virus, Limestone was figuring out what to do with Martha."

"They figured she was alone, she was an immigrant, and that

they could just make her disappear. So that's what they did," Luz said softly. "She must have said something about Rosario, or a witness said they'd been working together, and they killed Rosario too."

Dr. Aldana stared at them, the dampness of her eyes like fall leaves, wilting. Luz knew the look in them, the image of Martha growing smaller, like watching her fall down a well.

"I warned her," Dr. Aldana whispered. "When she told me what she was messing around with. I didn't know the details, of course, only that she thought it was big."

"But she asked you to hack something for her," Luz said gently, and then the tear-filled eyes were on her and she wanted to cry too.

"Yes," Dr. Aldana said softly. "She needed foundational code. I didn't know why. But she was brilliant. I don't know what I thought she had uncovered. A new way of programming, maybe, something that would make them faster, more realistic. A demonstration on Derby Day, shake things up. Not this."

Around them the parade audience jostled to make way for a cotton candy vendor. Luz had a sudden craving for the electric sweet, something to busy her tongue and distract her brain.

"She didn't set out looking for it," Ezz said. "But once you know the truth...you can't unsee it. We saw one of the unbound horses ourselves. It's unbelievable. They're...I don't know. Not alive. Maybe alive? I don't know! They're...real. They're real. I can't explain it. But if you know horses, you know it when you see it."

"Oh, Martha...," Dr. Aldana said, lowering her head again.

"She's a hero," Luz said. "She exposed something major. Through her own brilliance and kindness. And that's why we have to do...this."

Her tongue felt thick with only half the truth on it. The full truth was Luz's "this" had started before she ever saw Martha in the horse's memory. She wondered what Dr. Aldana would say if she knew about Luz's dark, green room, her vines and the plans she had for them.

"Do what?" Dr. Aldana said to the ground, and Luz was grateful when Ezz answered.

"What she already asked you to do," Ezz said, drawing the woman's eyes up again. Ezz glanced at Luz, passing her the verbal reins just as Luz collected herself.

"You're a hacker," Luz said. "The best. You taught me everything I know. You won all those awards that you taught me to aspire to. So you got her the code snippets she needed. It only makes sense: you were going to help them disperse the virus, weren't you?"

Dr. Aldana stared into Luz's eyes, the grief shining alongside the anger like two twin stars in one burning constellation.

"Yes," she said, sounding desperate. "But it wasn't complete."

"You were going to help them," Ezz said, her voice rising in a mix of admiration and disbelief. "Before you even knew what the virus *did*."

"Yes," Dr. Aldana said again, snapping this time. "I didn't need to know any more than the fact that Martha had been spurned by the same company that gets rich from the labor of people just like her. I didn't know anything more than Martha believed the virus would change things for the people she has worked alongside since she was a child. Martha was good: good hands and a good heart. Limestone can go to hell."

She was a little out of breath, angry and embarrassed, and her eyes flamed with both. She stood there with her rage flowering. Inside Luz was her own garden of anger, and it began to bloom.

"I'm guessing this is the part where you pull out your device," Dr. Aldana said bitterly. "Suggest we go to the police? Try to convince them to care about two Brown girls? We have no proof, no confession, no plan…"

"We have more than you think," Luz said sheepishly, and watched Dr. Aldana's eyes jerk up. "But we still can't go to the police. Limestone hired a fixer and he's already down here trying to cover everything up."

"But what about the virus?" Dr. Aldana said, looking sharply back and forth between them. "It wasn't complete. It would take me some time before I could finish it – I need more Limestone code and…"

Ezz held up the cufflink.

"We finished it," Luz said. "But there is something else you can do."

CHAPTER 43

LUZ

With one text from Ezz, Ty met them at the corner to debrief. Luz felt strangely relaxed. She felt as if everything that had happened, the coals that had been stirred inside her, should have sent her into wildfire. Instead the flames building in her body felt merely warm and pleasant.

The three of them made their way back to the Pink, walking, enjoying the sunshine, the lull in crowds between parades. It was the time of day during Derby season when everyone returned to their hotels and homes to rest, and it reminded Luz of the times she was still allowed to visit the backside to see her parents – when they would be resting in the shade with the other workers while Señora Cecelia would come around selling tortas and sodas. Sometimes the radio would be playing or sometimes her mother would be singing while other folks hummed along, low, texting or relaxing. Seeing Dr. Aldana had brought it all back…the summer days walking back and forth between Skyhorse and the track, the sun shimmering on pavement tricking the mind into thinking things would be the same forever.

"There's something you should know," Luz said out loud as they were crossing the street that would take them to the gates of the Pink. She meant it for Ezz, but when she and Ty both looked at her, Luz realized it was for both of them. The truth. "Something I…"

She trailed off. They were standing outside the gates now, and paused. Her heart sank at the thought of Ezz hearing what she was about to say, and then stepping through the gates without her, closing the iron in her face.

"What's up?" said Ezz. Her brows were crinkled in concern, but Ty's face was flat. Luz couldn't read her expression, was rattled by the guardedness of it.

"We've all been working on exposing Limestone. On getting justice for Martha and Rosario. And I've been helping, obviously. But I've also been working on something else. I have…another project."

Ty's eyes had sharpened, two jagged points in the flatness. Luz looked away and focused on Ezz.

"In the lair. In the first room. The plants."

Ezz didn't say anything, just stared. Luz swallowed.

"I think I'd better just show you."

They made their way through the leaf-shadowed passages of the labyrinth in silence, then down into the dim tunnel of the stairway. Luz trailed her fingers along the cool, dark wall just in case – the time she'd lived here had not been happy, per se, but it had been safe, which she thought was a form of happiness. She had been able to breathe here. This might be the last day, if Ezz chose not to understand.

The door to the first room was closed, as she had left it. She slowly swung it open, and the smell of soil and green wafted out into the hall in a silent greeting. She glanced back at Ezz and Ty, just in time to see them exchanging a glance. She couldn't read it. She couldn't worry.

She walked to the work bench, leaves brushing against her

Poison Ivy tattoo like a kiss. Ty and Ezz squeezed through the growth after her.

"I swear this was almost empty a couple weeks ago," Ezz said, gazing around. "What are you feeding these things? Steroids?"

"That's part of what I want to show you."

Ty's face had relaxed, taking in the swarming vines and leaves with a combination of awe and pleasure. Luz hid a smile. She knew a nature girl when she saw one. But watching her smile was like watching a popsicle in the sun – Luz waited for it to melt when Ty saw what Luz's green lab truly contained.

"I've been really…," she started, then her voice faltered. She thought of her parents working for Cavehill for so many years, every dawn spent in the shade of the triple spires. And how it all counted for nothing, the ladders raised and out of reach. Others' careers were cut short when ICE came to drag them away – when they had asked for too much, Luz knew now, when Annie Claybelle had picked up the phone and used it as a gun. None of the horse owners, none of the people in seersuckers who came to watch the warm-ups, none of them gave a shit. Everyone was silent. And the races just went on, the dust from the track swirling around and stinging Luz's eyes even when she was miles away. She swallowed. "I've been really…angry."

Luz and Ty watched her, saying nothing, and she used the moment of silence to turn away, tracing the bold but delicate shape of a kudzu leaf sprouting on the worktable. It seemed to reach out for her throat.

"So I've been trying to figure out what to do with that anger," she went on. "I've been trying to think of how I can make people see where my anger comes from. This industry runs on our blood and sweat, and they don't care about our work or what happens to us. They just look away and go on with their business and make their money. I wanted to figure out how to make it so they *couldn't* look away. And I've realized that it's more than just making them see – it's making them *do* too, which my friend Zarita is pretty good at. But I still have this room and what's in it and I need to decide what to do with it."

She went to the far side of the worktable, where black pouches lined the table. These were each labeled *Functional*; she barely recognized her own spidery handwriting, written in the dead of night after trial upon trial. She had whispered to these seeds in the thick of midnight. She had made them what they were, encouraged them to take this current form with water, light, chemicals, electricity, love.

"Do you want to see what they can do?" she said softly, not daring to look at Ty or Ezz. She didn't want to see the fear, if there was any. She didn't want to see the realization spreading from pupil to mouth: *there is something wrong with this girl.* They might be right.

"They're seeds?" Ty said softly. She didn't sound afraid. Only curious, like a horse's ears pricked toward a sound that they were deciding the danger of.

"Yes, but they're –" Luz paused. "Special."

Luz picked up one of the pouches. It felt light in her palm, surprisingly light, even though she knew exactly what it contained: ten seeds, each one shiny brown and shaped almost like a kidney bean, but flatter. Even before Luz had worked with them they would grow fast, like a mouse's heartbeat traveling through the dirt and roots. Kudzu, the plant that swallowed the South. But Luz had turned the mouse into something with wings, something on fire.

"*We both strive to see evildoers punished,*" she whispered. Poison Ivy's words felt natural in her mouth. "*But, while you have your gallery of rogues, I have my grove.*"

She opened the pouch, angled its small dark mouth toward her palm. Out fell one seed. She stared at it, still deciding whether to change her mind. The sight of it, like a kernel in her palm, made her think of Thunder Over Louisville, when she and the other kids would light off fireworks behind the backside, the Roman candles and the Black Cats hitting the sky like frying pans, cast iron sparks. No one minded because the equinibots weren't real horses – they didn't balk at noise. Now Luz wondered what memories they were storing away. She thought of the little white poppers that the little kids would fill their hands with on Thunder, flinging them at the ground and watching their tiny explosions. These seeds were like that.

"Step back out into the hall," she said. She didn't look to see if they obeyed.

She stared down at the seed in her palm, imagining that it had already begun to tremble. She took a deep breath. Then she turned her palm like a boat tipping at sea, and the seed began its long, fast descent to the floor.

Luz walked quickly to the doorway, where Ty and Ezz had indeed obeyed and stood just beyond in the hallway. Luz joined them, fishing in her pocket. She withdrew her device, pulled up the string of code. Like the metalbreds, the seeds would respond to a frequency. A green language that only her seeds could hear.

"Ready?" she said quietly, as much to herself as the other two girls. She saw them nod from the corner of her eye, was glad they didn't speak. She took one more deep breath. She knew it would work. She tapped her screen.

Someone might call it an explosion, but it wasn't. Not exactly. Not a fire. Not a scream of noise and air and metal parts. It was a crash of nature, of filaments becoming vines at a savage, unnatural pace, everything hurtling out of the tiny brown casing at once like springed guts, green and vicious. Not an explosion of fire, but vines: leaves and snaking tendrils, the spade-sharp leaves climbing the walls, wrapping table legs, then snapping them. The plant was hungry. It didn't have teeth – only the strength of its vines that Luz had given strange power, fueled by her rage. It was more than enough.

When she looked at Luz and Ezz, they were both behind her, backs against the far wall of the hallway. The green fingers of kudzu had slowed now and crept just to the edge of the room, where they seemed to consider the boundary into the hallway, wavering. Luz knew they had reached their growth radius, that the vines wouldn't reach this far. Not with just one seed. But twenty? Spread around? They would fill the hallways, would overrun the laboratory, crack the screens and snap legs of tables and humans alike. They would break down spires.

"Holy shit," Ezz whispered.

"I know," Luz said, almost ruefully. "I know."

"What are you going to do with it?" Ezz said. "What...what is this for?"

"It's for Derby," Luz said. "It's for all of them."

"You're going to unleash this at Derby?" Ty said, and Luz had to look right at her, to ascertain whether the trace of a smile she heard was actually there. It was. If not on her mouth, then in her eyes. Luz recognized that cold, sad look. She knew it from the mirror.

"Yes," Luz said.

"This is what you've been working on?" Ezz said. "You've been planning this for how long?"

"Long enough."

Luz looked again at Ty, watched the clock behind her eyes ticking. She didn't know what it was counting down from, or to, but she thought something might explode there too when zero was reached. Maybe they were all counting down to a zero, all the time.

"But what about the horses?" Ezz said. "The metalbreds? The plan for exposing Limestone?"

"This all feels like the same thing," said Luz slowly. "I feel like, if we go forward with this virus like we're talking about, it has the potential to make Limestone fall apart from the inside. Batman stuff, right? Clean evidence. The bad guys all tied up. But…but I'm not Batman. I'm tired of being clean with these people. Besides, even with everything we have – Claybelle's texts and her conversation with Salt: all that shit – we still can't tie Benedict to Rosario's crime scene. If we can't prove it, I at least want to fuck some shit up."

Ty said something softly, and Luz looked at her.

"What did you say?"

"I have more proof that Benedict was at Rosario's crime scene."

Luz felt Ezz stiffen in the dim hallway. No one said anything for a long time, and Ty eventually must have realized no one would, because she shifted, reaching into the kit she still wore at her waist. Luz squinted at her fingers, which a moment later withdrew something shiny from a pocket. It was a narrow vial. It clinked when Ty shook it.

"What the hell is that, Ty?" said Ezz.

"It's a needle," Ty said, so low Luz had to strain to hear. "It's the needle Benedict used to inject Rosario with the K. He left it at the scene."

"And why the fuck do *you* have it?" Ezz's voice bounced off the dirt walls.

"I saw it the day you came inside the Mahogany to look at the police hologram," she said. "I was looking at the bleach stain on the floor and I found the needle under the wardrobe. And I kept it."

Luz wasn't close enough to touch Ezz, but she could feel the anger vibrating through every cell of her skin.

"Why?" Luz said. "Why the fuck, Ty? Why didn't you tell us?"

"Why didn't you tell *me*?" Ezz shouted. "What the fuck is wrong with you?"

"I had…I had a plan," Ty whispered. Luz never thought she could've pictured Ty crying, those steel eyes always locked tight, but she looked close to tears. "I was…"

"You were going to *what*?" Ezz kept shouting. "Give it to your buddy, the cop? Hide it? Are you even on our side? Have you been pretending to –"

"I was going to kill him," Ty said suddenly, loud. "I was going to kill him, and I was going to use this needle. His fingerprints are on it, I'm positive. So I was going to use this. Tie everything up."

The look on Ezz's face made Luz cringe, the look she was afraid she would receive when Ezz learned about her vines – the face of someone who realized that they were talking to a monster. But if Luz was a monster, Ty was something more vicious. And somehow with this realization, everything seemed suddenly very clear to Luz.

"How do you know his fingerprints are on it?" Luz said calmly. "He probably would've worn gloves, right?"

"He doesn't wear gloves," Ty said, staring at Ezz instead of Luz. "He uses a bleach solution to clean bodies and his hands."

This hit Luz squarely in the chest, remembering the night tucked beside the shedrow, the figure of Brian Benedict spritzing his hands in the moonlight.

"There was bleach on the floor of Rosario's room," Ezz said, her voice grating.

"Yes," Ty said.

"You've known this whole time."

"I had an idea."

"How?" Luz asked, but knew as soon as the word left her lips that this was one thing Ty would not answer.

"I'm sorry," Ty said instead, and extended the vial to Ezz. Ezz shoved it back into her hands, her eyes flames.

"Put it back where you got it," she hissed. "I hate you right now, and I don't know if I can forgive you, but I will say this: it might be a good thing you took it."

Luz almost jerked in surprise.

"What?" she said.

"Think about it," Ezz said. She refused to look at Ty. "Darden or whatever his name is sent the Special Police into Rosario's suite to get the evidence Benedict left. He only got one piece, and Darden was sending him back to get it again. Thanks to Ty" – Ezz spoke of her like she wasn't there – "there was nothing to find. Now maybe if we bust out all these murdering motherfuckers at Derby, we can tell the private investigator to go back to the scene and look for the needle." She glared at Ty. "Which *you* will return to the scene. With everything we're going to show them at Derby, the Special Police won't dare interfere with the investigation. The public is going to be watching on that day, and every day after."

"Watching how?" Ty said. Ezz ignored her and looked at Luz to answer. The answer sank in.

"You're thinking of the Jumbotron," Luz said, raising an eyebrow, and Ezz nodded.

"If we put the evidence up there, everyone will see. The detective dude will have no choice but to ask the right questions, and then actually hear the answers."

Luz nodded, something like a hot air balloon taking off in her chest.

"And no one will be able to look away," she said.

"Exactly."

"We'll need to find a way to get into the exec suites," Ezz said. "We have to make sure Benedict and Claybelle don't just hop on a damn yacht when their faces pop up on the Jumbo."

"Should we –" Ty started, and Luz could hear the plea in her voice, could see she was immediately embarrassed by it, but Ezz cut her off.

"Luz and I will work on the plan," Ezz said sharply. "*You're* going to leave. Take that needle back to the Mahogany and keep your mouth shut. You're good at that, right?"

Then Ezz turned her back, and Luz sat very still, hoping Ty wouldn't actually go, that she would see what Luz saw: Ezz a builder of walls, always hoping someone would care enough to knock them down. But after a moment Ty left, wordless. Even when Luz and Ezz began to hatch the plan for Derby Day, Luz sat wondering if she would always be caught between two places, two needs, two cliffs too high to climb.

CHAPTER 44

EZZ

From the roof of the Pink, Ezz could see the three spires of Cavehill in the distance and, in the other direction, fireworks at the waterfront. Shavon's clippers buzzed in her left ear. It was past midnight and Ezz watched the bursts of color silently.

"You're quiet," Shavon said. She'd barely turned the clippers on and was already starting in on her cousin.

"Just thinking."

"About that girl," Shavon said.

Ezz didn't trust her voice to speak, so she just made a scoffing sound.

"Expected to see her up here," Shavon pressed. "Something happen?"

"Nah," Ezz said. "We're working on a project. She just needed to handle part of it."

"Then why she's sitting outside your gate crying?" Shavon said.

Ezz lurched and spun around, finding Shavon's eyes in the pink light from the rooftop.

"What did you say?"

"Damn, Ezzardine!" Shavon cried, grabbing her chin and jerking it sideways to examine her head. "You lucky I didn't put a nick in your shit! You can't just move like that when I'm shaping you up!"

"Fuck my hair, Shavon, what did you *say*?"

Shavon turned off the clippers, looking coy.

"When I got here ten minutes ago, Ty was sitting at the front gate all sniffly. Tried to act like she wasn't. Asked her if she was coming inside, and she said no. Then she left."

"She left?" Ezz said. She stood at the edge of the roof now, eyes scanning the distant dark edge of the fence surrounding the Pink.

"Why wouldn't she?" Shavon said.

Ezz went on staring into the dark until her cousin's hand found her shoulder, guided her back to the chair. Her eyes stung and she was glad Shavon was behind her. The clippers snapped on, and the buzz had just filled her ears again when Shavon's words joined the sound.

"It's hard to love someone when they don't let you," Shavon said.

Ezz sighed, thinking of the metal in Ty's eyes – the way it sometimes melted and showed her something warm.

"Exactly!" Ezz cried. "I just never know when she's telling the truth. I never know what's real, what's really inside her."

"That's cool," Shavon said near her ear. "But I was talking about you."

CHAPTER 45

TY

The needle was back under the wardrobe, and Ty was standing in another guest suite, willing her hands to stop shaking, when Camille slithered into the room.

"Hey," said Ty, and swallowed. She wasn't a crier, and certainly not in public. She glanced at where Camille alighted on a velvet armchair, out of the way of the final sweeps of Ty's silent Nanospeck. Camille sat looking a little more pale than usual, a flowing gray smock pooling on either side of her pulled-up knees.

"I was wondering if you'd come back," Camille said, a cat-like expression on her face. "You went from never missing a day of work to disappearing."

"I didn't disappear," Ty corrected, slipping the Nano into a loop on her kit. "I called."

"A-ha."

"Did you miss me or something?"

"Do you want the coworker response or the bratty almost-friend response?"

"You're not a coworker," Ty said. "It's not like you really work here...or at all..."

"Oh, fuck you," Camille said, but she wasn't kidding, and Ty turned, squinting.

"What's the problem right now?" Ty said.

"You ditched me at the Carousel party," Camille said flatly. "And then didn't come back, at the party or here. I don't even have the number to your device. I could've asked my mother, but I didn't want to draw any more attention to you..."

"Wait, you're mad because we left the party?" Ty said.

"You left *me* at the party," Camille said.

Ty blinked hard, the bodies of Martha and Rosario swimming in her brain. The disgust behind Ezz's eyes when she realized what Ty was capable of. Camille had not even entered her mind in the past few days – she had been a necessary rung on a ladder.

"I was the only reason you were able to go to begin with," Camille said. Her voice didn't change: it was steady and slow as an old-fashioned typewriter. Something about the heaviness slowed the spark in Ty ignited by defensiveness. She rested her hands on her kit.

"I know. I'm sorry."

They stared at each other.

"For what exactly?" Camille said.

"For leaving you. For using you to get to the party and then disappearing. That was bullshit. It's just..."

She trailed off and Camille's eyes seemed to scoop up each syllable.

"What?" Camille said. "You went into Rosario Vicario's room today. Why? Clearly there's more going on here than you've told me. Something really bad."

"What makes you say that?"

"*Because*, Ty, what the fuck!" she hissed, glancing at the door. "You ran out of the party chasing some girl, for one thing. And when you came to work yesterday, I saw you lurking around Darden's room. And I remember you talking to him at the party. And I remember you being upset that Brian Benedict canceled his reservation. Why?"

"You're reading into a lot of stuff," Ty said, shrugging it off, fighting back the rising feeling of near-panic. Hearing Brian Benedict's name out of Camille's mouth was like putting in earpods and, instead of music, hearing screams. "And what, you were spying on me again yesterday? Why didn't you say anything then?"

"I saw your face," Camille said, ignoring her questions. "I see how your face changes. How you have the face you put on when you're being normal – like right now – and the one that shows up sometimes when you start daydreaming. Some people are happy when they daydream. Or at least content. It's like your daydreams are…nightmares."

Ty stared at her, not daring to imagine which face she was wearing now.

"I was just cleaning the hallway," Ty said. "Why does everything have to be a big deal?"

"What's the deal with you and Brian Benedict?" Camille said flatly.

Ty let her eyes drop, adjusting the position of a few items in her cleanwork kit. The feeling of the assortment of delicate machines helped her feel rooted, kept her fingers from shaking.

"I don't even know who that is," she said without looking up.

"Look," Camille said, impatient. "You were doing recon at a high-level Derby party and Brian Benedict was the only high-level guest we had reserved at the Mahogany until he canceled his rez. I'm not stupid. I can connect the dots."

"None of that means anything," Ty said.

Camille took a long look at her and finally shook her head.

"You better come up with something better than that, Ty, because there's a cop outside with a Limestone exec asking for you."

The words took a long moment to sink in, a moment in which Ty stood staring at Camille's mouth trying to decide if the words coming out of it were serious. Camille nodded at the window overlooking the rear garden.

"He's on the patio waiting."

Ty was halfway to the window when her device pinged. She knew before she even looked that it was Madame Richmond, a series of texts shouting up at her from the tiny glowing screen.

Detective Segrest is here to see you.

Get down here.

If it had been a little cooler outside, the windows might have been open to let in the almost-summer air, and Ty could have eavesdropped for a moment before stepping out onto the wide verandah that overlooked the carefully manicured garden. As it was, the only snatch of conversation she was able to grab hold of was what her ears picked up in the two paces it took to bring her through the door and to the wide stairway.

"In any case, knowing when the investigation might close would be helpful for my business, as you can understand," Madame Richmond was saying, fanning herself even as she stood under the protection of the inn's awning. "We can't let the room until then, obviously."

"My team is working as fast as they can," Detective Segrest said, holding a sweating glass of water, brightened with frozen fruit bobbing among ice cubes. "Some questions have arisen that need answering. We believe that something was removed from the crime scene, and until we figure out what and why, we have some loose ends to tie up."

His eyes transferred to Ty, and she prayed her face didn't look how it felt.

"Miss Redson, hello," he said. "I was stopping by to chat with Madame Richmond and ran into your visitors."

Ty stepped past Madame Richmond and ignored Detective Segrest's greeting, squinting at the two men standing beside him.

"Dad," she said, nervous heart quickening into a tambourine. "What are you doing here? With…him?"

"Nice to see you again, Ty," Dr. Salt said, smiling warmly. Her father also held a glass of water, but Dr. Salt did not. His hands were hidden loosely in his pockets, the sleeves of his dress shirt rolled up to the elbow. He looked so casual; different than the tuxedoed evangelical that Ty had watched speak at the Limestone gala. With his sleeves rolled up like this, he gave the impression of a horse hand. Ty wondered if this was a PR thing. Out meeting the little people. Or perhaps a message to her specifically: *No cuff link to steal today, young lady.*

"You as well," Ty said carefully, determined to look nowhere but his very blue eyes, which now darted over Ty's shoulder at Madame Richmond, who still stood watching from the verandah.

"I think we can take it from here, Madame," Salt said with a grin, teeth so white and shiny Ty expected them to ping like a cartoon.

Madame Richmond had the decency to hesitate, casting her eyes down in the direction of Ty, who had swiveled her head around to watch her go. Employee and employer locked eyes, and for a moment Ty felt Madame's awareness of her age. Madame had daughters. Would she have left her own with three men in the garden?

"Thanks for taking such good care of my daughter," came Ty's father's voice, and it broke the spell, as he intended. Ty didn't turn, but kept watching Madame, watched her face register her own doubt and then decide to deem it unnecessary. The easier thing to do. A thing she could forgive herself for later if it turned out to be the wrong decision. She had an inn to run, after all. She broke from Ty's gaze, nodding at this small group of guests assembled oddly in the garden, and returned to the shade and quiet of the Mahogany. Only then did Ty turn back to the three men, alone.

"I wanted to thank you again for your help at the gala," Dr. Salt said, his hands coming out of hiding from his pockets and hanging by his sides. Free, but not loose. That's how she knew he knew. He knew what she did. Those hands wanted to be pointing at her, accusing her. But he didn't seem to have counted on Detective Segrest's presence, who stood by sipping his water and admiring the garden. He didn't seem interested in their conversation, but also didn't seem to have any plans to leave.

"It was no problem," Ty said. "Just in the right place at the right time."

"A habit of yours, it seems," Detective Segrest said, studying the garden, and she forced herself not to react. Her father, on the other hand, cast him a curious glance that the cop didn't return.

"I gathered you're investigating the death of Rosario Vicario, Detective," Dr. Salt said. His voice was a placid lake, but Ty could sense the alligator in it.

"Somewhat," Segrest shrugged, still admiring the swaths of tulips that Madame Richmond had installed for the season. "We have most of what we need. Just a few unanswered questions."

Something about his tone made Ty uneasy. There was something sharp buried in the core of it, and she wasn't sure where it might aim. Had he, like Dr. Salt, come to the Mahogany to question her? Two knives aimed at her heart, then, rather than one.

"A grave loss to the racing community," Dr. Salt said solemnly. "What she accomplished was a once-in-a-lifetime contribution to the sport."

Ty stiffened into an arch-backed cat.

"Then why did Limestone ban her until she was hired by a Limestone owner? Why did Limestone make Cavehill declare that home-built horses weren't allowed? You stand here praising her skill, but then you make all these new rules to keep people like her on the outside!"

"Ty," her father said, and she didn't need to look at him to know the expression on his face. His tone was a yellow light of caution, his face a red warning flag – he'd waved both in her mother's face enough times for her to know. She ignored both and stared at Dr. Salt, who had the audacity to smile.

"One can appreciate her craftsmanship and skill and still see the bigger picture," he said gently, as if scooping up a kitten that had wandered too close to the road. "The industry was undergoing massive changes after the ban of live horses, but it has always been the sport of kings! Which is not to say that what Miss Vicario accomplished was not extraordinary. It was! But horseracing has always been an industry of exclusivity. If everyone had a metalbred, where would be the kingliness of it all? And in the end, where was the harm? Miss Vicario won her first Derby and made a name for herself. The subsequent bans didn't stop her from being hired by the top owners in the country! In the *world*!"

"She is one person," Ty said. "And she slipped in the crack before you slammed the door. What about everyone else?"

"My dear," he said. "How many Rosario Vicarios do you think one industry needs?"

Detective Segrest and her father both stood listening, expressions unreadable, but Ty knew her face was an open book, and all the words were written in red. The only thing that kept her from spitting in his face was what she knew.

"But this isn't why I came to see you," Dr. Salt said, his tanned hands waving in front of his body as if rinsing his words out of the air between them. "I came to ask you for a favor."

This threw her.

"What kind of favor?"

"Your father tells me that you sing," Dr. Salt said. The kitten of his voice receded into the blue caves of his eyes. Something else looked out now, with much larger claws. "That you have an extraordinarily lovely voice."

She said nothing, floundering, and he seemed to revel in her confusion.

"Tomorrow is Derby Day," he said, his smile like a noose. "As you might know, Limestone hosts a very special private entertainment area for certain special guests on one of the higher floors of the New Downs. I would like to invite you to come, not only as a guest, but as a special entertainment feature. Based on your appearance at my gala, I'm positive you have a lovely dress to wear."

"You want me to...what?" she said slowly, realization dawning. "Come and...sing?"

"Yes," he beamed. "Come and stand in our little spotlight for the day. Allow us to admire your beautiful voice. I like to keep an eye on local talent. Perhaps, like Miss Vicario, you can make a name for yourself."

He smiled at her, and she didn't dare glance at her father or Detective Segrest, the latter of whom she could feel studying the conversation hotly as if from a sniper's nest. Ty wondered if his detective skills told her what she heard very clearly in Dr. Salt's invitation: *I know you're up to something, and I want you where I can keep an eye on you.* And then, like the fluttering tail of an ominous kite, tacked onto the end: *Do you want to end up like her?*

Her mind and her mouth tangled together, stumbling through tangles of tripwires, and this seemed to satisfy him.

"Good," he said to her stutter, and clapped his hands one more time. His skin had reddened slightly in the sun. "I will let your father go over the details with you. I should mention," he said, locking his piercing gaze on her one more time, "that you must not be late."

Then he turned to Segrest, his smile looking less like a weapon.

"Detective, if you're all finished with Madame Richmond, would you mind walking me to the street? I'd like to discuss any contacts you might have within the Special Police. I need to talk to someone about hiring a security detail…"

Ty didn't bother watching them go. Instead she locked eyes with her father, who looked like a bulldog preparing to wrench a bone from another beast. He removed his hands from his pockets now too, and Ty wondered if men were aware of habits like these. Was it a conscious or subconscious impulse for men's bodies to speak a threat when they were trying to convince their mouths to speak persuasion?

"It's a great opportunity, Ty," he was saying, and she was shaking her head before the words were even out of his mouth.

"Do you really expect me to believe that?" she snapped, but then reeled herself in. She didn't know what he knew, but she knew by now he couldn't be trusted.

"They're going to pay you," he said, frowning. "They're really doing *you* a favor. You just need to say yes."

"I have to work."

"Your boss already said she'd give you the day off," he said quickly. "For this."

"You talked to Madame Richmond?" she demanded.

He shrugged, and she saw the bulldog in his jaws bite down more firmly.

"Why do you want me to do this?" she said. "What do you get out of this? I don't sing in fucking public. Not anymore."

"Who cares? I told you once that even singing would be a better career than," and he waved his hand at the Mahogany, "this."

"Oh, fuck you," she spat before she could stop herself, but he didn't even notice.

"My boss wants you to do it, Ty," he said, and just like that his mouth was no longer relaxed. Like his hands, it was preparing for another version of this conversation. "And that means I'm telling you to do it."

"You're telling me," she growled. "You're *telling* me."

"You're goddamn right I am," he said, and in a flash he was one step closer. "You're God. Damn. Right."

She wondered if Detective Segrest was watching, if Dr. Salt stayed to see if the job was done. Probably not, she reasoned. He was accustomed to his orders being followed, to his creations doing exactly as they were programmed. She stared into her father's eyes, and tried to imagine wearing a mask, the same kind of mask her mother must have been wearing in the last few months of their marriage, as he grew inside Limestone and she grew outside it. Ty would need it now, and tomorrow at Derby. She didn't see a way to refuse what Dr. Salt was asking her to do, but an idea was occurring to her, and it helped her don the disguise.

"Fine," she said. "Sure. Whatever."

He looked surprised, but also pleased, the way a wolf might look upon finding its quarry hemmed in by thorns. She wanted so much to be more than a rabbit in his eyes. *One day I will make you afraid of me*, she thought.

"Good," he said, and that was all. He moved around her, back toward the inn. She didn't bother turning to watch him go, instead stared at the crush of flowers without blinking so that she would have something to blame her watering eyes for. She wasn't surprised when a moment later the tulips parted and Camille slunk out from between them. They stared at each other.

"You're the sneakiest person I've ever met," Ty said without emotion.

"I would probably hear that all the time if I had any friends," Camille said.

"I'm your friend," Ty said, and she meant it. She knew by the softening of those ferret features that the other girl heard, and knew.

"Based on that conversation, all three of the people who just left this garden hate you," Camille said languidly. She held a hibiscus between her fingers, spinning it. "Three different, special hatreds."

"Two at least," Ty shrugged. "The cop is just a maybe. But he's a cop. So."

"I heard him talking to my mother," Camille said, the sly look back in her eyes.

"Are you going to tell me what they said?"

"He asked to collect a sample of the carpet from Rosario Vicario's room," she said. "Something about a stain. I guess he means blood."

Ty's eyes rose to the window of Rosario's room.

"No," Ty said. "Bleach. Interesting. Maybe he really is trying to solve this thing."

The curiosity on Camille's face was almost like a stain of its own, but she didn't ask, and Ty admired her restraint. Or maybe it wasn't restraint, but the contentment that came with knowing one would get all the answers one way or another.

"So. Why does the head designer of Limestone want to keep an eye on you at Derby?" Camille said over the top of the flower, eyes like arrows. It was a comfort to Ty that the gaslight illuminating the conversation she'd just endured burned as brightly in Camille's eyes as in her own.

"It's a long story," Ty said. "And I'm going to tell it to you at some point. But here's the short version: they think I'm planning something that's going to fuck them over."

"And would they be right?" Camille said. She carefully removed a petal from the hibiscus and began to chew it thoughtfully.

"They would," Ty said.

Camille's smile spread, as if the garden would soon be on fire and she couldn't wait to dance in the glow.

"Well," she said. "I guess you just need one thing."

"What's that?"

"A big fucking hat."

CHAPTER 46

TY

Ty could hear the crowd from the barbershop around the corner – the night before Derby, and everyone was cramming in for a line-up, a freshening of edges before the parties and parades that tomorrow would be soaked in. Ty had worked on Derby every year in her working life, and tomorrow would have been no different until now, the now created by a young jockey's death and the dominoes that murder knocked down. Ty stepped into Bay's after squeezing between two big guys laughing and talking shit just outside, and found Shavon's eyes on her as soon as she was inside the buzzing gold light of the shop.

"I'm glad it's you," Shavon called over the top of the man's head she was finishing up. She raised her voice to draw the attention of all the people waiting, seated and standing. "Finally somebody with an appointment. Y'all hear that? An *appointment*! That means she's going ahead of some of y'all and don't say shit about it! I'm happy to take your money as long as you wanna wait, but if I don't get to you until midnight, that's on you!"

"You're worth the wait!" somebody shouted from the back, and everybody laughed and nodded. Shavon grinned briefly before grimacing.

"Y'all say that now," she said. "We'll see how you feel at 11:58. Come on, Ty."

She whipped the cape off the man in her chair and sent him smiling out the door, then dusted off the seat for Ty, who sank in with a sigh.

"Glad you could take me," Ty said, and enjoyed the feeling of Shavon getting right to work on her haircut, no instruction required.

"Of course," Shavon said, flicking her eyes over the waiting masses. "Relieved to see a familiar face, honestly. And a woman. People do this every year…all these dudes coming in at the last minute and all of them expecting to be the first in the chair."

"You open tomorrow?" Ty said.

"I think I'll open up in the morning for the *last* last-minute folks. But then I'm shutting down for the day. A girl invited me to a party and I actually wanna go, so I'm going."

"Good for you," Ty said, blinking affirmation as Shavon worked delicately along her ear.

"What about you? I'm assuming you're not working tomorrow if you wanted a cut."

"I'm actually going to the Downs," Ty said, and if she hadn't been getting a haircut she'd have shaken her head to indicate how stupid she understood this was.

"What!" Shavon crowed. "You must have a good feeling about a horse then, huh?"

"You could say that," Ty said. Under the cape her device buzzed and she snaked it out to peer at the screen. It was a message from Ezz.

We need a dry run. You off work?

In the chair at Bay's, Ty typed back quickly.

"Look at you," Shavon smiled, not even pretending not to see who the message was from.

Be there in five.

"Oh hush," Ty said. "It's not like that. It's business"

"You both stay telling yourselves that," Shavon said, smiling.

"If that's what you've gotta do."

Ty was quiet for a moment while Shavon went on cutting. The message from Ezz stirred her stomach – she hadn't been told not to come back, but it was also unclear whether she would be allowed back within the inner sanctum of Ezz and Luz's company. The text was like seeing a bird in the distance: too far to tell if it was a dove carrying an olive branch or a thunderbird leading a storm. Something about the barbershop was like a confession booth.

"We could have been something," Ty said, "but, I think...I think I fucked it up."

"Did you burn down her house?" Shavon said.

Ty looked at her while keeping her head still.

"No. What?"

"Did you put hands on her? Cuss her out?"

"Of fucking course not."

"Look, if you didn't steal from her, put hands on her, none of that...then this is the kind of broken that can be fixed."

"I don't know if that's true," Ty said. "I lied to her. I hid things. Important things."

"The truth is important," Shavon nodded. "But I don't think we can ever show someone who we are all at once. We do it in pieces, and sometimes the pieces come out in the wrong order. If you kept a secret and it hurt her, yeah, that sucks. But it means you can keep a secret. And with work, someone can then trust you to keep *their* secrets. A secret is only a secret until it's something you both share."

Ty's throat suddenly felt like a volcano, a sob like lava inching to the top. She nodded silently.

"It's okay," Shavon said softly. "Don't let her give up on you. She's always looking for an excuse, but you don't have to give it to her. Now stop moving around."

She pinched Ty's shoulder like a big sister would; Ty smiled weakly, and then they delved into the comfort of small talk: what Ty was wearing for Derby, the weather for tomorrow – "ordinarily I would hope all those rich fucks got rained on, but if y'all are going then here's to sunshine" – and Shavon was just brushing the explosion of tiny blonde fuzz from Ty's nape when the form of Ezzardine Clayton appeared in the doorway. The faint jingle of the door was drowned out by the buzz of conversation, but inside Ty roared an orchestra. She paid Shavon silently.

"Glad you had me cut you last night," Shavon said, and dapped Ezz up when she reached the chair. "Popping in here."

"I knew it would be," Ezz said, ignoring Ty. She slid her eyes over the rest of the shop. "Looking good over here, Shavvy."

"Booked and busy," Shavon agreed, and motioned at who was next to fill the chair, a young person with a neon green Caesar. He settled in looking relieved, as if he hadn't been at all sure this haircut was guaranteed. "You see how my little museum has grown?"

Shavon nodded at the portraits that had commanded Ty's attention her first time in the shop, and Ezz wandered over to take it in as if for the first time. She ran her fingers over the gold-plated tags bearing the name.

"You've got Granddad looking right," she said, smiling softly, then directed her eyes at Ty. The shock of Ezz actually addressing her almost left her dizzy. "You see this?"

"Yeah, I got the full tour awhile back. Did you say granddad?"

Ezz chuckled, letting her finger hover over one portrait, a young Black man sitting with arms and legs crossed, fine-featured with a barely-there smile.

"Lonnie Clayton," Ezz said, staring fondly at the portrait. "The youngest ever to win the Derby. He was fifteen. I have no idea if we're actually related, but I always say he's my great-great-great-grandad since we have the same last name. They erased so much of our history."

"Sometimes you've gotta make your own connections," Shavon said. "He's family if you say he's family. You're both tiny and love horses, so…"

"I'm not tiny!" Ezz protested.

"Like we don't all know you wore a high-top fade for years solely to give yourself a couple extra inches," Shavon teased. "You ain't got to lie to kick it!"

"I'mma kick your ass, how about that?" Ezz laughed. "Let's get the hell out of here, Ty. We don't have to take this abuse."

They headed for the door but were intercepted just as it opened by a young woman on the arm of a masc dreadlocked beauty.

"Ezz! Hi! Remember me? Donia. I heard there's a party at the Pink tomorrow night?"

"More than a party!" Ezz cheesed. "A celebration!"

"Word! What are we celebrating?" the girl said.

"It's a surprise."

With that, Ezz whisked herself and Ty out onto the sidewalk, where the far-off sounds of a marching band echoed down the street from what felt like every direction.

"A celebration, huh?" Ty said. "I guess the planning session went well last night."

"We've got most of the details worked out. I'll fill you in. We still gotta figure out how we're going to get into the executive area at Cavehill but…"

"I have to fill you in too," Ty said quickly. "I have a solution."

Ezz glanced at her, impressed.

"Well, okay then."

They walked in silence, Ty hyper-aware of the distance between them on the narrow sidewalk. Somehow Ezz walked just far enough away that their knuckles never brushed, and it made Ty wilt.

"Do you remember when there was only one parade?" Ezz

said, and Ty looked at her, glad to be pulled out of her own head. They stood waiting at a crosswalk. Around them tourists crushed close, live-streaming or laughing with friends. "They say this whole area used to be quiet during Derby – that the action was really only on Broadway and around Cavehill. But it gets bigger every year, flashier. Some of the old heads that come into Bay's always say that Central Park used to be for locals only. Can you imagine?"

"No," Ty said as they crossed the street, almost forced apart by a gaggle of already-inebriated tourists. "It's been a hub for the last parade for as long as I can remember."

"Everyone tells me I'm too young to remember," Ezz said as they strolled, the concrete entrance to the park just ahead. "But I remember going to Central Park with my parents. I remember going to see Shakespeare there. The big wooden stage, you know? They had an all-Black cast for *Midsummer Night's Dream* and I remember sitting on my mom's lap and watching and all the buds on the trees were white."

Ty nodded.

"I believe you. There's a lot my mom always said I was too young to remember, but I know I do."

"Like what?"

"I don't know. Stuff."

They were veering toward the entrance but everyone already in the park was pushing out, heading for the street, where they would gather to watch the parade go by. The parade wouldn't reach this end of the route for another half hour, but everyone wanted to be closer than everyone else. None of the metalbreds on display in the parades would actually be running in the Derby, but everyone who had money down liked to think that by observing the machines up close, they might get a glimpse of something like a giveaway, a hint at what made a winner tick. Ty wondered what they would all think if they knew the truth – that the glossy creatures flowing down the streets and around the track had a soul that was kept chained by an algorithm. Tomorrow she would find out.

"You've never outright said it," Ezz said when they finally made their way into the park. It spread out before them, golden in the approach of sunset, the distant shrieks of kids rising over the small hills from the splash park. "But your mom...is she...?"

"Dead? Yes."

Ezz's face crunched. Ty took a deep breath. On this day of all days, to be answering this question. Two years ago today – in one hour – she watched a bullet enter her mother's skull. She and Luis becoming shadows.

"She was murdered," Ty said.

"Do they know who did it?"

She could tell her. Ty could feel her tongue stirring in the bed of her mouth to form his name. But there would be no taking it back, and no matter what Shavon said about secrets and how they changed when they were shared, this was one secret she had to keep for a little longer.

Ezz was no fool. She would see the two paths Ty walked on, and recognize the one's disguise. She would think, perhaps, that to Ty, Rosario wasn't important. That Ty had been using her all along. And maybe she had been. Ty cringed from herself.

"This..." Ty said, swallowing. "This guy she kinda knew."

"And he killed her? Why?"

"It's kind of a long story."

"Okay, but it's a story I don't know," Ezz said softly. "So..."

Ty studied the sidewalk. This was Ezz's forgiveness. She was forgiving Ty for her secrets – the ones she knew – and for taking the needle, for having a hidden agenda. She was forgiving her for a harm Ty was still enacting. The softness in Ezz's voice only made it worse.

"My mom was an activist," Ty said. "Kind of."

"Yeah, I think I knew that."

"Well, she had this meeting scheduled with…" *Brian Benedict*, she thought. But she couldn't say it. "Somebody important. And I heard her talking to a friend about it in the days leading up to…that day. And she said she was nervous. She said she didn't trust him. But when the night came, she went anyway. Her friend went with her. He died too."

"Do you know why?" Ezz asked, and Ty couldn't help but think that if Ezz's parents hadn't died, if Ezz hadn't withdrawn from the horse world, that she would hear these pieces of a story and be able to piece them together: two activists dying side by side? A gun in his hand? Ezz's own grief had made her a non-witness. For Ty, this was both painful and a relief. They were walking across the sun-soaked grass now, slowly.

"Why what?" Ty said.

"Why she went, even if she didn't trust him?"

"I think she…," Ty started, then stopped. "I think she thought that whatever she was setting out to do was important. More important than…"

Me, she thought.

"More important than anything else," she finished.

She could feel Ezz looking at her, could feel her deciding whether to pull back the layers on this onion, to delve into everything she knew Ty was not saying. This is what Detective Segrest had done, and ultimately decided not to do. He closed the case and Ty's mother and Luis stayed gone, and life went on. For some.

"What do you remember?" Ezz asked. "From before? Your earliest memories?"

"I remember horses," Ty said. "With my mom. I remember her always gone, at a rally or something. Dragging me to the stables to watch her ride on weekends. She loved horses and she loved Louisville. Couldn't go anywhere without running into somebody she knew – horse people or protest people or friends from her job. Horses horses horses."

"It was horses horses horses for me too," Ezz said. Ty glanced at her and the ache written across her face was almost hard to look at. "Before my parents died, we would spend more time on horses than off."

"That would have been my mom's dream," Ty said, and couldn't quite keep the bitterness out of her voice.

"You didn't like horses?"

They were approaching the stage now, the amphitheater empty at its feet. On the wooden terraces children ran in and out of the shadows screaming and chasing each other.

"I did," Ty said, settling on a stone bench alongside Ezz. "When I was younger. With Joelle. But with my mom, they became a sort of...battleground? Maybe I would have loved them again if I didn't feel like I was competing with them."

"Real," Ezz said, tilting her head sideways. "Petty, but real."

"Petty how?"

"You couldn't put your shit aside and just get into what your mom was sharing with you?"

"It was more complicated than that," Ty said, bristling.

"How?"

"She never wanted to be alone with me," Ty said, and then stopped, surprised. She'd never thought of it this way, and now that the words were out of her mouth, they were too true. Now, free in the air, they swelled, too large to stuff back into the box they sprang out of. She took a deep breath and continued. "At home, she and my dad would fight nonstop. Sometimes get physical. When he would be at work or out and it was just me and her, she would grab our coats and say, *Let's go.* Always something. *Let's go riding. Let's go down to Cavehill.* She was always on the move. Never sitting still, never wanting to just sit and talk to me. I think I reminded her too much of my dad... His name. His attitude about horses. Maybe if I was…"

She stopped. She felt as if she had just vomited on the pavement, stared down at her feet as if her insides would be staring back.

"What?" Ezz said softly.

"Maybe if I wasn't me, she would never have gone that night," Ty said.

"No," Ezz said. "You're doing that thing that hurt people do when their pain has started making itself at home."

"What?"

"It's gotten under your skin," Ezz said, looking at her intently. "It's started to get comfortable. And you've gotten comfortable with it. You've started to believe maybe you deserve the pain. And you don't. Grief tells a lot of lies. Trust me."

"How can you talk to me like you're on the other side of it?" Ty said, sharper than she meant. "Like your grief is behind you? You don't even ride anymore, Ezz."

"And I never will," Ezz said, fast. "Maybe that's how I keep grief behind me."

Ty said nothing. She'd cried about her mother before, but somehow she knew that if she cried here, now, that it would be like wrenching the cap from a shaken bottle. Somewhere in her bones she knew she would explode at some point – it just couldn't be here. She'd rather save it. One more day 'til Derby.

"There's Luz," she said instead, nodding.

Ezz followed her finger to the figure of Luz, striding between the combatting hordes of youth, one of whom now stood like a director near the edge of stage right, explaining everyone's particular role in the violence they were enacting. One pretended to swing his sword in Luz's direction; with a snap of her neck she froze him with an icy glare, his sword fixed in space.

"She Medusa'd that ass," Ezz cackled. Ty laughed, relieved, and they both moved to greet Luz as she climbed the auditorium steps.

"Y'all okay?" Luz called, peering at them. Ty reminded herself to wipe the slate of her face clean.

"All good," she said.

"Those kids are eight and they're taller than me," Luz complained, hip-bumping Ezz in greeting. They were together again, all three. Ty was grateful that she had been allowed to return, without lectures and ceremony. "What the hell are they feeding these little mutants?"

"Chicken nuggets," Ty said. "And only chicken nuggets."

"Funny you said chicken nugget," Luz said, smiling broadly. "That's literally what our thing looks like."

"Our thing?" Ty said.

"Our clicker. Our signal. For tomorrow." Luz fished in her bag, made of collaged DC Comics fabric. Her hand emerged clutching a shiny black device the size and shape of…a chicken nugget.

"I cased it in two halves of a car key fob," she explained, handing it to Ezz to inspect. "If security sees it somehow they'll just think one of us drives a very, very old car."

"Which button?" Ezz said, studying it.

"Trunk."

"Cool." Ezz handed it over to Ty. It looked like any old-school fob she'd ever seen, before jewelry and fashionable-looking little doo-dads edged in and sent the bulky fobs the way of the dodo.

"So we press the trunk button and…what happens?" Ty asked. "Sparks fly? Will something explode?"

"It won't hurt the horses, right?" Ezz said, frowning, as if the idea of something exploding hadn't occurred to her.

"It shouldn't," Luz said. "The Aristidean component isn't a mechanical device that will short out. It's just barrier code. There's a mechanism that provides something like scene understanding – light estimation, plane detection – but ramped up to interpret audio input the way a horse would. It's all to make the metalbreds more realistic. The Aristidean component is integrated to bar the bot from making its own decisions. But the way Rosario and Martha wrote the virus, it will register as audio input, but interfere with and damage the Aristidean component."

"You might as well have told me that the Aristidean component is a microwave for tiny pizzas and I'd believe you," Ty said seriously.

"Save the pizza talk for a celebration if it works," Ezz said. "You ready to try it?"

Luz nodded once, and Ty deposited the clicker safely back in her hands.

"Then let's get to our spot."

Ezz led the way down the auditorium steps; when she reached the stage, she was met by the same army of kids armed with wooden weapons. Another kid took up a mock dueling stance before Ezz's palm connected with his forehead in a gently forceful mush.

"Don't even think about it, cub," she said, and marched backstage. Luz seemed to know where she was headed, and Ty shrugged at the kids, watching them go. No one pulled a sword on her and she felt mildly offended.

Backstage was a curling staircase that led up to one of the wooden towers built into the set. Ty had only been to this park once or twice in her life, let alone on the stage. She admired the ease with which Luz and Ezz climbed up to the ramparts, as if they were true royalty and through the correct pair of glasses this castle would gleam as gold and abundant as they themselves.

"Here we go," Ezz said when they reached the top; she stood to the side to allow Luz and then Ty access to the circular tower's nest. She looked Ty in the eye and winked, all tension forgotten, and in Ty's mind the sun was already down and Luz had suddenly decided she had somewhere important to be.

Instead, the three of them clustered at the edge of the wall, looking down over the park with a perfect view of the street, widened a decade ago, and thus the arrival of the parade.

"Perfect!" Luz cried.

"Timing and execution, babies," Ezz boasted, and leaned coolly against the wood. Ty leaned too – they had no job here, only watching. Again their arms brushed, and when Ezz didn't move to avoid it, Ty froze, reluctant to breathe, to do anything that might break this tiny, subtle contact.

"The band gets bigger every year," Luz said, shaking her head. "But I guess so do the crowds."

She was right – the sidewalks teemed with people, all of them cheering and swaying to the arrival of music and confetti and brass. The throngs sported hats and papier-mâché horse heads; by the end of the parade people with breasts would be flashing them to the street-sweepers, alcohol and excitement and nightfall all pouring into a single overflowing cup of abandon.

"If this works, they're going to freak," Ezz said softly. The tiny warmth of her on Ty's arm expanded as she pressed closer, like morning passing into noon on Ty's skin.

"What if the metalbreds go crazy?" Luz said, eyes scanning the audience rapidly. "Like the one Ty saw at the Limestone gala? What if someone gets hurt?"

"There are kids here," Ty added. She was concerned, but the concern was having trouble breaking through the noise of warmth besieging her brain.

"Is there a way to do only one bot?" Ezz said, but even Ty knew the answer. Luz was already shaking her head.

"No, it's a frequency, and they're all present. If I had a bunch more time and Rosario's brain, I could hack Limestone and find out all of their individual foundational codes…make a tiny virus to signal each one. But…"

Ezz waved the rest of the explanation away, nodding. In the

process her arm broke away from Ty. The effect was immediate relief, and disappointment.

"We're just going to have to see," Ezz said. "Let's see how many metalbreds they have, plus how many handlers. If it's too many then…then maybe we just don't. Today."

Luz said nothing and Ezz nodded. Today was the only practice they would get. They stood in silence, gazing at the marching band and the baton twirlers and, Ty noted as a new attraction, a woman in a bikini carrying a hand-cannon that shot roses out onto the onlookers. Then came the metalbreds.

Three of them, surrounded on all sides by rose cannons and shining brass instruments that crashed out the tune of a song Ty didn't recognize. A real horse, even a well-trained one, would be skittish with the flurry of activity and noise. But the metalbreds stepped briskly, unbothered, ears relaxed and nostrils unflared. Ty couldn't help but wonder if they were terrified, if the Aristidean component bound down their fear, forced their feet forward.

"What do you think?" Luz said under her breath.

"Only three," Ezz said.

"Nine handlers," Ty said, noting the walkers clad in Limestone gray, including the people on horseback.

"Three per," Luz said thoughtfully. "If they freak, they should be able to get them under control. At least for a moment. Plus they're surrounded by the band so…"

"Gives people time to run," Ezz said.

"I say we do it," Ty said. Her heart was starting to shudder. She had seen the wild freedom of the metalbred at Joelle's farm…something young and barefoot inside her wanted to see it again. It would be like watching a sword slice through manacles. Would they know right away, the horses? Would anything change? Maybe even with the bond of the Aristidean component fallen away, they would continue in this life, no idea of what freedom really tasted like, or what it meant to truly be a horse…

"Ten more paces and they're in range," Luz said, glancing at Ezz.

Ezz screwed her mouth up, thinking, eyes taking it all in, as if looking for a reason to call it off. The metalbreds trotted on, heads held high, as convincing as any real animal and as beautiful. The people on the sidelines reached for them even though they were too far to touch.

"Do it," said Ezz, and Ty watched Luz's thumb immediately shift to the trunk button of the old car fob.

"I'm not going to count down, I'm just going to do it," she whispered, and Ty understood that she was talking to herself, a reminder to *just do it*. Tomorrow. The horses trotted onward, and so did the noise; everyone on horseback smiled wide and bright in the late afternoon sun, the night before the most famous horse race in the country.

Ty didn't see Luz's thumb press the button, but she heard it – an audible snap, a sound as old-fashioned as typewriter keys or the click of a mouse. Two clicks: once pressing down, and again when the button rose.

High in the wooden castle, they were all holding their breaths, and down on the ground the glittering army of the parade shuddered into a new song, the crash of cymbals making all three girls jump, bringing Ezz and Ty's arms – and now hips – together once more. The cymbal made them think something had happened, something of note, and Ty watched Luz's fingers grip the rampart edge and lean far over, eyes round.

But the cymbals crashed again, and again, and soon they realized that the percussionists' enthusiasm was the only drama unfolding. The metalbreds' hooves were too far away to hear, and muted by brass, but the horses clip-clopped onward as perfect and obedient as always, their necks arched to the same equine geometry. The riders beamed as before, no helmets needed when riding the most predictable machine that existed.

"What the fuck?" Luz whispered, and the click-CLICK sounded again as she pressed the button once more, then again. "What the *fuck*?"

"What happened?" Ezz said, and Luz was too busy cursing, but Ty heard it – the relief. The kids who had clustered on stage with their swords had made their way to the parade's edge; Ezz's eyes rested on them, soft and relaxed.

"I don't know," Luz grumbled. "It doesn't work. I know I translated it right. Maybe we were just out of range? I was pretty careful with the mapping."

"Back to the lab," Ezz said, patting her back. "Add in as much geographical wiggle room as you can. We gotta leave room for shit to hit the fan tomorrow."

"Won't be anything to hit the fan, let alone shit, if our goddamn *thingy* doesn't work," Luz said, glowering. "What the fuck."

"It's okay!" Ezz said, patting her again. "We can go back after…"

"I'm going back *now*," Luz snapped. "We don't have time for this shit! I need to figure this out! We have like 22 hours!"

Ezz nodded quietly.

"Do what you gotta do," Ezz said. "I left a cheesecake in the fridge of your lab."

Luz turned on her, eyes glowing like an angry cat.

"A *what*?"

"A cheesecake. I left it in your fridge."

"What the fuck, Ezzardine?" Luz cried, and Ty watched them with wide eyes. "Did you think I was going to fail?"

"Of course not."

"Then why would my favorite *I-failed-and-I-need-to-snack* food be in my fridge?"

"Hey, technically it's *my* favorite I-failed-and-I-need-to-snack food too."

Luz surveyed her with a fiery glare before turning on her heel and stomping down the castle steps. When she was halfway across the stage, Ezz called after her.

"You can do it, Mer! I believe in you!"

"You also believe in dragons," Luz called back. "So fuck off!"

Ty and Ezz watched her go, the din from the parade quieter now that the biggest section had passed.

"You believe in dragons?" Ty said.

"Small ones," Ezz said, sighing noisily. "Why the fuck not? Have you ever seen *actual* animals on Earth? If a platypus is real then I'm not letting go of dragons."

"Maybe they live in the ocean," Ty shrugged. "At the very bottom. We don't know, like, anything about the ocean for real."

"I could get with water dragons," Ezz said, considering.

They had moved apart to let Luz down the stairs, and now, in her absence, the space between them felt vast, too vast, and hungry, as if waiting for something to float down and roost within it. The idea filled Ty with a vague panic – that this opportunity could be taken from her by nothing.

"Tomorrow is going to be wild," Ty said. She tried, for just this moment, to be on one path and one path only. Ezz made her want to forget the other one entirely. Not yet.

Ezz shifted her weight from one foot to the other, and like magic the warmth was back, Ezz's hip and side against Ty's, the bare skin above her elbow like the first riddle on a scavenger hunt.

"How so?" she said.

"Even if the virus doesn't work, the plants will. Right?"

"Oh, for sure," Ezz nodded. "That's tested. Those bitches are going to sprout."

"All over Cavehill?"

"Wherever we put them."

"This is *really* going to be wild," Ty said, turning her eyes back to the parade. Like magpies to diamonds, though, they were drawn back to Ezz's face when the other girl laughed.

"You're wishing you had never come to my party now, huh?" Ezz said. "In deeper than you intended."

Ty thought of the two paths she walked on, one beside Luz and Ezz, and the other a dark path through her own rage. Except for maybe the young woman who had spoken to Ty in the diner – Irma – no one knew what Ty knew. She was alone in this shadowed world. But she was also here, now. With Ezz.

"I'm where I want to be," Ty said, the gold sun in her eyes making her squint.

Ezz studied her, frowning, and in a flash Ty realized she knew this frown, knew what it was rooted in, and her skin awoke in a jungle of hope. Ezz raised her hand and cupped it around Ty's brow, so they could see each other without squinting, eyes open and – almost – honest.

"Good," she said softly.

CHAPTER 47

LUZ

Luz couldn't work in the green room anymore, taken over by vines, her worktable's legs broken. She had gathered the necessary supplies and relocated to the digital lab, where she hunched over the table with the chicken nugget clicker opened, its guts spread across the surface. She had figured out the problem shortly after she returned, leaving Ty and Ezz nuzzling in Central Park. A simple bracket missing in the code, which she fixed quickly. The mechanism would work now, she was sure. But would everything else? She was still sitting there when she heard Ezz and Ty making their way down the stairs from the maze above, their laughter soft and low. She coughed to announce herself, so they might turn back for the moonlight if privacy is what they envisioned. The idea of them sitting out in the silver together while she stayed here made her feel both relieved and lonely – was being alone worse than admitting she didn't want to be?

But they heard her, and kept coming; a moment later were sitting across from her at the table, their mouths a little puffy from kissing. She smiled at the thought that they would think she wouldn't notice, that the world wouldn't. She could feel Ezz's forgiveness, her opening, joining them in the room.

"How's it going?" Ezz said, nodding down at the clicker. She saw all the wires and circuits and perceived chaos where Luz found order.

"It's fine," Luz said. "Just need to sew it back up."

"So we're doing this," Ty said. Her voice was shiny with need. "We're doing this."

Luz nodded, glancing over at her device, where a text from Zarita flashed. A single emoji: a bird. Luz waved her hand over the screen to send it back into blackness.

"We're doing this," she said.

"It sounds like you two have already worked out most of the details," Ty said, and Luz could still hear the slant in her words, leftover hurt feelings like cursive letters. "But what else is left?"

"We already talked to Dr. Aldana. She's going to give Luz access to the speakers before she and her kids perform before the race. We sync with the speakers, play the frequency. Sync with the Jumbotron while we're there. Wait 'til we're ready, then click. Done. Boom."

"It sounds so simple like that," Luz said. She clicked the remote nugget back together.

"Simple is good," Ezz said, slapping her palms on the table. She was optimistic, hopeful.

"And what if someone notices what we're doing?" Ty said. "Derby has a lot of security. They're going to be watching for suspicious shit."

"Speaking of security...," Luz said, and felt the blush invading her cheeks before they even looked at her. The layers of Ty had perhaps been peeled back with the revelation of the needle, and though Luz had showed them what was at the core of her own onion-layers – her vines – there were other things she hadn't told them. "I may have...already hacked into the security communication network of Cavehill Downs."

Ezz's neck lengthened like a periscope.

"Pardon?" she said, blinking.

"This was before we ever had a plan or knew half the shit we know," Luz said quickly. "I'd been working on my vine project, not really sure what I was gonna do. I thought I was going to be doing it alone, so I just...learned as much as I could."

Ezz looked like she wanted to say more, but Ty jumped in.

"Sounds good to me," she said. "So we can listen in to what they're saying and we'll at least know if they're onto us."

"But we still need a diversion," Luz said. "Something to hold everyone's eye while we sync up with the system. Something that will get security riled up too, so they're focused on that."

They thought for a moment, three factories of wheels spinning. Then a slow smile spread across Ezz's face.

"Like, maybe, the reappearance of a metalbred everyone thought was gone?"

Ty's brow wrinkled for a blink until it dawned on her.

"Cloud Parliament," she said. "Joelle might..."

"She'll do it," Ezz said. "She wants justice for Martha and Rosario as much as we do."

Ty stayed silent, thinking.

"She'll be worried about them hurting the horse," Ty said.

"They won't get a chance to hurt him," Ezz said. "By the time they might try, we'll be sending out the virus to fry the Aristidean component. Besides, with all those witnesses? People who wanted horseracing banned because of animal abuse? It would look really bad."

Ty looked grim, but picked up her device. Luz watched her send the message to Joelle, thinking of what tomorrow would truly look like. She had told her mother she'd come home soon. But would she? Would Kentucky continue to be home? If Zarita's plans and her own aligned perfectly, she imagined Limestone crumbling, and people like her parents stepping up to lead. If her mother knew what she planned to do, would she throw her daughter in the back of their Toyota and drive north, or would she allow hope to kindle in her chest? What if Luz called and said, *Mami, do you want to help me bring it down?*

"So what about the seeds?" Ty said, and her tone pulled Luz from her own thoughts. There was a hunger in her voice, so subtle it was almost invisible. Hungry for what, Luz wondered? For violence? Even Luz wasn't sure, but she was wary.

"What about them?" she asked.

"We want them everywhere, right?" Ty said.

"Yes," Luz said. "But there are proximity rules we need to be careful with. You saw what they can do: if we drop them too close to where people will be, they can really fuck someone up."

"So?" Ty said.

"So," Luz snapped, "*so* we need to be careful, because there will be people there who have nothing to do with this. People like backside workers. People like the people serving drinks. People like children. *People.* We can't be so focused on the enemy that we forget who we want to protect."

"Right," Ty nodded, cheeks flushing. "Of course. I was just thinking about the Limestone executives, I guess. I'm sorry. That was shitty of me."

There was a moment of silence before Ezz coughed.

"The *enemy*," Ezz teased gently. "Wow."

"You know what I mean," Luz smiled. "Anyway. So okay. Tomorrow just before the race, when I signal the transmission, the kudzu will sprout almost immediately. So we have to have laid the seeds already."

"Exactly how many seeds do you have?" Ezz asked.

"Around two thousand."

"And how many did you drop to make all those vines appear in your lab?"

"One."

Luz could feel them looking at her, dumbfounded, imagining all her thousands of seeds exploding with the same green rage that they had witnessed in the lair. They couldn't quite picture it, but she could.

"Um. Wow. Okay. What about Millionaire's Row? The Limestone executive lounge?"

But Ty interrupted, no longer texting.

"I'll take care of that," she said quickly. "I have an in. Just give me the seeds and I'll make it happen."

Luz found herself avoiding Ty's eyes again, the hungry thing they contained. Ty may have told them one secret, but she surely had more. Ezz didn't seem to notice, too focused on the plans. Maybe, Luz thought guilty, she herself only noticed it because she too still had something to hide.

"Cool," said Luz, looking down. "I'll couple the frequency for the seeds and the horses. One click, and then bang, bang."

"So we're doing this?" Ezz said, laughing. "It's still not much of a plan. We're not, like, spies and shit. Just a bunch of girls."

"When has that never changed the world?" Luz said quietly, then took a bite of cheesecake.

CHAPTER 48

TY

Flocks of drones circled the triple spires of Cavehill Downs like buzzing, black eagles – journalists and security alike watching Derby unfold from the sky. The drones didn't make Ty nervous; what she carried they couldn't see. She walked along the bright tongue of the red carpet laid at the VIP entrance, three inches taller on account of her heels, platforms, velvet green. Even if the drones zoomed in on her, they would see only a young white woman wearing a gold dress sewn to look like coins, a hat that spread over her shoulders, hiding her bald blonde head. They would see a silk purse barely larger than her device, clutched in her manicured fist. They would see a bracelet encircling her wrist.

They wouldn't see the tiny tin of mints in her purse. Even if security emptied her clutch, they would take no notice of something the size of a container of floss. The label on the tin said *Peppermints*, and she was a young white woman entering a social scenario. Of course she would have them. Beside her, Camille held up her palm and breathed into it.

"I think I need a mint," she said, deadpanning. "Do you have one?"

"Shut up," Ty gritted out between her hard-smiling teeth. "Like, wow. Shut *up*."

They walked up to the security checkpoint barring the

entrance to the Downs and they both smiled, removing sunglasses, necks arching like swans.

"Check," the man in the booth said, and two other men emerged from behind him, bearing wands. Ty could see from their eyes that the two girls wearing dresses were already low threat. She supposed if there were jewels on display at the Downs, a woman in a dress such as hers might be given a second glance. But there was nothing seen as capable of being stolen present at the Cavehill – and robbing the gambling counters at gunpoint seemed very male in its stupidity – so there was certainly nothing to fear from two white girls in lace.

"Who should I give my ticket to?" Ty chirped.

"Up ahead," the first man said. "Are you two alone?"

"Yes," she said. And thought silently: *For now*.

The wands waved them through.

Camille and Ty were checked against a hidden list and given invisible stamps on their hands. Then they waltzed through security, immediately swallowed by the sweaty glamour of the Kentucky Derby. They were in.

Photos were being taken of them, not because anyone mistook Ty for one of the many celebrities arriving at this entrance, but because it was the photographers' job; any images of her would be scanned against a list of famous faces whose photos would be worth publishing online. Likely the images of her would be cast aside as soon as the photographers' editors realized she was no one. And *no one* she hoped to remain. Her hat hid her head and her sunglasses hid her face. Camille was a slightly different story.

"Miss Richmond!" called one of the closer paparazzos. "Your first event of the season! Who made your dress? Who are the shoes?"

Ty felt her muscles tremble, torn between pressing past the knot of cameras and staying near Camille. The plan was to split up – Ty heading for the Limestone suites and Camille for Millionaire's Row – but not this soon. Ty wanted to be photographed as little as possible for one thing; for another thing, she wasn't sure how Camille would hold up. Shelter-in-place Camille. Homebody Camille. Despise-the-public Camille.

But Camille was prepared. She didn't smile widely, but instead gazed patiently around at the many cameras, answering questions.

"A local designer," she said. "Clem Woodfolk. Look her up."

"Where are your sisters? Who's your friend?" The voices clamored over each other.

"Oh, I'm sure they'll be along," she said. Then under her breath to Ty: "Go."

Ty stepped quickly out of the wash of limelight. Her lack of reputation gave her cover. She slipped away, finally removing her shades, toward elevators where ushers waved rose-gold lights at all entering wrists, the scanner reading her invisible stamp and sorting her accordingly. The usher gestured her toward the lift that would carry her to the upper-upper floors, the fancy areas that she had always assumed existed but had never seen. The usher didn't know that she was entering not as a real guest but as a trick pony with a glittering harness. She would soon be surrounded by rich people. So what? She'd cleaned their toilets already, and was paid well to do so. It was good work. And even singing for them was bearable. She once sang for lots of people. But today she would also be singing for the man who killed had Martha and Rosario. The man she knew had killed her mother. As she rode the elevator up shining floor by shining floor, she tried to imagine her throat lined with honey. Otherwise, when she stood to sing the sound that might come out would be a roar. She swallowed, composing herself as the elevator began to slow. Almost showtime.

The elevator doors slid slowly open and she came face to face with Detective Segrest.

"Oh," she said, jumping back to keep from running into him.

He stood to the side to allow her out onto the carpeted floor of the executive suites, snaking his arm in behind her to hold the door open.

"Miss Redson," he said. "We meet again."

"What are you doing here?" she said, and maybe some part of her hoped it came out casually, but the slightest squint of his left eye told her he'd heard the whisper of a squeak in her voice and was looking for the source of her mousiness.

"Working," he said.

"On Derby Day?"

"I'm certainly not the only one," he said, and gestured at the half-dozen uniformed wait staff standing along one edge of the room, platters in hand, spines at attention. Ty always noticed the soldiers in the army of the service industry – she was one, after all. But the detective acknowledging them felt unusual. Pointed, somehow.

"Their jobs make a little more sense, in context," she pressed. "What sort of work does a detective have to do at Cavehill Downs on the day of the biggest race of the year?"

"Half of my job is watching," he said. "And here there's a lot to see."

Inside the elevator now, he allowed his arm to drop down to his side, and the doors began their slow reunion.

"See you later," she said, unsure of what else to say.

"Not if I see you first," he said, and part of her felt she was being trolled. She might have even called him a pervert if it weren't for the weariness in his eyes. But he let the doors shut without saying anything more, and she turned to face the room.

In a cleanwork uniform, she was accustomed to blending in, becoming part of the walls and carpet. Today she became part of the crowd, all the people in the room sufficiently warmed by bourbon and mint juleps, all wanting to marvel over her as they marveled over each other, hands reaching for but not quite touching the arching gold hat that Camille had pulled from a dusty pink box in her closet, another freebie provided for an event she would never deign to attend. Ty wished Camille were here now, someone to retreat to the edge of the room with, to escape the press of humid bodies that were clustered close and breathing the smell of money into one another's faces over and under and through the soft ribbon of violin. Ty's eyes found the source: a small circular stage near the center of the room, a pair of violinists and a cellist playing cheerily away while a thin Black man swayed at a microphone. Ty had mistaken the sound of his humming for an instrument.

"Oh, good," said a voice, and she knew it was for her by the sound and pitch of it, homing in like a missile from a distant cannon. "You decided to join us after all. Just under the wire."

Dr. Salt presented himself before her in a seersucker suit indistinguishable from the other seersucker suits revolving around the room. He looked down at his watch, which glinted. So did his smile. He was in no way remarkable from the other middle-aged men in the room, and yet as he stood before her, alone, it was like looking at a shard of glass sticking out of a pie.

"Of course," she said cooly. "You said I'd be compensated, and I don't pass up easy money."

"Some wouldn't call what you do easy," he said, and she was satisfied by the brief spark of surprise that passed through his eyes, expecting her to be cowed. Ezz had prepared her for how to play it. *He'll be watching you closely*, she said, and he was. "Most of us only sing in our showers."

"Well, I mostly do too these days," she said.

"Ah, *these days*," he said. "But you used to be quite an entertainer for one so young. What happened? Singer to cleaner seems like an unusual choice."

I needed an in to kill your boss, she thought, but instead she just shrugged.

"I wanted something more objective," she said. "A voice can be heard as good or bad, but clean is clean."

"I see," he said. "Well, I understand the need for stability. After...everything."

She looked into his eyes, seeing her mother. Was he in on it too? Did everyone at Limestone know what happened to her? Which particular type of cruel was he being?

"I think I'm on pretty solid ground," she said, thinking of everything in her purse.

"I'm sure," he said silkily.

Then came her father.

"I told him you wouldn't be late," he said. If Dr. Salt was silk, her father was burlap. He'd had a drink or two since being allowed in here among the seersuckers, and the flush in his cheeks made his rented tux look more rented. He smiled too much when he was drunk and no one had pissed him off yet. She felt a sudden hardening of her skin, wondering now if he, the corporate ladder-climber, knew – if he too had known all along. *Honey*, she thought. *Honey.*

"Not for something as important as this," she said.

"Good," both men said. She craved a dark corner.

"Roger will finish his set at 4," Dr. Salt said, motioning with his head to the man crooning on stage. "You're on then. Grab a drink! We couldn't convince Trouble to bartend for us, but the folks we *could* get still know what they're doing."

He winked and her smile felt perilously close to breaking. Her father said nothing else, just followed along after Dr. Salt like a crab scuttling on a beach. Embarrassing. The blush in her cheeks felt like a betrayal – why should she have any response to her father at all? She imagined life with him as a distant stranger – how her life would be with him ten years in her rearview. Maybe it would take that long, or even longer, to sever a connection as thick as blood.

"I don't see the resemblance," said someone on her left, too close. She knew it and she didn't. She'd heard it on TV. She'd heard it in the dark and dust.

Brian Benedict.

His suit was gray and one texture away from shiny, the way a shark's fin looks just a shade lighter than the body beneath the waves. She stared at him, plunging into an ocean of shame, because as much as she wished she were the brave voyager with a harpoon at the ready, all she felt at the sight of his too-close, too-polite smile was the same blank, paralyzing fear that a sailor in a liferaft might feel.

"If I hadn't known," he went on, gazing after her father in the crowd. "I wouldn't have guessed."

He turned to reflect her stare then, head-on, eyes like wet pavement. "I would say you probably look much more like your mother."

He waited for her to reply, and she realized, while floating in that concrete ocean, that the worst part wasn't that the man who killed her mother was talking about her mother to her face. In a movie, she thought, the sinister villain in the shark suit would be saying this because he was sending a message to the nosy daughter investigating her mother's disappearance. But standing here at the edge of the city's shiniest party, his hands clasped professionally in front of him, she realized it was worse. He wasn't making a point, not to her. He didn't know what she knew. He knew what *he* knew, and it was for his private enjoyment that he had come to stand beside her. A thrill for his secret amusement. If Martha's mother were in the room, he would have made his way across the room to say hello as well. Rosario's sister. The hanging threads of severed knots he tucked in his palm. She felt herself unraveling.

"Yes, we look alike." She swallowed. "Well, looked. She's dead. I don't know if you knew that."

His face didn't move, but in his eyes, there was something. A fraction more fin appearing above the ocean's lip.

"I think I do recall hearing something about those unfortunate events. My condolences."

"It was to be expected," Ty said, and her voice didn't shake only because she was saying something she truly believed. "When you shake a mountain, you should expect to get buried in the avalanche."

"That's one way to look at it," Benedict said, tipping his head back and forth. "I didn't know she was a mountain shaker."

She almost laughed. What an unnecessary lie.

"Everyone in the horse world knew that," she said, shrugging one shoulder. The lace of her dress scratched against her. She wanted to rip it off. "Maybe you were too high up the mountain to notice."

He was watching her then, actually watching her. She had become a harpoon after all.

"Your father brought you as a guest today?" he said. He wanted to know how easy it would be to have her removed.

"I'm here on Dr. Salt's invitation," she said, gazing out at the crowd, swaying a little to the music. "I'll be singing later."

"I'll be sure not to miss that," he said. He wanted her to flinch. She wouldn't.

"Brian! Come look at Helen's hat! It's *absurd*!" Another shiny guest, another mint julep brandished in the air.

"Excuse me," Benedict said, dipping his head slowly. The smile again, and then she was alone again.

She waited until he had been swallowed by the glittering crowd, then she slipped out her device.

How's everyone doing? She texted quickly. **I might have poked the bear.**

CHAPTER 49

EZZ

Ezz squinted at her device as she squeezed through the throngs of bettors, the snap and glare of the dozens of huge shining display screens sending purple glare across the texts from Ty.

"Poked the bear?" she muttered. "What the hell does that mean?"

She typed back quickly, but a message from Luz came in before she could press send.

Keep it together, Luz said. **We have two hours before the horses go to the gate.**

Ezz imagined Ty up in the same Limestone suites where Brian Benedict prowled, and her pulse went spiky. When Ezz had been envisioning this plan rolling out, her brain had skipped the part where Ty would have to actually rub elbows with the man they were trying to expose. A killer. She had gone straight to the image of him on the Jumbotron, two hundred thousand people in the stands all seeing him for what he was. But first they had to get there.

She also hadn't taken into account her problem with anonymity; she tried to keep her fingers from fiddling with the earpod that usually played jazz while she gambled, but today was filled with the chatter from the security channel. Everyone was accustomed to Ezz's earpod, Luz had argued, so no one would notice. But Ezz did.

"Ezzardine! I haven't seen you at the tables around town in weeks! I should've known you'd show up for Derby though!"

Security at the west entrance, move to the ADA ramp. Someone is blocking it.

"Ezzardine, I didn't get a chance to call you about Rosario. I'm sorry for your loss…"

I need two more of you at the executive entrance. We have a duplicate press pass.

"Who do you have your money on to win today, Miss Clayton?"

She made her way slowly through the brightly-colored hall, half-listening to the half-strangers. The gambling hall had been transformed in the years since Limestone took over, becoming something more akin to a ballroom, the act of placing a bet something like a performance. Ezz had kudzu seeds to distribute at the back of the hall, along the massive windows overlooking Cavehill's inner garden. But her main job today was to listen and watch, work the floor and act as an antenna.

She shook a few more hands, smiled and waved another half-dozen times, then made her way gradually over to the windows. She and Ty and Luz had all decided on breath-mint cases for the seeds; as all three of them got inside without issue, she supposed it was a good decision. Ezz reached into her pocket, withdrawing both her device and the mint case.

She checked the time as the seeds fell one by one. 2:42. Joelle would be arriving soon, if all went according to plan. Ezz couldn't think about that too long…she didn't want to let her mind linger on what might happen when the owners of Cloud Parliament saw their missing metalbred go galloping around the track.

How is CP getting inside? she texted.

I've got it covered, is all Luz wrote. Then a quick follow-up:
I think.

"You *think?*" Ezz mumbled to herself, and put her device away.

They were all being vague. They hadn't discussed it, but the possibility of getting caught lingered over them like Louisville's veil of pollution. Ezz imagined the Pink falling into disrepair, the sprawling stone walls crumbling while she sat in a cell. The thought filled her with a grief like helium, swelling her to popping. She shook her head. Focus.

The seeds felt like grain in her hands. She let each one fall. No one glanced her way. No one would notice the little brown pellets. They could be dirt from someone's shoe. They could be exactly what they were: seeds. She let her eyes wander to the ceiling of the betting hall, where the speakers jutted out from the corners like brass trumpets. Announcements about the race would come from those speakers, and so would the sequence that Luz would trigger, which would then trigger the seeds. Ezz moved back toward the center of the betting hall, not daring to let herself look back.

Ezz knew what those seeds contained. She was afraid of them, of what they might do when they sprang open. But she was more afraid of what would happen if they didn't.

CHAPTER 50

LUZ

Luz paused within the throngs of people to look up at the triple spires, the drones that circled their points like metallic birds. She wore a lacy green dress, the sleeves long to cover her tattoo, which someone might remember if they were asked about anyone notable seen lurking around the track. She didn't mind disgusing Poison Ivy in this way – the dress was like a forest, its lacework sewn in delicate leaves. She thought about the concept of disguise as she made her way slowly down the pathway toward the track, press pass around her neck as usual. A disguise was only a disguise if you were pretending to be someone else. She was here as herself.

Inside her small purse the two tiny mint tins slid back and forth beside her lip gloss. She'd started the day with several more tins, but they had made their way into the proper hands. All except one. Of the two left in her purse, she had hoped to deliver one to her mother. But the text she had sent late in the night had not been answered, and she hadn't slept a wink, waiting for her device to light up in response. But it hadn't. And she was here. So now she needed to do it alone.

Black uniforms were everywhere, all the workers and servers and hundreds of moving parts that made Derby happen. Some of them were white and some were Black, but most of them were

Latinx. Luz had to tighten her jaw as she stared around at all the white women in broad hats and all the men in their identically unimaginative suits who went on quaffing their drinks and laughing up into the empty blue sky, none of them noticing that the boat they all stood on was rowed by Marthas, that the walls of the building they stood inside were held up by her father, Otto, and her mother, Shery. And this work wasn't what made the servers in black and the hot walkers in brown and she, Luz Cabo Trejo in white, deserving of love, she thought. It was what made them human. Work, and breath, and dirt on shoes from walking. But here, they were invisible.

Not for long, Luz thought. She made her way toward the pathway across the track that would take her to the infield, which was already crowded with bodies less elegantly dressed than those in the stands. Khaki shorts and boat shoes would turn the grass to pulp by the end of the afternoon, beer sloshing on ankles. It would be easy to get swallowed up once she made it to the grandstand, but walking toward the starting gate was another story. The doubt was like a pebble in her shoe. This is where she needed her mother. She needed to get seeds on the track, but in a white dress and hat, she would be stopped. *Ma'am, are you lost? Here, this way...* Maybe she should've acquired one of the brown uniforms, turned herself truly invisible for the day. She pulled her device from her purse, telling herself she was seeing if Ezz or Ty had anything to say, but she found herself scrolling to her own message sent last night, the one that had dared to cross the divide and ask for help from her mother. Still no response.

She sighed and set one foot out onto the dirt. She would just have to risk getting redirected. A few seeds on the track was better than nothing, but it wasn't how she envisioned things. She put her device away and looked up.

And that's when she saw him.

She knew it was him, when his shape was just a smudge,

before his face swam into view. He walked down the track toward her, his brown uniform and his brown skin and the brown soil of the track all seeming to shimmer in the May sun. Then he was standing before her.

"Mija," he said. "Te ves preciosa."

"Hola, papi," she said, and she didn't know whether to smile or cry. How had he known she would be here? She hadn't sent him the message. So it must be...

She looked over his shoulder, far down the track from where he had come. Down at the distant gate she saw what she knew had to be the head and shoulders of her mother, peering down the stretch of sand and silt that separated them.

"Is she mad?" Luz asked her dad, looking back into his face. He was cleanshaven as always, his hair combed neatly. He had a tiny scar at the center of his chin that his mother always called "his trick." (It created the illusion of a strong cleft chin.) His amber-brown eyes were glowing.

"Ah, your mother," he sighed, grinning. "El perro que ladra no muerde."

Luz smiled at this, shaking her head.

"Bark and bite," she said. "I think mommy does a little of both."

"Like her daughter."

The last time she had seen him the trees hadn't bloomed yet, and now under the hot Derby sun, it felt as if whole seasons had passed since she had laid eyes on him. But there wasn't time now to reflect on all that she might have lost and gained since then. For now, there were things that needed to be done.

"What do you need from us?" he said softly, knowing.

The second tin from her purse was in her hand before he finished. She pressed it into his palm, and watched as he cracked it open, withdrawing one tiny seed.

He raised his eyes, baffled.

"Semillas?"

"Yes. All along the track. The whole thing, but just the edge. ¿Es posible?"

He frowned then, the frown she knew well, the frown that hovered on his and her mother's mouths when they'd learnd she'd been ditching Skyhorse for the greenhouse. She saw the battle in him, the struggle over his past and her future. He looked back over his shoulder at her mother, and that's when Luz knew the truth: her mother was on her side. Her chest swelled.

"Si," he said, turning back to her. "Lo haremos por ti."

I'm doing it for you too, she thought, but couldn't make her tongue work.

"Janila matyöx," she finally said, softly in the Kaqchikel she knew he thought she had forgotten, and he turned away just after she glimpsed the moisture in his eyes.

"Por ti, mija," he repeated softly. And then louder, laughing, back to pretending he was grumpy: "Salir de Guatemala y entrar en guatepeor."

Leave Guate-bad and end up in Guate-worse.

"Not even funny," she called. He always loved a good pun – the king of dad jokes. She wanted to watch him walk all the way down the line where her mother waited, but there was no time. He was dropping the seeds, and she needed to go. She raised her hand low by her waist, and waved at her mother. Her mother waved back.

Far off, Luz could hear a metalbred working up to a trot, and she imagined the sound and her heart matching beat by beat.

CHAPTER 51

TY

The seeds left their tin without a sound, spinning down to the floor along the back wall of the Limestone suite, behind the tables. Her father wasn't interested in her presence – it wouldn't be until she sang, all eyes on her, that he would come, pretending to be the doting father. For now she enjoyed near-invisibility, feeling only the occasional razor eyes of Brian Benedict. But it was easy to melt into the crowd that grew thicker and thicker as the big race approached, and she dropped a seed here and there as she made her way around the room. She eventually found herself at the front edge, where the light poured in through the bubble wall that insulated the suite from the outdoor terrace overlooking the track, and she pushed through. The material tensed at first, resisting her, before allowing her to slip through into the hot air beyond.

She moved to the railing, gazing down at the racetrack; from here it looked like a brown river encircling an island of revelers. A raised bandstand was in the middle of it all, rows of chairs arranged for the young orchestra that would eventually file up the stairs headed by Gina Aldana. Ty scanned the crowd, as if in the thousands of people she would be able to pick out the far-off forms of Ezzardine and Luz, each carrying out their parts of the plan. She almost didn't want to see them. She'd barely been able to look at them as they each went their separate ways, for though they each carried the same seeds, she carried a different purpose. Then she checked her tin, peering in at the four seeds remaining. She closed the tin, keeping them safe. She sent a quick message.

Out of seeds.

Luz wrote back quickly.

You got some by the door, right?

Yeah, Ezz added. **When everything goes down, I don't want Benedict running off before security can grab him.**

Ty felt her stomach drop, the heat of her secrets simmering. Instead of answering that she changed course.

About that... Ty typed. **The cop is here.**

What cop?

The detective from the Mahogany. Segrest. He's here.

What the hell? Ezz said. **Do you know why?**

He said he's working.

You don't think he knows anything, do you?

Ty glanced around the room, expecting to find that Segrest had reappeared without her noticing, watching every move she made.

I hope not, she wrote back. **But as much as I hate to say it, he's definitely sniffing around. I just don't know if it's for us.**

Everybody shut up, Luz typed. **I'm about to test the range.**

Ty leaned on her elbows, hoping the rail, at least, might be cool, might offer a chill against the too-warm sheen that seemed to have coated her like a second skin. She wasn't nervous, and yet the realization that she should be was like a lump under her flesh, cancer waiting to be discovered.

"For someone who I'd wager doesn't think much of Derby, you really dressed for the occasion," someone said, already leaning against the rail. Too close to be a stranger. Ty turned, the wide hat on her head making her feel like a planet revolving.

"Irma," Ty said, surprised.

Irma stood wearing a pantsuit that looked like it was spun from gemstones, a neat little hat perched atop mountainous wavy hair. A walkie-talkie clipped to her hip. Unlike the night Ty had run into her in the diner, when her makeup had been as tired as she was, she was fresh, a jeweled daisy in a crystal jar. She smiled at Ty a little ruefully.

"I never really expected you to call," she said. "And I understand why, given what you've been through. Which is why I guess I'm…extra surprised to see you here."

"I came for a gig," Ty said, feeling exposed. "I sing, get paid, then go."

"I hope they're giving you a good check," Irma said. "Lord knows they can afford it. But it's so weird seeing you at the Downs. Marianne would never come inside, you know? She would keep her protests outside. Looking back, she probably knew that if she came in, they'd be on her like mosquitoes."

"Turned out she didn't even have to come inside," Ty said, looking back toward the track. Her device had not sounded yet. Luz was supposed to be testing the virus range. Was no news good news?

"Are you okay?" Irma said, peering at her under her hat. "You seem a little on edge."

"I'm fine. Just been a long time since I sang in public."

"I remember Marianne telling me that you sang," Irma said. She folded her arms on the railing next to Ty, and Ty had to suppress a snarl. How did this girl always show up when Ty wanted – needed – to be alone? "Why did you stop? And I guess the better question: why did you start again?"

"Did they send you to interview me or what, damn!" Ty said, shooting her a venomous look, but Irma didn't even flinch.

"I'm sorry," she sighed instead. "I don't know why I always do this. My boss says this is why I can't work in sales. I never know what to say to people, and so I always end up saying the wrong thing. I could just talk about, I don't know, Muppets and Batman and Norteñas, but not everybody likes what I like."

Ty scoffed, darting her eyes past Irma as other Derby-goers joined them on the terrace.

"Yeah, well, I know a girl you'd probably hit it off with," she said, scanning the other guests.

"What are you doing here, Ty?" Irma said. Their eyes finally met and held, and Ty could see the steady knowing resting there in the center. Somehow the knowledge that these same eyes had rested on her mother, on days a lot like this one, made the hard thing in Ty's heart feel suddenly wobbly.

"It's complicated," she began.

Then Ty's device vibrated in her palm.

Luz.

We have a problem.

CHAPTER 52

LUZ

At Luz's back, Gina Aldana and the youth orchestra were arranging themselves in their seats, the flash of sunlight on brass, ebony, and maple like its own musical arrangement. But Luz couldn't look at them, at the children who she remembered playing only noise before they mastered the instruments they now held. She had watched some of them grow up while she still attended classes at Skyhorse. If she had stayed a little longer, maybe she would have met Martha. But she banished these thoughts. Instead she focused on crouching over the control box eyeing the wires like an open stomach before her, a tumor discovered.

No signal.

She was plugged in. The little nodules that communicated with her clicker were in place – it should have been a matter of pressing test and the nodules lighting up in confirmation. But nothing was happening. She fought the tears in her eyes. What the fuck. What the fuck fuck fuck.

My tests are failing, she texted the group. **It's like there's no signal. I don't know what to do.**

Fuck, Ezz wrote back. **What do we do?**

Nothing from Ty.

Luz squeezed her eyes shut. Time was ticking. The kids were

on stage doing their quiet warm-ups. Their day was going according to plan. Luz finally turned to look at them, kids from Mexico and Guatemala wielding bows and pressing silver keys. When they played "My Old Kentucky Home," everyone in the stadium would watch without seeing.

"What's the matter?" Dr. Aldana said, appearing next to her. She kept her face turned away, observing the children.

"It's not working," Luz whispered. "I can't get a signal."

"How can you solve this problem?"

"I don't know," Luz said, the tears swimming again. "They put a block on the whole infield, probably so all the people down here don't mess up the signal for everyone up there. It's more of the same, Dr. Aldana, it's always the same…"

"Luz," Dr. Aldana said firmly. "You may have left my classroom, but before that I taught you from the time you reached my knee. I have seen you teach a toaster to talk, not even loving the work. Turn down the voices in your head and listen to mine. You have solved many problems before. Now. How do you solve *this* one?"

CHAPTER 53

TY

"Shit," Ty whispered, squeezing her eyes shut.

"What's wrong?" said Irma, squinting.

"I...I..." Ty struggled to find words, a feasible lie. "My friend and I...we're...trying to do something...and it's not...working..."

"What, are y'all trying to blow up the Downs or something?" Irma said, laughing. A curl had escaped her up-do and she reached up to tuck it back.

"No," Ty said, but this entire conversation was outside the neat box she had arranged for this day, all the careful sweeping of facts and plans; her eyes were still scanning the ground far below, the watercolor of fancy hats, the winner's circle ringed in blazing red roses.

"Seriously," Irma said, her tone like a swallow dipping from a wire. "What are you doing here? I was just curious before, but now I'm suspicious."

Ty dragged her eyes back to Irma's face, and the frown told Ty all she needed to know – Ty was as bad a liar as she'd always been. She'd inherited that from her father.

"I'm not blowing up the Downs," she said quickly. "Please. That's ridiculous."

"But you're doing...something."

"I'm just working."

"Ty, what the fuck are you doing? I need to know that you're not endangering anyone at this track, or if –"

"The people at this track are endangered just by the sick pieces of shit that run Limestone," Ty snapped. "You want to talk about danger? *That's* danger."

"Say it with your chest," Irma said, scowling. "Whatever it is you're implying, say it."

"You know that girl they found dead on the backside?" Ty whispered. She stared at her device, waiting for it to light up again.

"The Guatemalan girl," Irma said. "The hot walker. Yes. I was opening the museum when the ambulance came."

"I know who killed her," Ty said, and she raised her eyes to Irma's just in time to see the clouds in them roll back to reveal something like lightning. "And he's in that room behind us."

They both turned to stare through the bubble wall. The violinists swayed, the sea of hats bobbing and dipping, drunken laughter. Dr. Salt and Annie Claybelle – when had she arrived? – stood surrounded by fawning guests, everyone grateful to be near enough. Nearby, Brian Benedict's hands encircled a glass of bourbon that glowed amber.

No signal? So the plan is fucked? Ezz texted.

"No fucking signal," Ty whispered.

"Your *friend*," Irma said, using air quotes. "Why do they need a signal? Are they in the pit?"

She pointed out at the infield, the thousands of people who couldn't afford tickets to the box seats packed in like inebriated tuna. Ty stared out at them, trying to imagine Luz somewhere among them, frantically looking for a signal. Running out of time.

I need to access the control room, Luz texted. **I'm on my way to look for it.**

"Fuck," said Ty.

You can't just go wandering, she wrote back quickly. **You**

could get caught. That press pass isn't a golden ticket.

Irma's hand snapped out, snatching the device from Ty's hands like a cobra's striking head.

"It's rude to text while you're talking to someone," Irma said, and when Ty opened her mouth to shout, her fingers grabbing the other girl's wrist, Irma shook her head. "Don't. Don't make a scene, Ty. Clearly you're trying to lay low."

Ty's eyes snapped back toward the executive suite, where no one seemed to be paying any attention to the two young women on the terrace. For now.

"Give it back," she growled, but Irma had already squinted at the message.

"Why does your friend need the control room?" Irma repeated.

Ty pulled her lips in, biting down. She'd already told Irma too much, and now she'd seen even more. Any minute Irma would be reaching for her walkie, barking for security. Down in the gambling hall, Ezz would hear it in her ear, but it would be too late for Ty.

Instead, another signal lit up in Irma's eyes.

"If you need the control room," Irma said, low, "I can get you there."

Ty almost laughed.

"What?"

Irma pointed down at her badge.

"I can get you anywhere. Where is your friend? Infield still?"

Ty nodded, once, scarcely able to believe it. But Irma's eyes held her and wouldn't let go.

"I'm supposed to be on stage in 30 minutes," Ty said. "But if I can get my friend and the remote…"

"The remote?" Irma said, crossing her arms, the crimson hat on her head tilting. Ty couldn't read her. She didn't know her well enough to read her, let alone trust her, but…here they were.

"Yes," Ty said quickly. "And it won't blow anything up. But it will…it will probably take Limestone down."

They were two girls searching each other's eyes for an agreement, two workers treading water, looking for shale beneath the current. After a long pause, Irma's arms came unfolded and came to rest on her hips, elbows hard angles.

"You *promise* you're not going to blow anything up?" she snapped. "Seriously, fucking promise me."

"I'm not going to blow anything up," Ty said. Something in Irma's eyes said *motion*.

"Good," said Irma. Like a viper, her hand snapped out again, grabbed hold of the gold lace at Ty's shoulder, and ripped it with one swift, savage motion. "Then let's walk fast."

"What the fuck!" Ty cried, snatching at her sleeve.

"Go with it," Irma said, pushing Ty's device back into her hands, then leading her.

They shoved through the bubble wall, ignored by the executives and guests watching the enormous screens in the Limestone room as they gossiped about the stats of the metalbreds displayed, arguing about who would be richer at the end of the day. No one looked their way, no one even interested in watching the track itself until closer to the race, when the hot walkers would lead the metalbreds to the chutes.

"Be cool," Irma said softly. She made her way straight for the service elevator, and Ty followed, the torn lace flapping against her arm. They almost made it, but someone was moving to intercept them. A pale white woman, blonde, her steel-gray dress billowing as she plowed toward them like a warship.

"What's this?" she said. "Surely our talent doesn't have cold feet?"

"Ms. Claybelle," said Irma, and Ty felt her stomach drop. Looking at her now was different than the night at Limestone's gala: here, her eyes fixed on Ty, there was the feeling of the air turning to ice. "I was just escorting this young lady for a quick dress repair."

Ty immediately recognized Irma's tone as her work voice. The slower sweetness of it had been wrung out, replaced with something rapid and nasal. Urgent, professional, slightly stupid. Claybelle blinked, only just registering Irma's presence. Ty could feel Irma's spine stiffening, hyper-aware that she had been rendered her invisible. Ms. Claybelle's smile broadened, a PR smile. She didn't give many interviews, Ty knew from her father, but she definitely still knew when to turn it on.

"Oh?" she said, smiling but cold. "Do we have a wardrobe malfunction?"

Irma's ruby nail pointed at Ty's ripped dress.

"Just a rip. I'll take her down to the seamstress."

Claybelle's gaze shot down to Ty's hanging lace, the beige bra-strap beneath exposed like bare cement under a circus tent. The woman's ice-blue eyes narrowed at the sight of it, then moved back up to Ty's face. Staring at her, Ty could see the shadows of everything she knew. Beyond her shoulder in Ty's periphery was the form of Benedict, watching.

"You have twenty minutes," Claybelle said. "If you are one second late, I'll ask security to bring you back up."

"Uh, sure," Ty said, trying to sound unconcerned. She didn't look at Irma, lest her eyes betray them both. She held her purse a little tighter and nodded.

"Yep, I figured she'd be faster through the service elevator," Irma said, then stepped forward and scanned her badge against the elevator pad. The sound it made was like a single raindrop, and then the doors were opening wide. Ms. Claybelle stared at them until they were closed safely inside.

"Text your friend," Irma said.

CHAPTER 54

EZZ

And Joel **STIL isnt ghere**, Luz typed, multiple words misspelled. She was either being jostled by the crowd or was so freaked out she wasn't bothering to correct herself.

"Shit," Ezz whispered. She sat watching a game of blackjack in the betting hall, the gambling wing they added three years ago. She was supposed to sit here and focus on the stream of security communications after she completed her task of dropping the seeds, but she couldn't stop glancing at her device, waiting for the text that would say everything was in place, that all they had to do was wait.

Ejecting two from the infield, the voice in her ear said. *White males, both inebriated.*

Not Ty. Not Luz.

"Deal you in?" the dealer asked her, but she shook her head, distracted. No way she could focus on a game. The cards that always seemed to reveal themselves to her like a mirage in a desert were just blank stretches of sand while she fretted about what was happening in the infield with Luz, the Limestone suites with Ty. She barely noticed the two men sit down at the table, towering cities of chips between them.

"You're back," said the dealer with a nod.

"Deal me in, Carl," said one of the men. "I'm feeling lucky."

The two men conversed in low tones while Ezz's eyes remained glued to her screen.

I have help for the control room, Ty wrote. **Luz, meet me by Millionaire's Row.**

What help? Ezz wrote quickly.

Two minutes, Luz wrote. No answer from Ty.

Fuck. Ezz raised her eyes to the betting hall, thinking she might go meet them anyway, plan be damned. But then her eyes fell upon the two men sitting just to her right, nearly shoulder to shoulder.

One of them was a stranger, but the other had a face she knew. White, beefy, hair cropped close to his head, beard nothing but a gray stretch of scrub on each cheek that somehow looked kept. A sand-colored suit, no tie. Unremarkable, but reeking of money. She knew his profile, the way he cupped his bourbon.

Mr. Darden.

She immediately lowered her gaze to her device, like many others in the hall. Her eyes stared at the message chain with Ty and Luz, but her ears became a wolf's, listening not just to the security channel now, but trying to catch the snatches of conversation between Darden and his partner that occasionally drifted toward her over the dealer's commentary.

"…flight leaves tonight. Did…came to do. If…partnership…my name on the check."

"Mr. Fix-It!" Darden's companion said, loud and a little drunk. He clinked the ice in his glass appreciatively.

"…one more thing. A little something…along to Claybelle…seal the deal. I went…myself and there was nothing else there. She'll…deal for sure."

Darden is here, Ezz texted madly, trying to keep her face as flat as the cards. **Luz, you said the cop at the Carousel told you he took something from the crime scene, right?**

No response.

Beside her the men lost and won chips, continuing to mutter. Ezz considered joining the game, starting up a conversation. She'd done it a hundred times before, chatting away while the cards flew, distracting them with her mouth while her eyes pried at the twist of their lip, the scratch of their wrist that could be a tell. She won on the table, but half the game was in the air. She was just uncrossing her legs to make a move when Darden's voice rang out loud and clear:

"Deal me out, Carl. We're gonna take a lap."

Ezz watched them withdraw, their tan suits understated in the noisy plaids and pastels of most Derby-goers. Her muscles twitched. She was supposed to stay in the betting hall – that was the plan. She glanced at her device. Nothing. Luz was somewhere making her way to a control room that might not exist, and it was fifty minutes until the horses ran. Shit shit shit. She made a decision. The plan was already unraveling, right? Fuck the betting hall.

She rose, arrowing after Darden and his partner just as they reached the door. They turned right into the outdoor corridor, brightly lit by sunlight. Ezz waited a breath, then plunged into the crowd after them.

CHAPTER 55
LUZ

She should've worn a hat. Ty had asked her if she needed one, but she said no, predicting that a wide brim would get in the way when she was trying to plug into the speaker system. But now, standing in the corridor, people pressing past on their way to the track, to the bar, to the betting hall, she felt exposed, her bare head like a thumb poked out waiting to be smashed.

Ty, where are you? She texted quickly, trying to look at ease. It was a beautiful day for a horse race, and she tried to look like she was part of it. Tried to look like she was not a girl with footage of a murder in her purse.

Almost there. Move to the east side. You'll see us and we'll just keep walking.

Luz picked her way through the foot traffic, smiling a silent apologetic smile for everyone she crossed in front of. She let her hair sweep down like a screen before her face. Should've worn a hat. *Pendejo.*

She saw Ty's hat first. Even in a sea of hats, the gold was like a knife jutting from all the pastel. She had someone with her but Luz couldn't see who – whatever "help" she had found. Luz just prayed that, whoever they were, they wouldn't ask too many questions.

Ty swept past and Luz fell in step beside her, not daring to tilt her neck to take in their new companion until they turned the corner away from Millionaire's Row. She glimpsed an employee badge first, and then caught sight of the face of the woman who walked beside Ty.

"You...," Luz started, her pulse jumping.

Irma peered back, an eyebrow raised.

"Aren't you...?"

They didn't have a chance to look at each other again until Irma stepped forward, steering them toward a concrete corridor that split off from the main walkway. Hair the same inky black as a horse's mane in a severe ponytail from the crown of her head to the bottom of her shoulders. Smiling eyebrows and sly eyes. Luz felt something wild gallop through her heart's chambers.

"You work in the museum," Luz said. "I saw you..."

"The day you were casing Cavehill," Irma said over her shoulder, closing the distance between herself and a door marked Employees Only. "I guess I shouldn't be surprised to see you again now."

Luz stayed silent, reeling. As soon as the door opened, the hum and warmth of machines rumbled out to greet them. The control room. But even as her stomach churned with butterflies, Luz felt sticky with doubt. Luz imagined stepping into the control room and Irma slamming the door behind them, police waiting at the threshold the next time it was opened.

Irma glanced at her, her eyes showing the kind of expression that spoke of equations already balanced.

"Your friend," she said, nodding at Ty, who studied them both, trying to parse together their connection. "She says you're going to take Limestone down."

"Something like that," Luz said, darting a glance at Ty, swallowing the butterflies that fluttered into her throat at the feeling of Irma's eyes on hers.

"I don't know how you're going to do it," Irma said. "But she says you're not going to blow anything up, and if that's true, well… I don't mind helping."

"Have you thought about what will happen if Limestone goes down?" Luz said. "You probably won't have a job."

Irma smiled ruefully, fiddling with her name badge.

"What did you say that day in the museum?" she said. "Does it bother me to work for a place that doesn't care if I live or die? Well, maybe it does."

Then she stepped through the door into the control room, and held the door open for the other two.

Luz took a deep breath and followed her inside.

CHAPTER 56

EZZ

Darden was headed for the Limestone suites. He made his way casually along the corridor, half in and half out of the sun; Ezz trailed at a safe distance, taking in his every move. If he carried the evidence he'd ordered removed from the crime scene on his person, Ezz guessed it was in his left breast pocket, for even while he chatted with his companion or raised a pair of delicate binoculars to his eyes to peer down at the track below, occasionally his other hand would rise to the pocket and give it one gentle, subconscious pat. Anyone who had spent any length of time around men like Darden knew that they had no qualms about doing dirt in broad daylight, and Ezz had gambled long enough to know a tell when she saw one.

It had to be in that pocket, Ezz thought, and sent another quick message to Ty and Luz. Still no fucking answer.

Darden paused at the rail to stand watching the infield. From here Ezz could see the distant shapes of Dr. Aldana and the Skyhorse kids finishing arranging themselves onstage. In another 28 minutes they would be lifting their instruments to their mouths, and if Luz wasn't hacked into the sound system by then, they would lose their chance of completing what Rosario and Martha had set out to do in exposing Limestone's secrets. Ezz chanced a sidelong glance at Darden, the binoculars still pressed against his eyes, then down at her device. Still nothing. If the rest of the plan was out the window, then Darden might be her only shot at justice.

Darden pushed off the railing, headed now for the elevators on which he would ascend to the Limestone suites. Based on what he said in the betting hall, he was going to place the evidence in Annie Claybelle's hands and then board a plane back to New York. Then he would just go on living his life, and so would Brian Benedict.

Before she fully realized what she was doing, Ezz had quickened her stride to pick up the pace and met Darden at the elevator. When he extended his fingers to press the button that would call the elevator and carry him up and away, she reached out and grabbed his hand.

CHAPTER 57

TY

Ty stood with her back pressed against the door watching Irma and Luz, both of them crouched at the foot of a glowing white wall of lights, each light blinking in its own separate rhythm. It was a control room like any other, and Luz seemed to plug in easily, the controls that she thought would be down on stage next to the Skyhorse orchestra placed here instead. Luz had popped a square of bubblegum in her mouth as soon as she'd entered the warm, buzzing room, and now Ty watched her jaw as it chewed, slow at first and then faster and less deliberately. She was panicking.

"Luz," Ty said, and nothing more. Her own device was blowing up with messages from Ezz that she couldn't stop to look at – she had to keep an eye out the crack of the door to ensure no one was coming – so she knew Luz's was too. She didn't want to distract her. But time was ticking away.

"I'm trying to figure it out," Luz said, her voice as tight as one of the orchestra's strings. "I have the nodules placed down by the stage where the speakers are, but I can't make this sync internally. I've got the Aristidean virus's sound sequence ready, but I won't be able to trigger it from in here: I need an unobstructed view to the infield where the other nodules are."

"Okay," Ty said. "So we go back out once you plug in. We

need to anyway, right? So we know when to press the button?"

Luz shook her head, chomping her gum vigorously.

"No," she said. "Because that's not the only issue. I can't play the horse-eye video remotely. I have to be in this room to launch the file. I can't do both."

"So we split up the job," Ty said. "I'll take the clicker for the virus and the seeds. You stay here and I'll text you when it's time to roll video."

Ty watched Luz pause in chewing her gum and knew exactly what was crossing her mind. Doubt. Trusting someone other than herself, allowing the plan to deviate, sharing the reins.

"I won't fuck it up," Ty said. "I promise."

Luz was quiet for a long time. Ty tried not to look at Irma, who was listening intently.

"You've placed all your seeds?"

Ty nodded.

"All of them," she lied.

"But you still have to sing," Luz said, shaking her head. "How are you going to sing and trigger the sequence at just the right moment?"

Ty looked down at her device.

Five messages from Ezz from several minutes ago: **Darden has the evidence he stole. He's about to give it to Claybelle. I'm following him.** Ten minutes before Ty sang. Fifteen minutes before the Skyhorse kids' music would flood the speakers of Cavehill Downs and provide cover for the sequence Rosario and Martha had built to unbind the metalbreds.

"I'm just going to have to figure it out," she said. "Aren't I?"

Don't worry about Darden, Ty typed quickly. **Don't engage with him!**

Guilt sank its fangs into her neck, raising her pulse. Ezz didn't believe that Ty had put the needle back in Rosario's room. Or maybe Ezz *did* believe her, but Darden had gone back to the scene and managed to find it anyway? Ty had checked under the wardrobe one last time before she came to the track – she had pushed it far back with a gloved hand. There's no way Darden had gone and found the second piece. Had he?

Irma drew Ty's attention back into the control room.

"I'll stay with you," Irma said to Luz, with the cautiousness of someone stepping into traffic. "I can watch the door."

The three of them were silent for a moment, each of them, Ty knew, harboring their own doubts – and harboring something else, Ty thought, glancing between the other two: a spark that couldn't be ignored. Ty glanced at her device once more. Nothing from Ezz. Shit. How did things get so complicated? She felt dizzy and tried to focus on the fact that Brian Benedict was only a few floors above her right now – she was determined to see her own plan through as well. For Rosario, for Martha, yes. But also for her mother. For her. Even if it meant Ezz never speaking to her again. Her heart seemed to gasp.

"Give it to me," Ty said quietly, her hand outstretched. The buzzing of the machines seemed suddenly muted. Luz had stopped chewing her gum, her jaw frozen.

"We *cannot* fuck this up," Luz said softly.

"I know," said Ty.

"We can't fuck it up, Ty."

"I know."

Luz stood and crossed the room slowly, the two of them looking into each other's eyes, all that they had lost floating between them like furious apparitions. Luz pressed the clicker into Ty's hands, and Ty immediately turned and slipped out the door.

CHAPTER 58

EZZ

"Can I help you?" Darden's voice was exactly as she expected – gravel turned smooth by the bourbon in his glass. His eyes were as she expected too, two pits, oil blue. Sinking into them could turn you into bones. Ezz had been an expert in table chatter for the many years she'd been a poker player, but in this moment her words failed her. All she could think about was keeping her eyes from wandering down to his breast pocket.

"I...," she began, but had no idea what to say. It's not like she could rob the man, reach into his pocket and snatch whatever was there, disappear into the crowd. A young Black woman at an event like Derby? She wouldn't make it ten feet, and likely not alive.

"I think...," she said, fumbling.

"Can we help you, young lady?" said Darden's companion. He'd had a few more drinks than Darden; she could tell that back in the betting hall. The whites of his eyes were populated by reddened blood vessels, squinted just a millimeter more. What happened next with him was as predictable to Ezz as the reaction of Derby security – he was looking for a fight. Ezz let her eyes raise and scan the crowded corridor for the gray uniforms of security officers. A few of them farther off, one on a walkie talkie nearby, not looking their way. Their chatter in her ear was benign. Hats and feathers and dresses…bright blue, yellow, then shimmering gold, a wide gold brim…

It took her a moment to realize she was looking at Ty, hustling in their direction, her face set in an expression of grim determination. Her eyes were locked on Ezz, her high heels striking toward the elevator where Ezz stood, hand blocking the button from Darden, whose eyebrows were knitting closer and closer together.

Ezz raised an eyebrow at Ty. Ty shook her head, hard.

Ezz stepped back quickly.

"So sorry," she said to Darden, her tongue coming unlocked. "I was trying to get your attention back there…I think you dropped this coming out of the betting hall."

She shoved her hand into her pocket, withdrawing a few hundreds where she'd stowed some cash, waving it in the air between her and Darden just as Ty joined them at the elevator. Ezz pretended she didn't exist.

Darden frowned, taking in the sight of the money, confused. He patted his pocket, the hip pocket this time, and doubtless felt his own money where it should be.

"I could be mistaken," Ezz said, rediscovering her poker smile. She made to fold the money in between her two fingers. Darden's lip inched up.

"I'll take that," he said, and Ezz's smile didn't change at the feeling of her money leaving her hands for his, but in her head she imagined her teeth all turning sharp.

"Excuse me," Ty said, ignoring them all. She tapped the button with one gilded nail.

"You don't have to excuse yourself, young lady," Darden's companion said with exaggerated courtesy. He sipped more. "Consider this *your* elevator. Consider us your escorts."

Ezz had become invisible, and that was just fine. She melted away, catching Ty's eye one last time as the three of them moved to enter the now-open elevator. Ezz tapped her chest once, shooting her eyes at Darden. Ty didn't move, but Ezz saw her eyes register the tip. The doors closed and Ezz stood there a moment, breathless, hoping.

CHAPTER 59
TY

The elevator was the size of a kitchen, but it felt like a vintage phonebooth while sharing the space with Darden and his buddy. Ty stared just to the left of the elevator buttons so as not to provide a full view of her face – she knew Darden hadn't truly seen her at the hotel, but the party at the Carousel was another story, mask or not. She was glad she had on the ridiculous hat to hide her distinctive bald head.

She smiled sideways, politely, as the two men delivered an endless stream of half-authentic compliments in her direction, and she was sharply aware of the gathering of sweat under each of her arms. In her tiny sequined clutch was the clicker Luz had pressed into her palm, and beside it was nestled the tin of four kudzu seeds.

As the elevator doors slid silently open, she stepped out, still keeping her face tilted away, using her device as an excuse for diversion. She pulled up Joelle's name and sent no words, merely a long string of question marks.

Silence.

Ty cursed silently, praying that Joelle and Cloud Parliament hadn't been apprehended before they ever reached the track.

"Back with us," a voice said, and Ty knew it was Annie Claybelle without needing to turn around. When Ty did turn, she was faced with Claybelle and Benedict together. They both shared the same slim smile. "My brother was telling me more about you while you went on your bathroom break."

The sharp blue eyes snapped down to Ty's shoulder, where the lace still hung loose like a snapped vine. *Shit.*

"What happened to that wardrobe repair?" Claybelle said silkily.

"They didn't have thread that matched," Ty said, trying to sound dismissive. "I'd rather wear it torn than with a poor alteration. Anyway. I don't think I realized until recently that you two were related."

Beside Claybelle, Brian Benedict's smile widened. Beyond them by the bar, Darden stood waiting patiently.

"Horses have always been a family business," Claybelle said, shrugging one shoulder. Her own dress, a cascade of lavender layers, rippled downward with the movement. It created a series of folds along her back. "Brian handles our PR. We're a good balance – he likes the spotlight. I prefer the background."

"I see," Ty said. This felt like walking on logs across water.

"I believe that's how Brian became acquainted with your mother," Claybelle said. Her smile, her eyes, did not change. But everything between them did. The logs all rolled once, fast, but Ty knew her footing now. "She was a bit of a PR issue for us, wasn't she, Brian? I never met her myself."

Ty stared at them, two snakes dressed in finery. Her mask was not as good as theirs – her lips twitched, teeth clicking together softly.

"There are always going to be people who don't appreciate what we do here," Claybelle said. She lifted a hand to wave at one of the fawning passers-by, her smile warming, then cooling. "But as long as we keep doing what we do best, we'll always come out on top."

"And what's that?" Ty said. She was supposed to sing in five minutes. "What do you do best?"

"Make fast horses and slow enemies," Claybelle said, but the pearly grin that tried to snake across her lips faltered as a chorus of cries went up around the room, the sparkling guests of the Limestone suite swarming over toward where the bubble wall had once been, lifted now to allow in the Louisville air, the far-off smells of the crowd and the track. Everyone was crowding the rail. From below came the rise of more spectactors shouting, calling.

"What in the world...?" Claybelle said, and glanced at one of the gilded clocks adorning the walls. "The horses shouldn't be on the track yet..."

She sailed toward the balcony, her brother at her heels, and Ty after both of them. Three feet from the railing Ty froze, her view of the track below unobstructed between the shoulders of Benedict and Claybelle.

Her hand spasmed toward her purse, then paused, waiting.

"There's a metalbred on the track!" someone shouted. "Is that...? Is that...?"

Ty's hand was buried in her purse. Her eyes were fixed on the side of Benedict's throat, where she could make out the throbbing vein of his pulse. She could have stabbed him right there if she had the needle. But then her gaze wandered to Annie Claybelle. From here Ty couldn't see the ice of her eyes, but she could hear her voice in her head: *Your mother was a bit of a PR issue for us.* Inside herself, Ty felt something take root. She was glad the needle was back in the Mahogany. She had something better now.

"That's not a metalbred!" came another yell. "Is it?"

Ty withdrew her hand from her purse, seeds in hand. Then she planted them. Easy. One, two. One, two. Only then did she look between the heads of Benedict and Claybelle. She could see the horse that had everyone screaming, everyone's eyes locked on the track: the gait that was too free, the wild abandon of the hooves throwing up dirt, the neck surging ahead not mechanical but urged by blood and bluegrass.

"Go, baby, go," she whispered

CHAPTER 60

EZZ

zz had just scooted into Millionaire's Row – almost stopped by a white usher until someone yelled: "That's Ezzardine Clayton, you idiot! Let her in!" – when the shouting began. She didn't realize something was happening on the track until she followed the hundreds of fingers pointing, the Jumbotron flicking away from an advertisement to magnify the events unfolding below.

"Cloud Parliament!" someone was screaming into the loudspeaker, drenching the Downs with their voice. "Ladies and gentlemen, the metalbred missing from owners Delilah and Stuart Sneed is on the track! Cloud Parliament, reappeared on Derby Day fifteen minutes until bugle, behaving very…oddly?! I can only call it odd! Jockeyed – actually jockeyed! There is a *rider*! –an unknown female…"

"Ezz! Ezzardine!" Ezz snapped to attention and found Camille Richmond waving her down, six seats over, standing up on her seat. Ezz clambered past the people staring slack-jawed in the stands and climbed up next to her.

It was like watching sunshine turned lightning, a bolt of gold splashing down onto the track and then whirling through the dust. Everything in Ezz seized, watching the horse's legs stretch and gather, stretch and gather, so different than a metalbred's stride, filled with horse-joy, every gallop swelling with memories of green grass and sweet feed and the buzz of grasshoppers. She could hear the drumbeat of Cloud Parliament's hooves; she felt each one, as if the pulse against the soil was in her own heart. And clinging to the powerful, graceful back was Joelle, arms bare and brown and a smile wide enough to see from Millionaire's Row and maybe the moon. She didn't need to urge Cloud Parliamenet forward – Ezz could tell from her easy grip on the reins that she was letting him go, along for the ride, bareback. The whole stadium was screaming. Ezz could tell from the pitch that no one could mistake the difference – this was a *horse*. Ezz looked down and found each of her hands in fists, the knuckles pressed together, halfway to her chin. She hadn't been on a horse since her parents died; she had surrounded herself with all the things that might take the place of that warm, solid memory. Now she wanted nothing more than to take Joelle's place behind those withers, to feel the same wind that caught the horse's mane run all over her face.

Gray-uniformed security guards were spreading onto the track, some shouting into walkie talkies, getting directions from whoever signed their checks. Ezz could hear them in her ear:

Who the hell locked the gates to the track? I need someone down here to handle this!

Several workers from the backside have blocked the security gate to the track! What the hell is going on here?

Interesting, Ezz thought. But no description of a girl like Luz, or Ty. No one looking their way.

Ezz glanced down at her device.

Luz: Ready

Ty: Almost

The blood in the valves of Ezz's heart began to churn, and she turned away from the track to peer far up in the direction of the Limestone suites. Ty must have the clicker – why else would she need to be ready too? She couldn't see Ty or her shimmering gold lace, but she could see the balcony, all the exclusive guests crowded at the rail outside. They would all still be watching when the metalbreds were led out to the starting gate and the sound of "My Old Kentucky Home" filled the sky.

Ezz turned to Camille.

"Seeds?" she said quietly.

Camille just smiled and gestured vaguely to the railing at the very front of Millionaire's Row. Ezz nodded. Her own tin was empty, and she felt hollow. She looked at the glowing numbers floating above the three spires – five minutes until the horses entered the track. Five minutes until something, or nothing at all.

CHAPTER 61

TY

She was still standing just behind Annie Claybelle and Brian Benedict when Claybelle whirled around, her face a portrait of rage. Benedict leaned close, and she whispered to him, then he was off to the edge of the room, conversing with the cluster of security guards waiting for instruction. Then Claybelle turned to Ty, eyes flaming:

"You get your ass up on that stage and sing. Now."

Ty said nothing, but turned and walked to the now-empty stage. Claybelle was looking for a distraction, something to draw the Limestone patrons' eyes away from scandal and back to the Derby she had always orchestrated. Ty would sing her private song here in the suites, and when her words had just begun to fade, the Skyhorse orchestra would take over. By then, Claybelle imagined, the stolen horse and its rider would be neatly in custody and the afternoon would unroll. Ty climbed the two velvet-coated steps, purse swinging on its gold chain over her shoulder. She clamped its satin mouth closed.

The Limestone band began to play, low, and a few eyes were pulled from the railing. Ty couldn't see, but beyond their heads, she hoped Cloud Parliament was still running.

"*Summertime…*"

She vaguely saw Claybelle's eyes jerk her way – it wasn't the song she had planned, but Ty couldn't remember what else she was supposed to sing, and the band immediately caught on and shifted on their strings. The music swelled and so did Ty's voice. Claybelle melted into the crowd, or maybe she didn't and Ty just stopped seeing her. She didn't know if her father was still in the room.

She sang about fish jumping and cotton and somebody's mommy and daddy. Something inside her was aching along with the words. The song seemed to go on forever, and from the elevated position of the stage she could see the Skyhorse children's orchestra taking their final seats, raising their instruments to their chins. It was almost time. Ty's voice wobbled, then found its feet again. She sang the possibility of morning and taking to the sky, but she kept thinking about cotton, and horses, and the green vines of kudzu that someone said swallowed the south but hadn't quite, yet.

She shifted her purse as the last few lines of the song slipped through her teeth. She could see the golden clock ticking on the wall. It was almost time. Somewhere Luz would be waiting in the dark, warm room, ready. She would be ready too.

"So hush little baby, don't you cry..."

She let the note linger, she let it waver. The band stayed with her, and then they all died together. There was light applause, and she moved to step down. She was already reaching for her purse, her fingers not quite shaking but not quite still. She had just lifted its flap to find the clicker when someone grabbed her arm.

CHAPTER 62

LUZ

S he stood with her back against the wall of blinking lights, tiny bulbs hot against the parts of her arm not covered by the dress. Still, she didn't move away. Irma stood at the door, peeking out through the crack.

"We're going to need to move fast," Irma said. "Once you run the video it's going to take about five minutes for them to realize someone had to be in *this* room to override the Jumbo."

"The file is just a copy," Luz said. "And I think I've made it pretty untraceable. Once it's in, we can leave."

Irma nodded, peered out the door again.

"You don't have to stay here," Luz said quietly. "You can go."

Irma just shook her head.

"If someone comes, I want to at least try to give you an alibi."

They looked at each other a moment. Luz had the sudden, uninvited thought of Poison Ivy filling a city with flowers.

"You know there are tons of security cameras, right?" Irma said. "Out there, I mean."

"I took care of the cameras," Luz shrugged.

"All the people filming with devices…they'll see a shot of you eventually. It's likely."

"And probably a shot of you helping me," Luz said sharply. She pressed her back against the hot bulbs, the heat keeping her grounded before anything else could carry her away.

Irma said nothing, then straightened up like a shot.

"Something's happening on the track," she said. "I hear people yelling."

Luz snatched up her device to text Ezz, but Irma had already grabbed her walkie talkie. She didn't speak, just turned the dial to raise the volume.

"Teams on A-Level, move to back and forward exits. Rider is rounding the last bend."

Irma raised her eyes to Luz's.

"What the hell? What rider?"

"Joelle!" Luz whispered, heart pounding.

"Who?"

Luz stood and rushed to the door, Irma jumping back to let her through. The control room momentarily forgotten, the two young women raced down the Employees Only corridor to the rail, pushing through the gathered crowd to see the track.

Where they stood commanded a view of the last bend, and Cloud Parliament galloped into sight just as they reached the rail. Irma gasped, but Luz was silent, watching the majestic golden body arching along the track, Joelle clinging to his back like a barnacle. Luz felt something shifting in her, in the muscle of her heart, remembering coming to the track to watch her parents groom and exercise the metalbreds and, before that, real horses. Looking down at the track, at the people leaning far over the rails to get a good look at the animal thundering down the stretch, Luz felt the gallop in her spine. She felt home. For a brief moment, her heart was every place her parents – and the world – tried to keep her out of. But also, her mother and father were here with her. This was a real horse. Even if it wasn't.

Then Irma grabbed her wrist, pulling her away from the track and back toward the Employees Only hallway, her walkie in her other hand. Luz could still see the track when she stood on tip toe.

Irma's hand on her skin felt like a satin ribbon.

"All teams to the front entrance!" Irma shouted into her walkie talkie. Luz jerked to stare at her, a spark of terror that she had been led into a trap. But Irma was still talking: "A trailer has pulled up to help the rider escape! All teams to the trailer to intercept!"

"Trailer?" Luz cried, bewildered. "What trailer?"

"I don't know," Irma said, a smile and a frown doing battle on her lips. "But maybe it will buy your friend some time."

Then she looked over Luz's shoulder, and her expression changed, the smile hefting something heavy, the frown defeated.

"And so will that," she said.

Luz whirled around. It took her a moment to find the reason for Irma's words.

Brown uniforms, almost blending in with the swirling dust of the track. Brown uniforms and brown skin, a throng of people rushing the track, forming a line. Backside workers. The sight of those those many brown shirts filled Luz's nose with the smell of her mother's detergent, all rose and sunlight as she washed her and her father's uniforms day after day after day. Dozens of shirts just like it barred the swarm of gray-suited security that had moved to the track to try and head off Cloud Parliament. Luz was too far to hear the words, which she could hear a trail of, rising in a smudged chant, but the distant shape and order of their bodies showed exactly what the backside workers had decided: *No*.

Luz's eyes filled with tears. All she could smell was her mother and her father and horses and air. All she wanted was to be down on the track with them. But the sight of the brown shirts forming a human vine reminded her why she was up here, and not down there. She raced for the control room.

It was time.

CHAPTER 63

EZZ

"Where did they go? Where did they go?" Camille was still standing in her seat, craning her neck for the backside workers. "All the backside workers held off security! Did you see? Now everyone's off the track. Are those bastards trying to arrest anyone?"

"Was that a real horse?" a boy nearby was asking his parents, still looking for Cloud Parliament.

"Of course not," his mother laughed, but she didn't sound sure.

They would see, Ezz thought, just as Skyhorse's stringed section on stage in the infield began to strum.

"Ladies and gentlemen," an announcer's voice boomed. A different announcer than whoever had been screaming excitedly about the sight of Cloud Parliament – they must have unplugged his mic. "Just a bit of pre-race entertainment to fill your afternoon!"

"Liars," Camille said beside her, finally coming down off her seat. "Ezz, are you going to be okay here alone? I'm about to go down and make sure no one is getting arrested."

She was gone before Ezz could answer, leaving Ezz staring after her with her mouth slightly open. The sound of the announcer's voice drew her back.

Here came the horses.

Ordinarily they were walked out by brownshirts, and a few still were. But a few people in suits walked beside a handful of the metalbreds, their backside hands mixed up in what Ezz had a feeling was becoming a protest. Part of her knew she should follow Camille, to see how she could help. But as she watched the horses file in, all she could will herself to do was stand and stare at the jockey box, where all the jockeys in their dazzling dresses and tunics had begun to assemble despite the preceding chaos, control panels in hand. Some leaned their heads in close together, no doubt discussing the reappearance of Cloud Parliament. Ezz didn't care enough to look for the jockey who had been hired to program him – if he'd been given a replacement model or if he and the owners had been forced to drop out. All Ezz could do was to stare at the box, the place where Rosario should have been.

Where she was not.

The violins rose, and so did the thousands of voices in Cavehill Downs. Once again Ezz found her hands in fists at her sides.

"*The sun shines bright on my old Kentucky Home…*"

The classic song never failed to give Ezz goosebumps, not because she was moved but because it left her frozen. The song always seemed as if it made time leap backward and then stand still within the sticky amber of the past. Trapped in a room wallpapered in seersucker, the gold tip of a rich white man's walking cane tapping at the door. She shuddered, then forced her eyes away from the jockey box, back to the horses.

Any moment now, the virus audio would blend imperceptibly with the Skyhorse orchestra, and the work that Rosario and Martha died for would untie the knots inside the horses. She knew her own ear wouldn't be able to pick it up, so she stared at the metalbreds, waiting, watching for any sign that the lock of the Aristidean component had met its key.

A text from Luz drew her attention down to her palm.

I hear the music, she wrote. **Is it working?**

Ezz stared at the message – surely this meant that Luz had triggered the virus. Or did Ty have the clicker after all? They all knew the plan: when the orchestra began to play, the virus would be triggered, and synced with the sequence for the horses would be the sequence for the kudzu. 1, 2, Jumbotron. Ezz raised her eyes to the line of twenty metalbreds, making their way toward the starting gate, slow and obedient, each step methodical.

She looked back at the jockey box, the many pairs of hands, all doing their jobs, none of them Rosario.

Her heart sank.

No, she wrote. **It's not.**

CHAPTER 64

TY

Her father's fingers dug into her bicep.

"Thanks for making me look good," her father said, his grin unblurred by alcohol. It would have been better if he were drunk, she thought. If there was something to blame for the green flame in his eye. And he did have a drink in his hand, like everyone else, but she knew when he was drunk, and this wasn't it. This was strutting. He'd be drunk later. No matter what happened, she thought, she wouldn't be sleeping at home tonight.

"It had nothing to do with you," she said, stepping down the second step off the stage. "Now, excuse me. I need to use the bathroom."

She tried to wrench her arm from his grip, but he held on. The announcer out on the track was saying something, and Annie Claybelle's guests in the Limestone suites all turned their attention away from Ty and her short, unremarkable performance. She was left under the eyes of no one but her father and a server, who stopped to top off her father's drink. Ty thought she saw a flash of blue as the girl carrying the bottle and tray turned away; by the time she looked again, though, the girl was gone, and her father was tightening his grip.

"Mr. Benedict pulled me aside," her father said, his voice lowering. He had looked like a snake before, and now his voice became one too, slithering through grass. "He said he had an interesting conversation with you."

"I don't have time for this," Ty said, pulling away again. She could hear the announcer saying something else, and one glance at the gilded clocks told her that the Skyhorse orchestra would begin any moment. She felt a tightness in her calf muscles, a poising to run as if she were one of those horses far below.

"I don't care what you have time for," her father hissed, pulling her closer. He maintained a slit of a smile. "This is my career, Ty. When the racing industry collapsed, I could have been sunk. Gone. Limestone picked me up and brought me in and I've been climbing the ladder ever since – and you will *not* fuck this up for me."

"Is that what you said to my mama?" Ty snapped. "How did *she* feel about your aspirations? How did she feel about your fucking ladder?"

"Watch your goddamn mouth, little girl," he said, a single microscopic drop of spit leaving his mouth and striking her cheek. It felt like a comet. She wanted to swing the purse like a mace and chain. But in the purse was the clicker, and she needed to press it.

"*The sun shines bright on my Old Kentucky Home…*"

Now.

"I need to go," Ty said, pulling away hard. She could feel her device vibrating in her purse. Ezz had no idea what was going on, and Luz was probably having a breakdown.

"Where do you need to be?" her father snapped, pulling her back again. "A meeting? One of the little secret meetings your mother was always going to? Little fake activist friends? What did they ever accomplish? Not a goddamn thing, Ty. Standing outside Cavehill Downs with their fucking signs and bullhorns. Riding horses on weekends like a goddamn child!"

"At least she wasn't climbing a ladder to nowhere," Ty snarled. People were looking now – she didn't care. "What's at the top of that ladder? Brian Benedict's ass, waiting to be kissed? They don't even know your name. You're a prop. So they can point at you for PR stunts – *oh look, we keep the old-timey horse people on staff so Kentucky doesn't realize a bunch of Silicon Valley suits waltzed in and whisked the industry out from under them.* Oldest trick in the book. You think as long as they're stepping on the workers from Mexico and Guatemala, *you're* doing okay. As long as somebody is underneath you. Way to go, dad. When's the last time they even asked you what you thought? You clock in and walk around and feel good about being in the room. Champion material! You're a *real* asset."

She saw the flame in his eye flare higher just as she pulled hard to get away. She could hear the Skyhorse kids playing their instruments, the song taking wing in the moist Kentucky air. She needed to be out in that air, needed to see all this come apart. She felt her arm break free from his grip, then felt his hands against her back, shoving hard. She was weightless and bent for a long moment, and then she was landing on the floor in fractions, hands, then knees, then chest.

"You little bitch!" her father called, and she heard it die halfway out of his mouth, as he realized that he had drowned out the orchestra, that he and Ty were suddenly more interesting to the Limestone guests than the horses walking out onto the track. Ty could see them on the Jumbotron – Luz hadn't plugged the footage yet. She was waiting for Ty to trigger the virus. All of this was falling apart because of Ty's stupid fucking father. She looked for her purse.

A foot away, just beyond her grasp. She stretched, half army-crawled, then heard her father's steps, hard and fast on the marble floor. Her knees and palms were screaming where they'd struck and couldn't move fast enough – she watched the tip of his rented shoe strike her purse, send it spinning ahead toward the balcony.

It opened. Of course it did. Her device had fallen close to her, slowed by its silicone casing. But the clicker skittered forward like a black plastic crab.

"Tyler," she heard someone call from across the room, one of his colleagues – not a tone of warning, but a waved hand, a single-syllable *easy now*. But her father's voice echoed over it like a clap of thunder.

"What *is* that? What did you have in your purse?"

Everyone was looking then. As she reached for her device on her way to retrieve the clicker, she glimpsed the messages from Ezz and Luz.

Is it working?
No. It's not.
I have to cue the video. Ty, wtf is going on?
Ty?
????

She had to do it. Thousands of people were out there singing "My Old Kentucky Home." She could hear the notes winding down. They would turn off the speakers when the song was over, and the virus would have no way to be broadcast. She heard scattered cheers. She glanced desperately at the Jumbotron, where she could see the metalbreds being directed into the gates, mechanical doors shutting at nose and tail.

She lunged for the clicker at the same time that she heard someone shout,

"Does she have a bomb?"

"That girl has a bomb!"

To her right she heard the elevator slide open. Out of the corner of her eye she saw Detective Segrest enter the suite. *Game over*, she thought. *So much for being covert.*

"Fuck it," she said out loud, and pounced on the clicker.

"Don't you do it," Annie Claybelle was screaming from across the room, gripping her brother's arm in a polished fist. Brian Benedict had a glass of bourbon halfway to his lips, frozen.

"Don't you goddamn dare!"

Ty felt instantaneous pressure on her chest in the moment before she fell backward, the sound of her dress tearing as her father used it to haul her toward him. She almost dropped the clicker, juggled it, but held tight. The last notes of "My Old Kentucky Home" were dying, the Jumbotron had switched to the flagman, the starting flag raised. Any fucking second.

Annie Claybelle screamed, and Ty didn't want to look but she did, thinking she would stare her in the eye the moment she pressed the button. Instead Claybelle's eyes were on Brian Benedict, who was clutching his throat, his face distorted like a claw had been taken to the inside. Choking, purple pain.

What the fuck? Ty thought, and she pressed the clicker.

Then she pressed it again, just to be safe. Beside her thumb, a tiny light turned green.

CHAPTER 65

LUZ

"I'm doing it," she said, her finger poised over the file tooth that would take over the Jumbotron. "We can't wait for Ty anymore."

The file tooth was the size of a Tic Tac but filled with the truth. All she had to do was insert it.

"Make sure you have everything you need before you do it," Irma said, standing in the door. "Because we'll need to run."

"We, Irma?" Luz repeated. "You don't have to stay with me."

"I want to see what you put up on the Jumbo."

"You'll be able to see it from anywhere in the Downs," Luz said, staring at the button.

"Do it."

She did it. The tooth made a soft sound like a single knuckle popping, and the machine's panel turned an obliging green.

"Go," Luz urged, and then they were running down the Employees Only hallway, the sound of their tall heels clattering against the close walls until they broke out into the sunshine. When they made it to the rails, panting, Brian Benedict's face was gargantuan above the universe of the Downs.

Luz heard someone laughing, a loose, familiar sound like a jay calling. She thought it was her mother somehow until she realized it was her. Nothing was funny, and yet she couldn't stop the laughter erupting from her throat like lava. She imagined her laugh setting everything on fire.

CHAPTER 66

EZZ

The video appeared on the Jumbotron in the instant before the flagman waved. Everyone's eyes flew upward to the massive screen, surprised, except for Ezz, who wasn't. She didn't want to see it again. She prayed that if anyone in Martha's family remained at the Downs, they were somewhere on the backside, and not here, where they would see what Rosario had made sure Ezz saw. Ezz didn't look at the screen. She kept her eyes on the flagman.

Oblivious, he stood near the starting gate with the flag raised, the edge of it fluttering in the breeze; in Ezz's chest her heart fluttered too, wondering. She pressed her knuckles together and imagined holding Rosario's hand.

The starting flag came down.

She'd seen it come down a dozen times, a dozen Derbys, a dozen years of horses and dust and money.

She knew the sound of the gates opening up, had been close enough before to hear the metallic screech that was masked by the chorus of thundering hooves. Those who hadn't yet noticed the Jumbotron, who still watched the gates with eagerness, bets clutched in fists, still let out the customary cheer when the flag dropped, when the gates sprang open.

And then the shouts wilted, steeped in confusion.

Because the gates had crashed open, but out of the row of steel mouths came...nothing. No blur of chestnut, no stretching white-socked legs, no blue-black streaks of lightning. The gates were open, yet the track remained empty.

Ezz's heart stopped. She slowly, slowly rose to her feet. In her ear, frantic security communications:

We just got word that something is happening at Limestone headquarters?! The glass is broken, the horses...

A gentle breeze was blowing, sending up slow dust curtains over the red-brown track. It was the only movement. Ezz's eyes darted to the jockey box, where three or four of the jockeys were on their feet as well, necks craning, palms lifted to shade their eyes as they leaned toward the track. Ezz watched their million-dollar hands fly across the screens of their panels, desperate for an answer that the code might provide, *something* in their directives and the Limestone framework that could explain why the metalbreds on the track were unresponsive.

Unresponsive, Ezz thought again. *Is that what they are?* Frozen, the way she felt? Did the virus corrupt more than the Aristidean component, something essential, now rendering them little more than incredibly realistic junk?

A group of butterflies, yellow as goldenrod, fluttered across the track in front of the gates.

And that's when Ezz saw the first horse.

A white muzzle edged outside the gate, disappearing again in an instant before edging out again a moment later. A face the color of a shining violin appeared, then a neck. The horse in the fourth gate stretched its body out inch by inch, hesitant to leave the close walls of the chute, but drawn by sunlight, by soil, by wind. By butterflies.

The cloud of flitting yellow seemed to be waiting, and it was then that Ezz heard the silence. No hooves, no cheers, no bugle. She could almost hear the butterflies' wings, swore she could feel

477

the infinitesimal breeze shifted by their flapping. The whole world was still, two hundred thousand eyes watching a chestnut horse wander uncertainly toward a butterfly.

One fluttering golden shape arced up, and then slowly came to a rest on the horse's nose, who startled backward, ears pinning and feet splaying for an instant before that massive shining body found its courage, danced its strong legs, and threw back its head to neigh.

And there it was, finally. The thunder.

Twenty bodies spilling from the gates, the dirt cascading, the ground shaking, every inch of the three spires seeming to quake as a herd of horses did what every horse's heart desires.

They ran.

And the mass of humans looked on, stunned, knowing what they were seeing was something beyond mechanical, the jockeys standing with hands on head, some of their mouths moving silently, panic and rage. For if the machines did this, what else could they do? Ezz stood watching with tears rolling down her face, and no one in the stadium said a word until, around them, everything exploded into vines.

CHAPTER 67

TY

"The horses!" someone screamed. "Look at the horses!"

For a moment all eyes were on the track again, away from Annie Claybelle screaming over her brother's toppled form, away from where Ty grappled with her father, his face red and sweating. As she fought to free herself, Ty could hear the sudden thunder coming from the track below, the deep rumble of stampede like a budding earthquake. Then from the corner of her eye she saw a flash of blue, turned toward it fast before it escaped, and saw a girl just before she ducked into the employee elevator. Black server uniform. Black corvid hair. A streak of electric blue along the bang that she tucked back behind her ear as she met Ty's eyes. A faint sliver of a smile, like a broken china plate, before the door slid closed.

And then the Limestone suites shattered.

CHAPTER 68

LUZ

She had dreamed of what it would be like, all her Poison Ivy fantasies coming true, the dust that her parents had toiled in for almost two decades rising up to meet her outstretched fingers. She was high above the track, the horses like toys, and they were beautiful, the way their necks arched in natural grace, the way they stopped when they wanted to stop, the way they galloped toward the edges of the track where friends in brown shirts with familiar faces waited with hands and fingers outstretched, mouths open and laughing. It was all beautiful. But there was nothing more gorgeous than when the vines sprang from sleep.

The jungle appeared like a hurricane in Millionaire's Row – nothing becoming a roaring something, chairs and tables upending, white tablecloths flown into the wind like sails over the sudden green ocean. A few small forests in the cheaper seats, lonelier vines, where the wind might have blown a seed or two – she hadn't anticpated that. She and Ezz and Camille had been discerning in where they dropped their seeds – not too close to the seats so that the average racegoer would find themselves wrapped in vines, but close enough. Close enough.

She could hear the screams, shock and fear, rage. She could see people standing, hands on head, staring around them, baffled.

One woman was attempting to yank her purse out of the green explosion, the strap breaking off in her fist. Luz could hear people calling to each other, the horses momentarily forgotten, as they tried to figure out where the jungle had come from, why this was happening, here, today. She watched it all from a high place inside her head, letting their confusion wash over her in what felt like a fine mist. She remembered so many early mornings, before the sun had begun to stir below the horizon, hanging over the fence and watching the shadows of her parents leading horses, guiding each elegant step. This felt like that. It felt like dawn. And above it all, the video of Brian Benedict looped over and over and over, the sound of Annie Claybelle's recorded voice repeating so clearly:

I'll take care of the girl.

I'll take care of the girl.

I'll take care of the girl.

Through the mist another sound broke through, Irma's voice. "Look! Look!"

Luz looked just in time to see the first spire crumble. Its black shingles were barely visible through the squeeze of vines, thick and green and hungry. The kudzu's embrace was like an anaconda, and the three spires that made Cavehill iconic wouldn't survive.

Irma was laughing in disbelief, and terror; when her eyes met Luz's, both girls seemed to hear the same music. One of Irma's satin hands was resting on Luz's shoulder, the other draped against her neck. When they kissed, Luz saw an explosion of roses behind her closed eyes.

CHAPTER 69

TY

The marble didn't crack, but the windows did. The screams were as sharp and rending as the glass, and Ty felt herself freed from her father's grip as they were both thrown backward, the front of the room by the balcony bursting in an explosion of green.

Ty had done this, she realized a moment later, raising her spinning head from the floor. The realization settled in as she gazed murkily around the room, the lavish Derby decorations rendered unrecognizable by sudden jungle. Vines clogged the balcony, the open air swollen with the spade-shaped not-quite-kudzu leaves. Furniture shoved bodily aside, chair legs snapped. Only a few people toward the back of the room remained on their feet, Detective Segrest among them, having just arrived in the glossy elevator, held open now by a single ambitious vine that had made it that far, the elevator door butting helplessly against it, dinging. Ty heard dripping – bourbon, a bottle on its side, its amber brown contents splashing slowly down into waste.

"What...what...what...," her father was saying. A stuttering lawnmower, he was struggling up onto one knee, but couldn't quite make it beyond that. Ty shoved him back down, staggering up onto her feet, starting to kick off her shoes, then seeing the broken glass and keeping them on. She felt unsteady, but clear-headed. Detective Segrest wasn't looking at her yet, but he would be. She wobbled forward, peering through Luz's wild garden in the direction of where she had last seen Brian Benedict.

She could hear people cursing, picking themselves up. She looked at no one, only made her way across the room, stepping over vines, methodical and single-minded.

"Miss Redson," she heard at her back. Detective Segrest. She knew that voice, knew it from over a year ago, when he had sat in her living room and asked her what she had noticed in the days before her mother had died. She had told him everything except this: this face, the face belonging to the body she now stood over. This had been hers to keep.

Benedict's face was frozen in that clawed expression, like something fanged had risen up inside and gnashed at the strings holding his face up. His eyes were empty, gazing at the air somewhere to his right, where his sister lay beside him. Vines encircled them both, a vicious green fist, and in the case of Annie, kudzu leaves lining the path all the way up to her throat, wrapped there like a leafed python with shimmering violet scales.

"Miss Redson," Detective Segrest said, nearer now. "Step back."

"That's the girl with the bomb!" someone shouted. "Did she do this? Did she plant this?"

They said plant instead of plan, or maybe they had meant plant, but she couldn't help it – she laughed. Her shoulders shook, staring down at Brian Benedict and his sister. She could only see pieces of Benedict, much of him obscured in green tentacles. Ty ignored all the voices and just stood laughing.

"Miss Redson, step back *now*," Segrest said again. "I need to see both your hands in the air."

"Call the Special Police!" someone shouted. It might have been her father. Both his bosses were dead, but he didn't know that. Still putting on a show. "He's just an investigator!"

She raised her hands in the air, reaching toward the ceiling, the only place unclogged with vines. She tilted her head back, gazing up. She wished she could go to the window, see the horses running. She could still hear their hooves. They were still running. Maybe they would run forever. She imagined the backside crew helping them escape, swinging up onto their backs and disappearing into the sunset.

She turned to face Detective Segrest, who was standing six feet away frowning, taser at the ready.

"No gun?" she said. "Am I not dangerous?"

"I don't know what you are," he said.

There was movement behind him, more people finding their feet. A tan suit rose from the nearby wreckage of a cocktail table. A bulky man, head like a train. He stood up, dusting himself off; one hand rose slowly to pat his left breast pocket.

"Darden," she said. Her voice sounded like glass on metal, and he looked up. "What ya got there?"

Detective Segrest didn't look to see who she was addressing. He took a slow careful step toward Ty, hand outstretched as if reaching for a spooked horse. One of Ty's hands dropped down from the ceiling where he'd ordered it, and pointed like a spear at Darden, who was moving toward the elevator.

"You!" Ty called. "Don't fucking go anywhere."

"Stop moving, Miss Redson," Segrest warned. "Hands in the air."

Darden kept moving, finger outstretched.

"He tampered with the crime scene in Rosario Vicario's hotel room," Ty shouted, both hands down now. "I know what you have, Darden, I know what you took!"

Darden ignored her, pressing the button, blood streaming down one side of his head, lashed by a vine.

"Ty Redson," Segrest shouted. "Do not move!"

But she was already moving, lurching forward, the sight of

that khaki suit like meat, like water. She felt starved for something essential, like the sight of Benedict and Claybelle's bodies wrapped in green and purple had been a drop of need in the bottom of an empty bottle. She needed to fill it now.

"They killed her," Ty was screaming at Darden. "And you helped them cover it up! You were just going to make it all disappear! I won't let you, I won't fucking let you!"

She shoved past Segrest, and Darden was before her, his eyes wide, body stiff. He looked robotic, like he had not been programmed for this scenario, in which a young woman charged him with her eyes filled with murder. She was going to kill him.

She almost made it.

CHAPTER 70

EZZ

The ceiling spun around and around over Ezz's head, her neck arched over the back of the chair in Bay's Barbershop as she rotated in an unending circle. Halfway through every circuit, her foot brushed against Shavon's leg, stuck out from where she reclined in one of the chairs along the wall. Neither of them moved to avoid it, and neither of them spoke. The shop was empty, the lights not yet flipped on. Ezz had come for a haircut but when she got here, decided just sitting felt better. The cool leather against her bare arms was comforting, as was Shavon's silence.

In the corner, the bright screen that had been transitioning from advertisement to advertisement finally went dark, then reanimated with the two polished white people who had been Louisville news anchors for as long as Ezz remembered, and whose names she still didn't know. They both had the shiny, slightly odd look of people whose final plastic surgery should've been three or four procedures ago. Their white teeth snarled the morning's headlines. Ezz closed their eyes against the noise.

"Fireworks this evening at the Waterfront! Wear your masks for the crowds and enjoy the last official night of summer in the company of your fellow Louisvillians! Food trains will be in attendance and dogs and ferrets are welcome."

"I'm so glad ferrets are making a comeback," the co-anchor said, laughing a marionette laugh, jaw nearly unhinged. "Maybe we'll see the living scarf trend make a comeback for next year's fashions. We may not have Derby, but we can still dress up!"

His colleague laughed on cue.

"Speaking of Derby!" she said. "Another of the bad actors in the Limestone-Cavehill scandal was sentenced today in front of Judge Harry Winkfield. We're being piped the update now…"

Ezz sat up mid-rotation, her eyes snapping open, and spun the chair to face the front of the shop, stumbling forward out of the slick black leather and standing rapt below the screen. Behind her she could feel Shavon standing close and silent.

"Maxwell Darden," the anchor continued, "originally of Sarasota Springs, was sentenced to six years in prison for tampering with evidence and felony menace. Judge Winkfield also decided to add on additional time for antitrust violations uncovered in investigations into the pending Limestone merger. Now, on to the weather! Smog warning in full effect today…"

"That's it?" Shavon said, still behind Ezz. "Six years?"

"More than I thought he'd get," Ezz said glumly. She slumped back to the spinning chair and slid back into it. "Horseshit."

"At least they let Joelle go," Shavon said, also returning to her seat. "I thought for sure they'd lock her up."

"Gina Aldana's recommendations helped. She's a respected member of the community or whatever. If it hadn't been for her, they might have melted down all the metalbreds instead of sending them all to Joelle's place."

"That's one plus," Shavon said. She paused. "Have you heard anything from Luz?"

Ezz shook her head silently.

"Damn," Shavon said. "I'm sorry." She sat quietly, then shifted, looking hesitant.

"What?" Ezz said.

"I…gotta open up shop. I'm glad you came by to talk. I know it's been lonely since Luz left. And with Ty gone. But…"

She pointed, Ezz following her finger with her eyes. Three or four dudes with rough hairlines were lined up outside, some of them peering in, eyes shaded.

"Oh," Ezz said, shaking her head, then nodding. "Right. Right. Sorry. Thanks for letting me hang out for awhile. Even if we're just being quiet…it…helps."

"Of course," Shavon said with a gentle voice. "Everything is going to be okay. Okay?"

Ezz nodded.

"And, Ezzardine, look…I wanted to tell you something."

Ezz looked at her, waiting, not wanting to hear. She was so tired of hearing everything except the thing she was waiting for.

"The Pink…all that house and it's just you. And you haven't been throwing parties. Which, of course you haven't. I'm not saying you should. But…I wanted you to know…you can sell that fucking mansion, okay? You don't have to stay there and keep being, like, this benefactor socialite if that's not what you want. I know you're lonely in that big-ass house by yourself. I passed the other day and all the trees are grown in. You're like the Beast from that Disney movie, locked up in a castle. And you ain't gotta be. You can sell it and come sleep on my couch again if you want. If *you* want to. Okay? Your parents wanted that house, but more than that, they wanted you happy. This is kinda like a reset for all of us. The whole damn city. The whole country, kinda. It's weird. I just wanted you to know…you can be somebody else on the other side of this if you want to be. And who that person is doesn't have to have shit to do with horses, or gambling, or anything else. It's up to you."

Ezz studied the floor, too aware of the stinging in her eyes. She didn't look up at Shavon until she was sure she could control the tears.

"Why did I have to be the Beast though?" she said. "I couldn't have been Belle?"

Shavon threw back her head, laughing, showing all her gaps.

"Not with that haircut you can't," she grinned. "Come back tomorrow and I'll hook you up."

They hugged, and Ezz fought back the stinging again when Shavon enveloped her in her thick arms, squeezing like the family she was. Ezz didn't look at her again, just made for the door, stepping out into the sunshine and past the waiting customers, who all grumbled with relief. Louisville – and everything – may have changed, but Bay's was still Bay's.

She made her way past Central Park, taking the long way just to have an excuse to pass the last place she and Ty had stood alone. She paused at the wrought-iron fence, rested her ams and then her chin on the cool metal, staring at the wooden castle where children had played below while she and Luz and Ty had stood attempting to fuck up the entire economy. Now hundreds were out of work. Limestone was shuttered after more and more allegations of money laundering came to light. All the backside workers had been taken on at Joelle's ranch while the Cavehill negotiations continued. Ezz had heard that Joelle built a second barn to accommodate all the equinibots, the creatures no one else knew what to do with. Ezz watched the park castle now, the golden rain trees deep green, laden with pods. The kids playing there today pelted each other with the pods, holding out their shirts in a pouch for their arsenals. The street was quiet – no parade, no confetti, no band. She remembered kissing Ty with the noise all around them, still feeling hopeful. They kissed thinking they would change the world. Maybe they did.

She continued down 4th and over, dragging her feet toward home. Shavon's words echoed in her mind, imagining the Pink sold, its walls painted white once more, the ballroom returned to disuse. If she sold it, would she tell the buyers about the lair under the labyrinth? She'd only been down there once in the months since Derby – the day of. She hadn't been able to find Luz at the track, and raced home and underground, waiting for her to come back. When Luz hadn't come, Ezz had surfaced, glued to the TV and her device, waiting for the news or the network to announce that they'd found Poison Ivy, the girl responsible for the kudzu that killed two people and caused millions of dollars in damage. But they never did, and Luz never showed up. To call the mansion quiet since May would be an understatement.

Ezz turned onto the short street that had become the Pink's. No neighbors out today – they avoided her anyway. The Black girl with the pink hair who threw massive parties was never going to be popular in the part of the city that rich white people envisioned themselves as having reclaimed. Never mind that they weren't close enough to really hear the music; whoever had owned the property twenty years ago had bought the houses on either side and leveled them for green space. That's what Luz had made her jungle playground, Ezz thought, her thoughts growing bluer and bluer. All her elephants and giraffes…

"Horses!" someone cried, and Ezz jumped. "In Old Louisville!"

It was one of her distant neighbors, an old white woman with hair dyed blonde; she must have been diligent about sunscreen because her skin was smooth and unspotted. The smile on her lips reached up into her eyes, the light there genuine. Ezz just stared at her, confused.

"How many do you have?" the woman said, stepping closer. She was still on her side of the waist-high fence, but Ezz thought they'd be toe-to-toe soon. "Which kind are they? Blood or metal?"

She pointed, and Ezz, still baffled, followed the trajectory of her finger, finding its endpoint in the wide green yard of the Pink. Through her tall fence, spread out among the bushes that used to be giraffes, were horses. Not topiaries, but actual animals moving through the wild-grown grass. Three that Ezz could see – two bays, one red dun.

"What the hell…!"

Ezz sprinted the rest of the block without a word, letting herself in the gate and locking it firmly behind her before running up the driveway. There were two more horses she hadn't been able to see from the road – an Appaloosa and a chestnut Thoroughbred. They raised their sloping necks from the abundant green grass they munched and blinked their brown eyes – one of the Appaloosa's eyes was blue – at her, ears twitching unconcernedly.

"Where…where did you come from?" Ezz said softly. Two of the animals from farther afield, closer to the bush maze, came wandering over, curious.

"Thought you might be lonely," someone said, and Ezz spun around, startling the Appaloosa, who jolted a few feet away then turned to look. All of them, Ezz and the horses, all stood staring at Luz Cabo Trejo.

"Luz," Ezz said, still. She didn't want to startle the horses again, or the girl, who stood halfway beteen Ezz and the front porch. She was half-standing – she must have been sitting before, waiting. Behind her in the shade sat Joelle, who raised a hand to wave, and another young Brown woman Ezz didn't recognize. "What…how? How the hell did you get all these damn horses over here?"

"We needed a little extra pasture," Joelle called, standing. "We're kinda full. Luz said she didn't think you'd mind."

Ezz gazed around, the wildness and neglect of the Pink's grounds adjusting slowly into a haven, a heaven in her eyes.

"No," Ezz said, quiet. "I don't mind."

Luz made her way down the steps and approached looking sheepish. The stranger came with her, and Ezz realized they were holding hands.

"I'm sorry I disappeared on you. That day at the

track…Irma," she nodded at the girl whose hand she held – they exchanged a quick smile like they couldn't help it, "had to sneak me out the back way because a bunch of Special Police showed up on our level. People Limestone hired that we couldn't even have known about. I stayed at Irma's for a few days until things died down before going back to my parents. I've been just kinda…reconnecting with them, you know? I wanted to call you, or come by, but I was afraid things were still hot. But now they've been sentencing everybody…nobody seems to know we were involved…"

"And you know why," Ezz said, suddenly angry. She turned away, keeping her eyes on the horses. "You know why that is."

"I do," Luz said quietly. "I do. But…"

Ezz waved her hand, swiping her words out of the air.

"It doesn't matter. We all knew this was a possibility."

"It sucks what happened to Ty. But she knew what she was doing," Luz said firmly. "Like you said, we all knew the possibilities. And I mean…Ezz…" she paused, eyes intense. "We did it. We fucking did it."

"Yeah, we did," Ezz said slowly. Then she thought of something, and raised an eyebrow. "How the hell did the spires comes down?"

Luz gave a grim smile.

"Zarita. I told her I'd help her with her demonstration at Limestone if she helped me with mine. So I gave her a batch of seeds and she dropped them on the spires with her boyfriend's drone."

"Wow," Ezz said. She wanted to say more, but what was there to say? It was September and Limestone was dead.

"The horses are so happy," Luz said. As if in answer, the red dun nickered. "All of them. All they want to do is run. Some of them look like they're grazing, but they're just letting the grass tickle their lips. Isn't that amazing?"

Ezz went on staring at the horses.

"Do you think she did it?" Luz said quietly. "Killed Benedict and Claybelle?"

Hands in her pockets, Ezz rubbed the edge of a deck of cards with one finger.

"Yes," she said. "And once I heard on the news that Benedict probably murdered her mom, it made a lot of things make sense, you know? I just wish she…"

She couldn't finish. The cards in her pocket felt heavy with bets she didn't want to place.

Luz nodded, wordless, Irma reaching up to squeeze her arm. Joelle stood watching from the porch, arms folded. They all watched the horses, and the horses ignored them, exploring the hedges, nibbling on the far-off maze. Ezz felt the tears again, starting somewhere deeper than the eyes. How did the sight of a horse feel like home? How did they smell like wheat and sun, and how did those smells align in her nose to carry her through time? It had been years since she'd ridden, had told herself after the fire that she'd never ride again. But looking at the animals now, she could feel her legs around their bodies, could feel her father's arm around her waist as they swayed back and forth down the trail, the back of her mother's hair ahead on the path, occasionally turning back to light the way with her smile. Her parents were dead, but the horses were here, and Ezz knew that they all shared the same bones, somehow, they were made of the same dust. She had felt like this with Ty too, and not just Ty, but all of them together, all galloping toward and part of the same shining something. They had reached it, maybe, but not together, and she wondered if it would always be like this: love like a funhouse mirror, sometimes showing you the back of your own head, sometimes showing just an elbow. Was everything always going to be in pieces, was everyone, or eventually, did you see everyone and everything all at once?

"I wanted to ask you something though," Luz said, and paused. Ezz glanced at her sideways, and only then did she continue. "That's why I came. With them."

She gestured at the horses, then fell silent.

"Yeah?" Ezz said. "What?"

Luz smiled, a bit like a bud opening on a vine.

"Want to go for a ride?"

CHAPTER 71

TY

Every day was the same.
Gray and blue walls.
Gray and blue bed.
Gray and blue cup.
Gray and blue toilet.
Gray and blue tray.
One window.

Her days revolved around this window, occasionally putting on the navy-blue outfit her lawyer had brought for court appearances and going in front of the judge to make concessions and agreements, to make various pleas. She'd had several of these appearances – the lawyer Ezz had sent her was good – a slim Liberian woman named Anna with a voice like a songbird. Ty liked her, and the judge liked her, and Anna assured Ty that they would "get her through this mess." Ty wasn't so sure.

Anna was coming today.

Not for a court appearance – the navy-blue outfit hadn't been offered when the guard had ordered Ty to prepare for her visit. Just a standard check-in then, when Anna would ask her questions and Ty would do her best to answer them, sometimes lying. She was allowed no other visitors, and Ty said that this was fine, but of course it wasn't.

"Redson, your turn," the guard said at 11:50 am, tapping on the wall outside her door. Ty stood while he reached through the bars to attach the leg restraints before opening her cage. Then he led her down the bright hallway, fluorescent lights mingling with sunshine, and toward the representation visitation rooms. There were other rooms for family visits, but Ty had never had one of those.

Anna was already inside, her papers and folders spread out like the lining of a rabbit's cage, covering the surface of a large round table. She waved cheerily when Ty entered, and Ty waved back. The guard removed the restraints, taking them with him when he left. He closed the door with a stern look, which Ty ignored. The look was part of his uniform. He wasn't one of the really bad ones, of which there were many.

"Still strange to see you with hair," Anna said teasingly. "The judge won't even recognize you this time."

"This is the worst part of being locked up," Ty said. "Someone told me I'd be allowed a haircut at some point, but I guess being cute isn't on the Bill of Rights."

"It should be," Anna said, raising a critical eyebrow at the brunette shag that had taken over Ty's scalp. Ty laughed and shook her head.

Anna went through dates and paperwork, asking her to sign things occasionally. Ty listened with half her mind. All the visitation rooms were on the second floor, but this room was her favorite: at the corner of the building, windows on two walls instead of just one, and wide, wide enough to let in the way the day actually felt and not just an impression of it. She watched the trees swaying back and forth in a gentle wind, ash and magnolia, everything the deep sleepy green of late summer. She wouldn't be out to bid it farewell before autumn took the reins. Maybe next year.

"I have a little reassurance," Anna said, "if you need it.

Witnesses recall you being close to Brian Benedict and Annie Claybelle just before the plants…appeared, but no one can say for sure that they saw you do anything suspicious, at least until you grabbed the device."

Ty said nothing, and Anna let the pause linger before continuing.

"They brought in a special botanist to examine the few unsprouted seeds that were found," Anna went on, shuffling papers. "They've never seen anything like it – clearly engineered for an attack of this kind. But they obviously can't link them to you, someone with no botanical or engineering experience whatsoever. A singer-turned-maid isn't exactly a criminal mastermind."

"I guess not," Ty said simply.

"Still, they can't prove that the device was linked to the plants, or to whatever happened to the Limestone horses. My argument has been, given your tie to Brian Benedict, that your device was linked to the Jumbotron and the footage therein. The rest was coincidental, and that multiple groups must have planned demonstrations for Derby Day, such as what we saw at Limestone headquarters."

"What's happening with that?" Ty said. This was the only point in which she felt nervous so far.

"They apprehended a young woman named Zarita Moreno-Mendoza at the scene of that demonstration," Anna said, checking her notes. "But they had to release her with no proof to link her to what happened with the horses or the plants. A Dr. Raymond Salt is under investigation, however. They found files that indicated he knew about the metalbreds' consciousness, so it's possible that he planned the whole thing to make a point."

"Cool," said Ty.

"There's a statement by a girl named Camille Richmond," Anna said.

"Oh, yeah?"

"She's publicly implicated her mother in the murder of Rosario Vicario," she said. "Claims she witnessed her allowing Brian Benedict entrance into the Mahogany on the night of the murder. Detective Segrest found a needle under the wardrobe in Rosario's room – the needle had Benedict's fingerprints. Then something about a bleach solution used at the scene that is connected to Benedict. So that bit is tied up, it seems."

Ty squeezed her jaw at the mention of Camille. Had she known about her mother the whole time? Everyone had their secrets, Ty included, though soon she could let hers go. The question was whether she would be alone when she was free of them. Maybe she would move after this. Better to be lonely somewhere new than lonely somewhere that held memories.

"No comments?" Anna said. "I've told you one hundred times we have attorney-client privilege."

"You've got it covered," Ty said, glancing at her, and Anna rolled her eyes, even if only half-irritated.

"Alright then. But there was *one* thing I wanted to ask you about for sure," Anna said, returning her gaze to her paperwork.

"Uh-huh," Ty said, her eyes still on the trees and sky, wondering when she'd feel them all again. Out one window was a city street; out the other was a stretch of green grass, a hill that rolled gently upward. From here she could see the occasional strolling couple, the occasional family with small children. A lone woman with long hair who could've been her mother. Couldn't have.

"On Derby Day, when you were in the Limestone suite, either before or after the incident, did you see anyone with blue hair? A young woman? Possibly dressed in black?"

Ty kept her eyes fixed on the window, watching the lone woman. She could be anyone. Anyone but her mother. She could be anyone but her mother, or Martha, or Rosario. Dead women.

Luis Funes. All dead. She thought of the stripe of blue hair on Derby Day, the closing elevator door, the smile like a flutter of distant lightning.

"I don't remember," Ty said, and she could feel Anna looking at her, but she kept her eyes on the hill beyond the window. The green was a safe place to rest her mind. She couldn't feel the easy wind, but she could see its fingers across the land, transporting her thoughts to an acre of bluegrass, elbows hooked over a chipped white fence, the smell of hay in her nose, the slow shadows of horses in the distance…

She saw their ears tip over the horizon now, followed by necks and withers, the graceful sway of riders on their backs, noon sun cutting through the angles of office buildings and parking garages. She heard Anna asking her more questions about a mystery girl with blue hair, but her words turned into noise. Ty was staring at four horses coming down the hill outside Louisville Metro Corrections, horses that couldn't possibly actually be there.

"You see, the Benedict estate requested an extended autopsy," Anna said. "The findings of the autopsy dispute whether the kudzu is what actually killed Brian Benedict on May 5th. It seems unclear at this point which killed him *first*, but poison was also definitely at play –"

But Ty was standing up, pushing away from the round table to the window that let in the light. It wasn't possible, but there they were: a black horse, an Appaloosa, a red dun, and a Palomino she knew by heart, all of them in a zigzag line, making their way down to flat ground. Four horses, four riders, and the person sitting astride Cloud Parliament had deep brown skin and pink hair.

"No fucking way," Ty whispered. "No fucking way."

"Is everything alright?" Anna said, the shuffling papers finally still.

Ty raised her arms, pressing her palms against the glass high above her head, her smile like a wound reopening and then healing all at once. She waved her arms like windmills, and far below, where the horses had reached the bottom of the hill, she saw Ezz see her. Then Luz. Then Joelle. Then Irma. Waving, waving, all of them waving, and the horses all prancing in circles like they knew why they had come.

Four horses, four girls. Ty couldn't hear a thing through the glass, but she could see the wind and it knew their names, and when Cloud Parliament reared up, pawing the sky, something mechanical at Ty's center came unbound, the rage that had held her still and silent flapping loose like a scarf, borne off on the breeze. Grief galloped wild inside her, but she didn't close her eyes against it – she stood watching Ezz, remembering. Ezz rode up and down the hill, one hand toward the sky, pink hair like sunrise, and beneath her, the golden body of Cloud Parliament, sunshine against metal in the moment before it becomes heat.

"I never saw a girl with blue hair," Ty said to Anna over her shoulder. "All I saw was kudzu. Did you know they call it the plant that swallowed the South?"

EPILOGUE

REBECA

This was a place that didn't smell like home. What was home without the hand lotion Martha always rubbed into her knuckles, burnt sugar? What was home without Martha's earpods, too loud, playing old pop music no one but their abuela recognized? Martha was home, and Martha was gone.

Rebeca stood with her feet on the bottom rung of a new fence, over new grass. It was a browner green, not the lake-colored fields of Kentucky. Beyond, her mother held the braided lead rope of a tired old bay carrying a six-year-old wearing a pointed birthday hat. It wasn't the Derby, but in this new town people loved horses, approached them with palms up and wide eyes. Rebeca had forgotten how kind hands could be, when they were open and not filled with money or metal.

She glanced at the sun and tucked the strand of electric-blue hair behind her ear, then made her way to the end of the ring where she would swing the gate open for the next eager child, the next curly-haired girl who looked at a horse and saw an altar. Martha would say these were their people, real horse people – Rebeca had never known there were so many.

Her Uncle Manny had told her this was the place where they sent horses with no future, and Rebeca couldn't help but wonder what that meant for her own. She stared down at her legs, browner now than they had been when they left Louisville under cover of night, and saw them for what they were: brilliant machines, made for carrying her where she wanted to go. Their job for now was to be still and silent. But not forever.

She stood at the gate watching old Laylah plod her way down the fenceline, head bobbing. Even now Rebeca tried to look for signs – old horse, or out-of-date equinibot? She could hear her sister whispering, *What's the difference, manita? Weren't you paying attention?*

Laylah came close, leaning in when Rebeca scratched just under the bridle. Rebeca imagined what life might come into those brown eyes when guided out toward the horizon, what dust the two of them might kick into the pale blue sky. She cupped the horse's muzzle and whispered, soft, into her ear,

"Patience, girl."

ACKNOWLEDGEMENTS

This book has been rattling around in my head for so long – one of those books that, every time I would start to push it aside in my head, a new article or interview about horses and the people that love them would pop up on my radar, calling me back. Thank you to everyone who assisted in that calling back – Lucie, Minda, and Kaitlyn, who first heard the threads of this story and knew it would end up as a quilt. Lucie, especially, for reading this absolutely massive book when you most certainly had more important things to do.

Thank you to Omaun, for tolerating my endless chatter, and for doing what you do best – just sitting and listening until whatever knot is in my brain works itself out.

Thank you to my sister, Julia, for your excellent and loving feedback.

Thank you to my father, Robert, who read this thing *three fucking times* and edited it too. Wow. May Editor Dad live forever.

Thank you to Hannah Drake, for your unwitting assistance in reminding me why this story needed to be written.

Thank you to Asha French for hearing about this book and saying "YEAH!"

Thank you to Ashley Woodfolk, for helping me to decide what the hell to do with this thing. This may not have gone the direction you envisioned, but you helped me see that this book needed to not be bound by rules.

Thank you to the Louisville Story Project, for your collection *Better Lucky Than Good*, which was released at one of those moments when I thought of setting *Cloud Parliament* aside.

Thank you to the Backside Learning Center, for your love and care and knowledge.

Thank you to Alexis Vasquez Garcia, for, in the midst of a global pandemic, giving me a virtual tour of Guatemala. Your wisdom and expertise are so deeply appreciated.

Profound thanks to Chris Davila – you truly helped me discover who Luz actually is, and your knowledge and care and sharp eye will never be forgotten. I'm bringing you *all* my books!

Thank you to Joy Priest – you imagine a different Kentucky and I learn from you every day. (Buy HORSEPOWER by Joy Priest, everyone.)

Thank you to every single living being who is working so hard to improve the lives of people and animals alike. Thank you to my mother, for always setting the example.

This book is for horse girls and girls who love horses and girls who have never ridden a horse but maybe wanted to.

Are you a horse girl? Well, do you feel the wind in your heart?

Then yes.